Retu D0430665

ELENORE SMITH BOWEN is the *nom de plume* of Laura Bohannan who was, from 1959 to 1962, Lecturer in Anthropology at Northwestern University, from 1962 to 1963, Lecturer in Anthropology at the University of Chicago, and Professor of Anthropology at the University of Illinois since 1965. She spent the better part of the years between 1949 and 1953 working among the Tiv of Northern Nigeria on grants made jointly to her husband, Paul J. Bohannan, also an anthropologist, and herself from the Wenner-Gren Foundation and the Social Science Research Council. She was a Senior Research Fellow at the East African Institute for Social Research in Kampala, Uganda, from 1954 to 1956.

Mrs. Bohannan received her B.A. degree in anthropology and classics and her M.A. degree in German from the University of Arizona and her D.Phil. from Oxford University in 1951. In addition to *Return to Laughter*, Mrs. Bohannan has written articles in anthropological journals and has contributed to a number of books on Africa.

RETURN TO LAUGHTER

BY
ELENORE SMITH BOWEN

ANCHOR BOOKS
DOUBLEDAY
New York London Toronto Sydney Auckland

AN ANCHOR BOOK

Published by Doubleday, a division of Bantam Doubleday Dell
Publishing Group, Inc., 1540 Broadway, New York, New York 10036

ANCHOR BOOKS, DOUBLEDAY, and the portrayal of an anchor are
trademarks of Doubleday, a division of Bantam Doubleday Dell
Publishing Group, Inc.

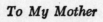

To My Mother

Foreword

IN THE SUMMER of 1961 I addressed a group of Peace Corps volunteers destined to be the first such group in Nigeria. I discussed certain themes in American culture in order to help this group of sensitive yet practical college graduates understand a little less badly the cultural load they carried as Americans. Five Nigerians took part in the orientation program, some of whom, although not educated at Oxford, would have been at home in its ambiance; and I thought it possible that these volunteers, in their openness and relative lack of ethnocentrism, might perhaps take these Nigerians as more representative than was justified, and hence underestimate the sorts of tribal suspiciousness, frenzy, and fear of witchcraft they might encounter. For, unlike earlier emissaries, these students were not going to Nigeria protected and confined by convictions of their own cultural superiority, capable of judging other cultures only from the perspective of the American Way, and determined to bring others to that standard if possible. Hence I was glad to find that members of the group had read *Return to Laughter* (then out of print) and I recommended in addition the African novels of Joyce Cary, to complicate their sense of the land to which they were going and of the social ambiguities that might be faced there, especially by the most well-intentioned visitor. Peace Corps volunteers, whether teachers or community development workers, know that they need the cooperation of those with whom and through whom they will be working. I felt they would find it illuminating to realize, in the fictional account of *Return to Laughter,* the ways in which the anthropologist was used as a pawn in the factional struggles of Chief Kako and his rival Yabo. The haunting conflicts Laura Bohannan faced between her sense of professional duty and her commitment to personal decency and friendship illuminate the near-universal problems of those of us caught, at some time or other—and who is not?—between his own culture's values and those of another.

A good many social scientists are novelists *manqués,* just as a good many novelists, wedded to a documentary supposed realism, subordinate both the reader and themselves to a mass of undifferentiated detail. *Return to Laughter* takes the form of a novel; its characters are said by the author to be composites, its incidents fashioned by the play of imagination upon her diary and field notes. As a novel, its spare references to British indirect rule may locate it in the genre of novels of colonialism. Mrs. Bohannan's enterprise, however, focusses less on the West African tribe among whom she worked and lived (and still less on the soon-to-depart British) and more on her own emotional hegira as a neophyte anthropologist. In this aspect she reveals some of the human costs, passions, missteps, frailties, and gaieties which lie behind the often too antiseptic reports of social scientists. In a recent article, the British philosopher, J. W. N. Watkins, argues that only by bringing the human person back into scientific reports can specialists in one field share the intellectual adventures of those in another, and hence truly understand their hypotheses and forms of thought. He writes:*

Paraphrasing Descartes, we may say that one method is to take the reader into your confidence by explaining to him how you arrived at your discovery; the other is to bully him into accepting a conclusion by

* J. W. N. Watkins, "Confession Is Good for Ideas," *The Listener,* vol. LXIX, April 1963, p. 667, at p. 668.

parading a series of propositions which he must accept and which lead to it. The first method allows the reader to re-think your own thoughts in their natural order. It is an autobiographical style. Writing in this style, you include, not what you had for breakfast on the day of the discovery, but any significant consideration which helped you arrive at your idea. In particular, you say what your aim was—what problems you were trying to solve and what you hoped from a solution of them. The other style suppresses all this. It is didactic and intimidating.

Watkins is talking principally of the natural sciences; what he says about the investigator's confessional colleagueship applies with perhaps even greater weight to those fields where the observer's participation inevitably evokes certain orders of data and closes off other orders. Yet anthropologists have been moving rapidly away from the tradition of being somewhat stoical and self-deprecatory aristocrats (necessarily gifted amateurs and rapporteurs in some areas, since they were seeking to embrace an entire, often vanishing culture), and moving toward the tradition of middle-class scientism, entering a tribe to map its kinship structure or linguistic patterns and to bring back fungible data for cumulative comparison. In this role, they aim to be distracted as little as possible by the personalities and particularities of their tribe, which is no longer "theirs" in any case in the older British style of "royal" anthropology, but shared with their university colleagues, and fragmenting in the face of Westernization.

Still, anthropology remains a collective endeavor in methods as well as in data, for all field workers belong to the club of the initiated and exchange experiences informally, if at times guardedly, although rarely in their publications. But outsiders, including students, cannot share this in-group understanding, and to that extent science as a large cooperative process suffers.

In addition, anthropology by its very nature requires

the cooperation of those being studied, and *Return to Laughter* suggests how great is the dependence of the field worker upon such cooperation. Thus, the opening through which this cooperation is gained tells much for the later fate of the venture—something which William F. Whyte makes candidly clear in his autobiographical appendix to the second edition of *Street Corner Society*. Beyond that, whom one sees first, and is seen with; whose wife gets sick, and who lives or dies; where one's own hut or camp is located; with what sympathy or paranoia one's aims are interpreted—all such matters are of course largely in the laps of the gods and witches, and can be guided by the field worker only in limited degree. In fact, *Return to Laughter* emphasizes again and again the way in which "her" tribe corrected Mrs. Bohannan's initial apprehensions, at times being more tactful and patient than she herself, and at other times shouting in the way we are all tempted to do with those who are only deaf because they do not know our language.

But it is no less important to see that, as in other branches of science, mistakes can be creative: they produce crises, fruitful enmities, and embarrassments, and make personal relations more dramatic than if one were always the smooth and poised observer. (In my own judgment, non-directive interviewing is often less useful than a more dialectical and argumentative approach, which may under certain conditions evoke different levels of feelings and behavior than the conciliatory and somewhat passive approach, which also has its uses.)

For Peace Corps volunteers in the field, as well as for anthropologists, there are hazards as well as opportunities in isolation. It is a strain to have to be always on guard, surrounded by curious if friendly people (or in rare instances shunned); as Mrs. Bohannan writes:

But above all else, it was only in the privacy of my hut that I could be my real self. Publicly, I lived in the midst of a noisy and alien life. If I wanted conversation in my own language, I had to hold it with myself. . . . I could escape my cultural isolation only by being alone for awhile every day with my books and my thoughts. It was the one means of hanging on to myself, of regaining my balance, of keeping my purpose in being out here before me, and of retaining my own values.

Educated Americans talk wryly about togetherness, but are still protected against prying and invasion by walls and doors, distance and money, night and travel. And in Mrs. Bohannan's tribe, as in so many others, where people are poor and live in a social network of tight blood-relations, and where the compartments of night and day are not much more solid than those of the thatched huts of the homestead, life is with people—no other way is conceivable.

Many times Mrs. Bohannan jangled this web, either because she failed to grasp what people said or didn't say to her, or because out of weariness or impatience or lack of empathy she tried to break through the subtle constraints intended to keep her in her place, at once privileged and walled off from aspects of tribal existence thought unsuitable for female European eyes. Thus, since Europeans are thought to disbelieve in witchcraft and to disapprove of it, her discoveries concerning it were made at the cost of risking acceptance by the Chief, and perhaps even her safety. And when she did begin to appreciate the ambivalence that underlay witchcraft, in which one had to fear only the nearest and dearest (not including one's spouse), who were precisely those who had reason and opportunity to harm one, she could also test the countervailing strength of the age-grade or group of same-sex peers who could rally to defend one from magic or from the charge of witchcraft. But she discovered that she herself could not defend, by the Western "magic" of station or mission hospitals, an intimate friend who was dying, for the hospitals were suspect and so were those who were supposedly guilty of wishing Amara's death (and whose confessions were extorted by practices bearing some resemblance to Chinese thought reform, as described in Robert J. Lifton's *Thought Reform and the Psychology of Totalism*). Furthermore, when smallpox hit the tribe, terror broke out as with a medieval plague, and Mrs. Bohannan, though herself immune, could not bring herself to rescue or nurture an infected and ostracized tribesman, lest she herself and those "boys" dependent on her be ostracized and perhaps destroyed for demonstrating in this way her contempt for the tribe's judgment and her own presumably malignant powers (for those struck down by smallpox are expected to try out of *Lebensneide* to bring their relatives down as well). Professional men and perhaps especially professional women in our society have a dream of omnicompetence in which they are never ruffled, angry, irrational, stupid, and tactless, let alone cowardly. Mrs. Bohannan discovers in herself all these failings—with the additional failing, quite alien to the tribe she studied, of wanting to be a superior person and without failings. For indeed the tribe is tolerant of weakness (and in fact quite intolerant of strength; it tries to pull Yabo down because of his contemptuous superiority); the "return to laughter" is, among many other moods, a willingness to accept the universe and the people in it for what they are, rather than for what they might be.

Even when most lonely, however, Mrs. Bohannan was only momentarily tempted to go native. For though the tribe, while shunning her, made her seek their forgiveness, she came eventually to realize that there was a certain callousness or thinness or indifference in the gay and sunny relations among people that so often exploded into laughter. Many anthropologists have so heavily embraced the doctrine of cultural relativism that they insist on accepting all tribal values (other than their own, toward which they are often less compassionate). And then it may come as a shock to them to find that after all they do judge their tribe. I recall in this connection a friend of mine who worked with a Latin American Indian tribe with apparently full sympathy, until one day he saw a dog kicked and couldn't stand it; Mrs. Bohannan reacted similarly to the teasing and tricking of a blind man; as she wrote, "where people laughed at human misery, our doctrine of kindness to animals, for the sake of mere kindness without intent to use or worship, seemed the wildest extravagance." A widening sense of empathy and dislike of cruelty has been growing in the Western world, a development that is one of that world's achievements (granted that systematic state cruelty in war and genocide operate on a different timetable). Of this and other matters, Mrs. Bohannan says, "I'd grown fearful of the constant temptation to question my own values that these people and this world afforded me." Indeed, despite the narcotizing daily round of field work itself (acquiring the language, writing down folk tales, witnessing ceremonies), such experiences repeatedly threw Mrs. Bohannan back on who she was and what she believed, and in this sense *Return to Laughter* is a kind of modern *Pilgrim's Progress*, played out against a background which perhaps seems more exotic than in fact it is.

For indeed, many of the same dilemmas, as the author realizes, can be discovered within our own society. Lower-class life in America may in some respects resemble the tribe more than it resembles the British university where Mrs. Bohannan studied anthropology. Moreover, the ethical dilemmas of field work are to be found everywhere. Thus, Mrs. Bohannan felt herself a trickster because she befriended people who could help her unravel tribal witchcraft, and she did not always explain to her respondents what it was she was really looking for. "Each time I had been thanked for sitting up with the very ill, for attending a funeral, or for coming to 'sit out death,' I had felt myself a sly ambulance-chaser, slimy with hypocrisy." But whose social life, quite apart from field work, does not involve comparable mixed motives, of friendship vs. status, sex vs. affection, loneliness vs. genuine concern? Nigeria acted for Mrs. Bohannan to bring out issues more easily rationalized in a familiar setting.

Because of the book's honesty in portraying the inner experience of field work, I was troubled at its initial appearance under a pseudonym, even though I was told by anthropologist friends of the author that this was done to protect the tribe, which itself for further insurance is not named. (The tribe emerges so vividly that one might think it required no protection, but not all readers can be counted on to view compassionately and without an axe to grind either the group as a whole or the fictional characters of the book.) The thought crossed my mind that the author herself may have feared that the book might hurt her reputation as a competent and objective ethnographer, perhaps particularly so among those literal-minded readers who could not separate the book's feeling-tone and subjectivity from its circumstantial chronicle. Correspondingly, I am glad that the author now is willing to have her own name on the book. For any assumption that an autobiography of affective experience is an ethnographic irrelevancy would, as I argued earlier, be setting a wrong model for what is truly scientific—a term I would define as a canon of ethical scrupulousness and choice of the most appropriate methods, not allowing these methods to be monopolized by any particular sect of methodologists. As a work of ethnography, and as a primer of anthropological method, *Return to Laughter* can stand on its own feet. It illustrates, for example, the advantages women can sometimes have in field work because they have access to all the private worlds of women as a member of their sex, and they are also able to penetrate such male worlds as magic and statecraft by virtue of their occupational role and the kind of assertiveness it allows them. (The old women of the tribe have a ribald assertiveness also, but this does not mean that they can come out of the Nigerian version of Purdah and enter the men's world, except on the periphery of gossip and joking.) The unhappy awareness in *Return to Laughter* of puzzles and contradictions gives the sense of a kaleidoscope in which another visit or another death or another episode of witchcraft would turn up new puzzles and interpretations. The words in which these latter are presented are necessarily ambiguous, as is any effort at cross-cultural translation. In fact all those who return from an extreme situation and try to explain it to the outside—whether it is war or a concentration camp or an alien tribe—face the problem of translation; and our canons of objectivity offer few and ambiguous guides. Obviously, the words with which one describes people and events, such as Mrs. Bohannan's reference to a particular "dowager" or to an "adultery," carry semantic freight with us that they may not carry in the other culture. But deadpan, seemingly scientific labels are no way around the issue, since they make empathy difficult and imply a deadpan verdict on the culture. Knowing the tribe in question only through *Return to Laughter*, I cannot judge whether the book's portraits are accurate for individuals or as composites; but they strike me as plausible as well as unforgettable, done as they are with gentle irony and an eye for the details of mien and behavior. Furthermore, as a study of witchcraft, this one says more than most I know about the nature and quality of the human ties and of the ecological situation, harsh and difficult, in which people struggle to make a living, to feel secure, to enjoy life, and to come to terms with death. It is, as so often among non-literates (and many literate people also, as in our own Middle Ages and even today) a world which is at once chancy and where nothing happens by chance, but only because human beings will it. What they cannot will, what they cannot imagine, is that life itself can be altered: man can help, or more readily harm, individuals, but not change the ground rules of existence; here one surmounts disaster only by laughter.

Like so many social scientists, Mrs. Bohannan, too, came to Nigeria with a scorn for do-gooders (one but only one of the anthropologists' sources of enmity for the missionary). But faced with illness and evil which Western programs could have alleviated, she felt less scornful of progress and of the reformers who had in the past pursued it. She felt frustrated and guilty when she could not help, even though she also felt disquiet at spending so much time handing out medicines, when her scientific conscience demanded that she finish her census of the homesteads. I share her values in this respect, and believe that the tension between wanting to help and wanting to understand is productive. New West African novelists are coming along, who are already looking on modernization (as Benjamin De Mott points out in a recent issue of *The American Scholar*) with the eyes of T. S. Eliot, and who fear deracination much more than they fear witchcraft, sickness, and needless early death. Other African writers and thinkers, of course, have gone over to the West as fanatical nationalizers, and would be unsympathetic both to the tribal values portrayed in *Return to Laughter* and to the author's vacillations and ethical uncertainties. Some of these nationalists have taken over the hard assurance that characterized many of the earlier colonizers, failing to see that beneath the latter's assurance, those men who appear so solidly in control are often tricked and manipulated by their own unconscious and by their seemingly obeisant subordinates.

To the lay reader and to the professional social scientist, most anthropological monographs also present a front of hard assurance, of findings or "results." Even the description of method is usually *ex post facto*. Nevertheless, journals (such as *Human Organization*) are beginning to publish discussions of problems, at once ethical and tactical, in field work in a wide range of milieux. *Return to Laughter* does more: it tells the story from within of what it is like to be an anthropologist in the field, as a human, all too human person.

David Riesman

August 1963

Author's Note

ALL THE CHARACTERS in this book, except myself, are fictitious in the fullest meaning of that word. I knew people of the type I have described here; the incidents of the book are of the genre I myself experienced in Africa. Nevertheless, so much is fiction. I am an anthropologist. The tribe I have described here does exist. This book is the story of the way I did field work among them. The ethnographic background given here is accurate, but it is neither complete nor technical. Here I have written simply as a human being, and the truth I have tried to tell concerns the sea change in oneself that comes from immersion in another and savage culture.

Laura Bohannan

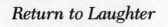

Return to Laughter

Chapter One

"I EXPECT you'll be all right." Tall Mr. Sackerton, the administrative official in charge of that district, fingered the thin mustache that marked him a confirmed optimist. Nevertheless, he seemed dubious as he gazed at the three-ton truck loaded with wooden boxes packed as half-hundred weight headloads, canvas parcels of bed, bath and tent, my three new servants whom I'd already learned to call "boys," three kerosene tins destined to become a stove, and the fifteen carriers who were to take me from the road to the resthouse near Chief Kako's homestead.

I crawled up beside the driver. Sackerton slammed the door: "You'll be all right at Kako's. I've told him you want to learn the language." As the truck growled off to a start on the muddy road, he shouted after me, "If you get into trouble . . ." but the rest was lost in the noise of the engine.

The truck alternately jounced and slithered over the dirt road; after last night's rain, the first of the season, it was a lake of mud with occasional reefs of laterite. To either side spread the grassland, dead gray grass patched with the green of yam fields and the brown of newly cleared land. Dotted about were their homesteads: circular clusters of round huts with thatched roofs like dinner bells, domed and golden in the sun. Men and women were out in the fields, hoeing and pulling grass. They straightened at the noise of our coming, shouted, and shook their fists

1

at me. Sackerton had thought to tell me that this was their form of greeting. I shook my fist in return.

Gradually we left the treeless, rolling plains. Mountains appeared above the southern horizon. The country grew more wooded; giant trees towered over the thin bush. We crossed narrow streams hedged in by vine-meshed palm and bamboo. Occasionally we passed a man—cloth tied around his waist like a towel, bow and arrow in hand, walking by the side of the road with a sleek dog trotting behind—or a party of people: an elder in front, leaning on his spear, followed by armed youngsters and by women whose heads balanced great yellow calabashes of farm produce.

Once a duiker bounded across the road. Excited, I chattered at the driver and got a fluent spate of sound in reply. We tried again: I more slowly, he more loudly. Eventually I was forced to the conclusion that he knew no more of my language than I did of his. I felt rather inadequate, and had to remind myself that there was no need to say anything: everything had been arranged. The driver knew where to let me off; the carriers knew where to take me, and I had been told how much to pay them. Chief Kako had been warned of my coming. And if anything should go wrong, I reassured myself, I had food, a tent and a cook. Furthermore, the cook knew about six sentences worth of pidgin.

That no one with me knew more English was my own fault, and my set intent. It had been the first advice given me. "Never use an interpreter," my professors had intoned, "or you'll never learn the language properly." "You'll learn the language more quickly," Sackerton had confirmed cheerfully, "if no one around you can speak anything else." The cook's bit of pidgin was my compromise between their counsel and my misgivings. I could at least get food and drink through him—when he was with me. Right now he was in back with my water, and I couldn't tell the driver to stop. As the truck went on and on, I sincerely hoped

2

that the other advice I'd taken would prove more immediately helpful.

About to go to Africa for the first time, I had conscientiously rooted about among my acquaintances for helpful information. On their advice I'd been inoculated for yellow fever, smallpox, typhoid and paratyphoid, tetanus, typhus, and only my own reluctance had saved me from a cholera shot. I had gone to a tropical outfitter in England, and had been expertly outfitted with all manner of folding equipment, with evening dresses (trouble to pack and seldom worn), a soda siphon (an unmixed blessing) and an elaborate set of silver, dishes and glassware (a nuisance, but good for my steward's morale). The outfitters said I would be able to get nothing at all in West Africa. The wife of a trader on leave told me I could get everything I might want there. Both were right, from time to time.

My main trouble had been that I had no idea of what I might need. My own imagination carried me no further than a typewriter, paper, notebooks, and a miscellany for reading: detective stories, desert-island stand-bys like Shakespeare and the Bible, and a terrifying handbook of tropical diseases. I had myself introduced to ex-traders and retired administrators. They all recommended a meat grinder to make goat meat edible and curry powder to make it palatable; unanimously they instructed me to trek early ("trek" in West African English covers almost any distance of walking), to sleep in the heat of the day, and at sundown to bathe, put on a sweater and have *one* drink with my quinine. I was grateful, but I wanted to know more.

Anthropological advice, though much less consistent, was equally limited. "Always take your boys from among the tribe you are studying, or there will be trouble." "Always take a boy who is a stranger; then he'll be *your* man." Circumstance made me compromise again. The tribe among whom I was going had a bad reputation with their neighbors; no outsider would consent to stay in the bush

3

among the "cannibals and wicked witches" under the protection of a mere woman. Within the tribe, trained servants were to be found only in the most sophisticated section (close to the administrative and mission stations); they regarded Kako's people as nothing worse than "thieves." (I soon discovered the basic principle behind such name-calling: the more foreign, the more suspicious; hence the worse the reputation. The character commonly ascribed, in bush, to Europeans suffers accordingly.)

The best advice, in the long run, came from the ripe experience of two professors of anthropology. One said, "Always walk in cheap tennis shoes; the water runs out more quickly." The other said, "You'll need more tables than you think." Both had added, without going into detail, "Enjoy yourself, and never, never be an embarrassment to the administration."

The truck stopped. Then I saw a small, weather-beaten sign that said KAKO; beside it a narrow path led off through the thick, high grass. I turned my back on it and tried to make my need for water clear to my boys by loud repetition. The carriers tossed my loads out of the truck and began to debate them, with shouts and gestures so violent that I thought a fight was imminent; actually they were only settling which one of them was big enough to commandeer, by force if necessary, the lightest load.

The carriers set off down the narrow path. I waved good-by to the driver; I wished it was for me and not the carriers that he was settling down to wait. And as I started off into the bush, I thought how nice it would be to be at home with friends or at least still sitting in the station drinking beer with the Sackertons.

The sun was high. The tall grass cut out any view and any breeze. Then the carriers began to sing, and my momentary depression vanished. Seeing them file down the path, boxes on their heads, made me feel like something out of an old explorer's book. True, I was not in traditional costume: neither Mary Kingsley's stays and petticoats, nor in the pith helmet, shorts and boots of the traveler's frontispiece. It's difficult to feel adventurous in tennis shoes, a cotton dress, dark glasses, a shoulder bag and a floppy straw hat, but I managed it. I even managed to feel competent, almost experienced. The water from the small streams we waded was running out of my tennis shoes just as I had been told it would.

Some five miles from the road, we halted by a shallow river. The carriers wanted to swim. My "small boy" Monday—six feet of gangling youth—set up my folding chair in the shade of the trees. My steward Sunday produced chicken sandwiches and my new thermos flask full of hot tea (I still don't know where he got the ingredients). I forgot that this efficiency was none of my doing, and I felt mistress of all I surveyed. Then I wondered how to indicate my preference for coffee, and had my chair taken away from me because the carriers were ready to start. Willy-nilly, feeling not quite so confident, I chased down the path after my entourage. I was unable to ask them to wait awhile.

My feet began to hurt. I had not yet learned the trick of walking without socks in tennis shoes. The water leaked out, just as the professor had foretold. However, he had obviously thought it an insult to my intelligence to add that I must wash them out at each stream; otherwise the pebbles and bits of gravel stay inside the wet shoe to create blisters, break blisters and finally work inside the blister.

Twelve miles as the crow flies. I began to regard every wind and turn in what I then thought an extraordinarily sinuous bush path as an enemy. I stopped. My entourage went on. I yelled. Sunday turned around, looked at me thoughtfully, and gave orders to Monday, who produced a knife and dived into the bush. A few moments later I had a passable walking stick—more staff than cane and very knobbly. Sunday made encouraging noises. Since there was nothing else to do, I hobbled on.

I don't remember now how long it took me to get there. Later I found it a pleasant four-hour walk, but later I had also discovered that the tall grass hid many homesteads where one could rest in the shade, chat and eat a roasted ear of corn hot from the coals. That first time, I dragged further and further behind. The carriers were completely out of sight, though I could still hear them singing. Monday, who had apparently been detailed to stay with me, gave me water at judicious intervals and finally took over my shoulder bag as well.

Walking had become an eternity. I scarcely noticed that we had turned onto an even narrower path. Then I saw all the carriers resting beside my boxes in a space cleared of all grass, in the middle, a tree, and under it, my folding chair. I collapsed into it. Slippers appeared. Tea was brought and more tea. Even more reviving than the tea and slippers was the sight of the canvas sacks containing bed, bath and folding tables disappearing to my right into a cracked mud hut—square, and taken with its narrow veranda, somewhat larger than my tent. I looked to my left, and saw three more huts. The cook had pounded one of the kerosene tins flat and was moving with it into one of the huts to set up the kitchen stove: the flattened tin was laid across the other two, on their sides as ovens, with the fire between them. Monday had extracted my keys from my bag. Whenever the cook shouted, he brought out pots and pans. Whenever Sunday shouted, he dashed into the square hut with some of my personal boxes. Obviously these four huts around a bare yard were the resthouse. We had arrived.

Sunday appeared with my money box conveniently open. As I dug out the shillings and pence for the carriers, I began to realize that keeping things locked from one's boys was largely a gesture. Even if I should continue that gesture . . . I looked at my very portable and rather flimsy safe-box and remembered Sackerton's story of the thieves who had carried off on their backs a four-hundred-pound treasury safe to get at the £50 inside it at their leisure. Keys clearly could not prevent my boys robbing me if they wished. Before long I made all the boys a speech, handed the keys to Sunday, and retained an inventory. Except for half a jar of melon jam (traced to Monday's sweet tooth), nothing was ever missing.

The carriers left, singing a swift song to speed them to the road. It was getting late, and they wanted to be back to the truck before sundown. Only the most urgent business or overwhelming curiosity, I soon learned, takes anyone but a witch out on the paths after dark.

The bed was up, and I wanted to lie down. My feet hurt; I ached with weariness. But Sunday, Monday and the cook disapproved, first softly and fluently and then, as I didn't understand, loudly and even more fluently. I caught the word "chief" and Kako's name. I looked at the cook. His meager pidgin English would have to carry me through my initial difficulties.

The cook stepped forward. "Kako come. Bring chop." I groaned at the thought of social effort. The cook reproved me, "You thank Kako too much!" and stepped back, his say finished. Sunday then repeated in his own language the greeting I had already learned and added another phrase. Parrot fashion I said over whatever he told me. With the added help of a missionary's really excellent word list (unfortunately only from the language into English), I learned "I greet you" "How are you?" "How are all your people?" "Are you sure all of you are really well?" I learned to receive gifts with both hands cupped (to take with one hand indicates that the gift is insufficient and to receive anything with the left hand is a downright insult), to comment as I received, "You have done well; I rejoice," and to hand the gifts then to one of my boys while I said, "Hasn't he done well?" to this the boy would then reply, "He has indeed. We all rejoice."

I was too tired to be quick; we were still on "thank you" when my visitors arrived. At their head was an old man, white-haired, with a white stubble on his cheek. A tattered indigo cloth was slung togawise over his shoulder. Indeed, it was by my boys' deference and not by any external sign of state that I recognized Chief Kako. He walked slowly

7

toward me, leaning on his spear, but with a firm step. Behind him came a small, naked boy, almost hidden by the bamboo chair that he carried on his head, upside down, like a hood; then two women, wrapped in Manchester cottons, carrying a chicken, corn and eggs. Then came a glorious procession of elders in bright red hats, long white, yellow and purple robes, and blood-red goatskin shoulder bags: these were the notables. I scarcely saw them. Kako's dignity of bearing reduced them to a gaudy backdrop for his own somber shabbiness.

Kako and I shook fists. The chicken, corn and eggs changed hands with all due etiquette. The little boy shed his chair and placed it carefully opposite mine. Kako sat down. I sat down. The notables spread sheepskins on the ground beside Kako, and they sat down. The women stood behind Kako's chair, stiffly, like Victorian wives. We all looked at each other and smiled.

The notables produced long-stemmed pipes and tobacco from their bags. The little boy filled Kako's pipe for him, dived into the kitchen and returned with a glowing coal perched on top of the pipe bowl. Kako puffed until the pipe was going to his satisfaction, then dropped the coal on the ground. A notable hastily picked it up and started his pipe with it. The little boy ran for more coals. Almost smelling scorched fingers, I brought out matches and handed them to Kako. He nodded benignly and repeated the thank-you phrases, but to my dismay he pocketed the matches. The notables continued to use the coals. They smoked. I smoked. We all smiled.

The sun sank lower. The conversation that had sprung up among the notables died down. They put out their pipes by holding a thumb over the mouthpiece, a toe over the bowl. I didn't know how to say good-by. In desperation I repeated the greetings. Kako and the notables replied gravely and the older woman kept a straight face, but the younger one giggled and the little boy laughed outright. Finally Kako stood up, pointed to the setting sun, said something to my boys, and departed with his train of notables.

I sat on in a sort of stupor, exhausted from the unaccustomed walking and by the utter strangeness of everything about me. Just at dark Sunday passed me with a lighted pressure lamp; behind him came Monday with a bucket of steaming water. I filed after them into my hut. The canvas bath was set on a grass mat. My wooden boxes, neatly set around the walls, perched unevenly on stones for the discouragement, or at least the easier detection, of termites. The mosquito net made a cool pavilion over the camp bed. Sunday set the lamp on a box, Monday poured the bath, and they retired, rolling down the mat that was the only door.

There are several varieties of canvas bathtub. Mine looked rather like a round water lily leaf, with faintly raised edges and room enough for a not very fat person to sit tailor fashion. A tin hip bath is real African luxury, and like so many luxuries these days, hard to come by. The canvas soon loses its waterproofing, turning the clay beneath into mud. Worse, a careless movement can easily depress one side of it enough for all the water to run out. But it is much more relaxing than the enamel basins in which one can set only one foot at a time. However, the bath is the main thing: to be clean and rid of general sweat and stickiness is one of the greatest pleasures of life in the tropics.

Sunday had apparently never heard that one should put on a sweater after sundown. Indeed, during all our time together, he persisted in regarding my sweaters as suitable noontime wear. He had laid out my mosquito boots and my most backless evening dress. There was no sign of my dressing gown. I hesitated. After all, this was the evening of my first day in the field as an anthropologist and on my own; I had looked forward to this moment through years of theses and examinations. It deserved celebration. I slipped into the dress.

At my call, by the simple process of carrying the lamp before me, Sunday led me outside into the yard and to my

9

deck chair, put the lamp on a box, then reappeared with a tray of cigarettes and drinks: gin, bitters, tonic, the one bottle of Scotch whiskey which my ration allowed me, the siphon, a bottle of filtered water, and, incongruously, the jar of pickled onions I had bought for the odd curry. A desire to use the first siphon I had ever owned tempted me to be extravagant and have some Scotch. I had a brief tussle with Sunday, who seemed to feel any self-service on my part was a slight to his dignity and beneath mine. I won. It remained one of my few domestic victories.

Sunday took himself off. I leaned back in my chair, content with my drink and with my lot. Monday's smothered laughter and a glow of fire marked the kitchen. The faint light of small kerosene "bush" lamps revealed Sunday's movements between kitchen and veranda, and touched the round hut appropriated by the boys. Beyond, I could just see the row of saplings that ringed the resthouse grounds.

I began to relax. It was very pleasant to be left alone, with no need to walk and no need to talk—in any language. The Scotch went down smoothly. I could smell the roasting fowl, but I was still too tired to feel hunger. I decided to have another drink. As I put my hand to the siphon, something rustled on the path behind the saplings.

"Birds," I told myself firmly, "or small, harmless animals." I squirted soda into my glass. Another rustle. I looked up sharply. It became very quiet, but I saw something move and caught the glint of eyes. I took a cigarette. The small, sudden flame of my lighter was greeted by a murmur, which ceased as soon as I turned to peer into the shadows. But the voices had already reassured me. "At least," I thought, "it's people, not leopards or snakes or elephants."

Yet I could not relax again. I thought of having Sunday bring me a book, but he was being very busy and I had begun to hope he was busy with dinner. I tried to occupy my mind by wondering about the jar of pickled onions. The voices and the movements behind the saplings became less restrained. I was very conscious of being watched.

It's no use telling oneself that it doesn't matter if people stare: We're not used to it. I tried to convince myself that only the distinguished are stared at. I tried to think grand and consoling thoughts of movie stars and of royal progresses. No use. I became more and more self-conscious, aware of every move I made, every sip I drank, every lift of my cigarette to my lips. I tried sitting completely still; perhaps I could bore my audience. They still whispered and giggled and watched. I admonished myself: these were, after all, the people I had come to meet. I had once been advised that one must let people get used to such exotic sights, if necessary, by parading through the village streets. With that recollection I smiled and tried to look gracious. I only felt a fool.

"Go talk to them then," I concluded. I drained my glass and got up decisively. But I found myself walking toward the veranda, and I breathed a deep sigh of relief as Monday followed me with the lamp and Sunday pulled out a chair at a table set with every kind of glass and cutlery I had brought along.

My relief lasted only through the soup. Then I realized that there was a slit between the thatch and the veranda wall and that, in the lamplight, I was fully displayed. Impervious to the stares of natives, generations of empire-building Englishmen in jungles and deserts have sat down in full evening dress to eat their custard and tinned gooseberries. An American like myself can only feel that she has been somehow tricked into going on a picnic in high heels. In any case, feminine evening fashions are not adapted to mosquito-ridden countries. I was thoroughly uncomfortable.

The chicken was tough. The canned peaches were slimy with custard. The coffee was very English. Then Sunday set before me a liqueur glass in which there reposed one pickled onion drowned in gin. I recoiled from it with a gesture of real disgust.

My unseen audience laughed.

Something cracked. Forgetting all anthropological training and all my blisters, I rose in wrath, thrust the liqueur glass away in a splatter of gin, seized the coffee cup and stalked to the kitchen, declaiming violently in English and not caring whether anyone understood a word—it sounded so good in my own ears. I made coffee, still orating loudly and shaking the measuring spoon at the cook. I retreated to the veranda and sat down sulkily to be served. The offending gin and onion had been removed. Cigarettes came, and my coffee. I sipped. It was good; I indicated that I wanted such coffee in the morning.

Good coffee and tobacco, soothing and stimulating at once, gradually made me regret my display of temper. A second cup of coffee—and a complete silence behind the saplings—made me sorry I hadn't greeted the people who had come to stare at me. "After this," I resolved, "I'll talk to anyone and everyone. I'm here to learn about these people, and there's no other way to do it." In this mood, I paid close attention to Sunday's "good night," repeating the phrase meekly until I had it to his satisfaction.

Inside the hut I found dressing gown, pajamas and slippers neatly laid out, and, beside them on a box: a fresh glass of gin and pickled onion. It held my gaze. Once in my childhood a plate of prunes had been given me again and again until I ate them. Smiling half ruefully—for only a frivolous memory would connect two such incidents and then point out that I had come to like prunes—I lifted the glass and sniffed at it suspiciously. Perhaps . . . I tasted cautiously. It was no longer gin and onion or even onion in gin, but that mystic union of two flavors which makes the olive the better half of the martini. I finished it, and tucked the mosquito net carefully in behind me. Just before I fell asleep, I reflected that whatever lessons Africa had to teach me they would, if gin and onion were any indication, be unexpected, not too easily learned, and perhaps in the long run more valuable as experience than as habits.

Chapter Two

EARLY the next morning, I sat contentedly on my veranda drinking coffee made just to my taste. My emphatic orders —"Fruit and coffee, and then leave me alone"—had been obeyed. I don't like being rushed into a day before I am ready for it. I need to stretch my senses awake, slowly, without disturbance, just as I need to stretch my limbs into life before I get out of bed. Certainly, it's not until my third cup of coffee that I am fully awake and willing to face the consequences of that condition.

I was still drinking my second cup when Sunday suddenly materialized at my elbow. Surprised, I looked up and met at eye level a bowl of seething gray ooze. At my irritated frown, Sunday vanished as rapidly and quietly as he had come; he knew some Europeans dislike porridge. Before I could rouse my sleeping wits, he was back with a large plate of eggs and fried toast.

It was well for justice that I could expostulate only through the cook's interpretation. While he crossed the yard and Sunday stood stiffly in the doorway, I reminded myself into patience. The English like a large breakfast. Indeed, in a country like theirs, where people apply the principles of insulation and central heating to themselves rather than to their houses, a large and greasy breakfast has a certain functional value which disappears in the tropics. The Englishman abroad maintains his traditions tenaciously; he drills them into his servants. I had asked for trained servants; I had, perforce, British-trained servants

I could scarcely communicate with my boys; they had misunderstood. I must explain.

Once more I tried to tell the cook that I wanted nothing but fruit and coffee in the morning. His air of reproachful resignation showed me that he thought his skill as cook was involved. I wanted to tell him it was not so; the chef who could tempt me to breakfast does not exist. But explanation without words is impossible. "Fruit, coffee good; eggs, porridge bad." We could say no more to each other.

A stir on the path released our deadlock. Once again Kako paced slowly into the resthouse yard, followed by his bright train of notables. He had come, as he had told Sackerton he would, to teach me his language. I sent the boys out to welcome him, while I searched for a notebook and gulped my coffee like a harassed commuter.

Once again we sat outside in the shade of the tree, smiling and shaking fists in greeting. Once again Kako and his notables produced pipes; the same little boy ran into the kitchen for coals; the same two women stood behind Kako. Today, however each action was a lesson. By the time their pipes were going, I had written and repeated pipe, pipes, coals, flint and steel. At Kako's prompting they showed me bags and spears, pointed to chairs, sheepskins and articles of dress, drilling me on each word by the simple technique of saying it a bit louder with each repetition. They opened bags: out came snuff stands, kola nuts, odd bits of cloth wrapped around shillings and pennies. With them, we came to an end.

Kako sent the younger woman and the little boy running. Through the cook he told me that now we were to start on the real pith of the lesson. I turned to a fresh page in my notebook.

Kako pointed to himself and pronounced his name. I beamed encouragingly upon him, for above all I wanted to learn people by name—as many and as quickly as possible. When Kako named, I repeated and wrote. When he pointed, I looked intently for identifying signs: that man was very thin; that one was lame; that one was reddish;

14

that one almost purple-black. All of them were elaborately scarred, and the more distinctive patterns of scarification proved the most reliable means of identification. Beards can be removed. What's worse, when these people shave, beard, mustache, hair and eyebrows all go, transforming a white-haired elder into a youthful billiard ball. However, this time—with all of them sitting together and in the same place—I was able to close my notebook and repeat all their names correctly. Kako informed me that I had done well.

The woman and the little boy returned, each with armfuls of leaves. Kako spread about a dozen out on the ground before me, and named them one by one; then the next dozen, and on and on. Some, he told me, were edible. By pointing at the farms to the north of the resthouse and the bush to the south, he informed me which were cultivated. Kako broke off; he needed all his attention for lighting his pipe with the matches I had given him. My instruction was taken over by Ikpoom, whose name and face I could easily remember because his eyes were so sad and he was so very ugly. Ikpoom, also pointing, taught me the words for path and bush, farm and fallow, earth and heavens, correcting my constant mistakes far more patiently than Kako had done. And I made many. Theirs is one of the simpler African languages, yet it was months before it seemed the only natural way to speak: a flow of fat, firm consonants and comfortable vowels, quite unlike the breathy hisses of English.

By nine o'clock that morning, I had several pages of words, and my tongue was limp from unaccustomed twisting. Unable to take in any more, I instituted a review by again naming the notables. I again got most of them right: the right man and almost the right sound. Kako looked on me with favor. Encouraged, I demanded the names of the women. They smiled, but Kako ignored my question and turned firmly back to the leaves. Rather reluctantly I began to name them. With every word Kako became more dour. I spoke more loudly; my pronunciation couldn't be that bad. Ikpoom's eyes grew sadder; the women seemed incredulous. The little boy could bear it no longer. He snatched from me the leaf I was naming and handed me another. The order had been mixed, and not once had I put the right name to the right plant.

These people are farmers: to them plants are as important and familiar as people. I'd never been on a farm and am not even sure which are begonias, dahlias or petunias. Plants, like algebra, have a habit of looking alike and being different, or looking different and being alike; consequently mathematics and botany confused me. For the first time in my life I found myself in a community where ten-year-old children weren't my mathematical superiors. I also found myself in a place where every plant, wild or cultivated, had a name and a use,' and where every man, woman and child knew literally hundreds of plants. None of them could ever believe that I could not if I only would.

Kako gave me that long and incredulous glare with which a brilliant father regards his backward child. Then he insisted that we start all over again. I stared at the leaves. I fingered the leaves, and drew the leaves. But the only leaf I could identify almost every time was the very distinctively pronged cassava leaf. I confused corn with guinea corn and at least three, very similar wild grasses. I couldn't and still can't, tell one kind of yam leaf from the next. The little boy, no more than eight years old, stood beside me and prompted me; he knew them all. I was discouraged. Kako lost heart. He became politely bored, and promised we should try again some other, unspecified time. Then he drew his toga more closely about him and withdrew.

I was left with the leaves and my notebook and a strong regret that I hadn't chosen to study a people like the Bedouin who have camels and a desert, both readily identified. I went back to the veranda; after one brief glance at my notebook, I stacked the leaves neatly in a corner. I was tired of leaves; I hadn't come here to learn botany. I moved outside again and occupied myself by staring at the stream

16

of people that had been filing along the path behind the saplings since early morning.

They were all going in the same direction, scores of them, almost on each other's heels. Most of them turned their heads to stare at me, and some shouted greetings, but none of them paused. Men passed, dragging recalcitrant goats, sheep and sometimes pigs by a rope around the animal's neck. Women in gaudy waist cloths balanced on their heads calabashes filled with greens and gourds, cotton, peppers or bundles tied in leaves. They were followed by their children, also with something on their heads: smaller calabashes with smaller bundles, or sometimes a tiny stool. A solitary boy, knock-kneed and naked, carried a tiny bamboo cage with a disconsolate song bird inside it. A young dandy clad in a very small cloth, but smeared bright red with camwood, headed a group of musicians— their drums slung over their shoulders, one of them piping a bamboo flute.

"A market." Excitedly I thought of going myself. Then I felt my blisters and decided against it. The boys, however, took turns at visiting the market; from them I learned it was held every fifth day and was only a few hundred yards down the path. By eleven the procession toward the market trickled to an end. From the east I could hear the dull roar of voices.

A man, who had been sitting all day by the path leading into the resthouse yard, looked up from his knitting. He nodded in the direction of the noise and said something. Word list and notebook in hand, I sat down beside him. "The market is roaring," he knitted on; it was a red and black scarf, I noticed, and he was using bicycle spokes as knitting needles. Like everything else that can be done while attending court sessions and other important meetings, knitting is man's work. Woman's proper occupation is weeding and cooking.

"Everyone comes to Kako's market," the man continued. I began to wonder what he wanted here and of me, and why he should prefer to sit here. He could not mean to go on to market later: people were already beginning to return, though still only one and two at a time.

After lunch, when I went outside again, the man was still sitting there. A rather burly young woman, with a clown's mask of white bath powder on her face, started to come past him, beyond the pale of saplings and into my yard. He shouted. She ignored him. He dashed toward her, his arm raised as though to strike. I jumped up, shouting and frowning at the man, greeting and smiling at the woman. She turned toward me, volubly. I could only greet and smile. She shrugged, then stood stock still and stared at me.

Another woman saw us; she too started in. Again the man tried to drive her out. I objected through the cook, but the cook refused to translate. He managed to tell me that Kako had placed this man here to keep the people coming to and from the market out of the resthouse grounds.

I was furious: so Kako meant to keep me from meeting people. Hastily and angrily I announced that anyone who wished to see me should be free to do so; I had come here to meet people and to get to know them; therefore I was going to talk to everyone who wished to greet me. My boys protested: no European did such a thing. They were quite right; mentally—and conditionally—I absolved Kako of unwarranted interference. Aloud I firmly overrode my boys: I was not like other Europeans; I had come here with the sole purpose of meeting people and talking to them. They refused to move from the entrance. I countered by dragging my chair out to the path. There I sat down.

By this time more people were leaving the market. One after the other they stopped, greeted me, and drew to the side of the path to join the cluster of people that just stood and stared at me. The cluster grew into a crowd. I found myself sitting like a smiling waxwork figure on silent exhibition to the curious. I sat on, determined to make clear by my actions what I could not explain in words. Surely

18

coming out here to greet people would prove that I welcomed them all.

I grew bored, and I was very glad to catch sight of an almost familiar face. It was one of the notables, Poorgbilin, the fat friendly one. I hailed him with loud cordiality, and escorted him and his wife into the resthouse yard. The crowd streamed in after us. I had been too successfully emphatic with the knitting man. He sat back, aloof and sullen.

Poorgbilin and I sat down in the shade of the tree. The crowd formed a tight palisade around us. Poorgbilin ignored them. I could not: they were so many and so close, yet so inaccessible beyond the barrier of language. I hadn't bargained for so many people. Poorgbilin had his wife take her market purchases out of her calabash. He named each object as she laid it on the ground: indigo, cotton, okra, palm oil. The crowd watched and listened, quietly, intently. Beniseed, beans, camwood—a word with one simple vowel safe between unspeakable consonants. I rushed at the word, and stuttered to an ignominious stop. Irrepressible laughter swept about me. I smiled, half embarrassed, at the grinning mob; they laughed again. Poorgbilin shook his head; his wife picked up her purchases. The crowd opened for them, and they left.

I also started to leave the yard, but no path opened for me. The circle of people merely extended itself, moving amoebalike as I moved, still I stood, still among them, just outside my door. I motioned them to one side. Many of them smiled; no one budged.

An old woman stepped forward, holding out a bottle filled with a thick orange liquid. Automatically I smiled and spoke: "Palm oil." A pleased murmur rippled about me. The crowd had found an amusement. They too would teach me their language. A youth waved some corn at me, calling out the word. I was silent. He spoke more loudly, shaking a corncob at me like a scolding finger. I looked at him, undecided: all my life I have had to avoid crowds for fear of fainting; I didn't want to offend anyone—they were

19

so many . . . I looked again at their expectant faces, and spoke: "Corncob." Two raised voices corrected me. Again I tried. Several more took up the refrain, chorusing "corncob" more loudly and yet more loudly each time, until the whole throng was screaming "corncob." Someone giggled at the noise; the shouting became a gale of laughter. A boy held out a banana. A woman poked a spindle at me. Again I responded. Again I became the target of their screaming.

More and more people. I could no longer see through the press of sweating bodies. A gang of tipsy youths elbowed forward. They pulled things out of the women's calabashes to thrust at me, yelling until my ears ached from their noise. I couldn't hear. I couldn't think. I could no longer distinguish anything individual in the laughing mass of mobile faces. There was no unpeopled air to breathe.

In all earnest now, I pushed toward my door. Those just before my hands tried to draw back; they could clear no more than a narrow lane. I slipped through, and collapsed in the corner of my veranda. They would not follow: I had learned in the station that a European's house is sanctuary.

They made no attempt to follow, though the pressure behind made those in front bulge slightly into the doorway. The rest flowed, like deflected water, along the edge of my veranda—crouching outside to peer through the slit between thatch and veranda wall, inserting head and elbows to see the better. Women held their children high and at arm's length over the wall: "Look at the European!" The European is their bogy man. The children howled in their mothers' stiff clutch. A drunken young man snatched a child: "I'll give you to the European!" The child writhed in desperation and fell terrified onto the veranda floor. His mother forced her way in.

The mob poured in behind her. I jumped to my feet.

They surged forward, laughing, shouting. Cheerfully, in friendliest fashion, they swarmed about me, penning me into the corner. The odor of recently consumed beer and the indescribably rotten smell of locust beans hit me like a blow. Nauseated and half faint I leaned against the wall. I called for my boys. Cassava, corn, indigo—anything with a name—thrust against my face. Words hurled at me. Again I called. No one could hear. A girl tugged at my skirts to show me her castanets. A bent hag reached out to touch my hair. The noise, the smell of hot, excited bodies closed over me.

A determined young woman shoved her way to the fore: broad-cheeked, a stubby pipe clenched between her teeth, her hair in a score of tight French braids close against the scalp. She put her hand on my arm. I moved to dash it away. She clasped my outstretched hand tightly by the thumb—the sign of friendship. She shouted her name: Atakpa.

Then she turned her strong, straight back square upon me, like a shield against the mob. Arms akimbo, she harangued them, and one by one, raggedly, they dropped their shouting. She spoke on, assured, without hesitation. She gestured at me with a toss of her head. There was a great roar of laughter. Then, without more ado, she grabbed me by the wrist, talking all the while, and drew me behind her, limp and unresisting through the crowd.

Out onto the path we went, the crowd parting before us and closing in behind to follow, in single file, for the path was narrow and the grass sharp. Atakpa released me. I followed her gladly, hobbling a bit on my blisters, but delighted to breathe fresh air. Eventually we turned aside into a rather small and ramshackle homestead. The thatch on the huts was smoke blackened even to the outside, and many of the roofs were bent and gaping. A plump baby sat in a litter of leaves and corn husks, eating dirt. Atakpa, again taking my wrist, pulled me into the central reception hut, on hands and knees through the low doorway. I stood up, coughing with the smoke and feeling, rather than seeing, the first of the crowd push in behind me.

Beyond me, invisible in the smoke and dark, an old man's voice exploded angrily: "Get out! Get out!" As I turned to go, Atakpa pulled me down onto a very low bench—actually a plank bed cut from a single tree trunk. Here, below the smoke, my eyes began to clear. While the old man's furious voice raged on, I made out the fire, a high platform over it supported by four teakwood posts, and close to the fire, the author of all the noise: a hale old man in dark red camwood and a ragged toga fallen from his shoulders. He rose, clutching the cloth to him with both hands, still snarling loudly. The crowd which had followed us disappeared—out of the reception hut we sat in, out of the homestead.

I sat on where Atakpa had placed me, dazed, without curiosity. I realized only that it was quiet. Atakpa vanished. The old man, Yabo, again lay back in his reclining chair and stared into the fire. I made out one or two old women in the shadows behind him. Atakpa returned with a young man. She introduced him. She pointed to him, to herself and then to the old man, repeating words. I smiled at them all, vaguely and without real interest. Atakpa began to scold. I shook my head. With a short, exasperated grunt, she tapped the back of my hand. I looked down and saw my notebook and pencil still in my hand, still open to the few erratic scribbles that marked the onset of the crowd.

While I still stared, Yabo stirred and growled at Atakpa. Soon I found myself eating a freshly roasted ear of corn. Then she brought what looked like a mass of wet, white clay and, in a separate dish, a slimy green substance. I smiled, rubbed my stomach, and waved my ear of corn in my effort to look well fed. Atakpa rather reluctantly removed the dishes: Yabo and the young man ate them. In their place, she brought me the dirt-eating child and once more started pointing and talking. To please her, I listlessly jotted some syllables of nonsense. But Atakpa had a genius for making her meaning clear. I suddenly realized that she was teaching me those anthropological favorites—kinship terms—and I fell to writing happily. This, I resolved, was the way I wanted to do field work: in quiet, among just a few people at a time, and in their own homes. But how? I might not find everyone as hospitable as Atakpa.

The sun was low when Atakpa dragged me back to the resthouse. I went unwillingly, half afraid that the crowd might still be there. I slumped together with relief when I saw the knitting man and my boys once more standing guard against passers-by. With an I-told-you-so attitude just short of impertinence, they inquired whether they were to let people in. I replied rather stiffly that the day was over. Privately, while I nursed my blistered feet and my shattered nerves in a hot bath, I wondered how to hit the happy medium between seeing no one and being hounded by a mob. I could not expect to be welcomed in their homesteads if I refused to receive them in mine.

Sunday came at my call. Once again he started to lead me out into the yard to my deck chair and my evening selection of drinks. I, however, wanted to stay inside, where I could not be seen. I motioned him to leave the lamp. Sunday pleaded; his frantic gestures of explanation included all the heavens. I was adamant. Monday came in, dragging my tent. He laid it at my feet. Sunday's finger pointed to an unmistakable hole in the thatch. A roll of thunder from the southern mountains completed the demonstration. In sudden comprehension, bowing and waving like animated puppets, Sunday and I pointed to roof and tent and ropes: he meant to give me a second roof of canvas inside my hut, hanging the ground sheet over the veranda and the tent itself over my bed and boxes. I would be underfoot inside.

I went out to my deck chair. There was no one about. Even the knitting man had gone. Only the swelling thunder broke a silence so clear that I could hear Sunday's muttered instructions to Monday as the two of them worked to secure me against the wet.

I, however, was even more concerned with my protection against people. I had come prepared to combat shyness and suspicion, expecting to be shunned and alone. I had known I must struggle to break through the fear and respect usually shown to Europeans—a respect that leaves one behind a glass wall, visible and untouchable. Today I had learned that these people were quite as willing to touch me as to stare. It was, it seemed, easy enough to make oneself the center of a curious crowd. But still withheld from any real contact.

Wrapped in my difficulties, I ate absently, inattentively waved Sunday good night, and sat on gazing blindly into the dark beyond my circle of lamplight. The heralding thunder, the approaching storm wind that blew keen under the thatch, roused me from my absorption and sent me to bed for warmth. There I told myself that it was only the thunder that kept me awake. Only the thunder, not the memory of raucous shouting, of smothered air, of people thrusting, handling, forcing screaming children at me. I tossed myself into bad dreams.

The pleasant rustle of rain in the thatch greeted my waking. I wanted coffee, but I lay on in bed listening for voices and wondering how many people were watching outside. The rain leaking through my thatch tapped against my canvas ceiling. It must be raining very hard. I sat up. No one would be out in this weather. I peered cautiously round the edge of my mat door. The rain-swept yard was empty. I went out.

Sunday brought papaw and coffee. I ate and drank, lit a cigarette and stared absently at the rain-pocked earth outside, tiny mud craters lifted and shifted by the pelting rain. Sunday appeared at the kitchen door, holding my umbrella over a precarious structure of dishes. I eyed him with foreboding while he tenderly unwrapped the dishes and set before me a repulsive plate of steaming sardines.

"Take it away!" I yelped. The missionary's word list had some very practical phrases in it. "Take it away!" Sunday started off with the coffee. In this language the pronouns depend on the class of objects; I had indicated a liquid "it." "Return with it," I countermanded. With almost aggressive resignation, Sunday brought back the coffee. I pointed at the sardines and repeated "take"; I did not dare repeat the liquid "it." Sunday first provided the correct pronoun. Then he gave advice. I resorted to the word list and discovered that I would get very thin and something else not listed.

Again I summoned the cook. As he so righteously pointed out, I had said only: "Eggs bad, porridge bad." With a sigh, I began a painstaking condemnation of every breakfast dish I could imagine. This time he seemed to understand. Sardines in hand, he turned to go. At the very door he turned around with the light of last hope in his eyes. "Beans on toast?" he suggested. I rejected his offer vehemently. The cook departed sadly.

I picked up the word list. Clearly I could not even influence my destiny until I could talk. The crowd had listened to Atakpa. But how could I hope to imitate her, when I could not make my own cook understand about my breakfast? I sat down to my task. The rain dripped from the trees, onto the thatch, through the thatch and onto the canvas. Against its tapping I mumbled words and phrases, over and over. Yet I was not really aware of what I uttered, for my ears were attentive to the rain, dreading any sign of its lessening, dreading the sunshine that would bring people forth.

The word list was dead. I tossed it aside impatiently. To learn I needed to hear people speak; to do my job I had to know at least a few of them intimately. Whatever else had been done yesterday, it had been made clear that I was prepared to see everyone. That could be turned to advantage. To set a guard at my gates now would destroy anything I had gained. In any case, no matter whom I might choose, I would give that person the power of selecting with whom I talked and thus what I came to know. That wouldn't work. What, then? I stretched out on my bed to think.

It was hot when I awoke, and clear. The yard was full of women's chatter punctuated with laughter and the teasing, off-duty voices of my boys. I peered out. About a dozen women were sitting under my tree, knee deep in calabashes and children. I hid behind my mat, wrestling with a sensation I came to know all too well: I wanted to talk to people! I couldn't bear to meet them. Even months later, when I could converse with ease and had my friends among these people, there remained that momentary pause, that same need to compel myself into their midst. It was very like the instinctive hesitation of the most ardent swimmer just before he plunges into the sea. I liked to be among them, just as I liked to be in the sea, but neither ever became my natural element.

I forced myself out into the yard. The women clustered about me, chattering gaily, thrusting small gifts of corn and eggs upon me. I accepted and smiled and wrote down names. I recognized Atakpa and greeted her. I sat down with them on the roots of the tree, but I could not give them my full attention. My eye was on the path. Two girls passed, saw us, turned back and came in. My heart sank. Atakpa was saying something. I paid no heed, afraid of another crowd, not knowing what to do to avoid it. Atakpa was shouting and pointing to something behind me. I shrugged my incomprehension; my eyes were fixed on the path.

Something soft and wet struck at me, below and behind. I scrambled away. It was a small, shiny tree frog. Atakpa was laughing, repeating the word she had screamed at me. If it had been a scorpion . . . I tried to grin, and resolved hereafter to pay attention to what was told me. The frog leaped at Atakpa. She jumped. I too began to laugh. Soon the frog, like a mouse at a bridge party, had all the women on their feet, giggling and screeching. Monday disposed of the frog, and we settled down again.

Atakpa said something about Yabo. I couldn't understand, but I remembered how he had chased the crowd from his homestead and wished I knew the secret. Several of the women began to chorus Atakpa's words, more and more loudly. Atakpa turned on them, silenced them, and repeated her speech softly. Gradually, with the help of my cook and the word list, I understood: so much shouting was bad; many people were a bad thing; I should talk to two or three at a time. I agreed heartily. Atakpa said I should come live with her at Yabo's homestead; there I could learn the language and no one would bother me.

For a moment I toyed with the idea. Then I remembered how small, how dilapidated and dirty Yabo's homestead was. Besides my boys seemed genuinely concerned: if I were to live any place but the resthouse, it must be in the chief's homestead. I suddenly recalled that Yabo had not been among Kako's collection of notables. Atakpa was still coaxing: it was not good to live in the bush alone. She threatened me with snakes, ants and witches. The boys were in complete agreement about the dangers she listed; there were few of us; we were some distance from the closest homestead, and again the whole group chorused: "It's not good to sit alone in the bush."

It took a long time to frame my questions and to understand their answers. At Kako's homestead would I see anyone besides his own people? "All the world comes to a chief's homestead, and they would all greet you—a European." Would they come as they had on market day? They were impatient: no crowd would push like that, uninvited (the boys were being tactful), into the homestead of anyone of importance, let alone into that of a chief.

I began to hope. True, I had planned to live separately at first, to avoid identifying myself with any part of the community till I knew something of the factions within it. By now, however, I was quite willing to shelter behind the chief's toga, if he would let me do so. But where would I live in his homestead and would he want me always underfoot?

The swift parting of the women and a flurry of greetings interrupted my vacillation. Kako himself stood before me, presenting a large and active ram prancing stiff-legged at the end of a rope. As soon as I had thanked him, he confided that his heart was troubled. With paternal concern he informed me that in my present location I was exposed to snakes and ants (he omitted the witches). It was not

27

good to sit alone in the bush. Would we move down to his homestead? He would build me a hut for myself, one for the boys, and a kitchen and reception hut right next to his own huts in his homestead. As quickly as I could, almost before I was sure that I understood him correctly, I accepted.

As we started off for his homestead to select the exact site then and there, I felt I was fortunate indeed to be among such kind, hospitable folk. Much later, when Kako and I knew each other from months of living within whispering distance, he confessed that he had been quite ready to insist on my moving down where he could keep an eye on me. He had not thought me able to take care of myself, and Sackerton held him responsible. I had, it seemed, been an embarrassment to the Native Administration. That afternoon, however, I felt only gratitude for his kindness. I walked back to the resthouse praying that Kako would build as promptly as he had promised, that I could move soon, and that until then it would rain a little every day and all day on market day. I vowed to pay better attention to words and frogs and leaves. I was not, as yet, concerned by snakes and ants and witches.

Chapter Three

I NEED not have worried. My behavior on market day had been unwise, but it had good consequences—mainly because two people had attempted to save me from my folly. Atakpa's exploit in stealing me from the crowd, Kako's invitation to come live in his homestead, turned me from a mere side show into an object of prestige. The lion hunters got busy. Everyone was determined to have me visit his homestead before I visited the homestead of anyone else. Through their industry I began to learn my way about the countryside; I met more and more people, and, best of all, escaped the throngs that kept coming to the resthouse "to stare at the white woman."

Every rainless morning of the entire fortnight after that first market day, I woke up to find from ten to twenty people sitting under my tree—not on my veranda, after the first time. I was ready to fight for morning coffee in peace and solitude, and I turned to my boys for advice. They were thoroughly pleased by this redeeming sign of European aloofness and guaranteed to keep people out in the yard until I woke (by what threats or persuasion I never asked). Then, they instructed, as I walked past the tree to my outhouse, I was to greet people, "Have you awakened?" On the way back, I was to say, "I go to eat and drink that my heart also may awaken. Sit then, until I come." My visitors actually did sit there, with only occasional shouts that I should hurry up. To tell the truth, I did try to linger over my coffee until I saw an elder among the waiting

29

people. Even if he had come merely to greet, the others were more quiet in his presence. Generally, such men came to invite me to their homesteads. I always went.

I thought I should enjoy those walks. The countryside was lovely: a range of mountains to the south, hills with scattered brush and occasional giant trees, stream beds shaded a cool green by palm and vine, gardenlike farms with neat rows of mounded earth over which the yam vines fell or twined up the stalks of interplanted cassava. But I was able to see remarkably little of it.

Stalking ahead of me, my host pointed out grasses and plants, birds and side paths. Even the most taciturn of these people becomes loquacious on the path—for there not even witches can overhear—and the talkative never pause. Not only my ears, but my eyes were busy. I had to look up, seeking landmarks visible above the grass, for I was trying to learn my way about the countryside. I had to look down. Across the ridges the paths are narrow gullies, eroded down to bare laterite; between ridges the paths are slick with mud. Even a few seconds' inattention to the path can bring stubbed toes, wrenched ankles and sometimes a fall.

I had to look at my notebook. Market day had firmly established it as my way of learning the language; forever after, anyone who pointed out any object to me insisted on my writing it down. Consequently, while my guide strode down the path before me, carefully watching his feet and talking a blue streak of information, I trailed behind—sketching paths, scribbling words, looking up, down and around—stumbling as I went. Every time I stumbled, I was crossly ordered, "Look at the path!" A second later, I was told, just as commandingly, "Write that down!" Finally, we would turn down a side path. My host, after a brief "This is my homestead," would fall silent, and then, for the first time, I had a chance to look about in safety.

Sometimes it was a homestead of only two or three families; sometimes almost a village with seventy to a hundred people. All of the homesteads, however, were alike in plan: a series of circles concentric around the open yard

30

and the shade trees in the middle. The outermost ring was formed by fruit trees, tobacco patches, and kitchen gardens for spices and sauce plants. Just within this was a circle of small mud granaries perched on hardwood stilts and of sleeping huts set a yard or two from each other—one for each married woman. Innermost were the reception huts which the men built in front of their wives' huts: here, or under the trees in the yard, children played while their elders did chores or entertained guests.

On a first, formal visit, my host and I usually sat outside, perhaps with some of the older men of the homestead also on chairs and benches beside us. Giggling women stood clustered about us to stare at me. The younger children peered out from behind their mothers' brief, wraparound cloths; the older ones watched boldly and intently. Only my host's senior wife came forward: she brought water to wash my hands, and fruit or roasted corn for me to eat. I did my best to make some kind of conversation. I didn't know then that I was supposed to behave like a prospective mother-in-law on her first visit, sitting stiff and silent until a chicken was caught and handed to me; conversation belonged to second visits. My hosts, however, did know how to behave. They sat, sober and untalkative while the chicken chase whirled around us.

African chicken is scrawny and muscular. At market my cook bought fairly young hens and fed them to a degree of plumpness. But a hen is not an appropriate gift. Prestige demands a rooster. The bigger the rooster, the greater the honor. Since chickens are sacrificed in many magical rites, a large rooster has attained his size and age through his strength, agility and speed. Everything that survives to ripe age in this country has to be tough. Almost always, it was the biggest, toughest, and hence most honorable rooster that was pointed out as suitable for me.

A single youth would begin the pursuit, between huts, through the two-doored reception huts, around trees, up the thatched roofs and into the trees. Soon others would join in the hunt, trying to catch a bird skilled in escape.

Meanwhile, taking my cue from my host, I pretended not to notice the chase—even when the rooster flew straight past me followed by a string of whooping, panting youngsters. Eventually, a triumphant boy would appear, the rooster, with its legs securely tied, clamped under his arm. The rooster was, however, still invisible as far as I was concerned and, also theoretically, still inaudible. Not until my host proffered me the rooster could I take notice of it, trying, as I had seen them do, to get an expression of surprised pleasure on my face: "You have done well. I rejoice greatly." I also tried, and was finally able, to hold between my cupped hands a strong, angry and ruffled rooster with seeming ease and without a pause in my flow of compliments.

The presentation of the fowl, or of any other gift, was the sign that it was time for me to go. My host, followed by all the members of his homestead, showed me to the main path; there he called a lad of six or ten to escort me back to the resthouse. And off we'd go: the boy swinging the rooster by its legs and carrying on his head the yams or other produce that the senior wife had given me.

The first four days, on my return from such visits, I went expectantly down to Kako's to see what was being done about the building of my huts. Kako always greeted me cordially. When I mentioned the word "huts," he smilingly led me to the site we had selected. Then, somehow, he faded away, leaving me in the company of a stiff, rheumatic old woman. Each time she succeeded in driving me into the gardens surrounding the homestead; each time— she had a commanding presence and a gimlet eye—she set me to learning the same batch of plants; each time I got them miserably mixed; each time she shepherded me straight from her kitchen garden back to the resthouse. My boys made a point of telling me she was Kako's senior wife, for they realized, as I did not, that her personal escort was a signal honor. At the time I added up the way she eased me home and the total absence of any building activity and got, as a sum, that Kako didn't really want me in his homestead. Annoyed, unable to discuss the matter with anyone for lack of words, I fell back on my own resources.

I decided to fill in, by systematic walking, the gaps left by my guided visits. I wanted a map of the scattered homesteads (about a quarter of a mile from each other) and the name of the head of each one. It was a task that had to be done, and one of the few I would be able to do satisfactorily while the people and their language were strange to me and I was strange to them.

I set about it, and it was well that I did so. As it turned out, only the good-for-nothing idlers who had no business of their own had time to come "stare" at me after first curiosity was satisfied. I soon became a sort of circuit anthropologist. The people who acknowledged Kako as chief lived over an area of many square miles. Except for occasional visits to particular elders for specific purposes, and the events that brought them into Kako's homestead, most of these people lived outside my sphere. But this larger group was subdivided into many smaller ones, and it was that group of Kako's which covered about four square miles on which I finally concentrated. The homesteads in this area could be covered easily and completely in four round-trip circuits, which I took in daily rotation; each was a full morning's walking and talking. This group of some eleven hundred people became the community in which I took part. Before I left, I knew all the men, most of the women and some of the children by name and by face.

It took the first few weeks, however, even to discover that this group existed, who of importance was in it, and where they lived. My days were a kaleidoscope of strange faces and unfamiliar objects, a maze of paths leading I knew not where. In the course of these walks I located the homesteads of many of Kako's notables. I turned, by a new path, into Yabo's tumble-down homestead. Atakpa immediately put me to shelling beans. When I tried to resume my walk, she led me off in the opposite direction to show me her farm. There, despite my protests that I could learn by watching, she taught me how to weed, knees straight,

33

back bent. My muscles were aching when she finally let me go. I began to wonder where I could find the oppressed, downtrodden women described by the missionaries. All those I had met were as stubborn and intractable as they looked. Just the same, I liked them—especially Atakpa, who was my age and merry.

On another walk I stumbled into fat Poorgbilin's homestead, and found it as large, clean and prosperous as Poorgbilin himself. He sent for chairs, for his toga (I had found him informally dressed in the youths' towel-about-the-waist costume), and for his wives. He spread food before me, and when I ate no more than a mango, he pointed out a plump and husky wife as proof of my need to eat a great deal more. He opened my notebook for me and had me write down the words for everything in our line of vision: huts, roofs, pots, chairs, stacks of mud bricks drying in the sun, bundles of thatching grass. Indeed, in every homestead through which I walked, even in the smallest and meanest—except Kako's—there were bricks and posts and stacks of building materials. Kako's delay could not be attributed to a shortage. But why should he bother to make a hypocritical offer?

On the second market day I went for a long walk, carrying water and sandwiches. At dark I returned to the resthouse, exhausted but unmobbed, with much of my map filled in and, since I had been going against traffic both ways, an almost shocked realization of the market's popularity. Everyone seemed to think I had lost my way, and everyone seemed to think that telling me where the market was would suffice to lead me to it.

What I did that second market day was even less approved than what I had done on the first. That night Kako's senior wife called to deliver a scolding palliated only by the presentation of five eggs. I returned profuse thanks and a firm statement that I didn't want to go to market. Possibly as a result of this rash statement, Kako and his notables all came the next morning: a market was a good thing; this was Kako's market; I must attend it; the very next market

34

Kako would send someone to carry my chair down to the chief's ramada, where I was to sit, be seen and be greeted. I gave in with what grace I might.

I had not wanted to spend every fifth day at market. The shape my life was beginning to take was not altogether of my choice. I had not wanted to spend over an hour every morning washing sores and handing out pills either.

First my boys, then Atakpa and her friends, then everyone else had begun to call for medicine. Conversation with other anthropologists had more or less prepared me for this. Their advice on what to include in a medicine kit had varied widely with the nature and activities of the people among whom they had lived. One had spent most of his time binding up knife wounds; another, in a more peaceable community, found himself treating hang-overs and indigestion. One, indeed, had refused to get involved in the matter at all, on the grounds that leprosy and tuberculosis are not to be cured with patent medicines.

There are, nevertheless, things that patent medicines, sometimes simple cleanliness, can cope with. I started modestly with those who said they had headaches or stomach aches. I learned to differentiate between the ache of surfeit and the ache of hunger, to dribble castor oil down a twig into the mouths of contrary-minded babies, and always to take temperatures, for these people called all fevers "stomach aches." I soon found myself dealing with old infections, boils, carbuncles and running tropical sores.

I felt it an obligation; yet it is one thing to come to an intellectual conclusion, quite another to act upon it without vomiting. And I often felt physically sick at my task. I knew then why washing feet and tending sores had been set as a penance by the medieval church. I had no desire to do penance; there was little enough I could do from a medical standpoint. Yet I could not refuse.

At first it had seemed to me a service I could offer to a community from which I was asking so much in the way of patience and information. That aspect soon vanished completely. I comprehended for the first time that it is

35

morally impossible to refuse help which it is in one's power
to give. That is a sentiment which I had heard since my
Sunday School days, but it is a sentiment which has little
meaning for the ordinary man in a complex modern society. If we feed a passing tramp or merely tell him of the
nearest relief agency, the matter is off our consciences. We
are often asked to give money. We are seldom asked to
contribute of our time and heart. The man whom unusual
circumstances might tempt to do so is very liable to find
himself unthanked and even lectured as a bungler by some
competent welfare worker—and with some justice. Charity
was once a virtue. It is now a paid and specialized profession.

Here the matter was completely personal, not even between myself and the community—as I had first thought it
—but between myself and this, that or the other individual.
That I refused medicine for those diseases which they too
considered incurable, like leprosy or elephantiasis—that
they accepted and understood. But that I treated some of
the ills they called "stomach aches" and not others, no matter what explanations I tried to give of suspected appendi-
citis, malaria-swollen spleens, and so forth, was invariably
set down to my helping the people I liked and turning
away those I didn't. Our viewpoints were irreconcilable.

Again, it was I who yielded. One old woman came to
me with a headache from weeding too long in the sun. I
gave her an aspirin. Two weeks later she brought me five
withered old women with swollen, aching knees. My medicine, she informed me, had cured a knee that had been
troubling her for years; she had brought her friends to be
cured as well. Not sure what part faith had played in it, I
gave them all aspirin. After a week they went away un-
cured and not quite sure who or what was to blame. Like
most compromises, it had satisfied no one completely and
had achieved nothing beyond the demonstration of a general willingness to be obliging and the setting of yet another
precedent for my general acquiescence.

As more and more people came to me with their ailments, I instituted an early morning sick call, partly so they could be sure of finding me, but even more so that I might get it all over at once. Even so, no matter where I went, no matter what time of day, they haunted me. I hated it, hated the unnecessary suffering they endured, hated my own incompetence, and felt quite unreasonably that it was somehow wrong for me not to be a doctor. I prayed, selfishly, that no friend of mine would ever turn to me for a help beyond my power to give. Outwardly, I cheerfully washed and bandaged, and brusquely told them their ills were not my business. Then I escaped to my other affairs as quickly as I could, for the sick made me forget that I was an anthropologist with a job of work to do; in their presence I could not pretend that I was living a high and light-hearted adventure.

It was hard enough, even without the sick, to remember what I was. I felt much more like a backward child than an independent young woman. My household supported me, right or wrong, against outsiders, but made their opinions known after the fact, and so obviously for my own good that I could not be justifiably angry. The advice they volunteered generally worked, though not always as I had expected, but I found it difficult to accept even the advice I had asked, for they would give no reasons or patently absurd ones. When we had slaughtered the ram Kako had given me, we kept what we could eat, but the rest, in the parts and portions the boys suggested, we divided among Kako, the elders and the notables. The boys told me I had to send some to Kobo, a man I particularly disliked. I refused. They insisted. I demanded reasons. They said Kobo was a good man, a man of importance, a highly respected man. I didn't believe it, and said so. Monday's delighted cackle told me I had caught out his two seniors. Nevertheless, they all persisted until I grudgingly gave my consent. Much later I found out that Kobo was a professional thief, and that by accepting meat from me he had been put into the position of a "child that is fed by its father"—a relationship which made it morally wrong for him to steal

37

from me. As it happened, he did steal from me; public opinion forced him to return his booty because he had eaten my meat.

At the time, however, I was constantly being given apparently arbitrary advice, until I almost gagged on it, yet I was almost always sorry when I ignored it. Nor was I always able to fool myself into a feeling of professional competence. Far from pursuing a schedule of research, I was hauled around from one homestead to another and scolded for lack of manners or for getting my shoes wet. Far from having docile informants whom I could train, I found myself the spare-time amusement of people who told me what they considered it good for me to know and what they were interested in at the moment.

I longed to make a stand. I knew of no grounds on which to make one. In cold blood I could find little reason for complaint, yet I found myself watching and waiting for an opportunity for self-assertion, an occasion when I would be so clearly in the right that I could have my own way and call it justice. I knew myself ignorant of the community about me. That awareness and my determination to get on friendly terms with them kept me quiet in our dealings. Almost without my realizing it, all my resentful claims to independence centered on my household and my overt grievances about mealtimes.

I thought myself entitled to eat when I was hungry: at one and at eight. My boys fed me at three and at nine, both sensible hours for the station life in which they had been trained. Offices close at two, and a cook must allow time for drinks. Indeed, parties can delay meals almost indefinitely: I've eaten lunch at seven and dinner at one-thirty of the morning. Under these circumstances a cook is judged by how well he has preserved the food and how late he is willing to stay up without murmur. I was not then concerned with these virtues, nor was I prepared to single out Saturdays for special treatment. For twenty years, on every Saturday, my cook had served a ground nut stew, palm oil stew or a curry, for on Saturday the offices close at noon

38

and much gin is drunk before one eats. Then the whole station sleeps, waking only in time for enough tennis to make club night physically possible. I had no club, no tennis, no office. Nevertheless, I got the stews and curries and meal hours my cook thought fit.

One overcast night, while I was still objecting to this schedule, I yelled for dinner at eight. By nine it hadn't appeared. Nine-thirty, and still no dinner, only whisperings from the kitchen and the sound of boxes being shifted in the boys' hut. The storm in the air made me irritable, and I was very hungry. I stood on my veranda and scolded across the yard at the cook. Nothing happened. I got really angry. In temper, and in the certainty that this time I was clearly in the right, I shouted that unless I was fed something, and quickly too, I would fire them all that very night and fend for myself until I could get a new set of servants sent out.

Sunday came, quite gray. He set the table, knocking the glasses over and chinking the silver against the china. He was normally soundless. I started to reprimand him, but a look at his face convinced me that it was sheer, nervous haste. Certainly he ran from the veranda to the kitchen and back again. Sunday was still nervous as he served the meal, and the food itself puzzled me. The chicken had been roasted almost dry in the oven. Everything bore the signs of overcooking. Had it been deliberate, keeping me waiting so long? I turned on Sunday with an angry message for the cook, but Sunday wasn't paying any attention. He was staring out the veranda door, holding the vegetable dish absently in his hands. He turned even grayer, and dropped the dish.

Sure that he was deathly ill, repentant then at my anger, I tried to make him sit down. He denied that he was ill, but he seemed incapable of moving from the veranda. I called the cook, and then, without waiting for a reply, hastened out to the kitchen. The cook was in exactly the same state. Monday was almost embracing the bush lamp in his desire for light. The cook insisted that nothing was wrong.

He was upset only because dinner had been late. I opened my mouth, stared at him, and again demanded to be told the nature of the trouble.

A child started to cry in the reception hut. "Who is that?" I asked sharply.

The cook answered readily enough, "People from Kako's. They are afraid to go back through the market place."

Then Monday, who was new to Europeans, and who had never been laughed at as "superstitious," spoke up. "There's fire in the market place."

"Fire in the market place?" I was puzzled. Surely, if the flimsy market shelters were burning, I should have seen the flames from the yard. I stepped outside. "There's no fire there," I told them. Sunday, carrying my pressure lamp in his hand and drawing obvious courage from it, came over and set it down by me in front of the kitchen. Monday, the cook and four people from the reception hut stepped out into its light. "See," I repeated. "There's no fire."

Just then, at treetop level down by the market I saw a ball of light moving slowly and steadily through the air. There was a gasp and a sighing from the people about me. It went out, not falling or dimming, just suddenly extinguished. Kako's eldest son, Ihugh, stepped forward. "Witches," he spoke the word softly. "My father must be told of this."

Another ball of light followed. We stared at it in silence. It too went out, all at once, absolutely.

Now they all insisted that Kako must be informed—but to reach Kako's, one had to pass through the market place. Who would go? They were all gray with fear.

Ihugh put his hand on my wrist. He was a tall, splay-footed young bruiser, whose face somehow suggested cauliflower ears and monumental stupidity, even now stolid and assured in his strength. "Come with me," he said, "and bring the big light. We two can reach Kako's. Witches generally avoid Europeans."

The other people refused to come with us. If I didn't mind, they would spend the night here. The boys were only too willing to have company. As Ihugh and I set forth, we could hear them shoving boxes in front of their door and generally barricading themselves.

Ihugh followed close on my heels. Slightly bent from his great height, he poured a soft, steady stream of chatter into my ear, but he was very silent in the market place itself. This was a particularly vicious form of witchcraft, he told me; nothing of the sort had happened for years. Who the witches were, what sort of thing their activities portended, he would not say, nor would he tell me what Kako could do about it. Kako must know, that was all.

We walked on through the night. Once something rustled in the grass. I jumped, and the lamp wavered. Ihugh steadied me. He might be dumb, I reflected, either too dumb to be afraid, or very brave. Everyone else had been terrified; in the dark some of their fear had touched me.

Kako's homestead was very quiet. "Ah." Ihugh barely breathed the words, "No one here has seen it." He went straight to the door of his father's favorite wife's hut, knocked, called Kako by name and pronounced the word "witches." Kako appeared immediately. He thanked me and offered to send Ihugh back with me. Both looked relieved when I refused his escort.

I walked more rapidly than usual back through the market place, but I reached the resthouse without seeing or hearing anything. "O.K.," I shouted my return to the boys. They came out of their refuge: now that Kako knew and I had come back with the lamp, they would finish clearing things away. They worked hastily and clumsily and soon had themselves barricaded in their hut again.

The air was hot and oppressive. I moved my chair outside to catch any breeze that might come. I was shaken enough to sit with my back against the wall, to take the lamp with me and my flashlight as well, and to jump at odd noises. My nervousness soon passed; it had resulted mainly from that of the people about me. But I was not sleepy, and I kept staring toward the market place.

So there were witches and a real terror of witchcraft. I

41

wasn't perturbed by the lights. I knew they had already been reported, though very rarely, by various European observers in this part of West Africa, and dismissed with that comfortable tag "electrical phenomenon." (I've seen the lights twice since, both times under much the same atmospheric conditions and both times late at night when everyone else was asleep.) I was upset by my lack of perception that something was wrong with the boys, and even more by their attempt to hide it. They were still whispering and moving about in the hut behind their barricades.

I wondered then whether there were any witches, or whether people just thought there were witches. I knew perfectly well, from books and lectures, that there were tribes among whom certain individuals actually pointed bones, brewed poisons, laid their spells, and performed all the nefarious machinations of black magic. I knew also that among other peoples no individual ever performed a single act of sorcery, that such peoples often used the word "witchcraft" where we use the words "coincidence," "accident," "statistically random," and that they were thus able to attribute to human causation what we so often attribute to unknown causes or the law of probabilities—any striking and not readily explicable event. All of us who had seen the lights knew immediately they were not stars, meteors or airplanes. They might have called it witchcraft for no better reason than I called it "an electrical phenomenon"; they too had sought a familiar pigeonhole.

No human being could have caused those lights. It would make all the difference to my work here if I had to cope with living sorcerers. Perhaps there weren't any, any who actually did anything, but just people who were thought to make things happen by some sort of remote control. It seemed likely. Ihugh hadn't jumped at that rustle in the grass.

I wondered whether I would, and how I could, ever discover anything about their beliefs, except through accidents of this sort, and then meagerly. Tonight had been an unusual opportunity, yet what had I learned? That cer-

42

tain lights were witchcraft; that people feared witchcraft; that the chief was the person to deal with witches, or was it thanks to some other qualifications or for some other reason that Kako had to be told? Indeed I was a stranger here. Perhaps I would always be a stranger. No matter how much they told me, they would withhold something. No matter how deep I went, there would always be something underneath.

Not until the storm broke and it began to rain did the whispering stop in the boys' hut or could I extinguish the lamp and go to sleep.

Chapter Four

EVERY night I sat on my veranda copying out the day's new words and phrases onto dictionary cards, tracing out the day's walk onto my sketch map, putting the names of people I had met onto the charts I was keeping for each homestead. I worked hard. The material piled up in my files. But I could not feel that I was making any progress —progress seems to imply some kind of forward movement, no matter how devious, toward some end. I myself might be learning something or someone new and different every day, but nothing seemed to add onto what I had learned the day before.

Certainly not the people. I had not even been able to separate those who actually lived in Kako's homestead from their visitors. And as for the general neighborhood—it was like trying to discover who was permanently in Grand Central Station by asking, since there were no distinguishing uniforms, the name of everyone who came through. There were so many people, and they would not stay put. Time after time I made a name-and-face acquaintance who proved to be a person easy to talk to, and make better acquaintance; then, overnight, that person would vanish: "He has gone traveling," I was told—perhaps for the day, perhaps for a week, perhaps forever.

Even names gave me trouble. They all meant something, and many were descriptive. Thus when I asked the name of someone I knew by sight, I sometimes took "The tall one?" as a name when it was really a question of identifi-

44

cation. Once aware of this mistake, I rejected all descriptive names, demanding and getting another. As a result, I often used the nicknames by which men are properly called only by their age mates (here men born within three years of each other formed mutual aid societies and behaved with an informality shocking in other relationships). Everyone had several names. Before I knew faces really well, I sometimes thought and spoke of one man as a set of brothers.

Women's names were even more difficult. I could not see why asking a perfectly sensible middle-aged woman her name should throw her into a fit of bashful giggles and cause a general embarrassment all around. Once the boy who was carrying my gifts back for me—when we were on the path and out of everyone's hearing—said it was his mother who had given me yams and told me her name. For a while I got all women's names from their children. Yet, although the women refused to tell me their names, they—and everyone standing about—were as delighted when I used the name as they were displeased when I asked for it.

I was finally enlightened by Kako's senior wife. Kako addressed her by a set of liquid syllables that should have been easy enough to say, yet, when I pronounced them, no one knew of whom I was speaking. The old woman must have grown weary of my garbling; at any rate, she finally told me to call her Udama.

"Oh!" Many things fell into place for me. "Then you're Ihugh's mother?"

For the first time, as her face relaxed in pleasure, I realized that this scrawny martinet had a twinkle in her eye. "Did he tell you that? I am pleased. It is well when a son points out his mother to persons of importance."

I didn't want to answer. Ihugh had told me his mother's name only because I asked for it; in my effort to place people, I was asking everyone for the names of their parents and ancestors. So I chattered, "Udama is much easier for

45

me to say. Kako told me another name; I cannot speak it
correctly."

Udama let me know, by words and expression, what a
stupid thing I had said. "A husband," she reproved, "never
uses his wife's name. Only her relatives and her own children use the name her father gave her." She looked me up
and down and shook her head. "You are a woman of importance, but you know nothing."

The young woman who so often accompanied Udama
gave me a sympathetic grin, but I addressed myself to
Udama: it was she, I felt, whom I must convince. "Will
you not instruct me? I have come here to learn, and I need
help."

Udama looked at me steadily, for what seemed a very
long time. Then, "Help me pull these weeds," she commanded, and thus adopted me, as Atakpa had done.
Udama, however, let me stop after a very few weeds and
began to mend my manners.

"Only unmarried girls may be called by name," Udama
instructed me. "To learn a married woman's name, ask her
husband the name of her father, and use that." She waved
at the young woman, who was weeding steadily beside us.
"One of Kako's little wives. Call her 'Daughter of Mul.'"

"My name's Ticha," offered the young woman demurely.
Udama stiffened, but Ticha, between weeds, remarked,
"It's the men who get embarrassed, and we three are alone
here."

Udama decided to ignore the interruption. Indeed, she
seldom heeded Ticha's teasing. "When you enter a homestead," Udama continued, "you must always greet the
homestead head first."

"It's enough just to call out his name," murmured Ticha.

"You should escort your guests out to the path when
they leave."

"Or just say you would if you had time."

"You should share your chair with anyone who is standing, but you must never sit on a sheepskin with a man."
Udama made a pointed pause, but this time Ticha made

46

no comment. "And you must stop wandering aimlessly about the countryside and start calling to return the gifts you have received."

"And that," concluded Ticha, "is truly so."

What had been given must be returned, and at the appropriate time—in most cases, within two market weeks. For more valuable gifts, like livestock, one should wait until the giver is in sudden need and then offer financial aid. In the absence of banks, large presents of this sort are one way of saving.

Fortunately, I had kept lists in the back of my notebook: as many as three pages of names opposite entries of two ears corn, one vegetable marrow, one chicken, five tomatoes, one handful peanuts. I couldn't remember; I didn't think anyone could. But they did, and I watched with amazed admiration as Udama dispensed handfuls of okra, the odd tenth-penny and other bits in an endless circle of gifts in which no one ever handed over the precise value of the object last received but in which, over months, the total exchange was never much more than a penny in anyone's favor.

For me this gift-exchange system was such a nuisance that I had to keep counting its blessings. It furnished me with a steady supply of eggs and vegetables. It gave me an acceptable reason for visiting. The truth, that I just wanted to meet people, aroused suspicion, but everyone thought it quite right and natural that I should walk four miles to give a woman tuppence in return for three eggs.

To me, the real point of such visiting was to learn people —who they were and where—and to become known to them. I went back and back to each homestead, thinking that some day I might become so familiar that they would no longer drop the activities in which they were engaged, that some day they might know me well enough to talk freely to me. Udama was willing to teach me manners; Ticha, how to evade inconvenient etiquette. She also showed me how to dress hair with an awl and how to use the local cosmetics. Ticha's irreverent gaiety made for good company—I thought her an odd wife for Kako and an odder companion for Udama—but the only information she could give me was on the local mode of frivolity.

Only Atakpa and her brother were willing to volunteer anything of importance. From them I slowly and painfully began to learn something of kinship and marriage, the names of some of the magical emblems I could see all about me, but much else that they told me I couldn't understand and copied down because they liked to watch me write. Occasionally the other people I visited were in a mood to humor me. Then they told me names and genealogies; with their help I recorded pot making, weaving, corn grinding, sauce recipes, and, over and over, the same confounded leaves. But only too often people were busy. Then they gave me the bare number of greetings and thanks demanded by courtesy before going their own ways and ignoring me completely.

In either case I was given something to eat: food is both a sign of welcome and the way to speed a guest. Fruit in the rind, corn fresh from the coals, some of the cakes wrapped in leaves and steamed for hours, all these—their between-meal snacks—I accepted with thanks and ate. In return, when they visited me, I offered kola nuts and tobacco. I was genuinely afraid to eat their porridge and sauces. Yams and other tubers are first boiled, and then pounded by mortar and pestle into a thick paste, rolled into a stiff ball and served in an open calabash. With the right hand, called the eating hand, one breaks off a lump of this paste and dips it into the sauce, which is in a separate dish. The sauce is sometimes thinned and cooled with unboiled water. Flies are thick at all stages of the cookery; sheep and goats often lick the utensils clean. Miles from any doctor and without transport, I had a healthy fear of dysentery and worms that made me very careful of what I ate and drank.

Unfortunately, it was only this porridge which really counted in terms of hospitality. No one could, or would, tell me how to refuse it without insult to my host. I tried

48

saying that I had just eaten. I was told that I was too thin anyhow. I protested that I was full. Almost inevitably someone would poke a fist into my stomach, decide I was not distended to full capacity, and renew the argument. I was adamant, yet always upset by the obvious distress my refusal gave them. But I could understand their attitude as little as I could make my own reasons clear to them.

I asked Udama about it. She took my question seriously and replied that I could eat the food at any homestead in Kako's country without fear or hesitation—except, perhaps, at Yabo's. I construed her words according to my own notions: Yabo's homestead was dirtier than most. I wrote down in my notebook that they had some idea of hygiene. However, Udama had not told me how to refuse food politely. On second thought, I decided she was too etiquette-bound to help me evade the least codicil of courtesy.

I asked Atakpa the next time I saw her. She merely laughed. Yabo, however, roused himself to answer. Although it was he who made Atakpa and her brother renew their instruction whenever the struggle of talking to me wearied them, although he insisted on my calling every day, he regarded me, I thought, rather contemptuously. He didn't always bother even to greet me. Now, in a surly tone, he curtly bade me not to accept any food from Kako.

Thoroughly bewildered I went home to consult my boys. Sunday and cook concurred: in their experience Europeans who ate African food indiscriminately always got sick, but they could not or would not tell me why it was evidently more insulting to reject some kinds of food, especially meat sauces, than it was to refuse other sorts. I commented, casually, that Udama thought it unwise to eat Yabo's food. They agreed. I asked why. After some thought, the cook said that it was a bad homestead. When I pressed him to explain, he would say only that it was dirty. At that point I produced Yabo's countersuggestion, that I must not eat Kako's food. I was watching them keenly, or I might not have noticed that pleased flash of interest—so often noticeable when someone hears a guess confirmed—which mo-

49

mentarily touched their eyes. It endured only a second. Then they were poker-faced and evasive: it was odd; they had no idea; they didn't know the people here. Left alone on my veranda, I meditatively opened my notebook and drew a line through the conclusion I had first based on Udama's comment; in its place I set two questions: what was up between Kako and Yabo? what were the implications of eating someone's food?

All this intrigued me, but from a practical standpoint it left me just where I was, and a practical solution emerged long before I could answer my questions. The whole affair was typical of my career during the entire time I lived there: difficulties, the causes of which no one would tell me, would suddenly beset me and just as suddenly disappear, for reasons equally unknown to me. Sometimes I found out—not always in time. I knew I was acting in the dark. I knew good intentions were not enough, for the same action can have utterly unlike implications in two different cultures. In the same way that a grunt meaning "yes" in my own language meant "no" in theirs—a very simple reversal which nonetheless got me into one awkwardness after the other—many of the things I did meant one thing to me, something quite the contrary to them. I could only hope that I would do nothing irreparable while I was feeling my way.

The practical food problem was solved by a little boy named Accident—after his grandfather. He was Kako's youngest son, the skinny one who had carried his father's chair the very first day I came. Long before the other children lost their timidity, Accident attached himself to me. He hung around my kitchen for a few days. Then, either when he had made up his mind, or when he had learned how to elude Sunday's vigilance—I don't know which came first—he came to sit just inside my doorstep. I told Sunday to let him be; he kept still and never bothered me. And there, whenever he could force himself to rest, Accident sat—a silent, wide-eyed fixture.

Accident appointed himself my particular escort. Whenever I went walking, he skipped along behind, diving every now and then into the bush to pluck something for me to write or draw. "This grass," he told me, naming it, "is eye medicine. This one is eaten. It's good, too. I always pick some for my mother."

The other children in Kako's homestead soon followed Accident's example. For a while, once they were no longer afraid of me and until the charm of novelty wore off, the straggle of children followed me wherever I went. I encouraged them; they were an invaluable help for language lessons and for odd gossip—for among these people children may go and stay any place as long as they keep quiet. If a child old enough to know better starts to cry, he is angrily told, "Get out, get out!" If it was a child under two, the nurse was called and scolded. Here, as soon as a baby is more than six months old, it is handed over to an older brother or sister or cousin, who thereafter carries the baby about on the hip: out of the huts if the baby cries and annoys its elders, out to the farms to the mother if the baby gets hungry. I never saw these children anything but pleased and proud of their charges, never heard an angry word or saw a slap. But I have seen an old man introduce another, with deep affection, as "The brother who carried me on his hip." For this bond, set up in childhood, is sacred even beyond the other ties of blood.

Wherever I went, the children who followed me were accepted without question. Indeed, I began to suspect that theirs was largely a cupboard love. Accident allowed me to refuse food only once. As soon as we were out of earshot of that homestead, he informed me that I ought to have taken all the food and given it to him to eat. From Udama I discovered, to my great relief, that giving my food to be shared among the children would be highly commendable. Thenceforth Accident and I were inseparable: I was always offered food; he was always hungry. Some of these walks must have taxed him to the limit of his eight-year-old strength. Yet I was never altogether sure whether the hour he spent just sitting, after such a walk—the only quiet

51

moments of his life—was due to exhaustion or to the effort of digesting the numerous messes he had consumed on my behalf.

Some walks overtaxed my own strength. There was no way, other than going myself, by which I could learn how many miles I was being asked to walk. One "not far" excursion put me to bed for a couple of days after a twenty-five-mile round trip without food or water, whereafter I set out on a "far" journey equipped with lunch and water, only to find it less than four miles in all. At first I thought that their use of these words was incontrovertible evidence that they had no idea of distance. Then I figured out that "far" referred not only to space, but to time and social distance as well. The words "Yabo's homestead is far" might mean that his homestead was a long distance off or that he was but remotely related to the speaker. As far as Udama was concerned, it was "far" because her husband Kako disliked Yabo. Everyone agreed that it was further from Yabo's to Kako's than from Yabo's to Poorgbilin's, but everyone also agreed that it was no further from Poorgbilin's to Yabo's than it was from Poorgbilin's to Kako's. All this seemed to mean that Yabo and Poorgbilin got on together much better than Yabo and Kako, but that Poorgbilin got on equally well with both—a fact which seemed to rank, in local opinion, as something of a feat.

In any case, there was only one thing of which I could be sure in advance: if people wanted me to come, they would tell me "It's not far"; if they didn't want me to come, they would tell me "It's far," and if that failed to discourage me, they would add that there was water on the path: an even less reliable statement, for I sometimes found a river, sometimes general muddiness, and sometimes no water at all.

Consequently, when Atakpa invited me to go with her to collect her cousin Amara—"not far at all"—I suspiciously demanded details. Atakpa assured me that if we left in the early morning we would easily return in time for my lunch; also, since Amara was ill but could still walk back to Yabo's without any difficulty, I should have no trouble whatsoever. I believed Atakpa was telling the truth, in an impressionistic way, and I agreed to go, but I gave orders that Monday and my lunch were to accompany me. Just before high noon and after three and a half hours on the path, I congratulated myself on my forethought.

Two cousins could not have been less alike. Atakpa, stubborn and aggressive, bounced and elbowed her way through life. Amara was the only truly gentle person I met out here; indeed, she had a consideration and sympathy for others rare in this world. She was three months with child, and had been afflicted by that terrible disease which swells the breasts until, as though filled by some heavy substance, they stretch and drag below the waist. Everyone foresaw a difficult birth. Therefore, her father Lam, who was Yabo's brother, had arranged with her husband that she and her first born, a boy of three, were to return to Yabo's homestead where due magical and medical precautions could be taken.

We walked slowly back to Yabo's, Atakpa carrying the child on her hip to spare Amara. Irascible old Yabo, who generally bestirred himself only to shout maledictions, himself settled Amara onto a bamboo bed out under the eaves where the breeze would cool her. While he poked about among his herbs for medicine, he berated his wives for not having food ready. Amara's father Lam, thrust into the background by Yabo's busy fussing, set himself to amusing his grandson, who was looking about the strange homestead rather dubiously. The child refused to be distracted by adult attentions; he walked about the yard with the deliberation of the very young, investigating with the thoroughness of an adopted puppy. He found a gourd, and settled down rather soberly to play with it. Amara, Lam, Atakpa and her brother and everyone else in the homestead except Yabo stopped their work and beamed.

Atakpa's brother asked the child what the gourd was called. The boy pronounced the word. "Ah, our relative really knows things," everyone told everyone else. People scattered to collect things for the child's inspection: spindles, calabashes, leaves and grasses. Soon they found something the child couldn't name, a comb.

"It's a comb," Lam told his grandson. The child repeated the word rather inaccurately. "It's a comb." Lam raised his voice. "A comb!"

"A comb!" Atakpa and her brother joined in. The child tried again, but still not to their satisfaction. Yabo's wives swelled the chorus, "A comb!" They were beginning to shout. The child looked at me, and I found myself yelling with everyone else, "A comb! A comb!"

I stopped guiltily. Just this kind of thing had reduced me almost to tears. I looked at the child apprehensively, waiting for a wail of dismay. Instead, he picked himself up calmly and, ignoring his still-shouting instructors, went off to investigate an attractive pile of rocks. The shouting broke into laughter. Atakpa stuck the comb back into her hair. Envying Amara's son his easy management of a situation that had proved too much for me, I went my way.

Chapter Five

ONE MORNING, a few weeks after my arrival, Sunday brought with my coffee the information that Kako was starting to build my huts that very morning; would I come see that the foundations were laid exactly where I wished them? I just managed an unconcerned "Very well," for I had almost given up all hope.

At Kako's I found all the notables assembled under the mango tree in front of my hut site. The earth had not been scratched; not a brick, not a stick was visible. The notables sat, chatted and smoked their pipes. I tried to be patient. Ihugh wandered over and squatted down before Kako, who presented him to me as though we had never met before: "My son, Ihugh. He will build for you." I had not forgotten Ihugh's calm when there was fire in the market place, but he still looked too stupid to lay one brick beside another. I smiled rather artificially, and watched with foreboding as Ihugh scraped desultorily with a hoe at my site.

Still we sat. Two men strolled before us, hand in hand. They sat down on the ground before the notables and removed their red liberty caps. They had my sympathy; no one paid any attention to them, either. Eventually Kako tapped my notebook and pointed to them; "It's a ——," he told me. I carefully wrote down the word, and then under it everything that happened to these two. Until I knew enough of the language to understand verbal definitions, observation was my only way of learning—something more easily done for pots and other material objects than for social events. In this case, however, it was quite clear that the two men had brought a dispute for arbitration. At Kako's sign, one began his story, interrupted by questions from all the notables and punctuated by sarcastic comment and injured denial from the other. Soon everyone was saying so much, and so loudly, that no one could hear. Then someone screamed, "Shut up! Shut up!" until all had taken up the cry. Then a silence, and the case slowly warmed up to a shouting point again. Eventually, one man reluctantly counted out twenty-three pennies and placed them before Kako. Kako counted them solemnly. Half a dozen notables counted them again, apparently just to make sure (actually, anyone who counted could then be called as witness in subsequent disputes). Finally, Kako handed the pennies to the other litigant, and the matter was ended. The two walked away hand in hand, just as they had first come.

This diversion over, I had leisure to notice that I had been here for over two hours. I watched Ihugh for a while longer, then told Kako I was going. Kako's face seldom had much expression: now it showed frank surprise. "But," he swept his arm widely to the various paths leading into his homestead, "they're coming."

"Coming? Who?"

Kako's answer was brief, but it contained not a single word I knew. He realized this and repeated it, word for word, several times. Someone tapped me on the shoulder. I turned, and saw Ikpoom's ugly face. "Listen," he ordered, pointing down one of the paths.

"Mmmm!" Kako hummed out his agreement. He also pointed. I heard singing. Everyone stopped to listen, except Ihugh, who, however, also heard it, for he began to swing his hoe in time to the song.

"*They* are coming," Ikpoom explained, as though that made everything clear. He leaned back again.

The song came closer. Kako pointed down another path; thence also I heard singing. I began to wonder, rather

56

wildly, if building here began with a dance, perhaps with ritual. I stroked my notebook in pleasant anticipation.

"Look!" commanded Kako.

A file of singing youths, great bundles of grass on their heads, trotted into Kako's homestead. Some of the bundles, already made up into rolls of thatch, were dumped beside us in the yard. The rest were spread out in long thick strips; the young men squatted down, using toes and fingers to separate and twist the grass into thatch.

"Look!" called Ikpoom. From another path came another gang of youths, also singing: young men carrying trays of mud bricks on their heads; adolescent boys carrying two or three mud bricks; little boys of seven and eight with only one mud brick. I began to understand. Another gang came in with posts for the reception hut and bamboo for roof poles. I recognized some of these youngsters. I had seen them gathering these materials in the bush and working on them in their homesteads. Building had begun, long ago; during all the time I had thought Kako idle, the whole community had been at work.

From that day on, I spent hours in Kako's homestead, supervising, suggesting, learning the many processes by which earth, grass and trees were shaped into buildings for me and my boys. Each elder and notable was there to see that his own dependents did not shirk. While they were there, they arbitrated many cases, for people with a dispute like to get as many opinions as possible, and this unusual concentration of notables presented a fine opportunity. (One can call in the elders, but then one must brew them beer.) Meanwhile, most of the notables were busied with some kind of handiwork, working a hoe handle with a native adz, twisting hibiscus fiber into rope—anything that could keep their hands busy while their minds were on more important matters. I sat with them, listened, drew pictures and learned the names of things and activities as they came along. It was quite a happy time, though Kako, finding me capable of noticing and remembering the difference between a chair and a spindle, renewed his efforts to point out the differences—just as obvious to him—between one sort of grass and another.

I learned about snakes, too. Early one morning, just as work was getting started, one of the notables leaped up from his mango root. He had been sitting on a snake: small, green, shiny and responding with contented wiggles to the warmth of the day. We formed a respectfully distant circle around the snake, and debated it. There are two kinds of small, green shiny snakes. One is poisonous. The other is harmless. Moreover, according to legend it once befriended these people, when they were trapped by their enemies on the banks of a deep and rapid river, by stiffening itself into a straight, loglike bridge over which they escaped; therefore, it must never be killed. But no one could decide which this particular snake was. Eventually a youth took a long pole, slipped it under the snake, and then carried it well away into the bush and flung it aside.

I thought it a good time to inquire about snakes. They mentioned about a dozen kinds: some bite you and you die; others bite you and you don't die. Was there any medicine for snake bite? Indeed, though not many people knew it, for it was very potent; but those who knew never lost a patient. I cheered up. Then, with cursed persistence, I asked which snakes' bites they cured. They treated only the bites of those snakes which "bite you and you don't die." I became snake conscious.

I asked my boys if there were any snakes about the resthouse. In response they started bringing me the bodies of those they killed in their huts and on the grounds. One morning I woke to find a mamba draped around one of the roof poles. After that, every rustle in the thatch made me look up nervously, peering intently till I could identify lizard, mouse or snake. "Wait until we move to Kako's homestead," the boys comforted me. "There are lots of snakes here only because we are sitting alone in the bush. They seldom come where there are many people." I hoped they were right.

I was impatient to move into Kako's homestead, away from the ants, snakes and witches that haunt those who sit alone in the bush. I wanted to know Kako better, and I could not while we met only formally to discuss building or other matters of business. It was easy to see that he was a man of great intelligence. Indeed, his patriarchal appearance, his sober gravity, and the shrewd equity of his opinions in court cases made me think of him as a rather tattered Solomon. Other notables spent their wealth on display; he made gifts to his relatives and visitors. Other elders tried to shout down their opponents in furious contradiction. Kako seldom raised his voice and, as far as I knew, never lost his temper. He had everyone's respect, and everyone, with the possible exception of Yabo, mingled that respect with some fear. Clearly, more than anyone else in that community, he could help or hinder me and my work. But I did not know how to get on any but the most superficial terms with him. He had a natural reserve underneath his smooth manner. As a Native Administration Chief he had had far more contact with Europeans than any of the other elders. I felt that while both his suavity and his experience might lead him to show me a far greater surface respect and cordiality these same two traits might easily make him by far the more difficult to know personally. Perhaps when I was his neighbor and could see him continuously and informally, it could be managed.

The work on my huts progressed rapidly and well, until it came to the finishing touches. Two weeks from laying the first brick, five from Kako's first invitation, saw all the roofs up. After each heavy rain, Kako and I would walk solemnly into each hut searching for the slightest trace of moisture on the floor. Even the kitchen was finished; it had taken the longest because the cook had kept changing his mind until I decreed that his fifth plan must be his last one. He had done well for himself: there was a vent for the stove with a flue composed of beaten kerosene tins and mud bricks, to carry smoke and sparks out from under the thatch; stubby brick pillars raised the roof to admit light,

59

and a grill of sticks was designed to keep out rats and light fingers.

I found a carpenter, taught by a man who had learned from a man who had learned carpentry while living in another tribe and from a man said to have learned it from a European. Someplace in the chain of teachers the principles of straight lines and right angles had been lost. Still, I had a door and two windows, concocted out of provisions boxes, split bamboo and market-bought bolts. They were set aslant, and the door was a masterly example of what can be done by just missing a rectangle. But the windows opened to let in light and the door shut. I would have a place in which I could be truly private. They had even made a fence of close-set saplings around my cluster of huts, like that around Kako's own huts; such a fence is intended to keep out stray pigs and goats, but in the absence of a gate it merely channels traffic.

The main difficulty had come with the sanitary arrangements. At the resthouse these were modeled on what, in the stations, is called the bucket system: this works fairly well with metal tins that can be properly cleaned and with prison labor to do the removing. With a porous clay pot and a general groundsman who has his dignity, the system tends to break down: the pot is left unemptied. Consequently, I decided on a hole, a seat of poles, and thatch for roof and walls. Everyone, especially the groundsman, agreed that this would be much better. They could easily get it done in one day and on that day. Confident that they understood, I set off to make some return calls.

That evening, however, they informed me that only the hole had been dug. I found a pit over eight feet deep and a good four and a half feet in diameter. They were proud of it, so proud that I commented only that so large a hole would call for a rather large structure of poles.

Next morning, while I was drinking my coffee, a number of youths carrying long, heavy poles filed past the resthouse. By the time I got to Kako's, they had sunk four of these into the ground around the hole and were tying the crosspieces into the forks. The whole thing was about three inches above the ground. I explained that I wanted it higher. The rest of that day was spent filling in the holes and jacking up the posts.

I gave a sigh of relief: there remained only the platform. There could be no difficulty. I spent the next day walking and mapping. That evening I gazed in despair at the platform—knobby logs still covered with bark and dirt and, in the precise center, much too far from any one direction, a vacant place.

Ihugh looked at my face. "It's a good, strong platform." He objected to my expression.

While I groped for words, little Accident jumped up onto the platform. "See," he said. He squatted. I called the boys to explain; they could not be unaware of the habits of Europeans. They also expected me to squat on the platform. Like so many other cases of cultural misunderstanding, this one arose because it had not occurred either to them or to me that the way "we" did it was not the way "human beings" do it.

A tradition of never alluding to such matters struggled with the necessity of doing something about it, and lost. The desire to use euphemistic and allusive phrases was checkmated by a knowledge of their language so poor that I couldn't say anything about it at all. Common sense said, "Don't be a fool." Upbringing said, "Don't be vulgar." I compromised on "when in Rome," with the mental reservation that it would be much better to know fluent Italian.

I picked up four sticks, laid them in a square where I wanted the hole, and sat down. Apparently no one was shocked, but apparently no one understood. I spoke up, defiant to my own sensibilities, "This is the way we do it."

Accident's eyes gleamed; he was young enough to remember one had to learn about such matters. He shrilled at his father.

"Mmmm?" Kako was unconvinced.

"Mmmml" I nodded, emphatically, and stood up. Accident sat down on the platform and spoke—with gestures. "Mmmm!" I hummed, even more emphatically. All our audience sat down in turn while I hummed agreement and Accident chattered. Kako, enlightened, pointed to a new location for the hole. I quite sung out my hum of agreement. But they still didn't see what else was wrong with the platform. Then, their clothes being somewhat scantier than mine, one of them got a splinter. Comments flew as the new situation sunk in: they would get other logs, peel off the bark, smooth them down. In three days it was finished—even to a roof and a thatch screen with a roundabout entrance. And until, in the late rains, the water level rose almost to ground level, the groundsman and I were very pleased.

Under similar pressure I learned to modify many other of my minor inhibitions. Here only unnecessary exposure is considered immodest. If a man's cloth is disarranged, he is told to fix it, but the fixing involves taking off the cloth, shaking it out and then retying it. I came to appreciate their standards of modesty as perhaps the most sensible I had ever met, though I was never able to adopt their viewpoint altogether. I learned not to mind if, despite all precautions, people were yet able to peek in while I bathed —to discover whether Europeans are white all over. That wasn't my fault. But to my last African river I was scolded for not taking off all my clothes; my companions, putting on their dry clothes, always told me I was being very foolish. I rather thought I was, but, foolish or not, I could not change my standards when it came to my own actions.

Many of my habits, however, were being quite insensibly modified as my life fell into routine. Every afternoon, when the late yellow light gilded the sun-bleached world, I strolled about Kako's homestead, checking on the building and finding out who lived in which hut. Everyone is home then, the women cooking and grinding grain, the men loafing under the trees or in their reception huts, as willing to talk to "Redwoman" (so Udama had conclusively named me) as they were to play with their children.

During one of these hours of gossip, I discovered that Ikpoom would be my left-hand neighbor: I had thought that hut unoccupied; it had no water pot by the door; no smoke curled through the thatch in the evenings. Accident told me that Ikpoom slept there but, ever since his wife had gone away, he ate with his brother Kako.

Just before dark, I went home to bathe and to type notes on the veranda, clad in mosquito boots and the roomy decency of men's pajamas. This outfit had long since replaced the evening gowns favored by Sunday and tropical outfitters. Only on curry day, with a vague notion of keeping up my own morale and humoring Sunday, I wore one of my better cotton dresses. My evening drink had already been transmuted from a sundowner to a time killer between clearing my papers off the table and Sunday's setting it for dinner. Indeed, one does need more tables than one thinks: keeping things in and on boxes means shifting half of one's possessions before one can get at the other half. Eventually, delayed only by the much more pressing agricultural activities of my bush carpenter, I had five tables and kept only stores and attractions for vermin in boxes. Even the books, which are damaged more by mold than by mice, sat out on bamboo and packing-case shelves. Shortly after midnight, I would put my work away and play a game of solitaire or read while I drank my after-dinner liqueur turned nightcap. Something was needed to prevent dreams of work undone, of witches, snakes and ants.

At long last Udama informed me that the women of Kako's homestead had begun to pound my floor. I rushed down to watch, praise, and if possible, hasten their efforts. They were not to be hurried. A good clay floor cannot be made quickly, and Udama (who was the senior woman of the whole community) had determined that this floor was to be a showpiece. For three days earth was wet down, pounded with heavy hardwood paddles and left to dry overnight. On the fourth and final day, the pot of beer brewed for me on my boys' advice was ready. Men and boys carried in large chunks taken from termite mounds—much harder to work than ordinary earth, but giving a hard, polished surface.

The women formed a line headed by the dowagers of the homestead. To make the work easier, they danced slowly backward, pounding rhythmically at the hard chunks, beating the floor smooth, and chanting, so I was told, songs in my praise. I listened, and could not feel they were precisely praise songs:

> Oh, the Redwoman, our mother-in-law,
> Our mother-in-law has summoned me to work,
> I perish in her work and have no rest.

Still, it was a nice tune.

They were nearly finished, and my pot of beer was brought out. Another song and chorus, extemporaneous as all these are, was struck up. I listened more confidently, hoping for kinder mention.

> Alas, the Redwoman
> The Redwoman has come.
> Alas, she has come.
> We cannot weed our farms,
> Our children are not fed.
> Alas, she has come.
> We faint in her work,
> She gives no recompense.
> Alas, she has come.

Nevertheless, they drank my beer with gusto, and I had my floor. It had a marked slope from north to south, but it had a high polish. In two days more, we could walk on it. There remained only the whitewashing, then I could move in.

I moved in before the whitewash was dry, driven from the resthouse by ants, driver ants with bites like fire and in inexhaustible numbers. They came for the first time while we were still dickering for whitewash clay. They invaded the kitchen where Monday slept to ward off thieves. They

64

wakened Monday by their stinging and me by his screaming. The boys wanted to run. I drove them into battle
armed with my DDT and a spray gun. Dancing up and
down on the fringes of the ant carpet, Monday sprayed
with a will, the cook drew lines in the ground with his
matchet to deflect the ants, and Sunday, as fast as the
fire would burn, sprinkled hot ashes into a dike along
which we hoped the ants would march away. Holding
the lamp to illumine their labors, I encouraged, praised our
victory, and relegated ants to the rank of nuisance only.

One night several days later, the boys were asleep and
I was on the veranda absorbed in my maps and charts.
Something burned, like a cigarette forgotten between one's
fingers. A column of driver ants was moving along the
veranda wall and down one of the posts to the floor; there
it had broken under the movement of my feet. One had
climbed on my mosquito boots to sting me. I jumped away,
scraping back my chair in an abrupt movement that broke
the column even further. Grabbing at the lamp, I located
three other columns: one coming from inside my own hut,
one marching across the yard, one circling the boys' hut.
With mistaken zeal I started pumping away with DDT
even as I shouted for the boys.

The best thing to do with driver ants is to avoid them.
The worst thing is to break the column. If they are marching under your very bed, keep a judicious distance and
wait until they go away lest some foolish insect or animal
disturbs them. But don't meddle with them. Secure in my
possession of DDT and with the contempt of insects peculiar to those bred in cold and temperate climates, I had
organized the previous ant fight and I meant to do it
again.

The boys tumbled out of their hut and out of the
kitchen. With one comprehensive look at my dancing and
spraying, they hopped their way to me with the discon-
certing news that there were two more columns by the
kitchen. I bullied them into spreading coals, and having
seen the effects of DDT, they responded much more readily

65

than they had before. They were supposed to guide the ant columns out of our habitat and into the bush; either by their own clumsiness or through the innate unreliability and viciousness of the ants, the boys merely succeeded in breaking the columns. I had achieved the same result when I ran out of DDT. Frantically, I filled the spray gun with ordinary, kitchen germicide. The ants were unaffected by it; that is, they didn't die, but they were certainly annoyed. Their columns converged and broke to form a living, stinging carpet over the entire yard and inside the huts.

Jumping, hopping, dancing and swearing in a variety of languages, the boys and I retreated down the path toward the market. We didn't stop until we were well away from the ants. We had rescued only two lamps. "It's best," said Sunday with remarkable mildness, "to leave driver ants alone." I grunted and searched for a consolatory cigarette. They were still on my veranda. We stood. The bush lamp sputtered and, out of kerosene, expired.

"Ants," observed the cook, "don't come where there are many people. It's bad to sit alone in the bush."

I grunted again, mentally cursing my improvidence in bringing only a gallon of DDT. Sunday broke off some leaves from a bush and spread them out for me to sit on. I refused impatiently and went back to scout the ants; they were still in full possession. I stamped back to the boys. All three of them were sitting. Sunday silently plucked some more leaves for me. "Sit down with us," Monday spoke with all the certainty of youth. "The ants come when they will and go when they will. You can only wait."

It grew chilly outside, without shelter. I hugged my knees for warmth. My lamp began to flicker. I blessed the moon; then, suddenly and acutely aware that I had never paid enough attention to celestial phenomena, I anxiously demanded when it set. "Not before dawn," was the comforting answer. We settled down to wait out the ants.

By dawn the ants had reformed themselves into two fat columns. We moved back to the resthouse. Sunday and the cook set to work on coffee and a breakfast that, for once, I ate with pleasure. My cigarettes were undamaged on the veranda. But one of the ant columns marched up one post, through the thatch of my hut, and then down another post, occasionally dropping burning sparks of formic acid on anyone foolhardy enough to venture inside. The sun came up. I sat disconsolately on a box in the middle of the yard.

"The whitewash is still wet," the cook was at my elbow, "but we could keep away from the walls for a day or two."

I looked at my ant-infested hut. It might be days before . . .

"Kako's youngsters would carry your loads down to his homestead," Sunday broke into my thoughts.

"If they won't," Monday chimed in, "I'll carry them myself."

I jumped up. "Enough of this sitting alone in the bush," I agreed. "Let's go." And, that very morning, we went.

Chapter Six

IN MY HUT at Kako's I sat idly watching a June shower spin a wet beaded curtain beyond my open door. Against the sharp tapping of the rain I could hear the occasional crow of a rooster and the calls of frantic parents, "Come in and get dry!" For everyone knows it is mad to stay out in the rain—everyone but the children, who romp on through the puddles, slide in the mud, or stand wet and naked in the rain blissfully eating a windfall of mangoes.

It was little more than ten weeks since I had waved good-by to Sackerton, but already time had taken on a more individualistic and yet more seasonable aspect than I had been used to. Already the days of the week and the month were no more than a heading printed on my diary pages. I did try to keep count; old habit made me feel I ought to know the date. Yet, in July, when I went back to the station for supplies, I found I had lost three days.

I discarded any concern with "the right time" of day much more readily. Shortly after moving into Kako's, I forgot to wind the rackety alarm I had brought instead of my wrist watch. I set the hour approximately by the sun. I soon became more sensible. From the standpoint of work, it was convenient for me to have two hours between bath and dinner. I was fed at nine by the clock; Monday had the bath water hot at dark. I went on my own time zone: dark and seven by the clock were to coincide. Every few weeks for the rest of my stay in the bush, I readjusted the clock, blandly telling my protesting boys that it was not working well.

I learned to forget months and to live by moons: to anticipate the full moon for its dances and storytelling; to fear the dark of the moon when witches were abroad.

Cutting through the moons was, for me, a complicated combination of weeks. First, there was the cook's seven-day curry week, highlighting Saturdays. Then there was the five-day cycle of markets by which everyone made engagements. Finally there was the seven-day beer-brewing week which culminated on a named day impartially designating "Sunday" and "beer drink." All these weeks ran concurrently, Kako's market coinciding now with curry Saturdays, now with beer Sundays, until, one day, Kako's market, Saturday and Sunday all happened at once, and none of us could figure out just how. There was no year, merely a succession of seasons and agricultural activities uncorrelated with moons or markets. The rains began when it began to rain; when it began to rain, people started to plant. One could say that a man had done his planting late, but not that the rains had come late. There was the season of yams, of guinea corn, and of millet, and the hungry season when there was little millet left and only corn to eat until the yam harvest. It was the time of hunger now. The provident were down to one meal a day, the improvident or unlucky to one every other day. Old women scolded the young wives for having sold food during the time of plenty: "Wait till you hear your children crying for hunger and have only water to give them."

"When I have children, I'll be careful," women like Ticha retorted. "But now I want money for cloths."

Meanwhile people grew thin and drank more and more beer. "From the amount of millet that will fill one man"—Udama was a thrifty woman—"one can make enough beer to make ten men feel full. That way you can save the real food for your children." Everyone looked with greedy eyes at the burgeoning yam vines.

And yet the mango rains, as this season became in my

69

personal calendar, were for me one of the pleasantest times of the year. Early in the wet season, the rains still come tempestuously with thunder, lightning and a wind that bends branches and tosses mangoes to the ground like bright thunderbolts. In a storm these wind-felled mangoes rolled almost to my doorstep. Then, when they were thoroughly rain-chilled, I would crawl out under the eaves to gather four or five of the choicest. An epicurean feast and an act-of-God holiday.

The holiday aspect of rain was always uppermost in my mind. If I was caught out walking, I splashed happily home through the ankle-deep stream of cool, swift running water that purled down the paths. People called at me from their farm shelters—they have a catlike distaste for wet— and when the path led me through a homestead, heads popped out from under the eaves at the noise of my squelching tennis shoes: "Come inside, Redwoman," they coaxed, gently, as one tries to persuade the crazy. "Come inside. Take off your clothes and dry yourself by our fire." I only grinned in reply. They thought me quite mad anyhow, and the rain that made their bones shiver with cold was to me a respite from a steamy heat surpassed, in my experience, only by a Washington, D.C. summer. So I reveled in the rain, and, according to Ticha, gamboled in it like young sheep and goats. Then once home, I would towel myself dry and sink into a happy period of complete relaxation, too dark for reading and too wet for visitors.

"Once home"—it was not long before I felt that I had always lived here, not long before I found myself writing in my diary "at home" instead of "at Kako's." It was my home. I no longer remember just how it came about, by what individual steps my new life became so familiar that even now I can smell, touch and hear it. I have only to close my eyes. But if my recollections of this time are as vivid as my childhood memories, they are also as disconnected and unordered: small, particular incidents, a pointillist picture evoking the entire period between moving to Kako's in May and going back to the station in July.

I remember the way Ikpoom's black and tan goat jumped my fence every morning, to drink from the waterpots by my kitchen. I can still see the wet, polished skins of women swaying back from the spring with the large-bellied waterpots on their heads. I remember when I first realized that the early morning pounding couldn't possibly be what I had so far sleepily assumed it: the throb, thump and whir of machinery. My alarm clock, typewriter and meat grinder were the only machines in miles. Over my coffee, I asked Sunday. His conviction that no one could be unacquainted with so common a sound made for a long detour through thatch rustlings and bird calls. Finally I went out to look. It was the thump of hardwood pestles in waist-high mortars accompanied by the shush-shush of grain slowly crushed between handstone and granite slab.

Most nostalgically I remember the nights. At the rest-house night had been a silence in which one lowered one's voice. I had sometimes hesitated to use my typewriter; its clatter had seemed an intrusion into something that might pounce. Common sense has little power against an African night, and to those who sit alone in the bush, the night is undomesticated and strange.

But in a large homestead like Kako's, the night is tame. Even in the dark of the moon, when people stay inside their huts, one can always hear the sound of low gossiping when people wake at night. (I found myself unique in my notion of a "good night's sleep" of so many uninterrupted hours.) In the full of the moon, everyone sat outside beside the fires which encircled the moon-washed yard like a bright necklace set in darkness. The children romped about, calling riddles to each other with shrill laughter. The old men, full of years and content, sat close to the warmth, smoking their pipes, their children and grand-children about them. Here a young woman dressed her co-wife's hair into elaborate braids and puffs, using a bone awl, a wooden comb and liberal applications of castor oil. There a youngster sat at the loom he had brought into the brighter radius of my lamplight, and wove a cloth for his

mother while he listened to his brother's wives gossip as
they spun. An old woman fried that delicacy, gourd seeds
in palm oil, and everyone helped himself to the half-penny
worth allowable to all the members of the homestead. Two
sisters out in the pale moonlight pounded grain in one
large mortar, singing to the thump of their alternating
pestles; every now and then one would toss the mahogany
pestle high up into the air—and straight—clapping her
hands in time to their song until she caught it coming
down, and, thump, into the mortar just on the beat.
Women sliced vegetables for sun-drying, or made potash
from the ashes of yam peelings. Here an idle young man
sat beside his busy wife loudly singing a song in praise of
the father and mother who had reared her so well. And
always, somewhere in the distance, there was the sound of
gongs and drums and singing.

Through the night Kako wandered from fire to fire, settling minor quarrels, informally discussing the next day's
tasks, and generally just making sure that all was well. At
first I wandered in his wake, for loneliness often drove me
from my hut and my work, to seek the fellowship of human
beings. But Kako had little time for me, and I was glad to
be made welcome at Udama's fire. Soon I had my regular
place there, and was content to lean back listening to
Udama's strictures on the slackness of modern manners and
watching Ticha tease Ihugh's younger brother—her husband's son. It was almost flirtation, but no one, not even
Udama, seemed to mind. But then, Ticha was Udama's
"little wife." (A man with many wives, like Kako who had
seventeen, generally places the younger ones in the care of
one of the first three; these "great wives" then look after
the welfare and morals of their "little wives"; they farm
together, cook together, and mind each other's children.)
It was natural that she should be particularly familiar with
Udama's three sons, and they were all much the same age.
The marked reserve with which Ticha treated the sons of
Kako's other wives confirmed me in my opinion. Anyhow,
her giddy jesting made Udama's fire gay with laughter.

Occasionally the contented gossip of these nights was shattered by a voice raised high in complaint to the world at large; it was usually a man who had come home to find no food prepared for him and no good reason for his wife's negligence. Soon murmurs of "Hear our brother" rose from the other fires, calls of sympathy, and perhaps even offers of food. Then, one would hear the energetic thumping of pestle in mortar as the dilatory wife, shamed by this appeal to public opinion, set about her task.

Such public complaining always worked. It was my quite innocent use of it which finally established the family relationship between myself and my boys. My cook was a very good cook, but he had a temperament and a delusion: he believed that his best creation was corn starch pudding. I loathe corn starch pudding anyhow. In his, there was enough corn starch to enable him to achieve sculpture: cubist, abstract and some attempts at realistic representations of coiled snakes. When all appeal and admonition failed, I snatched the corn starch from him and threw it into the river. The cook sulked. Things began to go wrong, each trivial and possibly accidental.

One day I told Kako, who was going off to market with his notables, that I would follow later, as soon as I had eaten. No food had been prepared. It was market day; the cook might have some legitimate excuse. I told him not to let it happen again, and turned on my heel to shout after Kako to wait: my cook had cooked me no food. From their own domestic lives, the elders found the situation familiar. By asking leading questions, they drew the story from me in its true perspective. Their loud asides taught me that the corn starch was indeed at the bottom of it all. (There's no hiding anything in such a community.)

The cook, poker-faced, slouched to the kitchen door. I realized I had started something. I hoped I wouldn't lose a good cook over it, but the affair was no longer in my hands. Kako gave his decision against the cook by calling Udama and instructing her to feed me, for my "children" were either lazy or sick. Immediately, just like the lazy wives I

73

had so often heard similarly rebuked, my cook turned back into the kitchen and there clashed pot against pan to notify the public that he was making amends.

That evening, while I was still most uncertain about possible consequences of the whole affair, my three boys appeared in delegation to present the cook's apology and a petition. The cook would never do anything bad again. None of them would. If, inadvertently, they ever again gave me cause of complaint, would I please mention it privately and softly before I let an outsider know? We were "one family"; they were all my children; we should settle our affairs among ourselves.

After that I had no more servant trouble, no need to speak of firing or fines, no need to scold, no need to do more than state my wishes—and listen courteously to any countersuggestions. I had appealed to the community once, and I might do so again; and so, I now knew, might they. We ruled ourselves accordingly. From that day on, as befitted the "one family" we were called, we showed the world only our loyalty to one another; our differences we kept to ourselves.

During this same period my relationship to the community also underwent a noticeable change. I was no longer called "the white woman" I was "Kako's European," sometimes even "our European." Kako, for reasons of his own—which I learned only when it was almost too late for remedy—was doing his best to have me identified as his "child." His intervention between me and my cook was one step toward this end: the incident showed us as his dependents, among whom he should keep the peace. He encouraged the women of his homestead to include me in all their activities.

At the time I noticed only that finally I was being invited out, that I was no longer restricted to the self-made projects in my notebook. First Udama, then her married cousin who was living at Tar's homestead not too far from us, then all the other important matrons, began to ask me to weeding parties. I was aware that it was largely a matter of lion

74

hunting; that my hostesses asked me for prestige's sake and not my own. Nevertheless, being asked to such parties at all made me feel a part of their daily life; it even gave me one thing about which I knew more than my own boys.

Generally women weed their own farms, but sometimes, because it is much pleasanter to get a month's work done in one day and in company, several women who have adjacent farms brew beer and summon the women of the neighborhood to weed and drink. No man between five and eighty dare venture near such a party. Each woman takes one line of yam mounds. Abreast, dancing as they move, singing obscene songs, they weed their way down to the end of the farm. Meanwhile, in any homestead within earshot, the men prick their ears at the songs and shake their heads disapprovingly if they do catch any of the words, for the songs the women sing in the evening while they drink their hostesses' beer are full of virtuous sentiments and fit for the ears of husbands.

One day I went to one of these weeding parties close to Kako's. Since I had come with Udama, who called me "daughter," I was expected to join in the weeding. My hostess showed me a short row, slightly less than the amount of work expected from an eight-year-old girl. "We know Europeans, like albinos, can't stand much sun," the woman said kindly when I flagged. "Go sit under the tree and start some yams roasting for us."

"Madam!" I looked up from the coals and saw Monday. "Madam!" He was advancing upon us, waving one of my handkerchiefs like a flag of truce and shouting loudly that I had forgotten it. "Go away," I yelled. But Monday was young, curious, and overconfident in my will to protect him; he had determined to find out what actually went on at these feminine get-togethers. Udama turned on me: had I broken my promise not to bring or tell any man? I denied my responsibility for Monday's gate-crashing; again I shouted at him to go back. Monday, still etiquette-distance away and not wanting to hear, was deaf. He came on.

75

With a whoop of pure anticipation, the women surged toward him; they screamed obscenities as they ran. Monday gave one frightened look; he swiveled on his heel and bolted for safety. Only the Furies could have caught him. The women, panting and laughing, returned to the tree. There they proceeded to mime in dance just what they would have done to Monday had they captured him. I appreciated his speed. When I got home to scold him, Monday still looked unsettled, but he seemed only faintly sheepish and not at all repentant. At least, he asked me to teach him some of the songs. Sedately, I refused.

Not all my social involvements were due to Kako's urging. I always felt welcomed at Poorgbilin's, and I was on familiar terms in Yabo's homestead. One day Atakpa came to fetch me. In great excitement she dragged me off with her to Poorgbilin's. Once she had me on the path, she began to explain. Only a few hours ago, Poorgbilin's fifth wife had borne her first child, a girl. Poorgbilin, as husband and as homestead head, had to name her; he had named her "Redwoman" after me, and Atakpa, who had been there visiting, had been told to bring me the news at once so that I might come give the mother two tenth-pennies "to tie around the namesake's neck." Atakpa outlined my new responsibilities: later, I was to make more gifts of coins "to tie around the waist," still later to help buy the girl's first cloth (I was vaguely surprised that Atakpa should imagine me still around thirteen years hence); I must always assist in medical matters and in payments to a diviner investigating the magical complications of my namesake's illness. I was not quite a godmother. The baby and I were one; we each took on all the relatives of the other.

Under Atakpa's eye, I handed over my gifts. I stood for a long time watching the pink-purple baby, wriggling and howling as the midwives smeared her with camwood for warmth and luck, put castor oil on her hair to keep her head cool, and painted her eyelids with antimony because it looked nice. For the first time I felt that it mattered to someone whether I came or went. In calmer moments I reflected that my pennies probably had something to do with it. On the whole, I preferred to believe Poorgbilin's statement, "Now, even if you go, your name will not be forgotten here."

I should have been content. The women accepted me. The children hunted me out. Indeed, it became difficult to find any time to myself. Once, after an afternoon rain, I went out with the fixed determination of seeing the sunset. Kako's homestead lay on the sheltered side of one of the foothills to the mountains that rose to the southeast. On the path leading down to the stream and swampland below was a convenient outcrop of bare stone where I often sat; it was not too far off the path, and yet hidden in the grass. There I went to smoke and look. A green field of yam gardens and grass, dotted with trees and occasional circles of bright thatched huts, rose gradually from the swamp. Behind, clear in the rain-washed air, the slopes of the hill Telemkpe glided through two thousand feet of grass and farms to the girdle of dark rain forest that hemmed the bare, baboon-haunted summit. Now Telemkpe was vivid in the saffron light of the storm-setting sun, a beacon before the threatening rain clouds piled high behind it. Truly, it is a country just this side of Eden.

I sat on, watching each fluctuation of beauty as the light was slowly drawn upward from the foothills. "Redwoman, Redwoman," a shrill, mosquito cloud of children was suddenly upon me. "Redwoman, didn't you see us burning the swampland? Come down with us. It's not good to sit alone." Children tugged at my clothes, unaware of anything but kindness in relieving my solitude.

At the edge of the swamp was a strip of land reclaimed and drained for growing corn and rice. Women and children were burning the stalks of the last crop, pulled and piled to dry as well as the rains permitted. The still moist debris popped and crackled in the fire or smoldered out. The children screeched with excitement as they darted with flaming grass brands to relight the pile, then the next. My nostrils pricked with the acrid smoke. I too caught the fever. I careened about with them, burning grass, laughing, slapping at the flying sparks. The sun set unwatched.

As I walked swiftly home through the brief twilight, I held careless debate on the pleasures of solitude and of sociability. I easily concluded that the delights of solitude were the more sophisticated, but which was the better, the preferable or the more valuable (and in reference to what) was a question I dismissed with the unthinking compromise that perhaps they were complementary.

In any case, the pleasures of sociability certainly depended on being able to communicate. As my grasp of the language improved, I began to be able to relax in company: *savoir-faire* assumes a certain conversational facility. Much of my early desire to flee into my hut and slam the door had been due to sheer exhaustion, for it had taken an intense concentration to find even a few familiar sounds in the stream of syllables so fluently and easily directed at me. Now this flow of speech resolved itself into words, known and unknown, just as the crowds began to dissolve into a number of people, friends or strangers. Within Kako's homestead I could even recognize some of the legs—all I could see from under the low thatch—that flashed past when a storm broke, and some of the voices that called outside my door. "Come out, Redwoman, come out. It's not good to sit alone."

I should have been content, and I was—as long as I thought only in terms of enjoying myself and of feeling at home. My dissatisfaction lay wholly in the part I was being assigned. I was rapidly being absorbed in the life of the women and children. All the magic, all the law, all the politics—over half the things professionally important to me —were in the hands of the men, and so far not one man had been willing to discuss such matters with me, not one man had taken me with him to the meetings of the elders which, I knew, often took place. Was there a moot? I was at a weeding party. An inquest? I had gone to visit my namesake. A ceremony? I heard women gossip of it, afterwards. I had been identified with the women: unless I could break that association, I would leave the field with copious information on domestic details and without any knowledge of anything else.

I didn't like this situation, and I tried to change it. My efforts seemed futile. I never accepted women's invitations without first asking Kako if anything "of importance" were happening that day. Kako always smiled while he uttered the many polite phrases which boiled down to, "Don't bother your head with such things, my child. Run off and amuse yourself." On my visits I always called first on the homestead head. Poorgbilin always led me straight to my namesake, Tar to Udama's cousin.

Daily I went to Yabo's. It was always assumed that I had come to visit Atakpa or Amara. Atakpa's brother Cholo sometimes spent a few moments teasing me. Amara's father Lam would answer my point-blank questions, if I could find him. (Lam never said no to anyone; he knew when to vanish.) Yabo made no bones about snarling at me if I tried to interrupt his thoughts with my questions. One day he spoke viciously to me. I wanted to tell him a great many things, all of which would prove how immensely superior I was and how necessary it was to treat me with respect. A limited vocabulary restricted me to an irritable, "You and Kako, you are just alike. There is only one difference: *you* know nothing!" I swept about on my heel, all set for a grand exit that was quite spoiled by my having to crawl out the low doorway. I muttered my way home, composing and trying to translate into their language the speech I had wanted to make.

A few days later there was a commotion in my reception hut. Sunday, who had entered it with dignity, flew out of it and into my hut; he announced that Yabo demanded to see me. I'd had enough of Yabo's rudeness. "Tell him to wait," I snapped; I tried to recall the nasty comments I had composed on the path. Sunday saw the gleam in my eye. He hastened back out, but there he hovered between two equally fearful poles, like one of Newton's planets. "Go on, tell him!" I shouted out the door. "Tell her," growled

Yabo from the reception hut. Sunday seemed permanently fixed halfway between the two of us. Both of us saw his irresolution; simultaneously we roared out of our lairs to browbeat him. Sunday side-stepped and let us collide.

My next clear recollection is of Yabo leading me by a bruising grip on my wrist out of Kako's homestead, and of Sunday panting up breathlessly behind to give me a notebook before I disappeared. As soon as we reached our destination, however, I swallowed all anger: Yabo had brought me to my first funeral.

I saw the body, a stiff bundle wrapped in mats, lying in the middle of the yard. Then I noticed the people. Under one tree sat the notables and Kako. Our eyes met for a moment; his shifted. He didn't greet me. Perhaps I should have challenged him then. But I didn't. I was too glad to be there. I looked around. Under another tree, the chief mourners sat silent with bowed heads and vacant faces. A group of strangers crowded under a third three; some of these also had their cloths tied about the waist like a sash, in sign of grief.

Yabo moved over to the elders and notables. He pulled me down beside him onto one of the hard plank benches. There was a long wait, while more and more elders came. Yabo only grunted at my questions. I located Ikpoom. Since other people were moving about, I went over to him. He told me that a woman married into this homestead had died in the night; she had five children; the strangers were her relatives; she would be buried today. We were shushed. I went back to my seat.

I was prepared for ritual, for funeral orations perhaps, for anything but what actually happened. It was a debate, conducted with all the noise and irreverence of a court case. And I understood not one word of it. First the strangers orated. Kako and his elders objected to everything they said. The strangers spoke even more hotly. En masse, they advanced to the center of the yard. The notables left me behind quite alone under our tree, as they too marched grimly out into the yard. Old men stuck out their chins pugnaciously; they shouted and waved their barbed spears in menacing gesticulation. Only the mourners remained silent and dejected under their tree. Finally Kako and some of his elders, either convinced or outshouted, returned to our tree and sat down again.

Not Yabo. He, Poorgbilin and a few others were still arguing and brandishing their spears in dangerous persuasion. It looked like the beginning of a fight; I hoped it was merely their style of rhetoric.

Kako tried to quiet Yabo, who turned upon him with a snarl. Kako jumped up, backed by his followers. He and Yabo argued bitterly. Meanwhile, the strangers unobtrusively and prudently withdrew to their own tree. In the midst of all this shouting, one of the mourners led forth five children. I caught Ikpoom's eye and he nodded: the dead woman had been their mother. Once again I expected some note of consolation and mourning. Once more I was mistaken. I watched in astonishment as the children were bandied about by the wrist, from one elder to the next. Before long Yabo reached the end of his brief patience. He seized the eldest child and flung her at Kako.

For the first time I saw Kako lose his temper and his dignity. Roughly, screaming at Yabo, he pushed the child aside. She reeled and fell against one of the elders. Kako paid no heed; he stood rigid and tight-faced as he wrestled with his anger. By the time the child had been set on her feet again, Kako had regained his self-control. He turned to the elders; in a soft, definite voice he put his views before them. At first there was appreciative laughter for some of Yabo's heckling. But slowly, with persuasive rhetoric, Kako won over all the elders. I leaned forward, as though by straining my ears I could make myself understand words I did not know. I might as well have been deaf. I had to fall back on what I could see, and that served only to confirm a rivalry I had already guessed.

Kako had secured his backing; he now resumed his debate with the strangers. Yabo found himself completely left aside. He began to dance up and down, shouting the first words I could understand: "I'm leaving." No one paid any attention. "I'm leaving!" screeched Yabo in the falsetto of rage. He was not heard. He started to walk out of the homestead. He was not seen. The elders were absorbed in the debate between Kako and the strangers. Yabo turned. Again he announced that he was leaving. No one asked him to stay. He started off again, but this time he wanted to take me along. I protested; I wanted to see the burial. Kako, lost in the heat of argument, paid no more attention to my objections than he did to Yabo's expostulations.

I had come with him, said Yabo, and I would leave with him. And willy-nilly, as I had come, so I left. Yabo dragged me by the wrist until he could fling me before him onto the grass-enclosed path from which there was no turning. Over his shoulder he shouted vituperations at the unheeding hullabaloo in the homestead behind us. Angrily he jerked me about to face him: "It wasn't the strangers. It was Kako who killed her." Then, as though he had said too much, he shut himself in a surly silence, and shooed me along the path before him, prodding me with the butt of his spear whenever I tried to linger, opening his lips only to hiss their "giddup" for slow-moving goats and women.

Back in my hut I poured myself a drink and tried to assimilate what had happened. Yabo's violence didn't worry me; he had merely treated me as he treated his own womenfolk—with the very important difference that he would not have taken one of them along on such an occasion. He had accused Kako of murder; he must have meant poison or witchcraft; Kako had been in his homestead when the woman died. I was too unsure of myself to repeat Yabo's words to any of Kako's people. My boys wouldn't talk. I never found out just what had happened that day, before my very eyes.

I had, however, learned that I could play Yabo and Kako off against each other, though not, as yet, very skillfully. Yabo would take me any place to show that I preferred his company to the chief's; Kako could not bear to let Yabo take the lead. Neither Kako nor Yabo was, by himself, willing to tell any European anything; neither Kako nor Yabo could stand the thought that the other was the more valued, by anyone or for any reason. Yabo had set the first, necessary precedent. From then on Kako, and in his wake all the other notables, told me of funerals and expected me to attend them. Again after Yabo set the example, I was notified of moots and inquests. Some of the elders always—and all of them sometimes—were amused or annoyed by my new role, but none disputed it. Not for any merit of mine, but because of the relationship between Kako and Yabo, my work flourished like the green bay tree.

Chapter Seven

I DIDN'T want to leave, but I had to. Thanks to my inexperienced buying, I had run out of some supplies and was dangerously short on essentials like kerosene. I had to go back to the station, but I did not want to go. I was still blinded by my first dazzled enthusiasm at being accepted by the elders, at being invited to all important events. I knew why Kako and Yabo took me. It did not occur to me to wonder why the others tolerated me, nor to wonder where they would stand if either Kako or Yabo turned against me. I thought I had a place of my own amongst them, that Poorgbilin and some of the others liked me for myself. I did not then see that most of the community, like me, was engaged in playing Kako and Yabo off against each other, that most people, like Poorgbilin, followed whichever was the stronger, that I might at any time be made into a political issue. In my innocence I thought that I myself had broken the ice and that no more obstacles would be placed in my path. I was quite sure that they were all willing to tell me what I wished to know. My only limitation seemed to lie in how much I could understand, and I feverishly set myself to remedy that. In this mood of intense working excitement, any interruption was an irritation; a prolonged interruption of ten days—for no better purpose than shopping—seemed intolerable.

It would take a full ten days. I could not wait, as I had originally planned, for the "little dry" of August, a two- or three-week intermission in the rains. This was July: the paths were wet and the streams high. I couldn't even take the shortest path to the motor road: one of the bridges had washed away, leaving a ford too swift and deep for safe passage with headloads. I would have to make a detour.

I consulted Kako. He suggested that I go north and spend the first night with an elder who "really knows things." The second night I could stay at Chief Nder's, who was close to the road and "knows the things of Europeans." To clinch matters, Kako added that Nder had eighteen cows. Since just one cow is a sign of affluence in a tsetse-ridden country where even dwarf cattle have a habit of dying early, I was as impressed as Kako meant me to be. Furthermore, I was fairly sure I had heard Sackerton (who called Kako "reactionary") mention Nder as a "progressive chief"; it might pay to see the difference between the two for myself. Since my trip would thus combine business with necessity, I began to regard it with less distaste. I sent off messengers to make arrangements.

The day before I left, Atakpa came around "to say good-by," so she loudly announced. My reception hut was full of people who had come for the same purpose, and to give me small bits of food "to eat on the path." Atakpa fidgeted about in the background, apparently waiting for them to go. They were still there when I excused myself for lunch. Atakpa dashed out after me and caught me just outside my hut door. "Come out to my farms when you have eaten," she ordered in her usual bossy manner. "I want to give you something." Then, in a conspiratorial whisper, "I have something to tell you, a secret."

"But . . ."

Atakpa broke off my protest. "I'll wait for you on the path," she hissed in the best cloak-and-dagger tradition, "behind the big locust bean tree at the first fork."

I nodded, hypnotized into consent by her air of mystery. It was not like Atakpa to be either coy or surreptitious; my curiosity was at high tide.

After lunch, Atakpa joined me on the path. She had not hidden behind the big locust bean tree after all; she had been sitting comfortably in any empty farm shack near by. "Well?" I demanded eagerly.

She looked around to make sure we were alone. "I'm going to be married."

I felt cheated. There's no secret about marriage. Nevertheless, I congratulated her and asked when the wedding was to be.

"That's just it," she said impatiently, as though I should have known. "Yabo doesn't know about it, and I won't tell him, for he would never consent. I am running away, tonight. No one else knows. I told *you* because we are friends, and a friend's heart is angry if such secrets are not shared. Now promise me you won't tell." I promised.

Atakpa went into a rhapsody about her handsome young lover. Between glowing praises of his general excellence, she told me how she had been meeting him at markets, how he had been brave enough to come at night to the outskirts of Yabo's homestead to serenade her, and what a wonderful farmer he was. "Yabo will be very angry," she concluded a bit nervously, "but my uncle Lam is my marriage guardian, and I can get around him, so it will be all right in the end." She didn't sound altogether convinced.

Technically, Yabo had nothing to say about Atakpa's marriage. A daughter should be able to turn to her father for aid and comfort, but men have been known to overlook the obligations of kinship rather than forgo their claim to some money. To avoid this possibility, some other close male relative is here appointed a girl's marriage guardian— the man who supervises all matters connected with her marriage; it is he who receives the bridewealth (the sum paid by the groom to legalize the marriage and legitimize the children) and who must repay it, if his ward seeks a divorce.

Technically, it was Lam's business. But I couldn't see Lam going against Yabo's wishes, or Atakpa's for that matter. He would be crushed between them. I remembered Yabo's volcanic temper and his basalt ruthlessness; I looked at the stubborn thrust of Atakpa's jaw, at her stubby pipe jutting out at a defiant angle. Father and daughter were of the same temper. It was hard to see what the outcome of their clash might be. Yabo might forgive her. She was his favorite. Atakpa pampered him; she brought him his pipe and cooked him special messes, and she was the only person in his homestead who dared tease that irascible old man. But Yabo might equally well do everything in his power to break his favorite's marriage so that he might bring her back home.

Certainly I should miss her. Her fiancé's homestead was about four miles from Kako's. All her interests and activities would keep her there. Atakpa had been my first friend, and now I would lose her. I said my farewells rather sadly. As I turned down the path, Atakpa ran after me with last instructions. "I didn't tell Amara why, but I made her promise to see that you do not sit alone. She is my cousin, and you are my friend. She is sick. Look after her." Again I promised, and we parted.

Next morning, over the hubbub of arguing carriers and last good-bys, I heard Yabo come storming down the path. He shoved his way through to Kako. Without any preliminaries he demanded that his runaway daughter be seized and brought back to him. Kako listened patiently for a while, but Yabo's cursing lamentation had no periods. Finally Kako interrupted: let Yabo calm down; Lam must be sent for. He dispatched one of his younger sons to fetch him.

Yabo muttered and threatened. As the minutes passed, he began comparing the messenger to a turtle for slowness, a water monitor for stupidity, a lizard for . . . He bit off the insult: the boy was returning. He was alone. Lam, he informed us, was not there; just after Yabo left, Lam had also gone off.

"Where?" thundered Yabo.

The boy retreated to Kako's side. "Lam told your wives he was going traveling someplace on some sort of business for some length of time."

Yabo exploded. I hid a grin. It was just like Lam, and, under the circumstances, not a bad idea at all.

Kako had to shout to make Yabo hear: Lam was Atakpa's marriage guardian and nothing could be done until his return; he, Kako, wanted to hear no more about it until then. Yabo quivered, baffled fury in every limb. He turned his back on Kako and lectured me on his daughter's frivolity, Kako's general weakness of character in refusing to take a high-handed line, and Lam's iniquity and cowardice in sneaking out of a difficult situation. I tried to look surprised and appropriately sympathetic. Finally, since he showed no sign of ever coming to an end, I yelled a loud good-by at him and left.

The carriers had already started off down the path. This time they were all people I knew, and Ihugh, by Kako's appointment, was at their head as their "elder": his job was to supervise their efforts, keep them all together, and perhaps strike up a song, but he carried no more than a horse-hair fly switch. Kako himself escorted me half a mile down the path. There he gave me a rooster "to eat on the path" and turned back.

One of the carriers had fallen behind to wait for me. It was Cholo. "Didn't my sister tell you she was going to elope?"

After a second's thought I decided Atakpa had not meant me to tell anyone. "No," I lied.

Cholo raised his arms and lifted the box he carried a few inches over his head, the better to frown in disapproval. "She did very wrong," he said bluntly, "not to tell you, her friend. When you come back, you must let her kill you a chicken so she will know your heart is not spoiled toward her."

At that I burst out with it. "She told me not to tell anyone."

"That's all right then." Cholo grinned. "Maybe you can get her to kill you a chicken anyhow. But if I can think up the reason, you must save me a drumstick as my share." He trotted ahead to rejoin the others, who were already singing one of the, by now, familiar songs about my working people to death.

I swung into pace with their song. We had a long day's trek before us, but I had got used to the climate and was in good shape from my constant circuit walking. I had no worries about my feet or about keeping up. I had no worries at all, and almost no thoughts. There was only the path to look at—the grass screened off all other vision—the path and the carriers before me. The heat and monotony of such walking induce a peculiar division in the mind: thoughts and memories come and go quite independently, without notification of their beginning nor of their ending; they have their own existence: quite often one tunes in in the middle, and sometimes one listens and more often one doesn't.

At one point I found myself reflecting on the saw that it is the experienced traveler whose baggage is neat and compact. I had come, new and green, with neat canvas bundles and wooden boxes; the boys, too, had had their loads neatly wrapped in mats. But now—I glanced ahead at the carriers—we looked like a raggle-taggle of Okies. Chickens cackled inside baskets and rolled mats. The sooty, kerosene-tin stove would have disgraced a junk yard. Sunday, with my interests in mind but without permission, had swathed some bottles of beer in wet cloths—a messy bundle passed from one protesting carrier to another and eventually thrust upon Monday who, as a small boy, was always stuck with the dirty work. Odd bottles of palm oil, which the boys had bought to trade to advantage in the station, clanked about in a bucket.

My appearance matched that of my loads. My straw hat had long since raveled into uselessness; Accident now wore the remnants and I went without. As a result, whenever I took off my dark glasses, I revealed two unwholesome goggles of white skin patched against a tanned face. My tennis shoes were disintegrating: keeping three pair in use all the time, I still wore out a pair every three or four weeks; I hadn't brought enough. Cotton dresses, sturdy

89

enough to survive the most brutal machine laundry, were tissue in the hands of Sunday and Monday. The two of them shoved everything into cold water, scrubbed violently with the bars of harsh soap available in the bush markets, and then, one at each end, they began to twist and wring. Having a tough linen sheet tear in their hands had rather surprised them, but it hadn't made them any more gentle in their work. I had been forced to replenish my wardrobe by making skirts from the Manchester prints that appeared in Kako's market: a bit gaudy for the station, but much admired in bush. Dirndl skirt and cotton blouse were, in fact, the most satisfactory bush costume I found: they combine a loose fit, hence coolness, with full covering against grass, mosquitoes and the odd postures one assumes crawling in and out of huts. The shirts, however, were beyond my skill: a tailor was on my station list. From the tailor, my mind wandered to the cold beer in Sackerton's refrigerator, and then became blank as the walking told on my energy.

It was late afternoon before we reached the homestead Kako had recommended. It was large and clean, but my heart sank. The old man who "really knew things" was badly stricken with palsy. He lay shaking on his plank bed and was barely able to stutter out a few greetings. He seemed to want to talk, but each word made him shake worse than ever. In all, I spent no more than two minutes with him. His brother, a very light-skinned man with a hatchet face and a disagreeable mouth, asked me to come inspect the reception hut they had cleared for my use. He also suggested that I might want to rest awhile in the shade, as, indeed, I did.

I settled under a tree. The boys bustled about making camp. Ihugh came to announce that he and the others were going off to bathe and eat. No one came to talk with me. I looked about: the homestead was unusually quiet; there was a generally depressed air about the people that puzzled me—I had seen nothing like it in any of the homesteads I had ever visited.

Then the elders of the neighborhood came in to greet me. One of them carried a rather unusual spear of really beautiful workmanship. To fill the silence that followed the greetings, I asked about it. It had been his father's, he told me, and his father had received it from his father. Soon the old man's eyes were shining as he spoke of the wars and hunts and feats of courage in the old days "before the white man spoiled our land." We sat long. I forgot my host and his troubles.

Ihugh came into my reception hut while I was eating dinner, to tell me that they had all returned. I had seen and heard them come back, so I nodded and wished him good night. Ihugh, looking stupider than ever, shuffled his feet. "This is a bad place." He blurted out the words, then disappeared, stooping through the low doorway with remarkable agility, before I could ask him why.

I asked Sunday. He set the custard carefully down before me; then, "It's a den of thieves."

"Come, now," I protested. "Kako said this would be a good place to stay." Sunday permitted himself only a non-committal "Did he?" before he too vanished. I dismissed the matter with a mental shrug, "More name calling; just suspicious of strangers."

I was tired, but not at all sleepy. I stretched out under the mosquito net to read Jane Austen's account of a life so utterly unlike the one I was leading or any I might want to live that it gave me escape without envy. Pages later, I crawled out from under the net to pump the lamp, and saw —in a ring outside my low wall—a neat row of black tufted heads: all my carriers. I blinked and looked again. They were sitting perfectly still, neither moving nor speaking, with a fixity that seemed to portend an all-night wait.

I stepped outside and called Ihugh. "Didn't they give you a place to sleep?"

"Yes, indeed," he replied loudly. Then, in a whisper, "This is a bad place."

From under the eaves came another whisper. "Don't put

out the light, Redwoman. We want to sit here. It is I, Cholo, the brother of your friend, who ask this of you."

I said they could have one of the bush lamps. I couldn't sleep in the light. Ihugh told me my boys had all three of them, lit, inside their hut. So they had, and boxes piled across the doorway. The symptoms were familiar. "Witches?" I whispered in Ihugh's ear. "Tell me."

Someone mumbled that I knew nothing at all. Ihugh himself hushed me with a touch of Udama's hauteur, "One does not malign a chief in his hearing."

"No one can hear us," I muttered crossly, "and if you will tell me no reason for your request, I shall not heed it. I will put out my lamp, now."

Ihugh caught my arm as I turned. "Hear me, Redwoman," his heavy voice slowly measured out each syllable. "There is reason. But you must not ask me, nor any of us, for we are just children. How can we know the things of elders? In our ignorance we might tell you what is not true, and thus mislead you. It is because we are children, your carriers and your children; therefore you must not act in anger toward us."

I didn't in the least believe that Ihugh didn't know what it was all about. But I had only one lever with which to pry his knowledge from him: my light. I hesitated to use it. Ihugh's clever little speech had labeled me as cruel and irresponsible if I did so. It had also informed me—and all the listening carriers—that if I demanded information I should receive lies. I could no longer regard Ihugh as a stupid bruiser, though in so big a man, I excused myself, it is difficult to be sure where body stops and character begins. In any case, body or soul, there was something very solid and reliable about him. When Ihugh began to get nervous the average man was already terrified. I didn't want my carriers to run away.

I handed Ihugh the more powerful of my two flashlights. He thanked me. Cholo murmured, "There speaks my sister's friend." They had got what they wanted.

I had not.

92

My second chance to find out something about witches had gone by like the first. But it was not this disappointment that kept me awake that night. By comparison I cared little what witchcraft there might be in this silent homestead of a palsied old man. (Indeed, that was all: palsy is considered a disease caused by witches; where the homestead head cannot protect himself from witchcraft, no one else feels secure; in a strange place, unprotected by their own elders, the carriers were afraid.)

I had lost an illusion. For the last weeks I had thought these people wholly open and sincere with me. Now I felt myself thrust right back to the beginning. I would have to start over again. Again? Had I ever started in actual fact? Had anyone ever willingly told me anything? lost his suspicion of me? I had been a blind fool, and yet . . . It could not have been wholly an illusion. Only yesterday Atakpa had shared her secrets with me; only this morning her brother had told me I was entitled to her sincerity. But the alternative, that I had lost a real gain by awkward, hasty questioning, was too bitter to contemplate. The whole miserable circle of misgiving and self-reproach wheeled around all night while I lay there, conscious of the silent figures crouched around my hut and of every nervous stab of light from the flash I had given Ihugh.

I got little sleep, so little that I honestly thought I had not slept at all. I was tired and cross: the boys had started packing at dawn; the carriers waited for us impatiently, twisting grass into head pads. I was nervous, too, about my farewells: our host could not have been unaware of our behavior in the night; such suspicion seemed poor return for any hospitality. But I did not see the old man, and his cold-faced brother made no sign that he had noticed anything odd. As soon as my loads were ready, almost before I had completed the necessary string of thank-you phrases, the carriers shot out of the homestead. Not until we were a good two miles down the path did they slacken their pace and begin to sing.

As the heat penetrated my body, still chill from waking,

and as the monotonous rhythm of walking stretched and relaxed my muscles, I too began to shake off some of the night's depression. I wanted to forget. Later, sometime, somehow, while I was in the station perhaps—then I would think about it. Not now. I only hoped that no one would mention it.

No one did. As we approached Nder's, the carriers turned their minds to quite other matters. "A rich chief like that," Cholo commented during one of our rests, "ought to kill us a goat. Tonight, we'll eat!" It was a comment I could not ignore. Money was precisely one of the shortages that was driving me into the station. I had enough cash for the carriers and for a few roosters and some oddments, but not enough for a goat. I made this observation into the air. Udama had taught me that possibly embarrassing statements of fact should never be directed at any one person in the group concerned.

After only the briefest pause, Ihugh spoke, also in to the air: what Nder wanted to give the carriers was their business and his, certainly not mine; however, if Nder ever visited me with an entourage, it would not be amiss to provide them with some beer or meat. I digested this information in silence. Ihugh had probably given me an exact statement of the case, but I suspected that the immediate result would be an increase of Nder's prestige—and possibly Ihugh's at the expense of my own. With a bit of sophistry, I persuaded myself that it would be petty to forbid the goat just because Nder might think me poor and stingy. "The goat is not my affair," I agreed. They all chorused their relief, "Truly, Redwoman, it is not your affair." And for the rest of the way into Nder's, Ihugh kept drawing my attention to all the botanical points of interest along the path. It was, I supposed, my reward for not being difficult. They were always very nice to me, when I did what they wished. "You give me and I tell you," I muttered in English. "Bah!"

Kako had been quite right. Nder knew how to deal with Europeans, especially when they arrived hot and bothered

94

from their walking. (On this visit I discovered no other sign of his being "progressive.") Under his shadiest tree, Nder had set his own deck chair for me to rest in; a wife brought a pot of hot water for my hands and feet; a child spread a clean mat, so that I might sit barefooted. Nder himself stayed only long enough to apologize for the reception hut he had provided: it was the newest and largest, but the walls had not yet been built; he had tied heavy, tightly woven mats about the posts; would it do? I reassured him. At that point I could see no advantage in the solidity of a wall.

Nder left me to rest and wiggle my toes in comfort. From the corner of my eye I saw him give Ihugh a goat, and I soon heard a happy chatter of conflicting advice while the carriers watched Ihugh dismember the animal. I counted Nder's cattle: one bull, five calves and twelve cows. They were very much in evidence. The bare, central yard which usually serves as a meeting place had here been transformed into a log corral, large enough to come within six feet of the inner circle of reception huts. In the center of the corral was a thatched shelter to protect the cows from rain and heat, and under it a trough of water. Nder did his cattle well. Any grain chaff, husks or refuse a cow might possibly eat was tossed into the corral; most of it got trampled into the mud and rotted there. It stank. Perhaps that was why the animals seemed so restless.

At just the right moment, when I had rested but was not yet bored, Nder came back to give me an enormous rooster for my "children" and a duck for myself "because it is the food of Europeans." My thanks were heartfelt. One gets tired of goat meat every market day and chicken every other day. I blessed the unknown who had given Nder this hint. We settled down to a more than pleasant conversation. Nder excelled at paring himself down to a basic vocabulary, at avoiding all grammatical difficulties, and at speaking slowly. He had talked to Europeans frequently. His experience had also led him to prepare a list of things suitable for me to know. The few questions by which I tried to lead him beyond that went politely unanswered. However, what he wanted to say included a great many things I wanted to hear. We retired with mutual compliments—he as pleased with his successful reticence as I was with my new information.

There was no question of frightened, huddling carriers that night. Nder's wives served up huge bowls of porridge and two pots of beer. And, of course, the goat. Even Cholo had all he could eat. Replete and content, they all came with Ihugh to bid me good-night. Then they sat about their fire and sang and shouted and sang. Everyone else went to bed. They still sang. I was glad they were happy, but their exuberance kept me awake. Then one of Nder's eighteen cows began to bellow in accompaniment. For a while, they tried to make more noise than the cow, but finally, with laughing and joking, they gave it up and became quiet. I blessed the beast, and turned over to sleep.

It was the last kind thought I had about those cattle. Now that the carriers gave the bellowing cow no further competition, the other seventeen provided her with chorus and obbligato. I began to wonder quite seriously why the lowing of cows is considered a fit subject for poetry and why cows are popularly believed placid. These had no calm. They chased around in the corral; they stamped. They kicked at the logs that shut them in. The thud of hooves on splintering wood, then a clatter of falling bars, a noisy leap—something large swerved against my mats and dented them in.

"A! A! A! A!" a rapidly rising crescendo of comment from nearby huts. "That old mother cow jumped out again!"

I sat up in bed. A clatter of rolling logs, stamping of hooves, and the sudden blows that battered against my mats made it evident that the other seventeen were following the old mother cow in her victorious leap for liberty. I fumbled my way out of bed and straightened the mats again, thanking my lucky stars that the posts were frequent enough and the roof low enough to have prevented their charging straight into my bed.

With the innate perversity of inanimate objects and large animals, the old mother cow and her horde stayed in the homestead to make our night wretched. Cows rubbed itching shoulders against my mats, buckling them dangerously. I took up my staff and banged away at each bulge, with the avowed purpose of keeping the mats from being torn down, but not at all displeased when I hit cow.

The cattle lowed and grumbled confidences to each other only a few inches from my bedside; they breathed heavily, a sour stench that penetrated my mats and my mosquito net and made me hold my nose. I presume the fragrant breath commonly attributed to these beasts applies only to those fed on clover; a cow on any other diet does not smell as sweet. In our tradition kine peaceably chew the cud and ruminate. Not these: they kicked and bellowed and scratched and chased about the homestead. It began to rain. Malcontents from beginning to end, these cows refused the shelter provided for them in their corral; they wanted to come into our huts. As I banged viciously with my staff, rushing from one side of my reception hut to the other, trying to keep the wet cattle from breaking in upon me, I came to a conclusion: I have a fondness for small animals only.

I was not their only victim. I heard angry voices as a cow knocked the door of a hut over onto a couple who had no desire to be interrupted. The cow stuck in the doorway. By now everyone was awake. A furious husband, matchet in hand, struggled in the rain with two men who tried to restrain him. He shouted vituperation indiscriminately at the cow stuck in the doorway, at his erring wife and at her lover. Nder himself flapped out to reason with the husband, who would not listen. Nder's high-pitched protest reached me. "But you might hurt my cow!"

I laughed out loud. It might be indiscreet, but I couldn't help it. Cows and a grand passion! At Nder's call, four men dragged the struggling husband away. Two others, afraid

97

to go near enough to be of any use, hovered about the kicking cow. I laughed myself into exhaustion. Man's fate is cruel, that others see his misfortunes as farce. If we must suffer, we should at least be allowed to suffer in the tragic manner.

Just before dawn, with a ruckus that woke us all, the cow extricated herself. There was wild confusion as the ungrateful creature charged her would-be rescuers and everyone else in sight. I wondered what would happen to the wife. I didn't feel I could ask Nder. I no longer had any expectation of hearing anything from my boys or my carriers. The night's events would, I supposed, remain an anecdote, an incident I could end at fancy whenever I wanted to play solitaire with my imagination.

With such an early awakening, we made too early a start. The truck had not yet arrived. We settled down by the motor road to wait. "Those cows!" Cholo yawned, "Why doesn't Nder use them for bridewealth? He could get many wives with them." He and some of the others drifted into earnest dispute over the precise number.

It seemed a good moment, now, while they were all interested. I risked a question. "What happened, once the cow was out?" They all replied, simultaneously; from their babble of cross-interruption I gathered that the wife had barricaded herself into the hut and the lover had fled while the cow was chasing people. Heartened by this response, I asked what would have happened if the cow had not got stuck in the doorway.

Cholo answered, with the dampening common sense characteristic of his sister Atakpa. "Then no one would have known, and nothing would have happened. Those cows! Now if I were Nder . . ."

I hastened to forestall another dissertation on cows versus wives. "I mean if the husband had caught them."

"All his kinsmen would have helped beat up the lover."

"The husband said he would kill him, and he had a matchet."

Cholo snorted, "That is just what one says at such times. A fight, yes, but it is not a matter for killing."

Ihugh agreed. "That is the way it is. It is necessary to frighten wives from time to time, but it is foolish to feel the anger one should show. Some men are fools; they feel a great rage and let it be seen. Such men cannot keep a wife; all women shun them."

"You mean, a man doesn't divorce his wife for adultery?"

"Of course not," Cholo was amused by my question. "Do you give away a chair because someone else uses it? The bad thing about lovers is that they tempt wives to run away. A man lets a wife go willingly only if she is lazy."

"Mmmm," a brooding voice came in sadly. "The trouble with women is that they run away."

"The trouble with women," Ihugh corrected, "is that women are trouble, and they make trouble between relatives, between friends and between age mates. Yet one must have wives, for without children the homestead perishes, leaving no sign that it has ever been."

"Women . . ." someone else began, and until the truck came, I had to hear my sex thoroughly trounced and defamed.

On the drive back to the station, I turned their words over in my mind. Their discussion had been pessimistic, but it had also been what we call a "civilized" conversation. Cholo had been very much the cynical man of the world; Ihugh's viewpoint was very much like a medieval friar's. But the main thing for me, at that time, was that they had replied, and freely. My limitless optimism and its deflation had been equally foolish, equally based on illusion. Kako and Yabo had used me; I had used them. But social utility of this sort need not exclude real liking; indeed, it can be a firm foundation for friendship. Through the rivalry of two men, I had gained a foothold. The rest was up to me. One cannot make friends with a community. One has to make friends with individual people. What Atakpa or Yabo or Ihugh might tell me had nothing to do with the confidences anyone else might make. There are degrees of acquaint-

99

ance. I knew this of my own world. I had been incredibly naïve to think it would be different here. Frank sincerity on one topic—among them as among us—does not imply a loss of reticence over everything else. Ihugh had not refused to tell me anything except one specific incident. I had generalized too widely. "Why, they'd tell me anything"; "They're all liars, every last man of them": both comments belong in the mouths of fools. I had said both. Very well, I should not do so again.

I must go slowly, I realized, much more slowly, and I must learn to judge more accurately my particular standing with particular people, and I must also learn the public rating of permissible topics. I must be content to learn by degrees, to penetrate deeper and deeper, level by level. There was no short cut. I could force the pace a little, but I must also acquire the sensitivity that would tell me how far. Above all, I must learn to accept, with what patience and humility I might, the fact that their voice, not mine, was final.

Chapter Eight

I ENJOYED my stay in the station and profited from it. I put in several days' intensive work with an English-speaking mission boy, with whose help I began to make sense of grammar and syntax. The Sackertons were hospitable and left me little time to be dreary in the station resthouse. I was delighted when they asked me to spend Christmas with them. Since I did not realize I would need a break before then, I set about preparing for five months' stay in bush. I went to the canteens, and I scoured the station for books.

Supplies were brought into that particular upcountry station by river (in the few months during which it was navigable) and by a chronically erratic train service. One could not count on a constant stock of anything. Sometimes there was nothing in the canteens but sardines, dried milk and canned artichoke hearts, or nothing but damson jam, tomato purée and canned snails (shells sold separately). Sometimes even the staples disappeared: no flour, no kerosene, no milk, no tea. Once even the gin supply had been known to fail. I was lucky. I got everything I needed except salt, bitters and yeast.

I investigated the club library—for the past twenty years an orphanage of unwanted books: Oppenheim, Orczy, Sarasin, P. C. Wren, Dickens, Thornton Wilder, Zane Grey, most of the Sitwells, and a battered Rabelais. One could find modern popular Britannica abducted from ships' libraries and abandoned here; it had journalistic the-world-as-I-see-it books and psychological the-world-as-I-fear-it books. I took the Rabelais and went on to the mission bookstore.

The mission bookstore had branched out from Bibles and hymnbooks. By the door was a glass case of pencils, fountain pens, paint brushes and knitting needles (but no paints and no wool). There were shelves of writing tablets, notebooks, account books, school attendance books and, mysteriously, a few leather-bound, lock-and-key logbooks at fifty shillings each. Behind the rows of five-shilling Bibles, Lives of Jesus in Basic English, prayer books and pamphlets ("A Christian Looks at Polygamy," "English Gardens," "Is Bribery a Sin?") lurked a whole shelf of *Mrs. Beeton's Fish Cookery*. Among the textbooks—Latin grammars, geography, African midwifery, arithmetic—I spotted Carlyle's *History of the French Revolution*. On one table were books in Basic or simplified English: Lamb's *Tales from Shakespeare, Tom Brown's School Days, Jane Eyre*—I wondered briefly what on earth a polygamous people who ideally had several wives would make of Jane's objections to bigamy. On another table were the pocketbooks: detective stories, plays, novels, biographies—all sorts of books that one would not expect to find in a mission bookshop: Darwin, Apuleius, Congreve and Voltaire. Again I was in luck: I found several books I wanted to reread, ten readable books I hadn't read, and a scribe.

A young man stepped forward from the loafers at the door. He volunteered to carry my stack of books and papers for me. Instead of walking behind me, he trotted along by my side and made conversation. He was not at all the usual type of malcontent that forms the largest element in the stations and towns. I asked him what he was doing there.

"I'm afraid of being bewitched," he answered promptly and cheerfully. He explained that his grandfather had been a man of great wisdom and magical powers and that all his uncles had suspected his father of having decamped with certain articles of magical equipment on the old man's death. "But he didn't"—Rogo was positive—"I know, for I am my father's eldest son and on his deathbed he gave me all the magic he had. But my uncles won't believe it, and now they're after me. So I can't go home."

"Never?" I felt very sorry for him.

"Oh yes," said Rogo, "as soon as I am old enough to be a witch myself. Then I shall go home, intimidate all my relatives, and become an important elder like my grandfather. Meanwhile, I do anything. I'd like to be a clerk, but I know only my own language."

"Can you write?" I was surprised.

Rogo told me that he had been a child when the British had first established schools. The chief, anxious to oblige them, had sent out policemen to capture some children for the school. His youthful catch was locked up and forcibly instructed. All the parents, Rogo's father among them, tried threats, bribery and persuasion, but the chief was deaf: the children must stay for several months, until the administration was convinced that the chief was willing to help; then those who wished might leave. Rogo was one of the few who acquired a taste for learning; he remained at school for five years, until his grandfather died. Then he and his father had to find refuge elsewhere. "Therefore," concluded Rogo, "I only finished learning to write."

On a sudden impulse, as I paid him for carrying, I handed him a sheet of paper and a pencil and asked him to write something for me. He took almost two hours over the page, but his writing—actually printing—was very legible and he had recorded a truly magnificent animal fable. I told him that if he wished, he could come with me to write fables: first on the basis of eating money and so much per notebook, and then we'd see.

Rogo made two conditions: under no circumstances would he follow me within witchcraft range of his own home (Kako's was far enough to be safe); he must be free to leave my service whenever he wished, at a moment's notice and without my bearing a grudge. "I wander," he explained, and indeed, there was an elfin, elusive quality in his triangular face with its cat's-whisker scars.

On the morning of my departure, I was not really surprised to find no sign of Rogo. The truck was loaded. I was about to get in. Then, suddenly, he was there: neat, clean, showing no traces of last-minute haste or apology. I saw him into the back of the truck with the carriers, before I climbed up beside the driver. Once more I waved good-by to Sackerton: "Until Christmas."

It was good to get back to Kako's, among a people who laughed out loud and shouted and sang as they worked and walked. I also laughed and shouted greetings. Like my voice, my gestures grew larger and more expansive, and I suddenly realized what a hobble British decorum places on American exuberance.

It was a homecoming. Going away had done far more for me than any length of continued residence. Someone who returns is no longer a stranger. This time it was the carriers from the station who sat in isolation, while the people of Kako's homestead clustered about me in greeting and little Accident danced with excitement. This time, when the carriers left, Kako turned to me, "And now that the strangers have gone . . ."

I glowed at his words, and nodded to everything he said. While I was gone, a mad man had tried to get into my hut; Kako had told Ihugh to sleep in my kitchen. Now he suggested that I keep Ihugh on as night watchman. I consented gladly: the market brought many thieves and strays, and the kitchen could not be locked. Monday had slept there, but he was courting one of Kako's daughters and I felt his presence could not always be relied upon.

All that evening, all the next day, people flocked in to welcome me, and to tell me what had happened in my absence. No one gossips with a stranger, and, knowing no gossip, I had been unable to see below the surface of daily events. Now for the first time, because I could ask about people by name and because absence is a legitimate reason for ignorance, I began to learn. "Mbana? She won't be back for some time. You know her daughter by her first husband who married a man from Nder's. Well . . ."

Through just such homecoming gossip, the pattern of their lives began to spread out before me. Mrs. Grundy is the anthropologist's best informant.

Whatever else people had to say, they all told me what had happened to the thief who lived nearby. This man was one of the most expert thieves in the whole tribe, and their standards are high: a really good burglar can knock a hole in a mud hut and remove all its contents—including that cherished possession, a bicycle—without waking the sleeping inhabitants. This one had been living with his three wives and their children in a neat homestead filled with the profits of his profession and the fruits of his periodic imprisonments: his wives' huts had wooden doors (he could afford a carpenter) and wickerwork furniture (jailbirds' skill); the yard was bordered with the flowers he had learned to appreciate in prison. His wives were the best-dressed women in the community, but they were not happy, for their husband was a strong man with a violent temper who ruled his women with an iron hand which they respected—and disliked.

One dark night, when he had chosen to sleep in his reception hut, all three wives quietly arose and took the wooden hut doors off their hinges. Onto these doors they loaded all their possessions—and all their husband's. Then, doors on head, children in hand and on hip, they walked away. The next morning their husband woke to a homestead stripped of wives, children and goods. The wives' homes were all distant, and in different directions. He couldn't decide which wife to chase first. He stormed about the countryside telling his tale to people who found it so funny that not even fear of his trigger temper and heavy hand could keep them from laughing in his face. The mere mention of his name was enough to make people double up with mirth. When it turned out that everywhere he went, the courts refused him return of bridewealth, wives, children or goods on the grounds that he had previously helped himself to liberal compensation, there was a new gale of laughter and universal approval. A topical song,

"The Robber Robbed," became the hit of the day. I was told that Poorgbilin's women had worked it into their program for me.

There seemed to be no way out of that program. Before I had gone into the station, Poorgbilin's senior wife had announced that she and the women of her homestead would come honor me with a dance. The phrase she used applied to one particular dance, generally done only by women; they slowly shuffle round and round in a circle; as the hips go one way, the hands—with a cloth stretched taut between them—go another. Three minutes of such monotony bored me; if they came to perform especially for me, I should have to watch for at least two hours. I had put it off until after my return. It had been a vain hope that they would forget. Poorgbilin's senior wife reminded me of the affair with the first words of greeting she spoke. I said I had to settle in first and was very vague about a suitable date.

As soon as I could, I went off to Yabo's to find out what had happened to Atakpa. Fortunately, Amara was alone and had time to warn me: the mere mention of Atakpa's name sent Yabo into paroxysms of rage; he had beaten one of his wives for asking whether she might go visit her; Lam had not returned, and Kako had forbidden Yabo to follow his daughter, but Yabo had sworn to seize her if she left her husband's homestead or . . . Amara broke off as Yabo appeared. By the time he reached us, she was asking me about the dance Poorgbilin's wives were giving me.

I might have been able to put off Poorgbilin's wives indefinitely; I could not put off the whole community. And everyone I knew, men and women alike, kept asking me just when the dance was to be held. I surrendered. I suggested the day after the next market. Poorgbilin's wives said that would be too soon. We agreed on the day following the second market.

In a rather by-the-way fashion, I informed my boys of the date and asked what I should give the women besides the usual pennies one presses on the foreheads of outstanding dancers. "Beer," they said. "Fine," I agreed. "One pot."

Sunday disapproved: one pot was not enough. I said I would give no more, because when people drank too much I couldn't understand what they said. Sunday looked mulish, and began a protest. Rogo interrupted him, "It doesn't matter about the beer, for she can't give them porridge either." The boys sighed with relief; they clearly thought the dilemma solved. I was out of my depth and knew it. "You mean," I cautiously checked up, "if I give no porridge I don't have to give as much beer as I would if I gave them porridge as well?"

"Of course," said Rogo. "Therefore you must give them a ram."

I thought he had gone mad. I looked at Sunday. He agreed with Rogo. So did the cook and Monday. I became stern, for I had an uneasy feeling that something was being put over on me. I reminded them that I had seen such dances before; I knew that no one ever gave anything more than a chicken to the person who organized it, perhaps some beer, and a few pennies. Many people gave less.

"But they're coming to honor you!" Sunday almost wailed.

"That's nice of them," I retorted. "A chicken, a pot of beer, and don't try to fool me like this again." I cut through their objections. "And I wish to hear no more about it."

But I did. They held audible conversations just outside my door. Rogo wrote a fable illustrating the virtue of generosity and, for good measure, told me of the feasts spread by his grandfather. I did not believe their advice disinterested. I knew their prestige was tied up with mine. I thought their motive could only be a desire to increase that joint prestige by a display of my affluence. I also was interested in my prestige, but if I were to live within my grant, I could not afford to hand about gifts of that magnitude and so out of proportion to what was customarily given. And once is enough for precedent. If I cut down then, for anyone, it would be an insult. I called the boys together and explained all this, slowly and fully. In this case, I concluded, I had seen with my own eyes what was customary;

the ram must not be mentioned again. To give them time to digest my lecture and to avoid all argument by the most efficacious local remedy, I took myself off for a walk.

It seemed a good time to walk the four miles to see Atakpa. Accident was palpably pleased when I asked him to show me the way. Atakpa's elopement was a sensational scandal, and Accident was a precocious gossip even by local standards. He skipped at the thought of seeing another stage of the story for himself. Accident was soon chattering about Yabo's contemptuous treatment of Ihiev—of whom I had never before heard. I lost interest in his story: it was very long and seemed to concern only Yabo's general dislike of the weak-spirited. Yabo was something of a bully, but he liked to fight for his triumphs.

Accident brought me up with a shock. "How in the world," he marveled, "could a futile little man like Ihiev have imagined he could get any place with Atakpa?" All interest again, I demanded details. Ihiev, Accident told me, was actually and even now, Atakpa's husband. He had become infatuated with her a good five years ago and had hung around her—at Yabo's, at markets, even out on her farm. Atakpa first ignored him, then took a delight worthy of her father in making a fool of him. She even set him to weeding her farm—woman's work.

Desperate, Ihiev turned to Yabo for advice. Yabo wickedly said that girls were always difficult: marry her, he recommended, and then things would be different. His own hopes and Yabo's insidious suggestions completely blinded Ihiev. He went off to scrape together all the money he could: borrowing from his relatives, selling his livestock, and even going off to do road work in the station. Eventually, he accumulated ten pounds. Yabo calmly pocketed them, saying mendaciously that he would hand them to Atakpa's marriage guardian, Lam. When Atakpa returned from her farm, Yabo pointed to Ihiev and told her: "There's your husband." Atakpa refused to have anything to do with him.

For a long time, months it seems, Ihiev tried to coax and

persuade. Finally, encouraged by his age mates, pushed on by his relatives, and maddened by the knowledge that he was the laughingstock of the neighborhood, Ihiev told Yabo that he was Atakpa's husband; if she wouldn't come with him willingly, he would carry her off by force. "Go right ahead," said Yabo.

Ihiev, said Accident, was a little man; Atakpa was, I knew, a strong, tough woman and, to judge by events, in no two minds about this situation. Approaching her warily, Ihiev made a grab for her, and a tussle royal rolled through the homestead. Yabo tucked up his feet on his chair and grinned maliciously. The women came to their doors and shouted encouragement at Atakpa. Atakpa's uncles and brothers shrugged off Ihiev's calls for assistance: Atakpa was Ihiev's wife, and if Ihiev could haul her off, well and good; but she was their niece and sister and they would not lay violent hands upon her. Atakpa finally knocked Ihiev out with a piece of firewood. Yabo scolded her mildly: she should discourage him more gently; what if he wanted his money back? Atakpa's grinning brothers revived Ihiev and advised him to go home and rest a bit before he tried again. "He never has," Accident wound up, "but he won't ask for his money back; the fool keeps hoping that some day Atakpa will relent, but she just laughs. And now she's run away."

Atakpa was not at home, to my surprise, for I remembered Yabo's threats to snatch her. Her husband, as her fiancé considered himself, pulled out a chair for me and explained that he was "sitting empty and useless" because his first wife had taken a great fancy to Atakpa. The very morning after the elopement, she had taken Atakpa off to her home to show her off to her family as "her new wife." He was pleased that the two women were going to get on well together, for "if your senior wife doesn't like the little wife you bring her, one of them runs away." Also, he thought it a very safe place for Atakpa at the moment. Nevertheless, he was a bit irked that he, a man with two wives, should be left without anyone to cook for him.

I asked about Ihiev. Smirking and stretching himself to his full height, he commented rather smugly, "Atakpa needs a real man." More seriously he pointed out that Lam had never received a penny of Ihiev's money; therefore Lam, Atakpa's marriage guardian, considered her unmarried and had agreed to take five pounds as down payment. They hoped to have the money by the end of the month. Then, no court would give Atakpa back to her father. Yabo's greed had cost him his daughter.

What, I asked, would happen to Ihiev's ten pounds? "Oh," Atakpa's husband answered carelessly, "he can try to get it back from Yabo, but I don't think he'll succeed." He returned to his own affairs, deviously. Was it true that Poorgbilin's wives were going to honor me with a dance? I said it was, but how had he heard? Everyone knew, he replied, and asked me to further both my affairs and Atakpa's by buying one of his sheep for the dance. "I'm not buying a ram," I yelled; his mentioning it was the last straw. He looked so genuinely surprised at my outburst that I broke down: why should I give a ram when others gave a chicken? He shrugged off my question and I left, charging him with greetings for Atakpa.

It was Accident who made me see the difficulty. As he talked, I again realized that learning the language and learning the culture were mutually dependent. I had misunderstood because I did not know the full social implications of the words. Accident was upset by what he had heard me say. "It isn't right not to give Poorgbilin's women a ram. They are bringing you new yams and all manner of vegetables for sauces, and firewood, and eggs and chickens."

"Then why didn't they tell me so?" I too was protesting.

"They did tell you. They must have told you, for I myself have heard you tell other people that they were coming to honor you with a dance."

Back home, I again summoned the boys. I told them I would buy a ram. I complained bitterly that they had told me nothing of the yams and chickens; they knew, if no one

110

else did, how little I understood of the language. They could not grasp the nature of my difficulty. Like everyone else, they assumed that if I used a word at all, I must be fully aware of all that it implied.

The next problem was adjusting the amount of produce, chickens and firewood to the size, age and dignity of the ram. I put Ihugh and Rogo in charge; together they scoured the neighborhood for a suitable beast. Meanwhile, all the women of the community were busily acting as go-betweens, rushing now to Poorgbilin's, now to me, to discover exactly what preparations were being made on both sides.

Interest in the dance grew every day. Nobody talked—to me, at any rate—about anything else. I commissioned Udama to brew my beer for me. The usual go-betweens watched it anxiously at every stage. I watched it too, and discovered that Udama had put most of the women in the homestead to work and that the one pot I had ordered had grown to six. This time I made no objections. Beer making is hard labor, and all the women working at my brew made sure I was informed that one potful was for them and no one else. I felt they would have earned it. Steeping the grain, grinding the sprouted kernels, and endless boiling alternated with periods of fermentation. The young women sat about the large, black beer pots in the midst of the yard, stirring with long guinea corn stalks, ladling the thick potion from one batch into another, and trying to shield their faces from the heat of the fire. Meanwhile, the old women kibitzed from the shade, but at each crucial moment of the brewing they hovered over the pots. It takes long experience to know the precise moment at which to take the pot off the fire or the exact point at which to stop the fermentation. The experts in Kako's and among the go-betweens never agreed, but they always said Udama should have done something else. She got quite irritable at having her judgment criticized by all comers and challenged them to name an occasion when her brew had soured or been too sweet.

I was also beginning to hear about the costuming of the dance. For everyday wear a woman here wears a hand-spun and hand-woven cotton cloth around her waist, not tied at the sides as is that of the men, but with the over-lapping ends tucked in just below the scars on her stomach. For market days she puts on a Manchester cotton cloth which she wears in the same way. But for great occasions she brings her gala dress out of the pots into which she sealed them, with leaves and clay, for storage. From these pots come African vogue: tennis shoes; the kind of long knee socks Englishmen wear with their shorts, but for African consumption, in greens, reds and yellows; lengths of sleezy silks and rayons; T-shirts, which to my mind are always unbecoming to women and especially to the ma-tronly type in a country where corseting is nonexistent; and gaudy scarves for the head. Nor was this all. Amara told me that Poorgbilin's senior wife had gone to visit her mother whose sister had a daughter-in-law who was said to have an umbrella.

As the day of the dance grew still closer, I began to no-tice a one-way traffic in enamel basins (usually there are three or four of these in each homestead). All those in the neighborhood were now flowing to Poorgbilin's homestead so that each woman could arrive with one on her head: to bear my gifts in their usual calabashes would be unworthy of the event. Poorgbilin's women began to call in outstand-ing gifts; those on the wrong side of the exchange ledger brought them firewood and farm produce and eggs. Thanks to the interlocking chain of obligations, I was myself twice pressed for an early return of gifts which, through a de-vious route, would eventually reach one of Poorgbilin's women and then come back to me.

Our own preparations gathered speed. The ram was brought to my door. It was white-haired with age and had a broken bleat, but it was imposingly large. I placed it in Ihugh's charge, specifying only that it be kept downwind from me. My boys, who usually demanded their pay in shillings, brought back these same shillings to be changed into pennies for the dancers. They spent the day before the dancing pressing their best uniforms. Sunday thought I ought to wear my red sweater for the occasion. Since I could never convince him that it was too hot for sweaters, I retorted that a hostess must not outshine her guests. Sunday stiffened with righteous formality and lectured me on my responsibilities: I must uphold the prestige of my household. We compromised on my usual shirt and skirt, but my brightest skirt and, as a special concession, high-heeled sandals.

On the morning of the day my groundsman swept my yard clean; everyone in Kako's tidied up the ground about his own huts. Sunday rushed me through lunch. All my available chairs were outside. Almost an hour before the sun had reached the place appointed (about four o'clock), the elders and notables began to arrive; they brought their wives and their chairs and their children. Everyone was dressed in his best and reeked of *Binta el Sudan*—a nauseating perfume sold throughout Africa and measured out in the local markets by an old 30-30 shell. Kako marched the few paces from his reception hut to mine. At his official arrival (he had spent most of the day telling me what to do about chairs and people), I went out to greet my guests. We settled ourselves in a semicircle in the shade.

Giggles and the tentative thump of drums announced the coming of the dance. We craned our necks for sight of the umbrella. Poorgbilin's women marched in. They were dressed in gaudy oddments of European clothing and their faces were ghastly under a liberal application of powder. Each had an enamel basin filled with farm produce on her head. I started to smile in greeting, but was poked by Udama who stood behind Kako and me. "They're not here yet." My boys piled the produce in an imposing heap by the kitchen. The firewood, carried by girls not yet of age to dress up, was stacked beside it. The enamel basins were pyramided in front. Everyone admired, and everyone pretended not to notice.

113

Then they really arrived. Poorgbilin's senior wife squatted before me to present five chickens. Udama, afraid I might miss my cue, poked me again and primed me with the most fullsome phrases of overwhelmed gratitude. The musicians came to the center. To their gongs and drums the women swayed and shuffled in a circle before us. Every now and then a solo dancer would perform in their midst or sally briefly from the circle to dance just in front of me. I thrust pennies at them. My boys, resplendently clean and pressed, shouted compliments and now and again dashed into the circle to stick the coins onto sweating foreheads. Elders gave their children pennies, pointing out the dancer to be rewarded. Poorgbilin's senior wife stood by the drummers, holding the umbrella as though she were presenting arms at parade, and shouting praise songs. The very old women of their homestead marched about inside the circle with leafy branches, striking at dilatory dancers or those who began to get out of line. It got hot and hotter. The audience, joined by an occasional resting dancer, drank my beer dispensed by Ihugh in calabashes and tin cans. The dancing grew more excited and the music louder. Shouts of encouragement from the audience—and ever more beer—spurred on the dancers.

Then, just before sunset, Ihugh appeared with the ram. Sunday took it from him, handed me the lead rope to hold for just a moment, and then in my name handed the ram —not to Poorgbilin's wives, as I had expected—but to Poorgbilin himself. Poorgbilin, looking his fattest and glossiest, in turn called upon the women of his homestead to admire the magnificent beast that I had so generously given them to eat. Loudly, for my ears, they called out the anatomical grandeurs of the ram: never before had they seen so fine a beast. I then stood up and called all present to witness how expertly the women had danced and sung, how the produce they had given me proved not only their generosity but their skill in farming, and how the whole occasion was a sign of affluence and good character on the part of every member of Poorgbilin's homestead. Then Kako rose to congratulate us both and to demonstrate to everyone present how everything that had been done had been done well and redounded to the credit of the whole community. The dance was over, but no one left until we had finished the beer.

Guests all gone, I idly asked Rogo, "How did you find a ram that pleased them all so?"

"We bought it from Poorgbilin," he said with great satisfaction. "It took some time, because Poorgbilin was so fussy. We found several that he turned down. Then he told us there was a fine animal at Ember's. We agreed as soon as we saw it. So Poorgbilin bought it from Ember and we got it from Poorgbilin."

For the second time I got a bad jolt over that dance. "And if I hadn't changed my mind and bought a ram? or refused this ram?"

"There had to be a ram," Rogo was unperturbed. "If there hadn't been a ram, there wouldn't have been a dance: Poorgbilin's women would have sat at home with angry hearts."

I put my hands to my head; pitfalls safely passed in ignorance make me giddy with what might have been.

"It was well, as it happened." Rogo had no uncomfortable afterthoughts. "Everyone knew how much you wanted to give and how much Poorgbilin thought was right for his women to give."

"Why doesn't anyone ever tell me?" I moaned.

Rogo looked perplexed. "We do tell you. Anyhow, you know things, Redwoman." Rogo amplified this, their greatest compliment. "It was very wise of you to refuse to buy a ram from Atakpa's husband the other day. Yabo would have been furious that you wished to help her, his kinsman Poorgbilin would have had to veto the dance, and Kako would have been annoyed that you gave opinion in a case he will not judge."

It had come out all right. No one's feelings had been hurt. Everyone had a wonderful time and we had all gained prestige in the process. Indeed, it had been the best of all possible events. But just how long would my protecting angels continue to guide my fool's feet?

115

Chapter Nine

"Boy!" I shouted out the door to attract their general attention above the evening noises of Kako's homestead. "Boy!" At their chorused "Coming," I became specific. "Rogo!" While the call for Rogo echoed around the homestead from one throat to another, I glanced again at the text in my hand. It began lucidly enough with a list of misfortunes, but it ended in what seemed to me a *non sequitur:* "And that is why my mother-in-law should not lean against teak trees."

"I am here, my mother." Rogo hesitated in the doorway as though the hut were a trap. One could not call him shy, but he had a catlike facility of living among people without ever becoming domesticated.

I waved the paper at him and told him to come in. "It is what you wrote this morning, about bad luck and teak trees."

Rogo padded across the floor to stare at the paper. "Because of the dance," he explained.

I leaned back and waited in silence. I had grown used to their mode of exposition, though I could not yet follow it: first they give the conclusion, then the minor premise. The major one is then supposedly obvious; to ask for it merely proves one isn't of normal intelligence. Fortunately, prolonged silence makes most people talk.

"The ram," he amplified.

I got the next link and primed him. "Something I don't understand."

Rogo nodded. "Yesterday on the way back from the funeral you sat down on a teak root to rest. The roots are not so dangerous, but leaning against the tree itself makes women barren."

"You were right to tell me," I approved. Rogo had taken to interlarding his animal fables with short essays on the words he heard me misuse. I was delighted to have him concerned with my actions as well. I told him to write more about women's taboos: those on food, those on sights —Rogo cocked his head to listen—those on objects. "And why, if you meant me, did you write 'mother-in-law'?"

Rogo was still listening, but not to me.

"Rogo!" He was at the door and out of it. "Rogo!" This was too much. "Rogo!" It was no more use shouting at him than at a cat, but I would scold him when . . . Rogo came back in. It suddenly occurred to me that I had never seen him look embarrassed, apologetic nor out of countenance. "I will sleep in the kitchen, Redwoman." The complete irrelevance of this handsome offer left me gaping like a desperate goldfish. "I went out to ask Monday about his sweetheart, because now that Ihugh has a wife, he . . ."

It was I, this time, who dashed outside. Now I could hear the singing on the path which had informed Rogo and the rest of the homestead that Kako was bringing his son Ihugh a wife. The women were rushing out to meet them. Udama paused briefly at my side. "Not a bit of camwood," she moaned, "and how am I to catch chickens in the dark. Why didn't Kako tell me?" She hurried off to make hasty arrangements. From the path we heard shrill ululation. The young men were bringing out their hand drums for the dancing. Ihugh, still damp from a quick bath sluiced from waterpots and with his best cloth slung about him, ran over to me: "Some money, Redwoman, for tobacco and the wedding chickens." I counted out his back pay. Ihugh tried to look composed and indifferent, as a bridegroom ought, but as the shouting and ululations came closer he shifted from one foot to the other, from kitchen to reception hut and back again, driven by the question that occupied us all: what was she like?

The procession wound into the homestead. The women of Kako's homestead were a dancing guard of honor; matrons escorted the bride and sang, "Lo, a stranger comes." The bride was supported by her mother. We could see little of her, for a cloth was draped over her head, but she was tall and well made. Rogo grunted his deep appreciation; he had an eye for women: "Tonight Ihugh will eat meat!"

"A feast?"

Rogo did not stay for my question. With the other young men, he began dancing behind the procession that now led the bride to the hut of Kako's second wife, where she would stay as an honored, and secluded, guest. The marriage celebrations end when the bride is put into the care of her mother-in-law.

Ikpoom's slow voice corrected me. "The bride is a handsome woman; thus we say her husband 'eats meat.' All those who have 'eaten okra'—a short, skinny bride—will envy Ihugh tonight." Ikpoom and I joined the crowd watching Udama and the senior wives of the homestead take the bride into the hut. They placed her behind a mat partition. The young people scrambled noisily in after and began to dance. Over the thud and pat of drums we heard the marriage song: "Like a hawk the bridegroom swoops. Who shall withhold his prey?"

"They will dance long," I thought I heard Ikpoom sigh. "Ihugh will no longer wake at night and we three will no longer sit together when men's hearts are afraid to be alone." During the time Ihugh had been my night watchman, I had often found him sitting quietly, next door or in my reception hut, with Ikpoom. Rogo was sometimes with them, or someone else who could not sleep that night. I had come to count on their being there; it meant that I was not completely alone for that hour when I had done with work but could not yet sleep. We often sat in silence. We were not seeking conversation, but human companionship; our disjointed, idle comments were antennae, satisfied by the sound of reply. Yet the very aimlessness of what we said revealed a great deal. I came to know Ikpoom as a kind, humorous man whom life had taught a great and patient sadness. The group centered about him, protectively. "Ikpoom wakes at night," Ihugh had told me privately, "and it is not well that he should be alone." Asking questions had become so associated with my professional life that I felt they would be an intrusion here. "Witches, or women, or both," Rogo once guessed, but he knew no more than I. Now I wanted to reassure Ikpoom: "Rogo will sleep in the kitchen now. He wakes at night."

Ikpoom didn't answer. Ihugh was pressing a twist of tobacco into his hand. A man who marries for the first time must give tobacco and chicken feast to all the married men in the homestead; the dancing in the bride's hut will not stop until he has done so. Ihugh killed chickens. Udama killed chickens. She pounded porridge. A few men drifted off to supervise the rich wedding sauce: chicken, sesame and tomatoes. But still the dance went on in the hut, as cruelly persistent as a shivaree. It was well after midnight before the laughing dancers let the bridegroom inside. The big, six-foot message drum beat out the names of Ihugh's ancestors and the words: "A woman has come." So the marriage was announced.

Early next morning Kako killed a goat for the bride and poured the blood over the threshold of the hut. The bride's mother asked her if she was pleased with the groom; the answer was apparently satisfactory, for her mother accepted the cloth Ihugh gave her and went home. The dancing started again. The drum call had been heard, and visitors came; they gave the bride a penny to see her face, and another penny for camwood to rub over her body. For more important guests she was led outside, supported by Udama and Ticha (Kako's youngest wife); they unveiled her for a brief moment, then took her back inside the hut. Except to be shown off in this manner, Ihugh's bride had to remain in seclusion for at least a week. She was a lovely girl. I complimented Kako on his choice in all sincerity.

Ihugh, his huge body relaxed, his bruiser's face illuminated with pleasure, sat in front of the hut. Loudly, so his bride could hear even behind her partition and be complimented, he described the perfections of his wife's figure: a clear skin, teeth filed to a delicate pointed palisade, a straight back, pointed breasts that stood out firm and high, elaborate stomach scars exciting to the touch, plump calves . . . "Redwoman," Ihugh interrupted himself, "you are my mother and must help me buy my bride some beads to tie just below the knee. She has such lovely legs!" I was amused by Ihugh's unusual garrulity and chalked it up to the much advertised power of women. I gave him two shillings. Ihugh's thanks followed me down the path.

These days, no matter how busy I might be, I made a point of visiting Amara every day. At first I had been concerned with keeping my promise to Atakpa, but I soon found myself going to Yabo's for my own relaxation. Yabo was never dull. Cholo had been born with the American art of "kidding." But mainly it was Amara who took me there. She could no longer walk out of the homestead and occupied herself in various light domestic tasks. Spinning was beyond me, but I could and did help her shell nuts, prepare vegetables for drying, and sometimes just keep her company during the morning when most people had gone out to the farms. Yabo sometimes listened to our chatter. More often he leaned back in his chair and dozed. But he stayed about us, or rather, about Amara.

It was difficult to put one's finger on Amara's attraction. True, from my point of vantage, she was an excellent teacher: she had Atakpa's intelligence without the aggressive impatience that sometimes made Atakpa shake me by the shoulder and scream at me. But it was more than that. Being with Amara was being at peace. The hours we spent together were utterly without event, but they were nonetheless important to me, though I did not realize then, while Amara was still there, how much I depended on her. She had the same effect on others. She never complained, never asked anything for herself. Other women gave yams and received eggs and grain in return. Amara gave something which made us give her love. Even Yabo was gentle with her. I fled to her, from the busy life which had engulfed me, as to a refuge, for the quiet hours with Amara were the exception.

The hunger was at an end, and now, in August, with harvest and plenty, people grew fat, merry and sociable. My determined and systematic visiting gave way to the rush of events. Indeed, I no longer had a schedule so much as an engagement book for dances, weddings and weeding parties, interrupted by unpredictable events such as funerals, meetings of elders to arbitrate family quarrels or to perform ritual. I had Rogo's texts to keep up with. I hovered in the vicinity of very expectant mothers, for I wished to see a birth. I had abandoned any thoughts of becoming mistress of my environment or of forcing myself upon the community, but I was happy in it and, because I had no time for introspection, I felt myself a part of it in a much more real sense than ever before. Nor was I, this time, the victim of an illusion. I was involved in their sociability. No one had put a seal on it; no one had paused to question the extent to which I might be involved. There was no time and there was no occasion. I myself gave no thought to it beyond reminding myself that I really must not get too tied up with homesteads I knew best. But always something happened and took all my time.

Now it was Ihugh's wedding. Every day people came to look at the bride. Every night people danced and sang in front of the hut. Udama ground camwood, carried yams in from her farm, and started a beer brew for the bride's coming out. I was her shadow. I had determined to record this wedding in detail. It was in Kako's homestead: it would not be difficult to attend the nighttime celebrations. Udama, as Kako's senior wife, was the most important woman in the community; her own strong character and strict sense of propriety made her the local Emily Post. If anyone knew what ought to be done at a wedding, she did; if anyone could get it all done, she could. And while Udama discussed her preparations with me, I began to realize her deep attachment to Kako and her loyalty to her own small unit in the homestead, the unit into which the bride would fit: Udama's own children, her little wives, and their children. I had always thought it a miracle of self-restraint on both sides that Ticha and Udama never quarreled. During the wedding celebrations I discovered how well the two women worked together and how fond Udama was of Ticha despite her flippant levity.

It was ten days since the bride had come. Udama had pestered Kako into buying new cloths for all her little wives; she had coaxed me out of five shillings for chickens; she had bullied the finest drummer of the community into leading the music. Bringing a bride to her mother-in-law's hut is a great event. And it was a cloudy day. Udama and I, and everyone in the homestead, peered anxiously at the sky, hoping no rain would spoil the festivities. It cleared for the night. The moon, just past the half, shone bravely onto the yard. Everyone came out to dance, including my boys in their best uniforms and Rogo in what I hoped was a white cloth and not one of my sheets.

Now the wives of the homestead sang and danced their way to the hut where the bride had been secluded. Still singing and dancing, they led her out into the yard. Ihugh's younger brother pounded the gongs strongly, giving the basic beat; the hand drums came in with a second and then a third rhythm; then Udama's drummer enchanted the music with a rhythmic obbligato that set even my muscles atwitch. Udama danced alone, opposite the group surrounding the bride. Now, still facing them, dancing backward, she led the way to her hut. The men formed an escort on either side of the women, prancing, leaping and whirling in a dance around the swaying, graceful women. Only the bride (and I in the discreet background) shuffled along; she was still officially shy and timid.

We reached Udama's hut. There the bride was handed

to her mother-in-law. The women scrambled into the hut after them. I tried to follow. Udama herself stopped me. "You must make up your mind," she announced loudly, so all could hear, "whether you wish to be an important guest or one of the senior women of the homestead. If you are an important guest, we will again lead out the bride, so you may see her. If you are one of us, you may come inside, but then you must dance with us."

I had longed to be accepted, but I had meant something rather different by it: the privilege of going my own way with their full confidence. Udama now pointed out that I could not at the same time claim the guest's privilege of doing more or less as I wished and the family privilege of going behind the scenes. How much of Udama's announcement was a formality, how much it might affect my life or what obligations it might bring with it, I could not foresee. But my hesitations were gone almost before she stopped speaking.

I went inside the hut. It was jammed. Under the grain platform in the center crouched Udama's youngest children; every now and then they flung grass on the fire to illuminate the hut. To the left of the door were the musicians, stamping and swaying to the excitement of their own drumming. I looked for the bride. She was way back, half obscured by the women who danced all about the fire. Someone was smearing her with camwood. Udama did not let me look long. "Dance," she ordered me.

"Teach me then," I retorted. Duly, she and the other senior women began my instruction: my hands and feet were to keep time with the gongs, my hips with the first drum, my back and shoulders with the second. If I were to dance at all, I had to concentrate on the music and my muscles, but while I danced, my anthropological conscience nagged that I was missing something. In response to my conscience, I craned my neck to watch the younger matrons decorate the bride. Whenever I looked, my feet subsided into an absent-minded shuffle, and then I was poked in the ribs by indignant old women: "Dance!" Kako

123

and everyone else outside took turns peering into the hut to grin at my efforts.

After an hour, "Sing!" I was ordered. "Everyone else is singing." My voice trailed along uncertainly and clashed with theirs, for they were uninhibited by any doctrine of true notes and never hit just where I did. My conscience perked up. I had lost sight of the bride, but in teaching me to sing, Udama was making the words clearer and I got some of the verses of their wedding songs. My feet lost time again as I began to consider possible translations of songs that, if put into equally vernacular English, would seem unpublishable. Someone poked a finger into my ribs. I began to shuffle with renewed vigor. Udama stopped me. It was the turn of the solo dancers. No, I decided, as I watched the young man with the stick and the woman who danced opposite him, not publishable unless I brushed up my Latin. Then little Accident, who fancied himself as a dancer and was a superb mimic, took the floor with a brief announcement: "When I grow up . . ." and began to dance. Really, for a child . . . The hut filled with ribald mirth. No, not publishable at all. Because Accident was a child, I was shocked. But only briefly. Here, in this company and on this occasion, there was no obscenity in the dancing or the singing, nothing but a vivid portrayal of one of the pleasures of life frankly enjoyed.

Early the next morning, Udama and Ticha took the bride down to the spring "to show her the water." Then they went to Udama's farm "to show her where to weed," for a bride cannot have a farm of her own until her husband clears one for her—impossible now, until the next rains. Ihugh's wife, on her mettle before her mother-in-law, settled down to work with a will. The wedding was over; she was no longer the bride, just one of the young matrons of the homestead. I got bored out on Udama's farm and revolved excuses for leaving in my mind. Udama never heeded my pleas of headache—"Go take some of your own medicine"—or of paper work—"What else have you to do at night?"—but even the feeblest social obligation won her instant approval. I remarked that the rush of festivities had kept me from visiting my namesake. Udama frowned. "You should go there, Redwoman."

"You are right," I assented. "I'll go now." I escaped down the path.

Just outside Poorgbilin's I stopped short. There beside the path was a very small mound of fresh gravel and, on it, a tiny cowrie shell belt. A child was buried here.

I went on in to greet Poorgbilin. He was leaning back in a deck chair, his paunch loosely swathed in his toga; he looked cool and serenely comfortable. "Redwoman! Come in. You are welcome." We exchanged greetings. Poorgbilin turned slightly in his chair. "Your namesake is dead." There was no grief in his voice; he might have been speaking of something wholly indifferent to him. "Your namesake and my child. They tell me she coughed once and died. I buried her."

I nodded. "I have seen the grave. Now I will go greet her mother." Poorgbilin's casual voice made me want to stop my ears. He called his senior wife. Together we went to the mother's hut. At first sight, she also looked calm. She was sitting under the eaves, quietly shelling beans. "My mother," I addressed her softly.

She never glanced from her task. "I am no longer your mother. My child and your namesake is dead. There is nothing left between us."

Awkwardly, I tried to express my sympathy. She interrupted me. "It is nothing. She just died. Children often die. It is their nature."

I had nothing to say. Nothing in my own life or in my own land had prepared me for this. Poorgbilin's senior wife sat down beside her and took a handful of beans to shell. "I have borne ten children." Her voice held the same emotionless comment I had heard in Poorgbilin's. "Of the ten, seven died; but three are living. Now I have grandchildren. You too will someday hold a grandchild on your lap. Then you will know it was not in vain." Here was true comfort. I left quietly. Indifference there might be, but it was acquired in a hard school. A stoic mask worn long enough can mold what it first concealed.

I told Udama about it. She was not interested in the acceptance of grief. She was entirely taken up with the thought of grandchildren. "Poorgbilin's senior wife was right. You will soon know it, when you hold our grandchild."

"*Our* grandchild?"

Udama nodded. "Ihugh's wife is a strong young woman. It will not be long." I agreed. I said it would be delightful, but I still did not see how it brought me grandchildren. "Europeans are queer people," Udama observed to the pipe she was filling. Then, pulling her worn cloth over her thin legs, she told me the facts of life.

While she spoke, I wrote dutifully for my conscience and Udama's pleasure. I had often wondered how to get at a subject anthropologically advisable for me to record, but, except in physiological theory, remarkably the same the world over. People, I had found, are sometimes willing to answer intelligent questions; certainly if questions are to be answered intelligently, they cannot be asked foolishly. And it would have been thought foolish of me to ask what every child knew. However, I had also discovered that almost everyone is glad to find someone more foolish and more ignorant than himself. Udama was not the only one to take my education firmly in hand and embark upon a program of enlightenment referred to as "opening Redwoman's eyes."

I thanked Udama for her lecture. Meekly I said, "Thus Ihugh's children are born and begotten, and you are Ihugh's mother. But I am not. How then . . ."

Udama bristled, "Because my son has married and no longer sleeps in your kitchen, do you deny him?"

"Huh? Well . . . You mean?" I am not coherent in my own language when I am besieged by gradual realization; in a foreign language I twitter feeble-mindedly. "No! I don't. You mean Ihugh called me mother . . ."

"You feed Ihugh, therefore you *are* his mother." Udama

corrected me firmly but quite patiently now that she saw I meant no insult. "Listen, Redwoman, if a woman dies, do her children become motherless? Is not the woman who feeds them and cares for them their mother? Therefore these are not merely matters of birth. They are matters of deed as well. You and I, we are both Ihugh's mother; therefore his children are *our* grandchildren. But there is more. Kako has put some of his youngest wives in my hut, for me to watch and care for; therefore they are my wives as well. Ihugh's wife I treat as I treat them; therefore she is my wife and she is your wife, and her children are our children."

Dazed, but convinced I was struggling along the right track, I ventured a deduction. "Then, if Rogo calls me 'my mother,' it is because I feed him. But if he calls me 'my mother-in-law,' it is because . . ."

"Because he respects you, but must nevertheless say to you things you will not like."

"I sat on a teak root." In my own ears this did not sound very coherent, but Udama followed it with the same facility Rogo had used in the original connection. "And some young man told you you must not," she finished. "Therefore of course he called you 'mother-in-law,' or it would have been rude."

Udama meditated into her pipe. I wrestled with the implications of this dual aspect of kinship, by birth and by deed. She was the first to rouse herself. "You must learn more of these matters, Redwoman, or you will be like a child among us, a child who knows nothing of life, nor of death, nor of birth." She scrabbled among the ashes looking for a coal to relight her pipe. "You know Ava and her wives?"

I nodded. Everyone knew Ava and her wives. They were the model household of the community, one every husband cited when his wives disagreed. Ava was a tall, rather light-skinned woman who was one of the leading dancers and song leaders at all successful weeding parties. She was also the senior of five wives who lived with their husband and children alone in a homestead not very far from Kako's. The women were fast friends. Indeed, it was Ava who had picked out all the others. She saved up forty or fifty shillings every few years, searched out an industrious girl of congenial character, then brought her home and presented her to her husband: "Here is your new wife."

Ava's husband always welcomed her additions to his household and he always set to work to pay the rest of the bridewealth, for he knew perfectly well that Ava always picked hard-working, healthy, handsome, steady women who wouldn't run away. Many men envied him. Thanks to Ava he had peace and quiet in his home and did not, like so many others, have to spend time and money chasing after truant wives. My feelings were more mixed. If, before I came out here, I had expected to feel sorry for anyone in a polygamous household, it was the women. But these women did very well. It was their husband I felt sorry for. We tend to think of the henpecked husband as a rather weak character. But what man can stand up against five united women? If Ava's husband raised his voice to any one of his wives, all of them refused to cook for him. If he bought one of them a cloth, he had to buy four other identical cloths. Discipline of the wives was in Ava's hands, and stayed there. When the poor man got drunk one day and struck one wife for nagging—well, until he had given many and expensive presents to all his wives, the five of them slept barricaded in one hut. Yes, I knew Ava.

"One of Ava's wives," Udama went on, "will soon bear a child. I will be the midwife, and I shall call you, for I would have you see for yourself what it means to have co-wives to help you and to know that if you die in labor there are those who will care for your children."

I started to ask for examples from Kako's own homestead. I didn't. It could very easily be a tactless question. Again it occurred to me that I had really learned remarkably little about Kako and his wives. He had as little leisure as I. Our surface relations were pleasant. We were both too busy to make closer acquaintance without need for it. Also, when one is busy, one spends little time at home, and Kako's was home to me. Again, as so often, it was but a fleeting thought, and I soon forgot it.

A few days later, Ava herself stuck her head into my reception hut and called me without ceremony. "Come, Redwoman, my wife is in labor. Udama told me to fetch you while she banked her fire." The three of us walked to Ava's homestead. Her husband was sitting in his reception hut, whittling aimlessly away at a stick and pretending not to be anxious. It was his twelfth child, he told me, but this wife's first. He greeted Udama with relief.

We went inside the hut. The mother-to-be was sitting on a very low reclining chair, looking quite composed while all her co-wives bustled about her. Udama, after a brief and expert examination, announced that there was plenty of time. She and Ava began to lecture me on the benefits of being one of many wives.

"When an only wife has a child, who will help her so she may rest? Who will feed her husband and her other children? Who will tend her farm and bring her firewood so she may be warm? Who will comfort her in labor and who will stop her cries?"

No adult should be so weak-minded as to cry out with pain. The two times when people will yell out, circumcision and childbirth, someone stands behind to clap a hand over the mouth at the first scream. Hard, perhaps, but certainly easier on their relatives and neighbors. I could not, however, even for the sake of argument protest that any of the other services they mentioned could be performed by any other relatives. I had been there long enough to know that no kinsman will take over the duties of another; it would be considered wrong, and these were the duties of no one but a co-wife.

"Never," said Ava severely, "let your husband rest with one wife. Men are lazy. If they have one woman to cook for them, they are content. If you leave it to your husband, you'll never get another wife to help you carry the firewood and the water and to look after you when you are ill. And if you do nag him into it, he'll pick up the first good-looking wench he sees. You can't trust a man to inquire into a woman's character and industry. Let a man pick his own mistresses; he knows what he wants there. But they're all bunglers when it comes to choosing wives."

"That," Udama interpolated, "is why a man's father selects his first wife."

"And the first wife," Ava continued, "should get the rest herself, like me."

I replied mildly that men in our country generally couldn't afford more than one wife at a time. "Earn the money yourself by going to market," Ava advised. "It only takes a small chicken to start with, if you're a good trader." I explained that we had a law against it as well. Udama stopped Ava's incredulity. "Indeed, I think it must be so. Rogo told Ihugh that very few Europeans have even one wife because the bridewealth is very high and anyhow they don't have enough women to go around."

There was a stifled cry from the chair and conversation stopped. Two of the wives held her back in her chair, a third pressing back her head and holding a hand over her mouth. Ava and Udama were busy for a long time, mixing herbs, massaging, giving encouragement. Finally, at sunset, Udama called out to the father, "A boy." He flapped happily in the background while the new mother was led outside to be washed, and the baby made uncomplimentary noises about the hot water in which Udama washed him. An elder appeared. Ava told me he had come to "remove the blood" from all of us who had been inside the hut during the birth. I found myself lined up with the other women and having my legs brushed with a wet and squawking chicken while the elder mumbled his incantation. It was a unique sensation.

Ava gave Udama the salt, palm oil and camwood that are the midwife's due and we went home.

"A very easy birth," she commented as we parted. I had not thought it so, nor, by the look of her, had the mother. Perhaps it was easier if one didn't know there were such things as anesthetics. One must make shift to endure unavoidable pain. But it wasn't just a matter of suffering. I remembered what the government and mission doctors had told me about deliveries gone wrong and about the damage caused by native midwifery even when there were no complications.

I also remembered that my great-grandmother had her first child alone with her husband on the frontier; in her diary she had longed for another woman then. I tried to imagine her surrounded by four co-wives, and could not. More generally, though, I could see that where we multiply specialists and services, these people multiplied personal relationship and perhaps in this way were closer to my great-grandmother than I was. But not in detail, not my great-grandmother with co-wives. What she wanted of her husband wasn't readily sharable.

Here people looked for little in marriage. A man would turn to his sixteenth cousin twice removed before he turned to his wife. Here the important ties were between blood relatives. Again I remembered Ihugh's pessimistic lecture by the roadside: women bring trouble between friends and relatives and age mates. Perhaps it was woman's only remedy against such an attitude—to club together, as co-wives, when they were far from their own relatives. Certainly a woman in trouble turned to her guardian or her brother and not to her husband.

I was beginning to understand what they did. I could not understand what they felt. I could admire the way co-wives got on together and still know that I, born and reared as I had been, could never take such a relationship. I would have all the wrong emotions. However, I personally could never be involved in polygamy. Indeed, I could see no reason to expect I should get emotionally involved in any way. I forgot that I had friends who would expect me to stand by them. I forgot that what they thought right might conflict with my own morals and professional ethics. It is not easy to remember that one is living between two worlds.

Chapter Ten

I woke suddenly—to the unmistakable sounds of fighting men and excited women. I flashed my light at the clock: 2 A.M. The noises rose to an even higher pitch. I scrambled out to investigate. Ihugh came to my side. "We caught a man in Ticha's hut," he explained, "and my brothers are beating him."

There was little moonlight and I was sleepy-eyed. Even so, I could see a writhing knot of men swarming over the surprised lover like a mass of ants mauling a crumb. "Come," I spoke to Ihugh sharply, "he has done wrong, but you can't let him be beaten like that."

"Ticha is our father's wife. Kako has gone traveling with Ikpoom. Shall we not protect that which is our father's?" There was a certain angry indecision in Ihugh's tone, and a note of self-justification. "*I* haven't lifted a hand against him."

"What difference does that make? He'll be badly hurt. You can't let . . ."

The man was down.

"My age mate . . ." With a shout Ihugh plunged into the knot of yelping men and picked up the limp figure they were kicking. Secure in his great size and strength, Ihugh brushed aside his irate brothers. "You must not beat my age mate any longer." He picked the man up. "We are your seniors. Besides, our father will want to deal with him." Ihugh bore the man off and tied him up in Ikpoom's empty hut.

As suddenly as they had appeared, people melted into their huts. I lingered outside, looking at Ticha's tightly closed hut, not liking to call her but not wanting to leave without knowing her unhurt. "She would get caught!" An exasperated thought, which showed me I was more concerned with Ticha's welfare than with her behavior. Poor, silly Ticha . . . And poor Udama. Scandal is heavy going for the righteous, and the failings of one's "little wife" count as one's own.

Next morning I found Udama and her new daughter-in-law on the farm, resting under the thatched shelter that stood in the midst of the yam mounds. They had thrown two sweet potatoes to roast on the coals; at my entry they added another. The wood smoke drifted lazily out into the fresh morning air as we sat with our backs against the shelter posts, moving only to slap at a persistent fly or to turn the roasting potatoes.

I tried to start a conversation, but Udama, for the first time in weeks, forced me through my botanical paces on all the plants just outside the shelter. I felt myself warned off dangerous ground; it would be tactless to mention last night's events. But the daughter-in-law got bored with plants. At Udama's first pause she broke in: "What will Kako do to Ticha?"

Udama looked severe, like the unrelenting arbiter of manners and morals I knew her. To her son's wife she painted a gloomy picture of beatings, admonitions and marital disfavor which would no doubt deprive Ticha of new cloths, market money and the general pleasure of her husband's company for some time to come. Then, I think to impress her daughter-in-law with the importance of the matter, Udama ordered me to write down what she next said: an emphatic lecture on wifely duties in principle and detail; ending on a note of industry, she sent her daughter-in-law out to weed until the potatoes were done. Udama watched her go with the suspicion of a twinkle in her eye.

I risked a long shot. "I will tell Ihugh that you have instructed his wife well. But now that we are alone, Udama, do you really think Kako will be so very angry?"

"If he had been here—but then, she wouldn't have done anything so foolish while he was here. Just think, Red-woman, that silly girl actually brewed beer, telling me she wanted to sell it at market; then she didn't and thought I wouldn't notice. She prepared a fine meal in her own hut, not where she cooks with me; we could all smell the meat. But when people came around waiting to be asked to the feast, she said she hadn't been cooking at all. So, of course, we all knew she was expecting a lover. I warned her, but she would not listen. She never listens. Then, our husband's sons hid around the hut at night to catch her lover. If I had known that . . ." She broke off.

"It was careless of Ticha, and so she was caught." Yes, that was Ticha, but the statement didn't match the Udama I knew: she had attempted to stop the affair; she was, as always, put out by stupidity; she didn't quite condone the misbehavior, yet . . . I asked straight out. "Don't you consider adultery a bad thing?"

"It is a bad thing, yet . . ." Udama hesitated. "Kako is an old man," she went on slowly, prodding absently at the potatoes with a stick, "and Ticha is young. She wants a child. I too am a woman and wanted children. How can I blame her? I cannot say this to my son's wife. In any case, it is not the same. My son is young; *he* can give his wife children. Kako will know why Ticha has done this, and so he will only scold her. But he will be sad at heart, sad also because he is no longer very angry over such matters. A man knows then that he is old." Again she paused. "I am a woman; my heart cannot blame Ticha. But I have been with Kako many years now, and I too am old."

Udama twitched the potatoes off the coals and called her daughter-in-law. The conversation was closed. We turned to greet those of Kako's other wives who, with some of his brothers' wives, had wandered over from their farms —for brothers make their farms side by side—to rest and gossip. Every time a woman entered, one of us would break

134

off a piece of sweet potato and hand it to the newcomer, till at last we each had only a small bit to eat.

They chattered about farming: about the rains, the worms, damage done by monkeys and stray goats. They discussed the affairs of their married daughters: such a one had a stingy husband who would not give her enough cloths—"He lets her run around half naked, like a monkey" —and was too lazy to keep her hut in good repair; another would soon bear her first child; still another had run away from her husband, who had not had the common decency to come chasing right after her. But no one mentioned Ticha.

They worried over their sick children. They all condemned the common negligence of fathers in consulting the diviner—for it is only from divination that one can discover the magical, hence the basic, cause of toothaches, colics and infections. Many of them complained that their husbands were slow in performing the ritual that would remove this cause once it was known: only after such ritual could medicine be effective.

"My husband says my child's stomach ache is nothing to worry about. I made him give me some medicinal herbs for it, but he will not go to the diviner."

"The diviner named the ceremony that my child needs, but my husband says he has no money to spend on sacrificial chickens, it all went to pay the tax." The woman glared at her younger co-wife, for whose child their husband had found the money and chickens needed for a rather expensive curative ceremony. The young co-wife bristled.

Dreading a scene, we all started to talk. One voice rang out with overriding clarity: "Ticha has locked herself in her hut. She says she will remain there until Kako returns." Someone, in her haste to change the subject, had forgotten where she was.

The women could no longer restain themselves. "It may be weeks before Kako returns." "She will have to come out tonight or tomorrow morning to get water from the stream."

"I'm going to tell her just what I think of such goings on," announced one stern-lipped dowager who was thoroughly disliked by her daughters-in-law and little wives and who had consequently suffered much from their misbehavior.

One of the younger women began to experiment with a song taunting Ticha for her misdeeds. Udama broke in, "Ticha is *my* wife."

"Yes," replied the dowager unpleasantly, "Kako will be very pleased with the way you have taken care of her."

Udama ignored the interruption and continued with considerable dignity—striking in a wrinkled old woman clad for the farm in a torn cloth, and the caked mud of her work still on her thin legs. "Which one of us has never had a lover? Or never longed for a child? Ticha is my wife, and I shall tell all my wives to say nothing to her about this. Those of you who taunt her, taunt yourselves. Are we not all women, and human?"

The dowager's face was vicious. I rushed in without thinking. "Ihugh said the lover was Kako's affair. So is Ticha."

She seized on my words. "Like mother, like son. Udama protects her little wife at the expense of her husband; Ihugh protects his age mate against his father's interests."

This was strong provocation. To avert an unforgivable quarrel, all the rest of us babbled at random. The older women picked themselves up, collecting the younger ones with meaningful glances and standing between Udama and her tormentor. They drowned the possibility of further words in a feather fall of social comment: "Must get back to my weeding." "Better make sure there aren't any goats on my farm." We all scattered: they to their farms; I to pay a visit to Poorgbilin.

Poorgbilin's homestead was slightly more than a mile from Udama's farms. I walked slowly. When scandal stirs the smooth surface of daily life, nothing pretty is brought to the top. The dowager had used Ticha's misconduct as a weapon against Udama. Some old grudge rankled there. I wondered who else would be hurt before this was over. Adultery at Nder's—among strangers, against a background of rain and cows—had been faintly amusing and an item for my notebook. An item followed by a note to inquire into the general moral standards of faithfulness in marriage. My point-blank question had always been answered by the simple statement: adultery is a bad thing which nonetheless often occurs. Somehow, I had assumed from this that, as in the Western countries I knew, people approved a chastity which human frailty made difficult to sustain, that they—just as I—accepted Ticha's adultery as proof of her frailty.

Ihugh had tried to explain, there by the roadside. It was not the loss of chastity that mattered in adultery, but the old, passionate resentment of anything that threatens any possession—a resentment which can never be wholly suppressed and which makes for trouble between those who should be the closest allies. Among us, the problem lies between husband and wife. Not here. Here adultery was such a serious matter because it escaped the triangle of husband, wife and lover and confused those loyalties which they counted highest: the bonds between blood relations.

Ticha had forced Ihugh into a dilemma: in a fight a man should assist his age mate; a son should punish anyone who seduces his father's wife. No matter what he had done, even if he had done nothing, Ihugh would have wronged one or the other.

When Udama had talked to me over the fire, I had thought her caught between her human sympathies—between her fondness for Ticha and her affection for Kako—and the necessity of upholding moral standards. Her later conversation had shown her torn between the duty of a senior wife to defend her little wife against everyone (including her husband), the duty of the senior wife to her husband as a general watchdog over all his wives, and a mother's duty to keep her son's wife at home and at work

(two desiderata undermined by an interest in other men).
Udama too had to balance conflicting loyalties—a feat demanding that she be a little less loyal to everyone concerned than she ought to be.

And Ticha herself? She had been condemned for stupidity, but not for frailty. She had a right to a child. Kako was too old. But she must have known that before she married him, and yet she had married him willingly. To me it spelled vanity—wanting to be a chief's wife—and then, in frivolity, adultery. I caught myself up short. I must judge by their standards, not by my own. But an objective standard, not the excuses and accusations of those directly concerned. I would ask Poorgbilin about it. He wasn't involved. Besides, Poorgbilin was neutrality itself, a man who could discuss even his child's death without emotion—or with detachment. I turned into his homestead.

The children playing under the central tree looked up and started to shriek, "Redwoman's coming! Redwoman's coming!" At their cries, Poorgbilin himself squeezed out of his reception hut and came toward me. I was shocked by the distress on his plump face. "My wife is ill. I sent my son to Kako's, but you were not there." I asked which wife and what illness, but Poorgbilin was too concerned with hurrying me into his reception hut to answer.

I forgot Ticha.

A woman was sitting with her back against one of the posts of the drying platform, arms raised above her head and crooked back to embrace the post. Her legs jerked as though she were trying to run. Her whole body shook with a harsh sobbing.

"Can she swallow?" I interrupted Poorgbilin's babble. Only some alleviation of her pain mattered just then. At his nod, I ordered hot water and a drinking calabash into which I crushed two aspirin. He got it down her throat somehow. We sat anxiously until her body began to relax and then, as much from exhaustion as from the medicine, she slumped down and fell asleep.

Poorgbilin himself relaxed and dropped his weight into a

chair. He began to tell me more coherently of her illness. While he spoke, I stared at the woman's now quiet face and recognized Poorgbilin's second wife, whom he had named "Where I rest my head" as a sign of the peace he had always found with her. When he finished, I shook my head: "This is beyond my skill. I am not a doctor. The medicine I can give her can make her sleep sometimes, but if she drinks much of it, she will get used to it and it will no longer help her. It cannot cure what is hurting her. The dispensary cannot help either. You must take her to the hospital."

"She cannot travel." Poorgbilin looked obstinate.

"She must." I knew by now that his reluctance was a compound of past experience, of thriftiness (my free medicine might work despite my warnings), and of a dislike of the missionaries who had the nearer hospital and a fear of the African personnel of the government hospital. These latter were, of necessity, drawn from more educated tribes which unfortunately happened to be traditional enemies of these people; thus from their viewpoint going to hospital meant putting oneself in the power of the enemy. And someone would have to go with her, for anyone who wants to eat in hospital must have someone to bring food in for him. Altogether it would be an expensive affair.

We argued for a while, but Poorgbilin finally decreed that she was to stay where she was. In the long run, neither of us had the necessary conviction that she would really benefit by being taken to hospital. Poorgbilin regarded European medicine as a last and dubious resort—when it had to be paid for. I doubted whether she would survive the trip, and would not myself have cared to be exposed to the local hospital, which was understaffed and undersupplied. I sighed, promised Poorgbilin to return that evening with what medicine I had, and again warned him that I could not really help her.

Poorgbilin's senior wife stuck her head in the reception hut. She took a swift look at the sleeping woman, then in a whisper said that Undu wanted to see me. I knew Undu:

a weak child of six; abdomen extended; flesh puffed, flabby and of an unhealthy reddish tinge; joints swollen, and only a few tufts of hair left on his head. He was riddled with worms, and Lord knew what other illnesses. They had asked me for medicine for him since I first came to that homestead, and I had consistently refused. His father had taken him to the mission hospital. There they had told him that the child would die and had refused to treat him. That refusal was, I knew, one of the reasons Poorgbilin would not now take his wife to hospital. Again, I saw both sides: the people complained that so many who were taken to hospital died there; the doctors complained that only the moribund were brought to them.

Automatically I again shook my head. "I cannot help Undu."

Poorgbilin's senior wife gave me a queer look. "Undu wants to give you something. He cannot walk far now." Reproved, I followed her out and down to the other end of the homestead. When we were close enough to see Undu sitting patiently under the eaves of his mother's hut, Poorgbilin's senior wife stopped abruptly. "You Europeans, you Europeans, we fear you. If it pleases you, you will help a man. If it doesn't please you, you give no one help. And no man can tell when it may please you." She walked off.

The child I had come to see gave me no chance to reflect on her words. "Redwoman," Undu called, "I have a present for you." From bits of guinea corn stalk and raffia he had constructed two circles suspended from a sort of cross. As I took it in my two cupped hands and wondered frantically what to say, Undu talked on slowly: "You have given me so many things"—yes, empty cigarette boxes, some tinfoil and once a paper bag mended with Scotch tape—"and I had had nothing to give you. Then I remembered you had no bicycle, so I made you one."

The object took shape under my eyes: two wheels, a crosspiece, and handle bars. I thanked him and half out of gratitude and liking for Undu, who was patient and cheerful under his doom as very sick children often are, half to remove from my memory the old woman's bitter accusation, I sat down beside him and made him a canoe out of match sticks and an old envelope. Undu was pleased, but, in his turn, had to be informed what the object was.

"I will take it down to the stream tomorrow," Undu told me gravely. "Tomorrow I will be well again." I could only look at the child, and he saw the incredulity in my face. "Yes, Redwoman, didn't my father tell you? He has bought a goat and five chickens and a turtle for sacrifice. Tonight the elder is coming, the one who can perform the ceremony. And tomorrow he will fix it for me and then I shall drink medicine and I shall be well. If you come tomorrow evening, you will find me climbing that tree with them" —he gestured feebly at the boys swarming through the branches of the wild fig tree in the center of the homestead, racing each other to the top.

I caught my breath at his perfect faith: tomorrow, Santa Claus. I thought of Undu sitting here tomorrow night, waiting for the miracle to happen, of Undu waking up, still ill, the next day and the next. Sick at heart I managed to say, "Your father does well, and I rejoice. Now I must go," and I fled.

Tears were stinging my eyes. I almost ran into a woman, then recognizing Poorgbilin's senior wife I turned on her with my own accusation, pitching my voice low lest Undu should hear: "How can you tell that child he will be well tomorrow night after the ceremony! How can you let him believe it? He thinks that tomorrow night he will climb that tree!"

"We have told him the truth!" Her voice was sharp and impatient. "You do not understand."

We stared at each other antagonistically. The anger ebbed out of me. "No," I replied wearily, "I do not understand. Yet you too have spoken hard words to me because you too do not understand."

The old woman drew in her breath. "You are a guest here, and I was rude. Poorgbilin would be angry at me.

And yet," she was still resentful, "when you do not understand, we explain and explain, but you never explain."

This time I thought before I spoke, thought of my attempts and my failures to explain that I had myself only the smallest fraction of the skills represented in the making of my possessions, that I could not weave them a plastic raincoat, that I didn't know how to make the medicines I had with me; of my attempts to explain germs and fly-carried diseases, of my futile explanation that my skill at reading and writing had been acquired by working in school, not by drinking a magical potion which I would share with my friends if I were not so selfish. "I cannot explain. I do not know your language well enough, and many of the things I wish to tell you about do not exist in your country."

She also was thoughtful. "It is true that one learns by seeing with the eyes, not by hearing with the ears." She looked over at Undu. "That is why he cannot understand. We, who are old and have seen, we know that until these ceremonies are performed, no medicine can heal. Our forefathers told us so, and we have ourselves seen that it is so. But we also know that if the ceremonies are not performed correctly, or if they are not performed in time—for when the disease has grown greatly, the medicine may no longer be strong enough—or if the witches wish to prevent the cure, then it will not help. And we also know that evil works swiftly, but that the remedy of evil takes time. All these things Undu will know some day. A child's heart is swift. The heart that has learned wisdom is slow. And your heart, Redwoman, is that of a child."

I was silent for some time, half hoping she would leave me, but unwilling to make the first move myself. She stood on, quite serene now. I felt some answer due her.

"Perhaps my heart is that of a child," I admitted ruefully, "for today I have again seen how little I understand. The wisdom of your country and of mine are different. Yet our hearts are the same," I was speaking my creed almost challengingly. "It is only that in each other's countries, where we do not understand, we become children again, who have still everything to learn."

"May you learn swiftly then," she spoke the sentence as a farewell, perhaps in mockery, perhaps as a rather dry blessing. I watched her as she walked off. My questions, including that of how to behave over Ticha, had been given a hard answer: before I might use my knowledge in judgment, I must school my own heart to wisdom.

Chapter Eleven

THE NEXT DAY it rained. Ticha still remained in her hut. I sat brooding in mine. I had sent little Accident over to Poorgbilin's with pills and excuses. He took a long time. He had stayed to watch the ceremony for Undu. Tomorrow Undu was to go to his maternal relatives to drink medicine. I gave Accident a penny for his errand and another penny as well, mainly because I was glad I would not have to watch Undu's disillusionment. No one here would know, until he was brought back to be buried; I did not believe he could live. I hoped it would rain all day. Poorgbilin's senior wife had upset me more than I would admit.

Painfully I realized that despite my training I had thought these people would differ only in externals of dress and custom, that their basic reactions to the same basic situation would be the same as mine. I had willfully closed my eyes to all but obviously superficial differences. Udama might dress in a single ragged waist cloth and smoke a pipe; she was, nevertheless, *grande dame*. Yabo, I had felt, needed but a change in outward appearance to be recognized as the crusty old man who disinherited his daughter for an imprudent marriage. Kako, the reserved elder statesman; Lam, a very Mr. Milquetoast, and a host of other familiar types: the gossip, the flirt, the steady young man, the devoted mother, the scholar and gentleman (though his subjects were genealogies and magic), the canny horse trader (though he dealt in goats), the henpecked husband (though it took five wives to do it), the young ne'er-do-well, and the giddy matron. Ticha again. Perhaps I had not misread their characters. Perhaps love, jealousy, bereavement, all human emotions were the same. But this did not mean that two people of the same character and suffering the same emotion would react in the same way—if they had been reared in two different worlds.

I should not, I knew, have exploded over Undu. My anger sprang mainly from my private and unshared conviction that magic could not help; yet I was also convinced that faith in the cure is a powerful aid to any medicine. I should have held my peace. Undu's father, assisted by his relatives, was spending a great deal in the hope of helping his child. I had been blamed for refusing to help with my pills. I knew my drugs would be futile; I thought their ceremony would be just as futile. They thought the one was sure to help and that the other might. Here, where we each had our own convictions, we were opposed. Whatever our words, our disagreement was plain.

When I could not feel them right, how could my immediate emotional reaction match theirs? No matter what Udama had told me at Ihugh's wedding, I could not really become one of them. I was beginning to find the points beyond which I could not go, nor could they, I thought rebelliously, expect me to. Unless, perhaps, they too had thought the differences only superficial? Did they expect me to adopt their values? A child's heart indeed!

I looked around at my bamboo-and-packing-case book shelf for comfort: technical books, the Bible, detective stories, Shakespeare, my station haul, some philosophy. "The heart that has learned wisdom is slow." Here was wisdom, the wisdom of my own culture, and here I was more willing to admit my ignorance. Yet the very thought of it, there and for my taking, gave me a shock of pride. I needed to get back to my own for a bit. I had no intention of questioning my own values by any comparison with theirs. It was useless and stupid to get emotionally involved in matters I would do better to regard impersonally and analytically. I walked over to the book shelf, took down

Locke and settled down to read and acquire what was, surely, a more valuable kind of wisdom.

I flipped through the book first, a bad habit of mine acquired by leafing through thrillers before taking them home from the library. A sentence struck my eye, though I had turned the page before its sense sunk in: a thing cannot simultaneously exist and not exist. I amused myself by trying to translate it into the local language. No, not that way: if that meant anything, it meant "Whenever a thing is possible, it is impossible." I made a few more attempts and found them equally ridiculous. I was solaced by this failure. Poorgbilin's senior wife couldn't say Locke lacked wisdom. I turned to the beginning and started to read intently. What these people had to say to me went into my notebook. It was the lessons I could learn from Locke and his fellows that I would write in my heart.

I was looking for wisdom. I found it, on the second page. "It is not worth while to be concerned with what he says or thinks, who says or thinks only as he is directed by another."

Again I had been answered. I must learn, for myself and from the world about me.

Unsought advice is difficult to take, but can, with some effort, generally be dismissed as an impertinence. One must, out of courtesy, at least listen to the advice one seeks, though this very obligation makes it the more difficult to accept when it is unpalatable. I very rudely slammed Locke to, shoved him back onto the shelf and thus left myself no escape from the conclusion that I was behaving very badly. Discipline, I told myself sternly, and sat down to type notes until the rain should stop. Chores are the most satisfactory form of escapism; one can call their performance duty. I successfully put both Locke and Poorgbilin's senior wife into the back of my mind.

Around noon the rain began to slacken. I took up my shoulder bag and raincoat and went out, calling to the boys that I was going to Poorgbilin's. As I picked my way through the puddles and the mud, I heard a cry behind me, "She's come out!" I turned to see who had shouted at me. The words died on my lips. Not I was being heralded, but Ticha.

Face set, waterpot on her head, Ticha walked with a defiant leisureliness toward the path to the stream. Perhaps she had hoped that in this weather no one would be outside their huts to see. But at the cry, people crowded out under the eaves. The young men stood out in the rain, jeering, hurling obscenities at her, asking her detailed anatomical questions with a mock politeness of manner. She altered neither her expression nor her gait. The married women, I noticed, after the first shouts, had grown silent; now they seemed to watch her with a certain sympathy. The older men had not even appeared. Ticha was now almost free of the homestead.

One of Kako's sons ran after her, yelling a venomous taunt. Ticha turned, then. She looked full in his face and laughed aloud. There was complete silence. In that silence she went her way to the stream.

I retraced my steps and went over to the hut of one of Kako's brother's wives, a middle-aged woman who had watched the whole scene from her doorstep, placidly smoking her pipe and saying not a word. "Why did Ticha laugh?" I demanded.

She continued to puff at her pipe, giving me only a brief glance before she turned her eyes back to the scene in the homestead yard. The women had gone back into their huts. The young men were drifting irresolutely into the reception huts. Ticha's laugh had punctured their superiority and turned their sly glances from her to that son of Kako's who had flung the last taunt, an insult distinguished from the others only by the intense animosity in his voice.

"What happened? What did he say? Why did she laugh?" I demanded again.

This time the pipe was withdrawn. With a lazy, careless gesture the stem was pointed at Kako's son. "He wanted her and she refused him. It was he who made the others wait outside her hut last night." She spat and went inside her hut.

Quite illogically, I found myself thinking much more highly of Ticha. The malice involved in catching her with her lover seemed to lessen her own offense. Nevertheless, the more I heard about this affair, the less I liked it.

Once again I turned on my way to Poorgbilin's. As I passed Udama's farm, I was surprised to hear her call to me from the farm shelter. I went over. "What are you doing out here in the rain?" I asked her in astonishment. No one ever goes to the farms when it rains, and it had been raining since dawn.

"When I woke," Udama shoved aside some corn husks and motioned me to sit down, "I thought it would clear quickly." Udama was a good weather judge. I didn't believe her.

"Ticha came out," I announced briefly.

"Ah, I thought she might." I caught Udama's eye. So that was why she had come to the farms. "What happened, Redwoman. Did my wives insult her?"

"No, the women said nothing," and I described what I had seen, laying stress on Ticha's laugh. Udama brooded over my tale for a while, seemed about to speak, then filled her pipe instead. Once again she started to say something; then, quite obviously changing her mind, she asked me if I would like a roasted ear of corn. I accepted. While she poked about for a tender ear, husked it and raked out some coals, I came to a decision.

"Udama?"

"Yes?"

"Udama, yesterday I was told that I was a child, that there were many things I did not understand. It is true, indeed, but it is not well that I should remain a child. You have taught me many things. Help me again to understand."

"You are learning well, but you should spend more time on the farms." Udama's eyes rested fondly on her neatly weeded rows of yam mounds.

148

"No," I said hastily, "it is not that which puzzles me today. It is this matter of Ticha."

Udama looked annoyed and troubled. "You have heard and seen what happened. Also, I have told you that it is not good to speak ill of people or to gossip."

"Was it not of that which you started to speak just now?" I asked bluntly.

Udama sighed. "What is it you do not understand?"

There was so much that confused me that I had difficulty in answering. "Why people behaved as they did" was what I wanted to ask, but it was too general and vague a question to evoke any genuine response. All my specific questions were tactless. Still, I could not stop now. I blurted out, "You say adultery is bad, yet in your heart you do not blame Ticha."

"Do you not know what it means to want a child?" She gave me yesterday's answer.

"But she told me she wanted to marry Kako, and she knew then that he was too old. You all say a wife should not seek other men. It is true, she refused his son, still . . ."

Udama turned the corn with her bare fingers. "Yes," she said rather sternly, "she refused the son he pointed out to her. That is the bad thing she did. When I could not myself persuade Ticha to accept him, I then told Kako that unless he let her choose among his other sons, there would be trouble. But Kako said he had promised her to that son and that trouble among brothers is worse than trouble with wives, for where brothers are divided the homestead falls to ruin."

"Kako pointed that son out to her," I repeated. The words were meaningless to me. Quite automatically I accepted the information together with the parched corn, turning the one rapidly in my fingers to keep from being burned, as I turned the other over in my mind, searching for some hold.

Udama, having started to talk, now was not to be interrupted. "It was not right. I tried to persuade Ticha, because it was my duty to Kako. But it was not right. Kako

149

put Ticha into my hut and under my charge. It should have been to one of my sons that she was given, to live with him and cook his food while Kako lives and to be his inherited wife when Kako dies. It was that woman," she named Kako's second wife with a vindictiveness that startled me, "who inveigled Kako into giving Ticha to one of her sons. Ticha didn't like him. Who does like that woman's children? They resemble their mother. I argued with Ticha, but I cannot blame her. She is a well-brought-up girl and knows her duty. If Kako had shown her one of my sons, she would not have refused."

Udama was well launched. She poured out all the hate she felt for that woman, her co-wife, a hatred which had mounted with each small disagreement between them, with each irritation, and which had waxed the stronger for having to be hidden under the friendly comradeship that theoretically represented the true feelings of co-wives. In Udama's diatribe Ticha figured as a pawn in this hidden conflict. Soon Udama was speaking so rapidly and vehemently that I could no longer understand her words. I don't think I really wanted to. The tone was enough.

Indeed I had not understood, still did not understand, and might never wholly understand the tangle of desires, of hates, spite and love beneath the apparently simple incident and beneath gossiping judgments. I had caught Udama at the moment she had to talk; we were alone and could not be overheard. Probably no one else would give me similar confidence.

Udama was coming to an end, each word slower and less urgent than the last, like a clock running down. She faded out mid-syllable and sat, emptied. The rain rustled faintly on the thatch, single drops following each other unhurriedly down the slim blades of grass in which the thatch ended gradually and untidily. Rain glistened down the dark green yam vines and bent the broad outstretched cassava leaves. The faint wind left the rain unmoved but seemed to breathe moisture toward us.

Softly, as to someone half asleep, I murmured, half questioning, "Kako was willing to give his own wife to his son."

Udama's eyes were still vacant, yet she spoke with a certain weary passion. "To die barren, without children . . . what sign that you lived is then left on the earth? In old age your children work for you and feed you; the sight of them feeds your heart. When you look about and see your sons, many of them, and their sons and their sons' sons, then you are ready to die, for you know that your name will never be forgotten on earth. When a man is old and cannot farm, do his sons not hoe his fields for him? Shall a man who is old cease to marry wives and have sons of his own name, while his sons can beget children for him? Ticha's son will be Kako's son and mine; is she not his wife and my wife? Kako did not wish his son begotten by a stranger. Can I wish mine begotten by another woman's son? That woman's son?" Again she ceased.

"And now?"

Udama spoke very soberly. "Now there is hate and trouble in the homestead. Whatever Kako does, hate will remain in someone's heart." For the first time, Udama looked and spoke directly at me. "Once a wrong has been done, it never dies. People speak the words of peace, but their hearts do not forgive. Generations perform ceremonies of reconciliation, but there is no end."

The rain dripped on quietly, like the rain of an English summer's day, moderate and quite without tropical display. Udama and I sat on by the fire, glad of it and glad of silence for our thoughts. Man's passionate desire to be remembered—what else was our longing for some form of immortality? Udama's words rang in my ears as I pondered our own beliefs. If no one else, our God would remember us, even if only to judge and to condemn. More, our heaven and hell were promises that we ourselves should remember. And yet, of the two, who would not rather choose to be remembered? Was not worldly ambition of glory ultimately but the longing to inscribe ourselves so deeply on our time that we would be remembered and our names

151

not quite die from the earth? Our names and our blood. Two slim chances of immortality. We, indeed, could die without children and yet not be barren. We had wrought a civilization and achieved with it this measure of grace. But here, for Udama, for Kako, for Ticha—to die without children was to die barren, to vanish from the earth without trace. My thoughts wandered to Undu, his father's only son, and to Poorgbilin's second wife, who had borne no children and who lay so ill. Without explanation I said abruptly to Udama. "I must go to Poorgbilin's."

Her thoughts could not have been so far different from mine, for she answered as though we had been speaking of Poorgbilin's wife. "No, she is not ready to die. Go, and give her medicine to drink."

Poorgbilin had barricaded himself inside his reception hut with his wife. He pulled the upturned plank bed away from the entrance to let me in. She lay on her side by the fire, her head pillowed on one arm, not quite asleep, not quite in a coma. Poorgbilin stood sentinel over her. His fat face, usually so smooth, dropped in unhappy folds. He explained to me, quite methodically, how she had been since I had seen her: a bad fit in the night followed by the semistupor in which she now lay; what herbal remedies he had given her, what ceremonies he had himself performed for her. He had not slept all night. No one else had come near her. Food had been handed in to him. She had eaten nothing. If I would be kind enough to sit by her for a few moments, while he got a little sleep . . . I sat down by the woman, and Poorgbilin slept across the fire from her.

Once she opened her eyes, saw me and muttered, "They are killing me. Do not go. They fear you."

"Nothing at all will happen to you," soothingly I murmured the conventional reassurance to the ill. But having said it then, in reply to her words, suddenly made me realize what the phrase meant. I was standing guard over her in the barricaded reception hut while her husband slept. "Nothing will happen to you: I, who have power to prevent it, will not let you be bewitched," or perhaps only

"I myself am not bewitching you." She was asleep again. Poorgbilin made no sound. The homestead outside had the quiet of night, more than that of a rainy day. Once a rooster crowed.

The woman could not have been much over thirty. No, she was not ready to die, though my mind, unlike Udama's, was not on her childlessness. Poorgbilin must think a great deal of her to stay with her like this. I had seen nothing like it here, though I had seen a number of men with very sick wives: they concocted medicines, consulted elders and sometimes had ceremonies performed, but all of them had meanwhile gone about their own business. Perhaps, even in this unfavorable world, love sometimes grew between husband and wife.

Or perhaps the witchcraft they both seemed to fear was more than usually pernicious. Poorgbilin might be guarding himself. His wife's illness might well be one of those which could be caused only by witchcraft. Poorgbilin might think the witches were getting at him through his wife.

They both slept. Even the fire made no sound. Only my thoughts whispered on. Witchcraft was generally no more than a complicating factor in disease as it was in childbirth. Witches could drive people mad, torment them with leprosy, make them barren. Was that why Poorgbilin's wife had no children? Was that what they thought? If children were one's only hope of immortality, if that immortality could be snatched away, not by some power beyond us, but by human malice, the malice of kith and kin—if that were true, how could one live except in constant hate and suspicion. Was this what lay below the surface? Hate, jealousy, fear. I had wanted to know, and I had opened Pandora's box.

I lit a cigarette. It was difficult in that shadowy hut to remember the laughter and warm friendliness that usually characterized these people. My smoking could not help me control my thoughts. I grew restless, realized that it was late and I was hungry. I wished Poorgbilin would wake up, but I didn't want to wake him up. He needed sleep. I wished he would take the woman to hospital, wondered if she were really as ill as I thought, felt it somehow my fault that I did not have the knowledge and skill to help her and could not get her, as I would get myself, to those who did have it. Finally I cursed myself for thinking at all.

I crossed the floor and called Poorgbilin. He woke instantly, like a man who has been listening, even in his sleep. "I must go," I whispered. "Here is some more medicine for your wife. Do not give it to her unless she feels pain or cannot rest." Poorgbilin pulled himself to his feet, fumbled on the top of the drying platform, pulled a rag out of a pot and twisted the pills into it. He thanked me and moved the bed aside from the door to let me out. "I will return tomorrow," I promised, and splashed across the yard.

Undu's father hailed me from the smithy hut by the path. I crouched under the eaves to ask him about his son. Yes, they had performed the ceremony; tomorrow if it didn't rain, he would take Undu to his mother's people. The child was in his mother's hut now; the ceremony had tired him. "You have given Poorgbilin's wife medicine?"

"I have given her medicine for the pain. I told Poorgbilin it could not cure her. She is very ill."

He nodded. "She will die," he said calmly. "No one of us is bewitching her, though Poorgbilin thinks we, his brothers and his cousins, envy him his many wives and children. Her illness is too strong for us. She will die, though no man has wished it."

I looked at the barricaded reception hut.

"Yes," he had followed my glance, "Poorgbilin's heart clings to that woman. We have all told him that he has other people, other wives and other children. We have reminded him that he must attend his affairs, for his welfare and ours. But he will not hear. It is wrong for a man to set his heart on one woman."

Once more in this place I was stung to involuntary and unwise retort. "It is well when a man finds a woman—" I faltered; if this language had the verb "to love" in anything

154

approaching our meaning I had never heard it—"a woman who pleases his heart and"—I recollected Poorgbilin's name for his wife—"where he can lay his head. In our country we think it should always be so between a man and his wife. There a man does not marry many wives so he may have many children and care little for any one of them. He seeks one woman whom . . . Damn this language!" I exploded in my own. "I can't say what I mean in it."

Poorgbilin's brother ignored my lapse into English. He stared intently at the hoe he was hafting. "It may be so in your country. But here—here it does not do to get attached to women and children. They die so easily." He spoke in the ordinary, daily tones of one who states a well-known fact, but his eyes wandered from the hoe he held to the hut where his son Undu was resting.

"They die so easily." "She is not ready to die." "Poorgbilin thinks we envy him his many wives and children, we, his brothers and cousins." "They are killing me." "To die barren, what sign that you lived is then left on the earth?" "Hate will remain. And once a wrong has been done, it never dies." Their voices pursued me down the path, into my hut, and into my heart.

Chapter Twelve

It was the sick time of year, a time that started with the fevers and infections of the late rains and ended with the epidemics which usher in the harmattan winds from the Sahara. Already the low-lying parts of the countryside were slowly miring into swamps. Stagnant pools of water lay in every depression of the paths. At night the damp and the torment of mosquitoes kept people by their fires, where they could be swathed in smoke. Only the toads waxed larger, healthier and more numerous. They littered my yard. At night, flicking my flashlight nervously, I had to pick my way among the plump blobs of their muddy flesh.

Part of my depression, I told myself, must be due to the weather. But not all of it. I had wanted to get below the surface. I had dived too deep. To breathe again I must stay on top for a while. I had allowed myself to become too absorbed in the personal affairs of the few homesteads I knew best. I would have to continue to take medicine to Poorgbilin's wife. Everything else was to be different. I should spend most of my time visiting the more remote homesteads or, when it rained too heavily, working on animal fables with Rogo.

There was more emotional reaction than methodical sense in this program to improve my morale, but it worked. Rogo's animal fables had a puckish touch that delighted me, and if Rogo himself had any dark repressions, I did not know them. He held the world as he held himself, aloofly. My visits to the further homesteads also cheered me. There I was well enough known to be received without formality, but no one knew me intimately enough to shake me with criticism or with confidences. They knew I did not know the details of their private lives. Therefore I felt free to ask about ceremonies, marriage customs and kinship. It is embarrassing to ask a man to discourse on fraternal loyalty, if you know he has just done his brother out of two goats. Best of all, Poorgbilin's wife was getting better.

Toward the end of the week, I resumed my visits to Amara. On my way there, I told myself that there had been no question of the desirability of intimate knowledge; it was merely a question of regaining and retaining my professional equanimity. Amara's presence worked its customary spell. She made me forget I was here as an anthropologist and not as an individual; with her, it was safe to forget. And she reaffirmed my faith that it was not all ugliness beneath the pleasant surface. There was good as well.

Only one problem still threatened my new crust of composure: only one's close relatives could bewitch one; all disaster was due to witchcraft. How could one live sanely where hate and suspicion must fall on those one should love best? Rogo could, and did answer: Bewitch or be bewitched. But Rogo walked alone. Not everyone could; Undu's father had advised it, but his eyes had turned toward his son. I tried not to think about it. I went back to Amara who was loved and unafraid.

One cloudy day when I went to visit her, I found the reception hut full of elders. Yabo, so it was whispered, was a dangerous and evil-hearted witch. I attributed this rumor to the fact that respect and dislike usually add up to fear. Yabo was one of the most senior men of the community and he possessed a great deal of legitimate magic. He had to be respected, but he was universally disliked. It was an inevitable reaction to his brusque, contemptuous manner. Yabo often called even the most respected elders fools; what was worse, he had an uncomfortable way of proving it to the satisfaction of all but the object of his scorn. Consequently, people called on Yabo only when they had need

157

of him. A congregation of elders anywhere else might mean no more than beer. At Yabo's it was sure to mean trouble.

Yabo waved me to a seat already occupied by an elder whom he particularly despised. On general principles I should have liked to counter the discourtesy Yabo thus showed him, but, as Yabo well knew, I also disliked this man. He was a blustering, thrusting, stupid old blockhead who had a knack of calling on me only when I had something better to do. While I hesitated, Yabo routed the old man from his chair, nastily referring to his deepest ambition in the process. "Unless you learn to curry favor with Europeans, you will never become a tax collector." The old man and I both spluttered—he at the implication that he could have no other qualifications, I at the implied gullibility of Europeans. Yabo, grinning at our discomfiture, again motioned me to sit down and resumed the discussion.

They were talking about someone called Yaav, at Tar's homestead. I raked my memory. Udama had taken me there on weeding parties; one of her kinswomen had married there. Tar and Kako were not very friendly. Tar's was a large homestead almost three miles from Kako's. But I couldn't place Yaav. I began to listen, but I had come in in the middle and didn't learn much: Yaav had a stomach ache and they were all very worried about it. Someone kept bringing up a cow and was jumped on every time he mentioned it. The elders agreed that they all forbade the stomach ache, but they would not meet at Tar's homestead to forbid it there. Someone must go tell Tar, but no one wanted to carry the message.

While they argued, the would-be tax collector kept mumbling in my ear. I tried to hush him. If they thought they could rid Yaav of his stomach ache simply by forbidding it, it must be witchcraft and I wanted to hear all about it. The old dolt was not to be silenced. While I tried to listen to the discussion with one ear, my other ear was flooded with his protests: he was the wisest, most senior and most honest man in the community; he could not stand by without words, helpless, while the land was oppressed by the present tax collector; if he himself had not been absent on urgent family business when the appointment had been made . . .

"You!" Yabo screamed at us. "Shut up!" The debate had come to an end without our noticing it. Yabo had promised to undertake the errand. He would, he announced, send Lam. Immediately I resolved to go along: this was the first I'd heard of Lam's return and I wanted to hear more about Atakpa's marriage; I still didn't know how one forbade a stomach ache. I hung around while the elders shrugged and took themselves off to their various homesteads. I lingered while Yabo sent for Lam, instructed him and packed him off. Then I gave Yabo a flurried good-by and chased after Lam.

As soon as I caught up with Lam on the path, I asked him what had been done about Atakpa. Lam gave the weak man's sly smile of triumph. Some time ago, Atakpa's new husband had paid him five pounds. Lam was afraid to return to Yabo's with the money; he was sure he would not be able to keep it. After much indecisive self-contradiction, he decided to go to his father's mother's people. With their aid he located a bride on whom Lam made a five pound down payment. She was, he told me, very young. He had always wanted to marry a young girl, and this marriage had an additional advantage: by the time she was old enough to come to him, Yabo would no longer be angry about Lam's having approved Atakpa's elopement and would not try to bewitch his bride. "Atakpa's my ward, and I'm in the right," Lam concluded, "but that doesn't make any difference. Yabo wants to manage everything himself."

He turned down a side path.

"Don't we turn to the left?" I objected. I remembered the way Udama had taken me to the weeding parties.

"There's a lot of water on that path," Lam explained. "This way is longer, but there is no water." Except for a few knee-deep streams, he was quite right: there was no water—just mud, deep, sticky mud that twice pulled the

159

tennis shoes off my feet. The path I had known ran along a ridge and crossed only one small stream. By all natural laws, it should have been drier than this one.

I stopped at our third stream, balancing precariously on my stick to wash off a pound or two of mud from each foot. Lam reached helpfully for my elbow as I wobbled on one foot. All he did was pull at the straps of my shoulder bag. I made a wild grab as I felt it slip from my shoulder. Lam snatched simultaneously, missed, lurched against me, and triumphantly clutched my bag high in the air. I sat down plump in the water. I glared up at him, but Lam smiled reassuringly. "Your paper is dry. I saw you put it in your bag."

Lam tenderly bore my bag across the stream, hung it up high and dry on a small tree and returned for me. I picked myself up, letting him fish for my stick which was gently floating downstream, and slogged my way to the bank. I was still speechless when Lam returned and leaned my stick against the tree, beside the bag. He recommended taking off my skirt; he would wring it out for me. I continued to stand inside it, damply and obstinately, squeezing out what water I could. Lam seemed to think that only his quick skill had saved me from falling into the water with my bag and precious notebook. I was sure that but for his clumsiness I would have wet no more than my feet.

We went on. Lam, dry, picked his way through the mud with sure, bare feet. I lagged behind him, skirt slopping wet and heavy against my legs, mud dragging at my sneakers. I was far too miserable to inquire about Yaav's stomach ache. I dragged into Tar's homestead, wrung myself out once more and sat down to steam silently by the fire.

When I reached the semidry, nondrip state, I looked about for Yaav. I had paid no more heed to Tar's commiserating clucks over my bedraggled condition than that old man had to Lam's tale of what had happened to me. I couldn't see anyone who looked sick. I did see Ihugh sitting back in the shadows, and was thoroughly surprised. Udama might visit her kinswoman here, but Ihugh was his father's son. And by now I knew the community was divided into those who liked Kako and those who disliked Kako enough to back Yabo, who was the only man strong enough to stand up to the chief. Tar belonged to Yabo's faction. Ihugh had no business here.

There were no more greetings to exchange. Everyone was looking expectantly at Lam; a messenger was clearly awaited. Lam, however, looked apologetic and sounded nervous as he told them, baldly, that the elders forbade Yaav's stomach ache but would not meet here at Tar's to do so. He tried, ineffectually, to counter their demands for reasons with, "Ask Redwoman. She was there."

No one asked me anything. Allies for once, both Tar and Ihugh insisted that if the elders really forbade the stomach ache in their hearts and not just with their mouths, they would meet here and discuss the matter. Yabo had chosen his messenger wisely. Indignant demands for explanation fell short before Lam's obvious ignorance and disinterest. Tar was disgusted. "Are you a woman or a child," he shouted at Lam, "that you know nothing of the affairs of men?"

Even Lam was angered at this insult. He had been away; he knew nothing of the affair, but from what he did know of it, it was in this homestead rather than elsewhere that the cause was to be found.

The men were all on their feet, speaking and gesturing with heavy melodrama. Yaav's stomach ache was important, and I didn't know why. If only Lam hadn't pushed me into the stream . . . From the darkest corner of the reception hut came—as a ludicrous, puncturing interruption—a hiccough. At the sound, the quarreling men froze: mouths open, hands in mid-gesture. I started to giggle. Such a stupid reaction. It was funny. Another hiccough. Tar and Ihugh exchanged a glance of deep significance. I was still amused. I thought them annoyed at having been interrupted so ridiculously. A third hiccough.

"Is it I who have done this?" Tar spoke with menace

and shook his fist at Lam. "Go! Go back to the elders and ask them to explain this away."

His was the anger of fear. I forgot my damp clothes and sat up straight. Another hiccough. Something was very wrong here. It couldn't be the hiccoughs. Yet Tar had vanished into the shadows whence the hiccoughs were still coming with distressing, silly regularity.

"Redwoman, can you help?" Ihugh tugged me to my feet.

No one is hurt by a few hiccoughs, but I was sobered by the curiously tense atmosphere and did not protest. With Ihugh I went over to the darkest corner of the reception hut. There Yaav, the man with the stomach ache, lay hiccoughing. I had Ihugh slap him on the back, hard and unexpectedly. He hiccoughed. I made him hold his breath. He hiccoughed. I had him drink water, slowly, from the far side of a gourd. He continued to hiccough. I tried every remedy I had ever heard of. His hiccoughing went on.

Ihugh, Lam, Tar and the elder men of his homestead held a hasty, whispered consultation. Ihugh reported to me. We would stay until late afternoon; if the hiccoughs had not stopped by then, the elders must be notified that they must meet. I agreed that it would be worrisome if Yaav hiccoughed so long, but I didn't really believe he would. In any case, there could be no point in my staying; Ihugh could tell me what happened. I wanted dry clothes. But I was overruled: by Tar's shouted instructions for roast corn and peanuts to stay my hunger; by Lam's promise to bring me along if the elders did meet; by a general remonstrance that if I was still wet it was my own fault; and by the explanation into which Ihugh immediately and temptingly launched.

Ihugh and Yaav were members of the same age set. Since Ihugh was the most important among them, Yaav had called him because Tar's medicine was of no help. As was customary, Ihugh and two other members of the age set, together with a brother of Yaav's as witness, had gone to the diviner's to discover the cause of the stomach ache.

The diviner found various magical complications which could be remedied by the performance of the appropriate ceremonies; he also found traces of witchcraft over the cow of Yaav's father's father. "That," said Ihugh darkly, "is why the elders are afraid to meet. Whenever that cow is mentioned, the elders cease to talk. But now," Ihugh was listening to the hiccoughs that came steadily from the corner, "the elders can no longer refuse."

Even as I opened my mouth to ask about forbidding the stomach ache, Tar brought out the paraphernalia for a ceremony which he knew and which might assist Yaav. I became absorbed in watching.

Late that afternoon we left to report to the elders that Yaav still hiccoughed. Lam walked home through the mud. I went with Ihugh the short way, a nice, high, dry path. I was more than ever annoyed with Lam. Walking with him I had got wet and learned nothing about the mechanics of forbidding a stomach ache. Again I resolved to ask Ihugh about it. Then we came to the river. It had never been there before—not a river like this muddy torrent, but only a meek, sluggish little stream.

While I stared at it, Ihugh folded his cloth neatly and placed it on his head. He walked into the water up to his knees, his waist, shoulders, his mouth, then slowly up again onto the other bank. Ihugh, I calculated rapidly, was a good seven inches taller than I. I would have to swim. I yelled to Ihugh that I could not swim holding my stick and bag. He recrossed the river and took them from me, but on the way back he missed the ford. For a few astonished seconds I could see only two arms, my bag in one hand, my stick in the other, advancing slowly across the river, then hair, a head and finally Ihugh.

A little unsteadily, I kilted up my skirt and plunged in. A few steps, only knee deep, and I was swept down from the ford. I grabbed frantically at a projecting bush and pulled myself up on the bank. Ihugh was already back in the water. Before I had time to think, he took me firmly by the wrist and pulled me into the water. He stood upstream, his body breaking the current enough for me to walk. Then I was once more swept off my feet. Ihugh tightened his hold on my wrist, leaned into the current and plodded on. I was dragged through the water, unable to swim while he held me, unable to keep my head out of the water, trailing downstream from Ihugh's grasp like a sodden rag doll. I tried to touch the river bed, but I couldn't force my legs down through the racing water. I thought I was drowning. Ihugh jerked me up and to my feet. We were only knee deep. He hauled me up onto the bank.

I collapsed, heedless of the mud, gasping for air. Ihugh wasn't even breathing harder than usual. As he tied on his cloth, he remarked casually that we were the only two people in the vicinity who could cross the river at its present height without danger.

"Indeed?" I gasped. Ihugh just then looked big enough to wade Niagara, but how did I fit in?

"No one," he amplified, "could bewitch you, and no one would dare bewitch me without Kako's consent. He has never given it. I know, for I have never been ill." Ihugh handed me my bag. It was getting late and we must hurry.

About a mile later I told Ihugh that I thought such a river capable of drowning people without outside assistance. Ihugh sounded both superior and repentant. "I knew you weren't tall enough to walk across, but I thought you could swim. Would you have tried to cross that river alone?"

"Certainly not." I was emphatic.

"Of course not." Ihugh seemed to think my reply proved something. In a few moments he went on, "No one who cannot swim well tries to cross a deep, wide river unless his wits are clouded by witches, for everyone knows that you die if your head stays long under water. Could you drown if the water were only up to your neck? No. Only if someone holds your head under by force. And if you cannot see that someone, you know it is a witch."

"Q.E.D.," I muttered, but I told Ihugh that tomorrow I would go the long way with Lam.

Ihugh agreed. "Tomorrow I must sit with our age set. Your place is with the elders."

And the next day I sat in Tar's homestead, sneezing, among the elders. Between sneezes I scribbled in almost illegible haste in my notebook. There must, I thought, be at least three hundred people in the yard, all of them talking at once. They sat under the trees in compact, separate groups: the elders, the men of Tar's homestead, Yaav's age set, Yaav's full brothers, Yaav's maternal relatives and, tucked under the eaves and grain platforms, sat most of the adult men of the community: they had no part to play but they wanted to see for themselves what happened. Hiccoughs prolonged to this extent were so pernicious a sign of witchcraft that messengers had been sent after Kako. We expected him about noon. Meanwhile, the less difficult complicating factors could be settled.

One of the elders, picked for his good memory and his loud voice, was acting as chairman. Right now he was being given the tally sticks, for not only Yaav's age set but each of the other groups concerned had consulted a diviner and brought with them bundles of sticks—one stick for each factor named by the diviner. One by one, five men, each representing one of these groups, stepped out into the middle of the yard, picked up the sacred plant by which one swears, and laid one tally stick after the other at the chairman's feet, calling out: "The mother's anger, the affair of the goat, the quarrel between his father's brothers, what the grandmother knows," and the names of the ceremonies which had to be performed before Yaav could be cured. The lists were remarkably alike and all, without exception, ended with "the affair of his father's father's cow."

The elders disposed of the ceremonies with astonishing rapidity. It was only necessary for Tar to agree to foot the bill and for the elders to agree who was to perform the ceremonies and when: most were to be done the following morning.

Then we came to the "affair of the goat"—a rather Holmesian touch, I thought. The chairman bellowed out:

"Who among Yaav's relatives bears a grudge about a goat?" No one stirred. An elder repeated the chairman's question. Another elder yelled, "What about that marriage goat?" A thin little man was thrust forward by Yaav's relatives; he began to tell us about a goat. There were shouts of encouragement—and contradiction—from Yaav's relatives. Everyone was talking at once, and the goat's history grew hopelessly complicated. Despite the chairman's résumés and the occasional hints from a helpful elder next to whom I had purposely seated myself, my notebook was full of questions. "Where did the second goat come in?" "Whose father?" "How do they calculate how many kids it might have had if it (and which one anyhow) hadn't died?" Suddenly the man who had been shouting the loudest offered the thin little man two shillings. They haggled. The elders settled on three shillings. The money was paid. The two men sprayed water from their mouths in sign of reconciliation. The chairman threw one stick to his left, and picked up another: "What the grandmother knows."

As the left-hand pile of sticks—representing the issues that had been settled—steadily grew, I realized that the elders were busily arbitrating family quarrels. No wonder five different diviners had named pretty much the same factors. There were always quarrels between brothers; mothers always had something to be angry about; grandmothers always knew something scandalous; goats were always in dispute; certain ceremonies were always advisable; in such a community everyone knew in which closet the family skeleton was hidden. And now, thanks to Yaav's hiccoughs, old grudges were being brought to light, aired and settled.

By the time Kako arrived, this minor business was finished and the women of the homestead had produced great calabashes and pots of food. Kako had not even stopped by his homestead. He gave me an absent greeting and settled down to eat while the chairman told him what had been done. No one was eager to get back to business. Tar came to squat before Kako; their conversation was soft and

166

earnest. The elder beside me watched them cynically. "So?" I murmured; an encouraging sound of interest is far better than a specific question even when one understands what's going on, and I was lost.

"I'm an old man."

This was incontrovertible, but it didn't explain his sneer. Again I murmured noncommittal encouragement, "Mmmm?"

"Since I have been an elder, we have been called five times over that cow." He looked again at Tar and Kako. "Kako would be pleased to have Tar abandon Yabo."

Kako stood up. His voice held just the right note of sympathy. His rhetoric was superb. He spoke of the love between kinsmen.

"You see?" breathed the cynical elder.

I saw. When one took away the pretty sentiments, one heard Kako's real advice: let sleeping cows lie. He sat down to applause.

Ihugh stood up among his age mates. On this occasion he was making no pretense at bluff stupidity. He congratulated his father on his speech. He said that he and his age mates were edified by the wisdom of their elders. He paused, and concluded with one brief sentence: "We, Yaav's age set, ask you about the cow."

There was a silence and an uneasy stirring among the elders. Ihugh and his father regarded each other steadily across the yard. At Ihugh's sign, two of Yaav's age mates carried him out into the yard and set him down in the shade of a tree. Ihugh, still on his feet, pointed to Yaav—and looked straight at his father. "You, the witches of this land, have done this. We, Yaav's age set, ask why."

Yaav hiccoughed and hiccoughed again. No one said anything. No one wanted to gainsay Kako, yet, with the evidence of witchcraft so blatant . . . A hiccough, and yet another. I felt myself starting to hiccough. For one wild moment I was afraid the whole crowd, hypnotized by the sound, would begin to hiccough. The elder next to me swallowed. Kako rose to his feet. Our attention fixed on him;

we no longer heard Yaav's hiccoughing. Our eyes and our ears were for Kako. He raised his arm in menacing accusation: "Tar, it is you who know." Ihugh had forced the issue.

Tar began a hesitating account of his father's cow. Only he and a few very old men knew much about the details. For once, since most of the elders knew no more about it than I did, a fairly full account was given. Even so, I found the tale confusing. Yaav's father's father's great-grandfather had had only one daughter, who had, on her father's death, been sold as a slave by one of her father's brothers to settle some debt of his own. When her brothers grew up, they had demanded compensation for their sister and had been given a cloth. Their sons were not satisfied with the cloth and received two goats in addition. By the time of Yaav's father's father, however, the descendants of the girl's brothers had stolen some magic from the descendants of her uncle, and had been forced to give them a cow in return. Currently, as far as I could gather, the living descendants of the girl's brothers claimed that the cloth, the two goats and the magic did not even yet compensate them for the girl's sale, for who knew what wives their ancestors might have acquired with her bridewealth and how many children these wives might have borne? Therefore the cow should be returned to them and, in addition, an equivalent in value to the number of offspring it might have produced. The living descendants of the girl's uncle, however, maintained that the cloth and the goats more than settled for the girl and that the cow did not compensate them for the loss of the magic.

Indeed, Udama had been right. Quarrels never came to an end, despite the ceremonies of reconciliation performed generation by generation. Today it seemed unlikely that there would even be a ceremony of reconciliation. Neither side showed the slightest sign of ceding an inch. Their argument reached the point of frenzy. Kako made not a single attempt to intervene or quiet them. The elders themselves were standing up in the middle of the yard, shouting at each other. Kako and Yabo were in the thick of the fray, shaking their fists and raising their spears. Again the cry "Shut up! Shut up!" went round. It had no effect. Soon it was replaced by Yabo's "I'm leaving!" He and his adherents stalked to one of the paths.

"I'm leaving!" shouted Kako. The majority of the elders started to follow him.

"Wait!" A mighty voice, Ihugh's. He caught everyone's attention. "Is this to be settled by the mouth or by the hand?" In a silence broken only by Yaav's hiccoughs, the elders stared at Ihugh as he stood massively in front of the threatening phalanx of his age mates. Slowly the elders came back into the yard. Reluctantly they sat down again. Ihugh and his age set crossed the yard, moving in a solid body, until they stood directly before the descendants of the girl's uncle.

"It is you," said Ihugh, "who claim that the cow given you by Yaav's father's father is not enough. You wish Yaav and his brothers to pay you that debt. Therefore it must be you who have bewitched Yaav to make him pay. If the elders say Yaav owes the cow, we, his age set, promise that he will pay it. If you owe him money for the girl, we shall see that you pay it. But in either case, we promise that unless the elders agree to forbid your witchcraft and unless we hear you promise to cease bewitching our age mate, we will beat you and put pepper in your eyes."

There could be no doubt that Ihugh and his age mates meant it. Hastily Kako told them to sit down. Ihugh replied bluntly, "When we see that the elders have come as impartial judges, then we will gladly place our age mate's affairs in their hands." For a long moment Kako and Ihugh stared at each other. During that moment father and son had the same face, unquestionably of the same blood and the same spirit. The contest was decided in that moment and without words. Then the two masks—one of hulking stupidity, the other of patriarchal benevolence—again hid merciless ambition tempered by cold intelligence.

"Sit, my children, while we, the elders, meditate our decision."

"We who are but children wait to hear the wisdom of the elders."

Ihugh had won. The elders drew into little groups, consulted, circulated and sat down again together. Kako rose. With his most benign expression he discussed the benefits of harmony and agreement in the homestead. In long clauses he balanced possible wives and children against the rate of increase of goats and cows and the income derived from magic. He concluded that Yaav and his brothers owed the others a cloth of specified type and weave, but they owed Yaav and his brothers two hens and a rooster. In a murmur of applause Kako sat down. His decision saved everyone's face, for the two "fines" were of almost precisely equal value.

Yaav's eldest brother disappeared into a hut and came back with the cloth (he had been seen buying it at the last market). The eldest of the other side appeared with two hens and a rooster. Each accepted the offerings of the others. Including Yaav, they performed the major ceremony of reconciliation: killing a chicken, cutting it in two, roasting it, and each eating half. They took water into their mouths and sprayed it out as a symbol of dispelled anger.

It was all over before I realized that sometime in the process, Yaav had stopped hiccoughing. I put it down to concentration. Everyone else saw it as a sign that the reconciliation was sincere and the witchcraft withdrawn.

"You see," said Ihugh cheerfully, "all it takes to get things settled is standing up to the witches. The trouble with most people is that they're afraid to fight against odds."

"And you, don't you fear Kako's anger?"

Ihugh smiled, but he lowered his voice. "It has been said that I am too stupid ever to become chief. Today I have given my father a chance to refute that taunt. I don't, often. That would be dangerous. But he will not bewitch me for this."

"Kako, bewitch you?" I echoed slowly.

"All the elders are witches, Redwoman. That is why people fear them. But they are only people, Redwoman. One must be cautious, but I am not afraid."

This, then, was my answer. Witchcraft was their greatest terror, but witches were only people. Everywhere one must fight to survive. There is a measure of insecurity in all societies. We may consider it easier to accept defeat at the hands of fate; fate is unconquerable. But where disaster is held to come from the hands of one's fellows, there defeat is not inevitable, there one need not cease to hope. Only my overwrought imagination had shown me the reign of witches as a reign of terror. Between sneezes, I whistled on my way home.

Chapter Thirteen

WITH tropic swiftness, my sneezes turned into a cold. By the time we got home from Tar's, I was a leaden lump of misery. Nothing could catch my interest—not the mean, accusing face of that son of Kako's whom Ticha had rejected, not even Kako's frozen features, immobile though his fingers writhed about his staff as he heard his son speak. Ticha's shrill defense and a ringing in my ears vibrated painfully and senselessly in my head. Giddily I staggered past Kako, toward my hut, to close myself in against the world. Kako's voice was uplifted in cold and formal curse as he drove his son from the homestead: "Go. There was evil in your heart. Go!"

My eyes focused on Kako. "You can drive snakes out of Eden," I said wisely and in English, "but you can't keep them out." I wished people wouldn't stare at me so: one can't be sick in public. I was on my knees, aware that Kako held my head and that my groundsman was throwing sand over my vomit. There was a confusion of voices: "It is nothing, Redwoman," "The yellow pills, Sunday," "Keep courage," "Tea," "Nothing will happen to you, Redwoman. Our hearts watch beside you," "Fix the bed." Through the blur and the pain I knew I had to give instructions. With all my strength I listened to my voice and was satisfied with its clarity. "Now the white pills, Sunday. In the red box." Anxious faces. Then the dark and quiet of the closed hut and sleep.

My cold was a fever. Quinine quickly broke its first onset.

It would be over before I could get a doctor. "It's only a fever," I muttered over and over to myself. "Stay in bed, drink water and take your quinine. It's only a fever. Everyone has fevers." And for a week I lay there, shivering with ague, sneezing, burning with fever, coughing, dosing myself.

Then I was better, well enough to lie in my deck chair and do nothing. I wanted only dark and quiet. Tears of weak irritation ran down my cheeks because I could not shut out the bleating of kids and goats, the rustle and flutter of chickens on my thatch, the squalling of babies, the swish of grindstones, thump of mortars, shouted conversations and the constant drumming. Sounds that I usually managed to relegate to the background, noticing them no more than the hiss of my lamp at night, now tormented me. I could think of nothing more beautiful than the black-and-white sign at home, HOSPITAL STREET. QUIET.

I only wanted to be left alone. I could not bear the jostle of people. Their life was too strong for me; it hurt me as the light hurt my eyes. I didn't mind Kako. Once a day he came with Sunday to my door: "It is nothing, Redwoman. Nothing at all." I was not too ill to remember it was his neck if something happened to me; I had refused to let Kako notify Sackerton; I owed Kako a daily sign of life and recovery. It was the other people. They camped outside my hut. Women brought me eggs to give me strength. Elders came to assure me that no one wished to bewitch me, that I would soon be well. And I could not avoid them. I had convinced myself that while I had the strength to get to the outhouse and back, I was not really ill. If I were not ill, I need not be afraid. So I groped my way along the wall and out, leaning on my staff and Udama's arm. Dizzy with fever and with quinine, I reeled as I stood. I made poor thanks to the people who waited for my appearance and who planted themselves in my path to make their presents and give their reassurances.

No one here had ever believed that anyone could want to be left alone. To them the worst fate that could befall anyone was being left alone and solitary. "All work is better in company." "A man sits alone only to plot evil." "Not even monkeys walk alone." The very worst of the terrible consequences of the greatest moral and magical trespasses (fratricide, witchcraft, the breaking of treaties), following the leprosy, madness and dire disasters that befell such evil doers, was the most horrible fate of all: "and such a man will sit alone in a silent homestead."

The fate they abhorred was a necessity to me, and not only when I was ill. Being alone and quiet was essential to some of my paper work. But above all else, it was only in the privacy of my hut that I could be my real self. Publicly, I lived in the midst of a noisy and alien life. If I wanted conversation in my own language, I had to hold it with myself. If I wanted familiar music, I had to sing it to myself. If I wanted counsel from my own people, I had to turn to my books. I could escape my cultural isolation only by being alone for a while every day with my books and my thoughts. It was the one means of hanging on to myself, of regaining my balance, of keeping my purpose in being out here before me, and of retaining my own values.

With convalescence came a morbid dread of seeing anyone at all. I wanted to lock myself up in solitude. I was even shy of the necessary presence of my boys cleaning up and waiting at table. Now that everyone knew I was getting well, people no longer lingered outside my hut. But as soon as I stepped outside, I was pelted with shouts from the closest reception huts: "You can't get better sitting alone," "Come out where the breeze can cool you," "You mustn't shut yourself up any more." I was well enough to know how sensible this advice was. I was still weak enough to feel that I was being hounded with it.

Then we had three days of pouring rain, weather so unusual that I chose to regard it as a favor granted me by the gods—and I felt such a favor long overdue. During these three days no one braved the weather. No one came to greet me or shout at me. Bothered by no one at all, I felt steadily better and more cheerful. Best of all, the damp sent the cook in to demand our flour supplies for oven drying against mold. Underneath, I found a hoard of five detective stories, which I had never read before and which I had hidden from myself, and almost too successfully, against such an emergency. I sat down to them, really happy for the first time in days.

By the end of the three-day rain-granted peace and the five detective stories, in only one of which I had been able to guess the murderer, I had almost completely recovered. The next morning was blue and fresh; the soaked thatch popped and rustled cheerfully as it dried in the sun. I was gay with the clear morning air and that first wonderful moment of recovery when one's body feels as good and wholesome as newly baked bread. The people by whom I had felt persecuted were today familiar faces and old acquaintance; conversation with them, which had seemed so impossible, the most natural and pleasant thing in the world.

I gladly heard Rogo's news that Ikpoom had returned two days ago, that Kako had released the lover with a warning never to return to the neighborhood while Kako could remember his face, and that Ticha had gone home "on a visit." I decided to tour the homestead and catch up the rest of the news myself.

I was not even much put out when I entered Kako's reception hut and found him tasting beer. It seemed that this was a Sunday. The doctrine of Sunday, in its bush form, is a very simple one: one day in every seven everyone must sit around doing no work; therefore, one should dance and drink beer. Early on Sunday morning, the women put the grain to soak, for six days they worked brewing beer, and on the seventh (having laid down a new brew), one drank. Since people began to drink about dawn, they were—depending on the particular brew and the individual drinker —dancing and drumming drunk between ten when the beer was finished and twelve when the beer began to wear off. They were either sleepy or morose for the rest of the day. On Sundays, I did paper work.

Today, however, I quite happily joined Kako in his sampling. We agreed that one of the three lots was by far the best and the driest. It was also the largest—four pots, each containing about twelve gallons. Kako reserved these for his own dispensing and divided the other two batches— one a bit too weak, the other a bit too sweet—among his various brothers and cousins in the homestead. I felt sociable and promised to join in the drinking. It's a pleasure to be alive and well. I went back to get a glass and tell the cook I wanted ground nut stew for lunch. I felt like a holiday.

All morning I sat in Kako's reception hut, nursing along my beer. Although I was drinking very slowly, Kako got four large glasses down me. No one else resisted his hospitality. All morning Ihugh was kept busy ladling out the brimful calabashes that were passed among the guests who crowded Kako's reception hut. Kola nuts were divided and distributed. Pipes were handed from one man to the next. Snatches of song, snatches of conversation. Two elders demonstrated their skill in drinking together from the same calabash, mouths pressed close together into double funnel, without spilling a drop.

Outside the drums and the gongs began their intricate compulsion of thud and clangor. The young men danced, feet wide apart, leaping and crouching, and rippling muscles of their backs highlighted by sweat and sun. The women danced, shuffling, swaying, subtle movement of hips and stomach. Inside too the old men, bright-eyed now, sang songs of the days of their youth and their loves, of the days when they had been great warriors, great dancers, unsurpassed lovers.

I excused myself to Kako. It was time to go, now, before their speech became drink-slurred beyond my understanding, before usually meek wives became aggressive, before anyone became "mad drunk"—a queer state in which a man's body becomes suddenly stiff in a cramped, paralytic rigidity and his open mouth utters loud, meaningless roars.

I had waited a bit too long. Kako was urging me to stay. "It's free beer, Redwoman. Drink!"

I shook my head and stood up. Soon the singing elders would remember the feuds and hates of their long dead fathers, soon the dancing women would begin to giggle and lurch, soon the young men would leap yet more wildly and stagger through the homestead, stammering their strength and prowess to a laughing, unbelieving world. I did not like these people drunk. I could not cope with them or they with each other.

Kako pulled at my skirt. "It's Udama's best beer. You must drink some more."

"Truly, Kako, I cannot. I'm full." My protest was genuine. I was used to stronger, more concentrated brews. Their beer is a fermented gruel. Long before I could get the slightest lift from it, I felt distended and logy.

"Nonsense. One can always drink more beer. Take this." Kako held out the dripping calabash from which he had been drinking.

"No."

"Why?"

I have yet to meet the human being who will take an unfurbished "no" for an answer. "I must go drink medicine, Kako."

"Do that, Redwoman. Then return. Beer will take away the bitterness of medicine."

"But this medicine, Kako," I spoke slowly and impressively to gain time for thinking; common sense is not easily refuted, "this medicine is not a simple herb that anyone, even a young woman, can go gather in the bush. It was given me by an elder, a man who really knows things"—my doctor ought to be complimented—"and therefore it is taboo to drink beer with it."

I escaped while they were still trying to figure out how my last statement could possibly follow from what I had said before. After all, when my constant "Why do you?" "Why don't you?" pressed them too far, they put me off with "Because that is the way it is done" or "Because my heart tells me to." I would have been quite willing to use these evasions myself, but they would never let me get away with them. On the other hand, I had to admit that I never really accepted these answers either. In a sense, neither of us was prepared to abandon the "reasonable man," that mythical creature who always keeps his head and never acts without sufficient cause. Unfortunately, our conceptions of the reasonable were quite divergent and, being composed of our stock prejudices, were not to be reconciled by any appeal to reason. I had to fall back on a diplomat's substitute for real agreement: the working misunderstanding.

I edged my way back through the lurching dancers. I was in a party mood, but I could celebrate with them no longer. I should have to do so alone. But not quite alone. I closed my door on Africa and turned to my bookshelves. I wanted good company. Falstaff, I decided; the background noises would not be inappropriate. I rummaged through my stores for a worthy drink. Sack, Falstaff advised, and sack I had, but what I drank would follow native (very small) beer and be followed by a ground nut stew. I mixed a martini, dry but warm, and was soon lost in a roistering England I found vastly preferable to the austere blue-law and red-tape land of my acquaintance. Fat Falstaff rumbled genially, proud Percy glittered defiance, Ancient Pistol roared—a tremendous roar that shook me out of Shakespeare's tavern straight back to the homestead.

Shouts, crashes, a drunken storm of laughter, a furious feminine voice. Curious, it didn't sound like the usual Sunday beer brawl; it didn't sound like a clown dancing to an appreciative audience. I stepped out into the homestead yard, and caught my breath with astonishment.

Kako was drunk—for the first time in our acquaintance, gloriously, reelingly drunk—and Kako had a fat stick in his hand. His favorite wife was drunk. She stood with beery concentration before the door of her hut, with a pot in one hand and a calabash in the other: she would cook whenever and whatever she pleased; if Kako wanted gourd seed sauce instead of okra he could . . . She went into detail.

178

Kako shook his stick at her. The abuse with which she emphasized her first statement was Shakespearian in its gusto.

Kako took a firmer grip on his stick and tried to roar her down. He wasn't really angry. Her anatomical comparisons were too flattering. However, no self-respecting man will tolerate obscenity from his wife; to save his face, Kako shook his stick. His "Shut up!" lacked conviction.

The whole homestead was listening, entranced, to her vivid, vulgar imagery. "Shut up," shouted Kako, "I'll beat you." He almost purred at her reply. She elaborated. Someone snickered. Kako remembered his dignity. "You'll cook what I want when I want it. Get busy."

She was very drunk, for she turned her tongue to Kako's digestive difficulties.

He lurched toward her in real fury now. "I'll beat you!"

She raised her arm. The pot sailed at Kako and splintered at his feet. Involuntarily, he jumped back. Everyone stood back, shocked. Wives don't throw things at their husbands. She aimed the calabash, with a slow, drunken windup, and got Kako on the head. Kako just stood there in amazement. Things like this didn't happen to him. "I'm the chief." His voice was high with surprise.

In response, she reached down to the basket of yams and sweet potatoes at her feet. Kako danced under her bombardment, but he was closing in on her. She reached inside her hut and flung a heavy pestle with a defiant shout but a carefully wide throw. Kako retreated, and as he retreated, he shook his stick all the more menacingly. His embattled wife took careful aim with another calabash. It got him, square on the shoulder. It was the okra sauce he had refused to eat.

Kako stood stock still, staring at the stuff oozing down his body, as though he couldn't really believe it. His wife, with a final insult, stepped inside her hut and pulled the bamboo door closed. We heard her shoving something heavy into place behind it.

None of us dared catch Kako's eye as he made his way to Udama's hut, still mumbling threats at the one wife as

179

he called to another for water. With carefully impassive faces, people made their way back to their beer pots. My boys disappeared into the kitchen. I followed, and found them clinging to each other, weak with suppressed laughter. Only Rogo had a measure of self-possession; he looked up at me from his notebook, with a satyr's grin. "I am writing for you, Redwoman. If she only knew her manners, that wife of Kako's would know everything."

The boys became aware of my presence. They struggled for composure. Rogo mumbled one of her phrases as he wrote. The boys smirked. "I'm a chief!" Monday mimicked. They were off again: laughing, quoting, commenting. Kako, the dignified statesman, the respected chief, smeared with okra, dodging and dancing under the missiles thrown by a wife! Kako, the reserved elder, smirking with pleasure while the whole homestead heard his wife explain just how he did this and that! Kako, the sensible husband, foolish enough to order a wife who had drunk too much already to stop drinking.

"Indeed, Redwoman," Rogo put in, "drink and fear make fools of the wisest men."

The cook wiped tears of mirth from his eyes. "Only a fool provokes a wild buffalo or a drunken woman," he agreed sententiously. "Beat your wife only when she's sober."

Rogo nodded, "The hare disguised himself as a wildcat, but he could not change his character. Or, as Kako's wife said . . ."

At the memory they began to laugh again.

I retired to my hut grinning with the unrighteous mirth one feels when a bishop or anyone pompous slips on a banana peel. As I picked up my book, I almost thought that the spirits of Falstaff and all his crew, chased from sober England, had come to do their work here. At least, out here, people were not afraid to let go. There was always laughter.

Chapter Fourteen

Sᴜɴᴅᴀʏ brought a message with my early morning coffee:
Amara had been in labor all night; I was to come at once
with medicine. Yabo's peremptory voice was audible even
through Sunday's rendition. "As soon as I've had my coffee," I told Sunday. He had already told the messenger
that I could not possibly come until the sun was there:
Sunday's outstretched arm pointed to the second row of
horizontal roof ties—ten o'clock. "Where is the sun now?"
I inquired, gulping coffee. My alarm clock had broken; my
hut remained quite dark until ten. Sunday's arm went to
a spot halfway up the wall—about seven-thirty. Sunday,
having observed that being hurried through my coffee upset my temper for the day, took pains to protect himself
by protecting me during that crucial time. His having mentioned the matter so early struck me more as a proof that
he shared the general fear of Yabo than as any recognition
of my well-known fondness for Amara.

There was, actually, no point in hurrying. I knew nothing of midwifery, could not possibly do anything to help
Amara. Nevertheless, I skimped my coffee and set off hastily. I made my way over the muddy path as quickly as I
could, and I soon found myself behind Udama, who was
walking at a more leisurely pace. With her was a massive
woman with a large goiter and a husky voice. Udama explained her presence. "Yabo's senior wife has summoned all
the midwives. This case is too much for her."

At Yabo's instructions, Amara had been carried out of

the hut and placed under the shade of a tree in the yard. The breeze, he said, would refresh her; here, too, there would be space for all the midwives, and they would be able to see the better. Already about a dozen women had gathered around her. I recognized the senior women of Yabo's homestead and a middle-aged woman who was Amara's co-wife. She had appeared, with their husband, as soon as word had reached them.

I looked at the assembled midwives. Yabo's senior wife had indeed sent far and wide. One old crone, bent almost double and shaking with age, lived four miles away. "You have come far, my mother," I congratulated her, for I had occasionally seen her on the path, tottering, clutching at her stick, always balancing on her head a small calabash that quivered and slid as the old woman trembled, and yet miraculously never fell off.

Udama's husky companion pushed her way into the midst of the clustered experts. Amara was lying back in a sloping wooden chair, head lolling, eyes shut. Her co-wife supported her. The midwives argued, loudly and volubly, asking Yabo's senior wife for details, interrupting her replies and unanimous only in their disapproval of her treatment.

Yabo, with a sheaf of herbs in his hand, appeared at my elbow. Shouting down the midwives, he demanded my medicine. "I have none," I spoke loudly and to them all. "In our country also childbirth is the affair of old experienced women, or of doctors." Only Amara's kin seemed disappointed. The old women looked rather relieved that they were to remain in charge. They resumed their consultations.

Meanwhile Yabo crushed the herbs into a pot, poured water over them and told one of his wives to put it on the fire to boil. As I jotted down the names of the ingredients, he added that this was medicine associated with some magic most commonly involved in difficult childbirth; there was little use in performing the ceremony without positive diagnosis from the diviner, but there could be no harm in administering the medicine and it might help.

The midwives had reached an agreement: not an agreement on any one course of treatment, but that each of them was to apply her own remedies. One of them had begun to massage Amara with cruelly stiff fingers whose touch made Amara whimper. Several others had scattered into the bush to gather roots, leaves and grasses from which they would prepare those medicines they had found most efficacious. Soon the homestead was full of bustle. The old women commandeered pots, mortars and pestles, and the palette-like slabs of smooth, dark stone on which one grinds snuff and medicine.

I wandered about from one to the other. I tried to put my whole attention on herbal recipes. It distressed me to watch Amara. One woman prepared an oleaginous mess that was to be smeared on Amara's abdomen; it would gradually soak in and strengthen her muscles. Another produced an oily application to grease and make easy the "path of the child." Most of them were preparing medicine for Amara to drink: some were to induce violent labor pains; others would give the mother strength for her ordeal. The shaky old crone was boiling three kinds of bark and lots of pepper into a thick reddish mess with a nauseating odor; this was the most important of their medicines, for it was associated with the only magic controlled by women and would assist Amara far more than these other, purely secular doses.

As they finished their medicines, each midwife poured her brew down Amara's throat. After about the fourth gourdful, Amara complained that she felt sick. Her protest produced only yet another draught which would, they assured her, settle her stomach. Whenever their unfortunate victim closed her lips and would not swallow, they began to shout. "Drink, my child. It is medicine. Drink." They gave her no peace until all the potions were finished.

Udama drew me from Amara's side. "It will take time for the medicine to walk through her body to the place it must do its work. Come, Redwoman." She drew me into Yabo's reception hut. The other midwives followed, leaving

Amara under the care of her co-wife. Inside were Yabo, Amara's husband, her father Lam, all the men of the homestead, and Yabo's younger full brother Yilabo who had built a separate homestead years ago after a bitter quarrel with Yabo. They were in earnest consultation. It was time to visit a diviner. Lam and Amara's husband wished to set off at once. The others advised waiting until the midwives thought it necessary.

Soon there was a call from Amara's co-wife: "The medicine has begun its work." Again the midwives gathered around Amara, encouraging her, massaging, pouring still more messes down her throat, hopeful and confident. The hours passed. Amara, exhausted, could not respond to their shouts. She seemed to withdraw from her body, and her body from its task, until there was only an inert mass slipping from our hold.

Udama gravely walked to the reception hut. Standing erect outside, she called to Yabo, "The matter is too great for us. It has become your affair."

Lam and Amara's husband at once came out. Without a word, they reached for the spears they had leaned against the thatch of the reception hut. Without a word, they set off for the diviner.

Udama turned to me. Soberly she said, "Go eat your food, Redwoman. Then return. Nothing will happen while you are gone, for there is nothing we can do. There is magic in this, perhaps witchcraft. The world was so created that, as the field brings forth its fruit, so does a woman bear her children. Only evil willed by man can prevent it. Unless the elders seek out this evil and remove it, no medicine can help her."

I stood over Amara. She tried to smile at me. She was very ill. I was convinced these women could not help her. She would die. She was my friend, but my epitaph for her would be impersonal observations scribbled in my notebook, her memory preserved in an anthropologist's file: "Death (in childbirth) / Cause: witchcraft / Case of Amara." A lecture from the past reproached me. "The anthropologist cannot, like the chemist or biologist, arrange controlled experiments. Like the astronomer, he can only observe. But unlike the astronomer, his mere presence produces changes in the data he is trying to observe. He himself is a disturbing influence which he must endeavor to keep to the minimum. His claim to science must therefore rest on a meticulous accuracy of observation and on a cool, objective approach to his data."

A cool, objective approach to Amara's death?

One can, perhaps, be cool when dealing with questionnaires or when interviewing strangers. But what is one to do when one can collect one's data only by forming personal friendships? It is hard enough to think of a friend as a case history. Was I to stand aloof, observing the course of events? There could be no professional hesitation. I might otherwise never see the ceremonies connected with death in childbirth.

I marched over to Yabo. "Do you wish Amara to live?"

Yabo grunted his willingness to hear me out.

"There are doctors who can save both her life and the life of her child. They have stronger medicines than yours to bring forth the child. If those fail, they know how to reach up into the womb. They even know how to cut open the living body, bring forth the child and then heal the mother. I will send a messenger on a bicycle to the hospital and another for a truck. I will pay carriers to carry Amara up to the road and on it, until the truck meets them. I will write a paper to the hospital, asking them to give her the best medicine and telling them that I will pay. I have always spoken truth to you, Yabo, and I speak truth now. Give my friend Amara to me, that she and her child may live."

Yabo spoke more kindly than I had ever heard him speak, but with unmovable determination. "You are Amara's friend and your heart wishes her well. I am grateful. I will even believe what you say of your doctors. But can your doctors remove the magic? Can your people deal with our witches? These things I can do, but they can not.

Unless these things are done, my brother's child will die. Amara stays here."

I argued with him, passionately. The ceremonies could be performed for Amara, even in her absence, on a cloth she often wore. The magic would be less powerful, but surely it would suffice to ward off evil until her return, especially if she could have our medicine meanwhile. It would cost them nothing in effort or money.

Yabo grew no less firm, but far less patient. Nothing I could say moved him. I was only making a nuisance of myself. When I would not stop, Yabo simply ceased to listen and forced me to recognize his refusal by starting a loud conversation with his brother Yilabo.

Defeated, I sat on by Amara all that day, forced to watch her in pain and steadily growing weaker. I heard the diviner's report, saw the messengers dispatched to bring back experts in that magic which Yabo himself could not perform. I watched Yabo sacrifice chickens, make ritual motions and anoint Amara with sacrificial blood as he mumbled the magical invocations. Yabo, like Undu's father, was doing his best. But it could not help and they would not allow me to help. In silence and in bitterness, at nightfall, I left.

I returned the next day at sunrise. The midwives had not returned, but Yilabo's wives had come and all the women of Yabo's homestead sat in the reception hut, waiting. They sat around Amara, who lay there on a plank bed. She was alive, little more. Her co-wife supported her head in her lap. Their husband had gone to summon his age set to defend him if he were accused of killing his wife, and to support him when he accused others. For the diviner had discovered that four men had reason to bewitch Amara: her father Lam, her two uncles Yabo and Yilabo, and her husband. With this report before them, the elders must themselves identify the witch and settle the disputes and grudges which had driven the witch to this action.

During the early morning, the ritual specialists Yabo had summoned arrived, one after the other. Jovial, some of them, like hearty country doctors; they made their jokes and radiated confidence as they slit the throats of chickens and daubed mud, blood and feathers on the ritual symbols and on Amara's navel. Most of them were dignified old men, clad in ragged togas, who probed seriously and thoroughly into the findings of the diviner and muttered their incantations gravely. All of them, the ritual finished, prescribed the herbal remedies associated with the ceremonies they had performed and supervised the mixture.

Each time her co-wife raised Amara's head. Each time Yabo held the potion to her lips. Each time they called to Amara, as to someone far away, until she opened her eyes and weakly swallowed the medicine. Each time they had to call louder and longer to make her hear. And each of the elders, his task finished, took the spear he had leaned against the entrance and left the homestead. I marveled, for usually elders gather where there is serious illness and enjoy nothing more than magical consultations.

Yabo's eldest son entered the reception hut. "They refuse."

"They can't refuse!" Yilabo was a thin, excitable man, as highly strung as his brother Yabo, but without Yabo's stamina or intelligence.

"Oh, my father," Yabo's son began formally, to dissociate himself from any responsibility for the message he brought, "the elders all say you have refused their advice in the past. Therefore they will not come to advise and assist you now." He dodged out quickly, away from Yabo's condemnation of the elders as timid evil-wishing fools, weak-kneed followers of that smiling villain Kako. Yabo cursed his son as a bungling, easily intimidated idiot while Yilabo's high-pitched voice scolded Yabo for the contempt which had alienated the elders. The women stirred uneasily; who now would protect Amara from her closest relatives, from those who should protect her life but had the power to cause her death? They muttered secretly among themselves.

Yabo was the first to pull himself together. He rose, dominating the reception hut, his feet red with camwood in the sunlight that slanted through the door, his face and body gloomy in the dim light within. "There are four of us who might have willed this thing. When Amara's husband returns, we shall all be here. Then we ourselves shall discuss it. I, Yabo, forbid Amara's death. I am stronger than all of you, and I forbid it. The elders' refusal is therefore of no importance. Nevertheless," he added, "they shall repent their insult to me."

Perhaps none of us looked convinced. Yabo, a shrewd man though one not usually concerned with the comfort of his guests, sent his women off to prepare food. He ordered Lam to prepare some medicine which he Yabo had held in reserve. Then he engaged Yilabo in an enumeration of the magic they possessed, to see if any possibly helpful ceremony had been left unperformed.

Thus it was that when Amara's husband arrived with his age mates, they found a feast ready for them. They may have come to accuse. They found themselves eating greedily. While they gorged themselves on porridge dipped in a chicken and sesame sauce, Yabo skillfully told him of the iniquitous behavior of the elders who had refused to come, of his own unceasing surveillance and care, of the medicine Lam would soon have ready for his daughter, of the rite Yilabo would then perform. Amara, he said, was merely sleeping; let her gather strength; there was nothing to worry about.

When the women removed the empty pots and calabashes, Yabo divided some kola nuts and passed pipes among the young men. Replete, they sat back quite contentedly to see what would be done. Only Amara's husband was still tense and suspicious. Yabo radiated good will and confidence as he inspected Lam's medicine.

But Amara would not respond to her father's voice when he called her to wake and drink medicine. "She is not sleeping, yet my child does not hear." There was dread in his voice.

"Don't whisper then," Yabo snorted. He shoved Lam aside, shook Amara and slapped her face as he roared in her ear, "Amara, Amara, drink!" He roused her. As they lifted her head, Yabo held the calabash to her lips and spoke almost coaxingly as he poured the liquid into her mouth, little by little.

Yabo's senior wife stood over them, watching Amara narrowly. "She may still live," the old woman snapped, "if you men will only discuss matters now and quickly. If you delay, she will not have the strength to bear her child."

The confidence so carefully established by Yabo had already vanished.

"It is you"—Amara's husband pointed at Yabo in accusation—"it is you who are my wife's guardian. There is rancor in your heart because you covet more bridewealth than we agreed upon. The court would not take my wife from me; therefore in anger and jealousy you have bewitched her so that seeing her sick to death I would pay you more."

During his jumbled, vehement indictment his age mates cried out their backing: "Hear, hear." "That's right." "He is speaking truth." And when he finished, one of them jumped up to shout, "Leave our age mate's wife alone. We will not allow it."

Yabo admitted that he wanted more money, but he denied that he was bewitching Amara. "You," he accused her husband, "you are killing the child in her womb, for you wish to make her ill and thus make me drop my claim." His counteraccusation was brilliant. There was only one way for Amara's husband to clear himself of all suspicion: if he admitted that he owed yet more money for Amara's bridewealth, then he also proved that he had not yet purchased the power to bewitch the child she carried. Either way, Yabo won.

Accusation and counteraccusation. The men shouted, threatened, denied and attacked. Whenever they paused, the women urged, "Agree, agree that our daughter may live!" "Agree, that your wife and mine may live."

Amara might yet be saved, if only they would settle all the grudges between them, all their possible motives for bewitching her. Witchcraft comes from the heart, sometimes involuntarily; it can cease only when the witch's heart is freed of all hate and rancor. Has the witch a just motive? Remove it, quickly. A witch can, indeed, be forced to desist. The use of physical force is dangerous in these colonial days. It took a man like Ihugh to threaten it and convince the witches that he would use it, irrespective of the consequences. No one here would dare. And only the elders, sitting together and with unanimous consent, can wield enough witchcraft to fight fire with fire successfully. But the elders had refused to come.

Only the women were wholly free from suspicion. They were singleminded in their determination that Amara must be saved. Even if the witch's cause were just, let him abandon it that Amara might live. But although any one of the suspects—father, husband, uncles—would gladly have sacrificed his interests for her life, each knew that sacrifice would be in vain, for each one of them knew he was innocent of wishing her death.

Yabo knew he was not killing Amara. Why, then, should he forgo his claim to more bridewealth for her? It might be a motive, but he knew he was not the guilty one. As long as he persisted, however, the others, who also knew themselves innocent, suspected him, indignantly denied his counteraccusations, and just as firmly refused to cede any ground.

The women pleaded, forcing the men to look at Amara's motionless figure. Time after time, looking at her, one of them would suddenly yield. Yabo lowered his first price. Amara's husband paid it then and there. Together they performed the brief ritual of reconciliation, drinking water and spraying it from their mouths. Lam admitted that he had grudged Yabo's taking his daughter as marriage ward at a time when he was wifeless and without means of getting another wife. Yabo ceded one of his marriage wards to Lam. Yabo admitted that he had resented Lam's behavior over Atakpa's elopement. Yilabo and Yabo again went into the old quarrel that had caused them to live apart. Again their anger flared. Again the women intervened. Again those who loved her looked at Amara. Again each sacrificed his own interests that she might live. And yet again they made some compromise and were ritually reconciled.

Still Amara was no better. "You are speaking with double tongues," the women accused. "There is something else. Settle it, and dispel your hate, or Amara will die."

They were at a standstill. There were no evident motives. If there actually were no other cause, then Amara was being killed to satisfy that dreadful lust which takes possession of some witches: the desire to kill and eat the victim's body.

The ability to bewitch is a dangerous one, but it is a common human faculty and, like any other weapon, it can be used for many purposes. A good man uses witchcraft only as a last resort, and then not to kill. But there are witches who enjoy being feared, who delight in killing, and who hunger for human flesh. Such men are feared and hated. They walk alone.

Everyone turned to stare at Yabo. Here was the man. It was written in their eyes.

Yabo saw it. He turned on his full brother Yilabo with quick reproach. "How can our niece recover when you delay the ceremony?"

We had all forgotten the ceremony, and, having forgotten, felt guilty, abashed and relieved all at once. While Yilabo got ready the herbs and magical apparatus, Yabo, with apparent irrelevance, began a rambling discussion of family history, recounting the wives and children, sisters and marriage wards of two generations past. Once again he had broken the mounting tension; thinking this the only purpose behind his leisurely discourse, I gave all my attention to Yilabo's ritual performance.

Yilabo, however, was listening to Yabo. Even while he made the magical gestures, he would interrupt with his own comments and opinions. By the time he had finished and was squeezing the juice of some plants into a calabash of water, he was arguing stubbornly with Yabo. "No, you are mistaken. She was not his ward, but his uncle's."

Amara's husband and his age mates were beginning to follow their comments with interest. Lam offered his version, but was promptly squelched by both brothers. "You, you are just a youngster."

"Perhaps," retorted Lam, "but Amara is my daughter."

Yilabo, always excitable, made angry, nervous gestures. The wet herbs were still in his hand; Amara and I were sprayed with bitter water. "Do you not see what Yabo is doing? He wishes you to believe what he says so you will not think he has any cause for envying me that wife I inherited from our father. He has always been jealous of me for that. That is why he is bewitching your daughter."

There was a rising mutter from the age set. "Yes, it is Amara's relatives who are bewitching her." "It is jealousy over women."

Amara's husband sprang to his feet. He pointed at Yabo and shouted, "I ask you, I demand of you, what bitterness is in your heart?"

Yabo waited for silence. Then he leaned back in his chair and asked aloud, "Why should I bewitch my own ward Amara out of hate for Yilabo? What is she to him? Nothing." He pointed his pipe stem at Yilabo. "It is you who are jealous of me because I am the eldest and had the largest part of the inheritance. It is you who are bewitching Amara."

Yilabo dropped the calabash. His body trembled and his face was drawn with rage. "It is you, you!" Again he accused Yabo. Again Yabo twisted every accusation to his own advantage.

It had to be one of those two. Amara's husband had cleared himself. Lam was too weak a character to be seriously suspected. Yabo or Yilabo, which? We were utterly absorbed in the duel between those two. Only Amara lay unconscious of the fight for her life.

Yabo kept a deadly composure; every word struck home. Yilabo lashed out wildly, without plan. He was no match for Yabo. Yabo did not stir from his chair. He was shouting, overriding Yilabo's defense, invulnerable to his attacks—

yet his very superiority was a proof that he possessed the greater power of witchcraft.

Yilabo had been pushed past coherent argument. He screamed random accusations at Yabo, attributing every misfortune that had ever befallen him to Yabo's malice. Constantly he repeated, "It is you, you who are killing Amara. You! *You!*" Yilabo stood over Yabo, his whole being shaken by his desperate passion.

I too had begun to tremble. Here it was no comfort that witches were only people. Therein lay the tragedy. These men were torn with anguish, striving to save the life of one they loved. Amara could yet live, if they could only force a confession from the witch. Each knew himself innocent. Each therefore knew the other guilty. I knew them both innocent. I watched while each strove to break the other, to force his confession, to save Amara. I knew they could not. Their battle was the more terrible to me because it was in vain and fought against shadows.

They were frantic now; if the witch did not desist soon, now, it would be too late.

Again Yabo accused, with deadly effect. Ashen, trembling, Yilabo mouthed words we could not hear. We cried out. Yilabo's dagger flashed from its sheath as he sprang on his brother below him, defenseless in his chair.

Somehow Yilabo's wife had him by the wrist. Yabo slid away from danger. Yilabo's knees gave under him as he stared at the dagger. Slowly his hand opened. He watched it, as though it were not his hand, not his doing, not his wish. He looked on while his wife took the weapon from him.

"Your own brother." A chilly whisper. "Your own brother, who nursed you when you were a child. You would have killed your own brother."

There was no motion in the reception hut, no sound but Yilabo's harsh breathing. The moment of realization is infinite.

Amara's husband rose, slowly. Deliberately he loosened his toga from his shoulders. Deliberately he twisted the

cloth and coiled it about his waist in sign of war, or mourning. We stared without comprehension. Then, suddenly
afraid, we looked at Amara. The woman by her answered
us, "She still lives."

"She will die," and her husband's voice spoke more of
war than of mourning. "One of you two is killing her. Have
we not witnessed that brother would kill brother? What
evil, then, is beyond you? She is my wife. I do not consent.
Confess! Or my age mates and I will force you both to the
ordeal."

"So be it." Yilabo smiled. "My chicken will drink poison,
but it will live to prove my innocence. Then if Yabo will
not cease, you may beat him and rub pepper in his eyes."

"So be it." With a terrible glance at his brother, Yabo
too assumed the dress of war and mourning.

But they were afraid. They wanted to delay, to get wit-
nesses, elders. They stood in the yard arguing, refusing to
start.

Amara's husband turned to his age mates in passionate
appeal. "They are killing my wife! Make them go!" The
young men closed on the two elders.

Yabo raised his spear. "You dare?" he roared. "You
dare!"

I screamed as they rushed upon him, then sobbed as I
saw the tumultuous crowd jostle and drag the two old men
out of the homestead and down the path toward the ordeal
master.

My knees were shaking. I was afraid to go with them.
I forced myself out on the path to follow them. Amara's
husband was coming back. He saw me. "Let my age mates
take care of it. You come back with me and keep watch by
my wife. She will die. Help me guard her body. He will
kill her. I cannot prevent it. But he will have killed her in
vain. He shall not eat her body."

It was dark inside the reception hut, and very quiet.
The women still kept watch over Amara. Her co-wife still
sat with her.

The man stood looking down upon his dying wife. A

194

man must never call his wife by her name. He may never touch her in public. This man knelt beside his wife. "Child of Lam."

She did not stir.

Tentatively, he laid his hand on her forehead. "Amara, Amara." Perhaps he thought she heard, for he added bravely, "Nothing at all will happen to you, Amara, my wife." He clasped her hand in his.

We sat on, waiting in silence for Amara to die.

Chapter Fifteen

THE SUN sank lower, thrusting yellow fingers of light through the dilapidated thatch of Yabo's reception hut. Amara still lived, her hand held in her husband's. Still the others had not returned. Sunday came. I had sent for cigarettes, sandwiches, coffee and a bush lamp, for Amara's husband had asked me to watch the night through. Outside, the shadows turned purple, lengthening, spreading, slowly conquering the earth as their domain. We watched night fall.

Once we heard the sound of shouting men and lifted our heads to listen, but as they passed by on the main path we heard them disputing goats and chickens and knew they were only strangers, coming back from market. It grew dark. At the doors a faint gray. The embers themselves were gray with ash. Only my hands and the white cloth they had laid over the dying woman showed pale in the dark.

The gleam of fires flickered from the surrounding huts. The man and I sat on alone, absorbed in the darkness into which Amara was slipping. I could not tell his thoughts. I had been wrong too often. That he must feel something to sit by her thus, that he felt both hate and fear for the witch who was killing her, that much I knew. What else there was I could not guess.

One becomes weary of waiting for death. I had said farewell to Amara yesterday, when Yabo had refused to let her go. Last night I had wept and beaten my pillow in impotent fury. We all owe life a death, an inevitable death which we can meet. But the unnecessary death that wastes life denies all consolation. Today I had joined a wake over the living. The passions that had shaken us had been the fears of those who still hoped and fought, first for her life, but soon for their own safety.

Would they kill the witch? Such things were said no longer to happen, but here was a lonely night of fear, anger and approaching death. The lights of the station and the formal clink and chatter of silver, tongues and glasses at dinner were far away. The way of life and the rule of peace they stood for seemed even further away. I was not here as their representative, yet it should have been I who held Yilabo's hand when he would have stabbed his brother. In that dark hour I had no real faith in my ability to protect Yabo or Yilabo from harm, no real assurance of their safety. I had been drawn too far into their own fears and passions, away from my own convictions, yet not wholly into theirs. I felt miserably inadequate to cope with my world or with theirs. There remained only a shame of showing fear and a certain stubborn loyalty to Amara: at least I could watch by her body and guard it from the hungry ghouls her husband seemed to fear.

One of the women came in. She paused questioningly. Then, as we did not speak, she knelt to mend the fire. I welcomed the commonplace and almost forcibly pulled my mind from all other thoughts to watch her stir the coals, lay the tinder, at the first tiny flicker, place the slivers of wood and corn stalk; then the bright flame twining about thin, forked branches and at last the steady, reassuring glow of the three logs.

There was comfort in the fire, and the place I sat was familiar enough. Yet the presence of Amara, inhumanly bulky and still under the white cloth, made it strange and new again. The firelight gleamed on the mahogany chairs, on the grain platform posts rubbed smooth from the leaning of many shoulders. It leaped up to the dark mass of the platform, blackened and mossy with the soot from many fires. The cone of the roof escaped into darkness. Sometimes, as the wood broke and flared, the light touched the weapons that hung above us, the dark globes of dried indigo suspended from the roof, the hanging and strangely ornamented pots that held Yabo's magic, and the white and splintered animal skulls that stared down upon us.

The women joined our wake, sitting quietly in the shadows. An owl hooted in the distance, a mournful sound that drew us closer to each other and to the fire. A soft pad of bare feet outside; the faint rustle of a spear leaned against the thatch. Amara's husband called out sharply, "Who is it?"

"It's I." One of his age mates, tired and muddy, crawled in the doorway. "The oracle master was not at home. We have sent for him, but we cannot know until morning. I have come to tell you. The rest will wait there for him." He turned to Yabo's senior wife. "Give me a pipe. I have walked far and am weary."

The old woman broke a twist of tobacco into her curved, wooden pipe. She lit it with a coal from the fire, then handed it to the young man. I too began to smoke and he seemed to notice my presence for the first time. The old woman explained. "Redwoman does not agree to Amara's death. Therefore she is watching with us."

He nodded. "I also think so," he said obscurely, "for the elders would not come by day. Listen!" Again we heard the owls, still distant. He turned to me. "It is well that you are here, Redwoman. The witches are abroad tonight."

"What do you mean?" My voice was just steady.

"Can you not hear the witch owls calling? They smell death and are gathering for the feast of ghouls."

"They have smelled death indeed. She is struggling with death."

Amara's breathing had changed. Her fingers clutched the cloth. Her body, gross with the promise of life, twisted once sharply, convulsively, and was still.

Yabo's senior wife held her pipe from her mouth. "She dies."

Amara's husband still clasped her hand. "Bring me a feather!" he snarled at the old woman. Then to me, "Is she dead? She cannot be dead."

I could find no pulse. The feather below her nostrils did not stir. Still we grouped about her in a strangely indecisive silence, as though life might yet return. We were still as though enchanted.

Then, quite close, we heard the call of an owl.

Amara's husband tore out of the hut, grazing his shoulder on the low doorway. We heard him shout, "What have I ever done to you that you rob me of my wife and child? I have never eaten human flesh. You have killed . . ."

But even as he shouted, the women broke into a terrible wailing, a banshee lament torn from soul and body. Standing, hands clasped behind the head, body arched and shaking with the cry that began in a high scream and sobbed itself slowly down the scale into silence. The fitful firelight touched Amara's body with deceitful warmth and lent her face expression even as it turned the living into strange, weeping shadows.

Yabo's senior wife stripped Amara's body, tearing the cloth she had worn about her loins. She motioned the young man to leave. "Take your age mate into my hut," she ordered. "He should not be alone tonight." She knelt by Amara, lifted her head and tied the torn cloth about her face, masking it completely. That mask of death seemed to banish Amara from among us. The wild sobbing ceased. We were no longer with Amara, but with a corpse that must be readied for its burial.

The women scattered to their tasks. Only one of them still stood by the fire, singing Amara's dirge: a song told in a minor key and made strange by a scale not our own; a string of mournful phrases knotted between racking sobs.

The women washed the body and smeared it heavily with camwood. At their request, I lit my bush lamp. In its steadier light, the scene took on a sobriety and calm that matched the new mood of the women. There was sorrow in their faces, but the anxious fear that had marked their features for the past hours had vanished. Somehow we had returned to a saner world. I helped them lift the body—it was very heavy—so we might wrap it in the white cloth that had covered Amara during her last hours of life.

This task done, they called her husband. "Watch, while we go wash death from us," they told him. "Come," they said to me, "take your lamp, and we will go wash in the stream."

Outside the night was cool and clear. The familiar stars were low on the horizon, hidden from me by the dark fruit trees that surrounded the homestead. My lamp made a slight pool of pale light on the guttered path that led down to the stream. The high grass looked white and ghostly at our approach; as we passed, it closed ranks in the darkness behind us.

Tonight I felt that I too wished to wash death from me. Like the other women, I piled my clothes on a boulder by the stream. Momentarily I felt shamelessly naked among their decorously dark bodies. The shock of cold water drove death and nakedness from my mind and from theirs. Our own life absorbed us. The stream was shallow. We poured water over ourselves and splashed to keep warm. On the bank again, I tried, like them, to wipe myself dry with my hands: pressing hard with a downward stroke, using the side of the palm like a scraper, and ending with a quick, outward flip.

Going back up the path to the homestead, rather damp, chilly, and quite hungry, I felt wakened from fanciful fears. Like the women about me, my mind had turned to practical matters. While they disputed the relative value of the camwood each had contributed for the dressing of the corpse, my thoughts turned to food, food and coffee. Nevertheless, I asked Yabo's senior wife if I could eat in her hut. Even the sight of the bulky white bundle that had been my friend—an unwilling and unavoidable glimpse caught as I dodged into the reception hut for my picnic bag—couldn't bring back my nightmare mood of depression. Indeed, as I ate, I found myself wishing I hadn't promised to spend the night here. I no longer believed that anything menaced Amara's repose. To keep my resolution, I had to argue that it was my professional duty to stay up. Their ghouls and witches were no longer real to me.

My feeling for Amara seemed to have vanished with her life. It was with a wholly selfish reluctance that I went back into the reception hut to wait for the dawn. Amara's husband was huddled in one of the big mahogany chairs. He seemed to be sleeping. Below the continued dirge for Amara's death, the other women argued, not too amicably, about who should spell the singer and how often. I twisted on the hard wood of my chair, my thoughts a jumble of witches and soft mattresses, of ghouls, the price of cam-wood and Amara.

I had slept. Stiff, chilled and numb in that bleak dawn, I awoke to immediate recollection. No sleepy waking mur-murs today, followed by the sounds of opening doors, morning greetings and the first lazy thumps of the pestle. When the sky first lightened, the old women who had kept the last watch roused us with their crying. At their clamor, the others came out from their huts wailing, yawning be-tween their sobs. Still they cried and lamented: "Amara, Amara, why have you left us?"

As the sun began to rise, their dirge slowly died away, and they turned to their morning tasks. Amara's husband and I set off down the path together: he to tell Yabo of Amara's death, I to inform Kako.

Kako knew. In the still night he had heard the wailing. "We will have to meet for the funeral," he told me, "as soon as Yabo returns. Meanwhile, go rest. I will call you when it is time."

My boys were curious, but I was stiff and stupid with fatigue even after I had bathed and eaten. It would be at least three hours before Yabo could return and the elders could assemble. I fell asleep.

When, in the late morning, we met at Yabo's, I was curi-ously reminded of the first funeral to which Yabo himself had taken me. Again there was a homestead full of people clustered under the trees. There was one strange difference. There was no knot of mourners, sitting silent and numb, apart from the rest. Amara's husband sat surrounded by his age mates. Lam, too, had called his age set and sat among them, holding Amara's son on his knees. Apart from all the others and from the elders, sat Yilabo and Yabo; behind them were ranked all the male descendants of their father's father. There was an empty chair among them. Kako pointed to it. "You watched by the body, Redwoman, therefore today you must sit among them." He smiled briefly, "Don't worry. We know you do not know. We shall not ask you."

Yabo clasped my hands as I sat down beside him. "You know I didn't kill her."

"Yes," I said. "I know."

"We heard of her death while the ordeal master was mixing the poison. Then he refused to give the ordeal; he would not take judgment out of the hands of the elders. Now they will all think I did it, for they know my heart is strong."

There was a touch of pride in his voice that suddenly sickened me. I excused myself to go greet the women in the reception hut. Their dirges gave the day its unity. The formless, pulsing wailing had stopped. Two women were singing well-known laments; through their voices, sometimes in organum, sometimes in perfect counterpoint, Amara's cousin wove her smooth contralto in broken praise of the dead. Now and again one of the women would utter that slow, descending scale of sobs, a leitmotif in tone and rhythm.

The women of Yabo's homestead sat closely about Amara's body, with leafy branches in their hands to wave away the flies. The hut was packed. All the senior women of the neighborhood, all the young women who had known and liked Amara were crouched close together, covering the floor and even out under the eaves. In their midst, the fire burned hot and bright. The air was stale with their crowded numbers and there was in it a sickly odor, a sweet corruption, the perfume of death. I forced myself to mutter correct condolence before I retreated into the fresh air outside. There, once more by Yabo's side, I listened again to the singing and marveled that man has been able to lend death such dignity.

Yabo rose. Slowly, without evident emotion, he told us of Amara's death and manner of dying. I hardly listened. It was wearisome to recapitulate hours that had been so long in the living. I watched Lam dandle his grandson on his knee. He too seemed to be exhausted past interest. At one point in Yabo's recital, he made a flat denial, but then he relapsed into indifference. His age mates were there to fight for him. It was they who leaped up to shout and defend when Yabo or the elders attacked Lam.

Once again, as at my first funeral, I saw the debate grow hot, watched people shake their spears at each other, saw the elders divided in their opinion. This time too, though they sat apart and aloof from each other, I saw the mourners sit tired, too weary to argue themselves. They, and I, were anesthetized by fatigue.

Only Yabo stood alone. He alone was unable to leave his case in more capable hands. He had boasted that he was stronger than them all, and now he had to pay for his boast. His closest kinsmen had banded behind him, as they were in duty bound, but there was no one of them who had Yabo's skill and intelligence in defense and attack. Moreover, it was to Yilabo that they gave their genuine support.

I heard again what I had heard while Amara lay dying: the same arguments, the same motives, the same accusations. There was more noise. There were more people. But to me the shouting was mechanical. The urgency that had driven them while Amara might yet be saved had gone. Only the constant mournful singing that flooded through the sudden silences reminded us that Amara was still our concern.

Someone had killed Amara. The guilt must be fixed. Here too was something mechanical and the debate seemed unreal. Perhaps those of us who had been most closely concerned were too tired to care. I didn't care any more. Since Amara's death I had fallen into apathy. But it was more than that. There could be no tension today: Amara was past help, and judgment was a foregone conclusion. It would be Yabo. His guilt had been in their eyes yesterday. Who else among them was so ruthless? who else so selfish? Who else had so often braved the opinion of the elders and dared to walk alone?

Yesterday Yabo had defended himself with powerful conviction. He wanted to prove his innocence because he wanted to find the guilty one. Today, this motive gone, he was slowly entrapped in his own character and by his own reputation. He had always thought most of the elders fools; they were showing themselves fools again today. His contempt of them began to show, and it angered them. That same contempt of those who were there to judge him, of those who were believed to command the magical powers of the community, frightened the younger men. And Yabo's fatal joy in commanding, winning, making himself feared, led him to play on their every sign of belief in his evil powers.

As the hours wore on, Yabo's protestations of innocence became formal, set phrases. His repetition of the indictments leveled against him—"I, a witch?" "I wish her death?"—lost their first shuddering denial, became empty, then gradually were tinged with an evil, mocking pride that attested their truth. Before my eyes I saw their proof of witchcraft. Yabo had been accused, falsely accused, because he was feared. Now he embraced that accusation that he might be still more feared. A witch's reputation grows like a philanderer's: every new conquest is attributed to the same man; and his denials are called discretion.

Yabo would not have killed Amara, but Yabo was not unwilling to be credited with her death. He wanted to be thought guilty. At the end, he stood alone and upright, contemptuous of the accusers snarling about him, laughing at their horror of the crime, until they gave way before him in fear and loathing. In the end he was confronted only by his brother Yilabo, and I, too, believed when Yilabo cried out, "You deny it. With your tongue you deny it. But in your heart you know who has done it."

"Enough." Kako's voice put an end to accusation, even as its tone fixed the guilt. "Bury her, and give her child to its father, for it was not he who killed her."

Lam, holding his grandson close, carried the child over to Kako. The boy cried a little, when his grandfather left him in strange hands, but he was soon comforted when Kako gave him over to his own father.

From the outskirts of the homestead came the crunch of hoes biting into the ground. Yabo's sons were digging a grave. The singing grew louder. The elders sat immobile and withdrawn. Some of the women came out of the reception hut and began to move about in their own huts. It seemed hardly the right atmosphere for a funeral feast, yet I could not imagine what else they might be doing. No one paid any attention.

Yabo's sons came back into the homestead. They were covered with dirt. As they approached the reception hut to bring out the body, the singing ceased abruptly. Once again our ears were pierced by high-pitched wails, a chaos of sound, offensive and animal after the music of the dirges. Wailing, screaming, the women withdrew into their huts behind closed doors. No woman, no man whose wife is with child may look into a grave lest birth and death be confounded.

The men all rose to follow the body to the grave. Yabo drew me along, and Kako nodded approval. There are many sights forbidden to women, but only to protect the women from powers they are not strong enough to withstand. As a European, I was considered probably immune to many of these influences; my continued survival confirmed their opinion. Only some of the women interpreted my hardihood as a sign of more occult powers; they thought I might possibly be a witch. But today even the men looked curiously at me as I stood by the side of the open grave and watched them lower Amara's body into it.

They covered her with branches, so the soil might not touch her. Soon only a raw mound of red earth marked her grave. There had been no ritual, no ceremony of any kind. Just a group of men who watched silently and spoke only to give practical instructions. Everything that had been in contact with the corpse must be destroyed or washed. The women might come out; they too must bathe, and the gravediggers.

Still the elders lingered at Yabo's. Then, when the women had returned from the stream, I saw the reason for their former activity. They were leaving. The young men with their wives and possessions were leaving, some to live with Yilabo, some to go to other relatives. Lam left with his age mates. Amara's husband went off with his son and his relatives. Yabo sat, intent, but making no sign, as one after the other of his wives and children walked away and out of his homestead, without saying a word. The elders sat on, witnessing their departure and receiving the only farewells they spoke.

Yabo's senior wife came out, empty-handed save for her pipe. She offered it to Kako: it was the gesture of a hostess. She alone was not afraid to remain with Yabo. Yabo, sitting alone beside me, drew in his breath as Kako accepted the pipe, drew a few puffs, then rose to leave. As I got up to go with him, Yabo suddenly asked, "Will you come again to see me?"

He looked very old, left there alone in that empty homestead. I nodded, and repeated my promise to the old woman as I passed her.

By the time I got home, the boys all knew. "The evil at heart are left alone, sitting in a silent homestead. Yabo is a witch. He could not refute it. And it is thus that witches are punished."

Chapter Sixteen

THE REALIZATION of Amara's loss came very slowly. At first I was aware of no particular grief, but merely of an exhausted disinclination to do anything at all. Between naps I moped about Kako's homestead or just sat with Ikpoom. His silence was companionable, and when he did speak, it was of some commonplace topic that touched no chord of memory. Kako also came to visit me, as he had done in the days of my illness. He seemed to think I needed distraction. At any rate he fed me tidbits of information designed to rouse any anthropologist from apathy.

Kako puzzled me. Twice I had caught glimpses of the man behind the mask of dignified reserve, and what I had seen had been contradictory. Kako drunk didn't match the coldly ambitious politician, but it was only on the latter basis that I was able to cope with him at all. Both what he told me and what he wouldn't tell me seemed consistent with their notion of what Europeans wanted in a chief. Kako maintained the strictest silence on any topic —such as witchcraft—of which Europeans were known to disapprove. But whatever he wanted me not to know, he wanted even more to have me assured that from every standpoint of wisdom and ability he was well chosen as chief. He could not afford to let me think him ignorant. And now he was being kind to me. Our relationship was such that I wondered why, and what he hoped to get out of it.

Obliquely I sounded Rogo on the subject. Equally indirect, Rogo wrote me a text on elephants: intelligent, an almost impenetrable skin, afraid of little things like mice yet capable of running amuck, and never forgetting an injury. He seemed to think that Kako or the elephant—Rogo's use of pronouns and their antecedents would have protected him from libel charges under any law—indulged in altruism only for policy's sake. As proof, he cited a gloomy tale about the wild buffalo, the egret and the elephant. But he drew no moral.

Kako was as unusual a person out here as Amara had been. For the most part, these people were volatile, nervous and noisy. Their homesteads were quiet only when everyone was out on the farms. There was always laughter, cheerful shouting and singing, punctuated with brief, angry quarrels. On the surface they were gay, casual, frank and light-hearted, happiest in company and hating solitude. Yet they were moody. Sometimes, for no apparent reason, a man would shut himself up in his hut for days; there he would croon sullen songs to himself while his wives and relations coaxed him to "come out; it's not good to sit alone."

To hear them talk, the ideal man always kept his temper, for a quarrel once started would never really end. In fact, they distrusted an even-tempered man like Kako, as one who must be hiding and nursing his resentment. A hair-trigger temper was bad but natural. Most of them were suspicious of slights and very quick to take offense. They were equally ready to come to blows. Since men and women both went armed with knives, I used to wonder that so little damage was done.

There was always the threat of ultimate violence if all means of arbitration failed. It had taken me a long time to distinguish between the spear brandishing and dagger flourishing that was a reminder of this threat and that which was a sign of imminent fighting. Actually, they were seldom in earnest. I had heard mentioned with dread a few times in the distant past "when the witches were against every man, and brother raised his hand against brother." The community was intensely shocked by Yilabo's attempt at fratricide. They talked and compared his deed with stories from the past.

To kill a man in warfare was a glorious act, and he who had taken an enemy's head in combat was a hero. Murder, however, was rare. There had been a mad man who had killed three people before he was caught and put in the stocks—I was glad everyone at Kako's was sane. Once or twice young men, seeing their brothers or their children die bewitched and unable to fight the witch with his own weapons, had taken bow and arrow and gone forth to kill in self-defense. By their reckoning, no one died a natural death; like leprosy and madness, death was the work of witches. By my reckoning, despite the weapons and the shouting, there was little lethal violence.

It took great provocation to make them really lose control. Each man had a chip on his shoulder and believed the whole world ready to knock it off. Self-respect demanded that each show himself unafraid to fight. Only a coward would back down before his opponent. However, to give in to public opinion was common decency. Therefore, at the sound of furious altercation people rushed to witness. One might see two men locked in seemingly fatal combat, each gripping the wrist of the other, dagger at the throat of one, club over the head of the other—a magnificent display of matched strength. Only their eyes, cocked audience-ward, told that they were both waiting for someone to say, "Gentlemen, gentlemen!" Then, skin and reputation alike undamaged, they could air their grievances and accept arbitration without loss of face. Public opinion was police, judge and jury, and its expression in ridicule or ostracism made other punishment unnecessary.

I tried to resume my usual routine, but my very habits betrayed me. I was used to visiting Amara almost every evening; sometimes, unthinkingly, I found myself starting out on the path to see her. I always turned back. I didn't want to go to Yabo's and not find her there. She had been the only person with whom I could sit quietly, the only person with whom it was not necessary to be constantly on guard lest I give unintentional insult and transform friends and ready informants into men suspicious of the alien in their midst. Like the other mourners, my first indifference had come from weariness, the press of immediate funeral tasks and the release from an almost unbearable tension. Now we felt her loss.

I didn't even want to talk about Amara. It was with some reluctance, therefore, that I started to pay my calls of condolence to her relatives. But Udama insisted, and so did Accident, though for different reasons. Accident was still my shadow on most of my walks, loping ahead of me, diving into the bush to pick grasses for my inspection or to try at a bird with his slingshot. Whenever I went into a homestead, he sat demure and quiet during my call, a silent shadow behind me until food appeared. Then, eyes sparkling, he ate voraciously, not in the least put out when my hosts began to remark at his appearance, "I see you've brought your bag with you." Now Accident wanted his share of the mourning feasts.

The recently bereaved should not be left alone. The reception hut where he sits is always crowded with those who have come "to sit out death." When one visits a mourner, one takes tobacco and kola nuts so that he may have a good store for the entertainment of his callers. In return, one is fed well and generously. The mourner is not expected to make conversation, but people talk about those things they think might interest him, seeking to tempt him into social enjoyment and forgetfulness, just as the women prepare special dishes to tempt his appetite. Usually the atmosphere of good food and good talk does its work in a very few days.

As soon as the mourner feels himself able, he resumes his usual work. Then callers cease to come with mourning gifts, lest he be reminded of what is better forgotten. Until the bereaved again wears his cloth in ordinary fashion, no one mentions the dead to him, for his heart is not yet wholly serene.

There is no fixed period of mourning, only a recognition of sorrow that must have some expression even while every means is used to banish it. Death walks easily among them, with strong weapons of famine and disease. They have only a few weak foils to fence off death's inevitable victory. But death's easier conquest has taught them how to fight his second, sorrow, not with proud and stoic resignation, but with life and laughter.

Always before I had felt mirth an intruder in the presence of sorrow. The black-crepe sensibilities of our mourning customs are not easily abandoned. But then, never before, had their dead meant anything to me. I had felt myself a pushing outsider, coming with whetted and professional curiosity to observe the expression of grief. Each time I had been thanked for sitting up with the very ill, for attending a funeral or for coming to "sit out death," I had felt myself a sly ambulance chaser, slimy with hypocrisy. Then, when I had sat among them with funereal demeanor, I had soothed my sense of inner indifference by contrasting it to their outward indifference to the mourners' grief.

This time I genuinely grieved for Amara and found myself gradually cheered by the happy faces and merry chatter about me. Soon I was able to remember Amara with that glad affection of the memory in which we always hold those good hours which we knew would be fleeting even while we lived them. Here and now I learned that just as the happiest event has permanence only in recollection so too it is with life—our own lives and the lives of those we love. To grieve over loss too long is to lose all that remains.

A mourner myself, I sat many hours with Amara's husband, with her father Lam and with her uncle Yilabo and all those of her relatives who had moved to his homestead after the funeral. Her name was never mentioned. But with them I gradually recovered my good spirits and with them was delighted, rather than revolted, by little Accident's whole-hearted enjoyment of the funeral meats.

Possessed of this greater serenity, I felt myself strong enough to obey my conscience and visit Yabo as I had promised. Once there, I was remorseful at my neglect. For over a week Yabo had sat there alone with the one wife who had not left him. No one had come to "sit out death" with him. His first words reminded me that a witch must expect to be ostracized. As I stuck my head into the door of the reception hut, Yabo blurted out, "Then you don't think I killed her?"

"No," I replied, entering and deliberately sitting down on a bench close to him.

His expression was hard to read. "Everyone else thinks I did." There was a shade of complacency in his voice that matched only too well his behavior at Amara's funeral.

Irritated, I retorted, "If you did kill her, I didn't see it done. In my opinion you didn't. As for what the elders think, well, when you denied it before them, you spoke as one who speaks with a double tongue, not as one who speaks from the heart. But I heard you speak before she died. Then you spoke from the heart, and then you denied wishing her death."

Yabo almost grinned. "Yilabo didn't think so. Yilabo thinks I killed her. He is afraid of me. Even Kako is afraid of me."

I was too annoyed to answer. Yabo fumbled about and produced a kola nut for me. He watched me intently as I peeled it and took a bite.

"Aren't you afraid I'll poison you?" This was Yabo at his worst: proud, contemptuous, with a perverse delight in alienating everyone from him.

He made me mad. "No, Yabo, you won't poison me. Your heart is too weak for such a deed."

"Don't you fear me, Redwoman?"

"Does your senior wife fear you?" I countered. "She remained."

Yabo shrugged his shoulders. "Her guardian is my best friend; we are blood brothers. But you, who will protect you? Aren't you afraid of me?"

"No." I borrowed a leaf from his own book. "I am more powerful than you. My heart is stronger than yours. Why, then, should I fear you?"

Yabo collapsed in his chair and laughed in pure delight. Suddenly leaning forward, he stuck a lean finger against my breastbone, over the spot where the power of witchcraft is believed to reside. "Indeed it is true, Redwoman. You also have great witchcraft. I have always thought so, and now I know it. However, there remains much which you do not know. I will teach you, Redwoman. Kako is afraid to tell you," Yabo leered knowingly, "because he wants Europeans to think him righteous and innocent. Anyhow, I know more than he does. Come sit with me, Redwoman, and I will teach you the great things of magic and of the night."

All my other reactions were swamped by a great thankfulness, a greedy acceptance of so much luck. I was a European and a woman. There were things which must not be told me. I had become increasingly aware of a boundary across which no one would take me. Only a few slips of the tongue, some comments I had not been meant to overhear had given me occasional glimpses of this unexplored territory. Whatever his motives, Yabo was willing to take me some of the way at least. I accepted with gratitude. That day, and the next and the next I sat with Yabo listening and probing and, at his request, writing in a new notebook which I had promised never to show to Kako.

One evening I came home from such a session, tired and jubilant. I headed straight for my hut and my bath. I was waylaid. A woman ducked out of my reception hut. From head to foot she was smeared with ashes. She carried a frond of the magical plant that wards off witches. She was mad.

She bowed and smiled and genuflected and poured forth a stream of jumbled words that made no sense. Sunday apologized at my elbow. "She walked in and she won't leave. She's waiting for Ikpoom."

"For Ikpoom?"

"She's his wife." Rogo padded up to us. "I told you it was women or witches or both that made him so sad." In shocked silence I listened to the tale Rogo told against the broken babble of the mad woman. Almost a year ago Ikpoom's wife had gone mad. Kako had sent her home when he heard I was coming, for fear that she annoy me. But she had run away from her home, because she believed that her relatives were bewitching her. Twice she had made her way back to Ikpoom, whom she trusted. Twice Kako had sent her back. Then she believed that Kako also wished her to die, and when she ran away once more, she took to the uninhabited bush. Ikpoom had dragged Kako off with him in an attempt to find her, but it had been in vain. She had vanished without trace. This afternoon she had suddenly walked in, asking for Ikpoom.

Still she smiled and talked, bowed and danced. She was a young woman and handsome, under the ashes. Ikpoom's sad eyes haunted me. The thought that it had been on my account that she had been sent off to the people she feared and abandoned to her fate was almost intolerable. And Ikpoom had nevertheless been kind to me, and a friend. I felt a deep surge of indignation at Kako; he went too far in his calculating ambition to curry favor with the least of Europeans. Even so, I didn't really want her in my reception hut.

When I started into my hut, she came right after me. I had heard someplace that one should speak slowly and soothingly to the mad. I tried. I said I had to bathe and eat; I would greet her when I came out again. To my relief she seemed to understand what was said to her, though none of us could make sense of what she said. To my even greater relief she showed me a certain docility. Monday added his bit of comfort while he poured my bath water: only once had she been violent. She had come up behind a woman on the path and tried to strangle her, but, said Monday cheerfully, it was a woman she had always disliked. He did not think we had anything to worry about.

After dinner, Ikpoom and Kako came together to see me. What Kako had to say confirmed my first suspicion: he had sent her away lest I be irritated and tell Sackerton that he, Kako, was an inefficient chief. Kako never let his conscience get out of control. All my sympathies were with Ikpoom, who wanted his wife to stay with him if she wished. I had to agree that it was wrong for her to wander about the countryside mad and uncared for. And I was angry enough at Kako's inhumanity to imply that most Europeans would feel as I did about it. Kako contrived a bland interest in my information, and left.

Ikpoom lingered. "She will do you no harm, Redwoman. She is mad, but she still knows those who have a good heart toward her."

I wasn't going to admit, even to myself, that I didn't share their optimistic faith in her judicious choice of victims. But there was something else on which I could speak as I felt. "I am sorry, Ikpoom, that it was on my account Kako sent her away. I wish you had told me."

"I almost did," Ikpoom paused, then picked his words carefully. "I knew you were my friend. But many of my friends have told me I should not care so what happens to a wife, especially since she is barren. And you, you are a European. You live with us and you know many of our ways, but your heart was molded in your country. And one can never be sure. Not about Europeans."

I made an impatient gesture. These were words I had heard long since at Poorgbilin's and which I would never forget. "I think you ought to care what happens to her. For the rest, Ikpoom, our hearts are like yours."

"No," Ikpoom contradicted me firmly. "Yours may be, in some matters. But Kako was right. All the Europeans who have ever been in this land want the mad kept far away from them. If they see them, they catch them and put them in a prison where they die." He ducked out the door, then stuck his head back in. "It's the small madness."

His last words were meant as reassurance. No one worried about those who had the "small madness," and there were quite a few. They wandered about the countryside, talking to themselves—one of the most definitive symptoms.

Some went naked, some dressed eccentrically—one man went about wearing a basket. They did no work and no harm. Wherever they went, people gave them food and shelter for the night.

The great madness, however, was dangerous. I had seen only one case and had not at first recognized it as insanity. I had thought the young man merely a ne'er-do-well who was to be found wherever there was beer or dancing. Dressed in a gay cloth, wearing a string of rattles on each ankle like a morris dancer, he always demanded the center of attention. He danced extravagantly and always sang the same little song, "Oh! how drunk I shall be." Even when he pushed other dancers out of the way, he was always humored and laughed with. I was the only person who didn't know what was wrong with him.

He had often come to see me. Once he brought me a duck and danced with it outside my hut, most comically and still singing his song. Some weeks later I heard he was ill and went to his homestead to make my return gift. He was seated in the shade, held firmly in the stocks. A hole had been hollowed through a huge log; one of his legs had been thrust through it and was held in place by wedges; the log itself was tied to a tree and was long enough so that he could not reach the rope. He was wholly mad now. With a shock I remembered his song, that the word "drunk" also meant "insane": "Oh! how mad I shall be."

His relatives told me he had suddenly whirled round in his dance and pounced upon the nearest by-stander and half strangled him before they could pull him off. They had been expecting it. Everyone knew the course of such madness: from a fey gaiety, through alternate violence and stupor, to death.

Several times I tried to talk with him. Usually he didn't recognize anyone. His eyes were curtained from us. Sometimes he was talkative; like Ikpoom's wife, he poured forth words that had no coherence. Once he called me by name. In a low whisper he told me that he was mad and would soon die; there was one thing I must promise him: to take his children away into safety, away from the power of those who were bewitching him. It was the sane request of a loving father. But this man was not a father, had no children. It was the great madness. I hoped Ikpoom was right about his wife.

Ikpoom kept a good watch on his mad wife. He let her go wherever she wished in the homestead, but he was always a few paces behind her. When she wished to leave, he would coax her back. She almost always came without his having to use any force. Most of the time she sat under the eaves of her hut, talking to herself; whenever it rained, she sat there singing in a high, mad voice. After I heard just one such aria, I called her Lucia. She liked the name, and she liked me. Whenever I went in or out of the homestead, she came up to greet me: kneeling, smiling and talking, pleased to be greeted and asking only to be heard in patience. We all got used to her, but we never turned our backs on her. It might just be the great madness.

Only little Accident was completely at ease in her presence. He told me that before she went mad, she had always been nice to him and had given him "lots of good food." Now he gathered sauce plants for her and listened to her attentively. Accident was the first one of us to understand her at all. After he had explained, we too discovered that much of her talk concerned food, and we could piece out that she was afraid to eat and unable to eat—though she crammed food into her mouth whenever it was given her.

Accident was perturbed by all this. He was always hungry, always able to eat, and he always knew when he had eaten. He knew that the insane often talked confusedly, but he didn't really believe that confusion over food could be more than tongue deep. As we walked along, he would worry over this problem aloud and at length, always concluding that Lucia really knew better. "She's just saying so. I saw her eat a whole bowl of porridge with gourd seed sauce yesterday. She must have known. She kept patting her stomach, and it was full like this . . ." Accident made an expansive gesture around his own stomach, already distended with the meal he had eaten for me that morning.

Accident and I were on our way from Poorgbilin's to Yabo's. I warned him where I was going, for I had been seriously criticized for my continued visits to the man held responsible for Amara's death. Rogo, my boys, Udama, Ikpoom, even Poorgbilin had scolded me for having anything at all to do with so notorious a witch, one whom the entire community had ostracized. I credited them all with good intentions, so I took time to remind them that it was my work to learn the things of their country, that I had always called and would continue to call on anyone who helped me. My explanations did nothing to allay their uneasiness, but I could do no more than explain as well as I might.

Accident, however, hadn't hesitated a moment, nor did Yabo show the least surprise at his appearance. As usual, Accident started to sit down behind me. Yabo told him to listen carefully, if he wished to grow up into a man "who knew things." Accident was all ears and listened in fascination while Yabo told me how witches could transform themselves into owls and other creatures of the night, and of the precautions one must take to be able to re-enter one's own body which had been left behind, apparently asleep on one's bed.

Yabo stopped talking only when food was brought. The sauce, Yabo's wife told us, was a stew of greens and smoked antelope. Accident's eyes glistened with greed. When Yabo said, "Come eat, my child," Accident hastened to pour some water over his right hand. Without so much as flipping it dry, he pinched off some stiff yam porridge, dipped it into the savory sauce, put it in his mouth and swallowed as fast as he could to make way for the next bit. A good number of swallows later, hand halfway to his mouth, a thought seemed to strike him. Accident looked at the fragment of meat clinging to his ball of porridge. His hand drooped.

"Eat, my child," Yabo commanded. "Eat."

Accident muttered that he had eaten enough.

"Eat," repeated Yabo with soft insistence. "Do you think I would give you anything bad to eat?"

Yabo's question merely served to confirm Accident's suspicions. He turned faintly gray, but under Yabo's compelling stare he lifted the food to his mouth and swallowed it convulsively.

"Eat," Yabo insisted. "Eat some more." The grim amusement in his face terrified Accident. The child gave me a frightened glance of appeal. I intervened. "Accident has eaten enough."

Yabo bared his yellow, rotting teeth in a leer of assent. Accident gave a moan of despair.

"Come now," Yabo spoke to the terrified child with a gentle sweetness that matched ill with his gleaming eyes. "I would not give you human flesh to eat. Though to be sure, if I had, you have already eaten enough that you—or your father—would owe me a human victim in return, for us to eat together as you and I have eaten. However, this is merely antelope sauce. This is not your father's homestead. There indeed a man must be careful what he eats. Even your uncle Ikpoom's mad wife isn't too mad to know that. Even she knows enough to fear . . ."

"Shut up!" I blazed. I was furious with Yabo. "Accident," I ordered, "go out and wait for me on the path home." The child scrambled out of the doorway.

Then I turned on Yabo, stretching my command of the language to its utmost to tell him just what I thought of such bullying. I told him he deserved to sit alone, and I threatened never to come back. Both of us were shaken by the threat. I didn't really want to give up my sessions with Yabo. Yabo went so far as to explain and protest that it really was antelope sauce and he had said so. He made a halfway apology by promising never again to frighten any children I brought with me. Resolving never again to bring a child, I grunted and departed.

Accident had been very sick all over the path. To him, his vomiting proved that it had been human flesh—the only food that an honest and healthy stomach refuses. But he looked a lot happier for it. Now he was no more involved than if he had never eaten it in the first place. He had started to gorge himself, he admitted, before he remembered the talk he had heard about Yabo and Amara. With recollection, came the realization that he was probably eating Amara's flesh. If I would only give him a strong purge, he would be quite all right.

I promised, and searched out medicine for him as soon as we returned. Accident went off cheerfully enough, but I foresaw trouble with his parents and heartily cursed Yabo and my own lack of foresight. The insult that lay in refusing to eat one's host's meat sauces was now all too clear. I knew that witches were believed to raise their victims from the dead that they might eat their flesh. And because I knew, I had watched Amara's grave; it had not been disturbed. I knew that people always shared fresh meat, sure of losing nothing, for all hospitality must be returned and with its precise equivalent. I should have had the wit to put the two together and to the sum add the fact that what was believed to happen in the world of witches need match no physical occurrence. I should have realized that a witch would be believed to share his ghoulish feast with others and to delight in entangling the innocent in an obligation to return the gift—paying it, if necessary, with their own bodies. A father was answerable for his son's debts. Accident was Kako's son, and Yabo hated Kako. Again I cursed myself for my stupidity.

Delay couldn't help matters. It might make them worse. Rogo's little essay about Kako and the elephant aggravated my worries. I went straight to Kako and, pulling him to one side, told him the whole story. I repeated over and over again that what the child had eaten was antelope flesh. Kako lost none of his usual composure. He called Accident and seemed more relieved by the fact that he had been sick after eating than by my assurances that he had eaten nothing harmful. He scolded the boy for having gone to Yabo's at all. To me Kako said only that it was not my fault; I had not forced Accident to come with me; indeed, according to the boy's own story, I had warned him where I was going.

I renewed my apologies. Kako said if I were really sorry, it might be well to avoid Yabo in the future. Again Rogo's warning flashed through my mind, but, on professional matters, I could not let Kako dictate to me. I explained profusely, but I refused to abandon Yabo.

Kako smiled his usual bland smile. "You are a European, and may do as you wish." But his very blandness left me uneasy. This was not the end of the incident.

Chapter Seventeen

KAKO did not change his suave and paternal manner toward me. If I sought him out, he would converse with me at length. But these days he told me absolutely nothing; his talk was that appropriate between a chief and a strange European. Accident's mother wasn't speaking to me at all. Udama washed her rheumatic hands of my affairs. My boys gave me meticulous service and laconic answers. Even Rogo refused all conversational gambits. Everyone had advised me to drop Yabo; he was bad and dangerous. I went right on visiting him. For a while people scolded me, telling me I was foolhardy, foolish and obstinate. As I paid no heed to their advice, they stopped, one by one, paying any attention to me.

Amara's relatives had taken my behavior as a direct criticism of their leaving Yabo's homestead. I realized this, and tried my best to explain myself to them. It was no use. And after Atakpa's brother and I had failed to reach an understanding over the matter, all of them stopped talking to me. Cholo had started with the tactful statement that I was as stupid and headstrong as his sister. "Yabo is my father. Would I have left him without good reason?"

"Of course not, Cholo. But . . ."

He interrupted. "Yabo, my father, is a witch." Cholo was abnormally grave. "When sons, brothers and wives leave a man sitting alone, everyone knows he is evil. Then they too leave him alone. We cannot let such men go their way unhindered. To visit him means you approve of his actions. I cannot believe that of you, Redwoman. You were Amara's friend."

I objected that responsibility for Amara's death had never been proven.

Cholo looked relieved. "I forgot. You do not know." He embarked on a long, explanatory tale of past death and misfortune for which Yabo was clearly responsible. If he were not, how was it that those who left his homestead prospered while those who stayed with him became ill and died?

I was unable to give him a satisfactory answer. The explanations that satisfied me—dirt and coincidence—were unacceptable to him.

Yabo's homestead was the filthiest I had seen. No one ever swept. No one ever washed utensils. The yam peelings, grain stalks and other trash, from which careful housewives made potash, soap, brooms and scouring pads, in Yabo's homestead lay thick on the ground. In the rains the homestead yard turned into a compost heap. Regarding cleanliness as a sign of thrift and industry, people here thought Yabo's homestead unpleasantly dirty and smelly. However, their theories of illness did not allow me to point out any connection between dirt and disease.

They did not admit coincidence. If a tree had been too deeply ringed—for they let a tree die before felling it—the least wind might blow it over. That, they said, was the cause of its falling. But if, in falling, it killed a man, they did not think that man a chance and unlucky passer-by. Why that man and not some other? Who had bewitched him so that he would pass under that particular tree at that particular moment? Some snakes were fatally venomous. That was how a man died of snake bite. But not why. To answer why, one asked who: who had arranged by witchcraft that that man should not see the snake and be unable to avoid it? Why had he wished to bewitch that man? Nothing just happened by chance.

Our basic disagreement lay deep on both sides. I believed that even where witchcraft existed, its mumbo

223

jumbo was impotent save in so far as it made use of psychological suggestion or actual poison. And here, nothing at all happened. I had talked to enough reputed witches and heard enough from Yabo to know that no one ever performed a single act of black magic. They themselves considered witchcraft a psychic act. They themselves knew that its performance was deducible only from its evident result (someone's death, someone's madness) and the culprit only from the findings of the diviner, who merely named the relatives among whom there was sure to be hate.

To satisfy Cholo, I would have had to answer him in his own language and in his own terms. In that language and by their philosophy, there was only one possible answer: Amara's death proved the witchcraft; his age, position, character and the ill luck that haunted his homestead proved Yabo was the witch. That Yabo was innocent of murder in the physical sense was known—and utterly irrelevant. Neither of us could convince the other. Cholo openly attributed the lameness of my reasoning to a guilty conscience; he too ceased to have anything to do with me.

Yabo and I were both ostracized.

No one was rude to me. If anyone had been, I would not have felt so thoroughly excluded. I simply became invisible. Even Lam had the courage to pass me on the path without any greeting. If I took the initiative, my greetings were returned civilly. My questions were answered, briefly and unsatisfactorily. No one volunteered any information. No one would converse with me. No one came to see me. I was left alone.

I was helpless, encircled by a velvet curtain that seemed to yield wherever I touched it but which was, for that very reason, quite impenetrable. No one opposed me directly. They simply receded from me and left me in isolation. Once I had resented the chorusing people outside my hut—"Redwoman, come out. It's not good to sit alone." Now I could sit outside under my mango tree reading, without having anyone come to disturb me, except Ikpoom's mad wife and little Accident, as loyal to me in my disgrace as he was to Lucia in her insanity. A witch, a mad woman and a child—these were now my only friends.

After two weeks of such treatment, I turned stubborn. I would not give in to a public opinion which I could not share. At the moment I didn't like Yabo very much, but I didn't like Kako any better. Yabo was no murderer; I could not shun him as one. Anyhow, I was not going to forgo the information he was giving me. I needed it; it was my job to get it. And I gave Yabo the benefit of my self-pity. It is not pleasant to find oneself disliked. But to find oneself in the bad graces of one's whole world, intentionally ignored by a whole community, brings on again that nightmare aloneness of an unforgiven child.

I even reacted in a childish fashion: I'd show them I didn't care. I no longer tried to explain. I too withdrew into cold formality. To annoy Kako I daily engaged him in a punctiliously polite hour's conversation, about nothing. Daily I left him to go to Yabo's, defiantly calling out my destination to my boys, for all to hear. I told myself that it didn't matter, that I didn't care. Yet sometimes I could bear it no longer. To see the smile wiped from faces at my approach, to have my overtures rebuffed in cold monosyllables, in my own household to meet with nothing but robot, servile compliance.

I was very lonely. Accident sometimes took me grasshopper hunting, or showed me the pools where the fishing would be good as soon as the water began to go down. But even Accident had his own affairs. It was harder than ever to return to loneliness after his open friendliness.

I grew fond of Lucia. *She* liked to be with me. When I sat under my mango tree—trying to read, my daily interview with Yabo finished and no one else to talk to—Lucia came to bow and smile and talk by my side. She too was lost in a great loneliness and sought human contact. She was growing sleek, now that she no longer roamed about the countryside unfed and untended. She was getting much better. Every now and then a stray sentence would float to the top of her chatter. Every time I saw her, I thought of

Ikpoom's kind gentleness toward her and remembered the nights Ikpoom, Ihugh and I had sat in quiet companionship. Ikpoom wasn't talking to me these days. Nor Ihugh. It hurt.

In the nights, when it rained, Lucia sang. And I sat inside my hut, by my softly hissing lamp, playing solitaire. I had sat so for nights, laying out cards, stacking them together, hearing the parting crack and joining ruffle of the shuffled deck, playing Idiot's Delight while the rain whispered on the thatch and Lucia sang and laughed.

It had to end. I was burying myself within my own resentment. There was no one there to tell me I had lost my sense of proportion; no one to remind me of man's emotional dependence on those who form his environment; no one to slap me out of my self-pity.

Loneliness and the madness of Lucia's song pervaded my hut. I had come to this, to sitting alone and busying hands and eyes with a senseless dealing of pasteboard to exorcize all thoughts. Was self-isolation not akin to madness? Only Lucia's voice had life and seemed to have purpose, though it was a fey song alien to hearth and homestead. Her high eerie voice sounded as inhumanly natural as the wind and rain that shared the night with her. Madness must be a great loneliness. Lucia was lonelier, perhaps, even than Yabo. I wondered if shadows kept her company. Perhaps. Even so she had come seeking her husband; she had not been content to wander alone, veiled off from the world.

To live one must be of the world, not merely in it. Lucia was struggling back to life from her private grave. It was not easy. Her song reached our ears but not our understanding. And Yabo? My hands slowed among the cards. I had not approved his punishment because I had not thought him guilty of what he stood accused. Yet I could now see that he had refused his world. His world had finally spat him out. There were many known witches, but they walked delicately in the sight of their people. Yabo had been singled out not by the magnitude of his sins but because he had seemed to revel in them.

I had deigned to justify myself to my chosen friends, but when they had still found fault, I had shrugged and gone ahead on my way without apology. Like Yabo. But I was right. I slammed the cards together. Outside in the night and the rain Lucia applauded her song with mad laughter. What use was it to sit alone in my righteousness, even as Lucia sat alone in her madness?

Yet I could not abandon Yabo. Professionally, I needed him. Individually, I felt obligated to him. Only a coward could leave him in the utter loneliness that even now withered my soul, though this was not my only world. Let me be a coward, then. "To sit alone in a silent homestead." It was a terrible punishment indeed. I could not support it. And I valued this world; I wanted the good opinion of the people in it. I would give much again to hear Udama's strict instructions, Rogo's pungent aphorisms, to see Ikpoom's slow, ugly smile . . . It wasn't as though Yabo were a good man.

I was up early the next morning. Lucia was already under my mango tree. She had remembered that she had a farm and that it ought to be tended. She had cloaked her back against the sun with a tattered old cloth, as women do when they work long hours on the farm. Her song might have been a weeding chant. She had a hoe in her hand. True, she was scraping away at the bare earth under the tree, but she was making all the motions of weeding.

Ikpoom stood watching her. Joy at Lucia's improvement made his ugly face radiant. As she sang and weeded the barren ground, Ikpoom and I forgot all else. We spoke of her, talking in our old familiar way. The barriers were down. Now was my time. Surely I could trust Ikpoom's opinion. I liked him and respected him. I sought some formula for my night's decision. It was hard to put into words.

"Redwoman! Ikpoom!" Accident was gleeful. He had something to tell us, so funny that he didn't even notice Lucia and quite forgot his usual respect for his elders. Accident could hardly stop laughing long enough to speak, but he would not let us get in one word. We knew Ngun? That old, old man who was blind and had no children to lead him about? Surely I had seen him feeling his way along the path, testing the ruts with his bare feet, poking from side to side with his stick. I nodded. Ngun was a nice old man who bore his blindness bravely, but he was without wit or humor. I couldn't imagine any funny story concerning Ngun.

"Well," Accident told his story with zest, "I was out hunting birds with my slingshot, and I met him. He was all alone, shuffling along because the path was so slippery with mud. He was about to fall anyhow. So I yelled, 'Watch out, Ngun. A snake!'" Accident hugged himself with mirth, and Ikpoom howled with laughter. Only Lucia and I didn't get the point.

"Well," I prompted. "Go on. Tell me what was funny."

Ikpoom, still forgetting that I was in disgrace, gave me the explanation, his usually monotonous voice lively with amusement. "Ngun is blind. He can't see. He wouldn't know which way to jump." He began to laugh again. "There's nothing funnier than yelling 'Snake!' at a blind man."

"Funny!" I looked at Ikpoom as though I were seeing him for the first time.

"Yes," Accident put in. "He can't know where it is."

Ikpoom saw that I was not amused. He was a sensitive man and a kind one; he thought he knew what disturbed me, and he tried to set my mind at rest. "If there's really a snake there, you mean to tell him where it is. Only people get so excited when they see snakes that they don't remember. They just yell. So of course a blind man can't be sure."

They were both laughing. I looked at them, at Accident's glee, at Ikpoom's gargoyle grin, at mad Lucia singing and hoeing away at the bare earth, throwing pebbles behind her like weeds. Were these the people whose approval I had wanted? to whom I had almost been ready to submit

228

my conduct for judgment? I looked back again at the man and the boy.

Accident pointed the joke. "He keeps poking about with his stick."

"He's afraid to move and afraid to stand still," Ikpoom hooted at the picture, "and he doesn't know which way to jump."

"Quite." My voice was as cold as my heart, and, as always seemed to happen here when I was deeply upset, I spoke English. "Quite. Typical peasant humor, but I am not a peasant and you are a bunch of savages."

They looked at me, puzzled by my tone. "What is it?" Ikpoom was concerned.

"Don't you know the words?" Accident groped for my trouble.

I looked at them across a gulf I didn't really care to cross. "Perhaps it is the words." I had to say something. It was just the way they were. It was no use being angry at them. It was just seeing what they were and knowing what I had almost done that had made me almost sick in revulsion. "I will get my paper." They were still friendly. That was what I had wanted. I didn't want it right now, but why spoil it? I went into my hut, but not to get my notebook.

"There is nothing funnier than making a blind man jump"—in fear and to avoid a danger he could not locate. Just then, their laughter was a symbol. A symbol of everything that has held me silent and disgusted before those of my own country who laugh crudely and maliciously at the pain of others. The little boys who tie tin cans to dogs. The hearty hulks who play cruel practical jokes. The fine pincers of malice exposing pain to the laughter of a callous world.

I could never have laughed with Accident and Ikpoom at such a story, but it was only because I heard it when I did that I was so nearly sick over it. My revulsion was within and against myself, because I had forgotten who they were and who I was, because I had come so close to begging their liking at the price of my convictions.

Ikpoom was a good man by nature, but he was a savage. They were all savages. For the first time I applied the word to them in my own thinking. And it fit. What could I want with them? What could they offer save poverty of life and of spirit? Taking from the earth a bare sufficiency for the year, they gorged themselves at harvest and then went hungry. Wasteful, improvident savages. Why should I hope to find anything of personal value to me among them? One does not seek wisdom among men who live and sleep so close to the earth, the very vermin their superiors.

Slowly the grim facts of their environment crept back into my memory. The mold and mildew that rot the stored grain. The termites and boring insects that honeycomb the walls and eat through the roof supports. The deadly diseases that lie like a miasma over the hot earth: malaria, sleeping sickness, yaws, leprosy—an hour's rosary of killing and maiming diseases. Improvident? Callous? What else could they be.

It was not just to blame them, but I could no longer be charmed by them. The lush vegetation covered a harsh ground; the vine-draped groves by the streams were haunts of disease and poisonous fungi. Nature had given this land a warm beauty to cover its cold, selfish indifference to the struggles of those who lived upon it. Man is not nice about means of survival. The land could fascinate, but in that fascination there could be little affection. The people seemed to me as the land. At first acquaintance they had laughter, a proud bearing, and a grace of speech and movement. Underneath? Whether it was their nature or their circumstances, today they seemed harsh and cruel.

With a new appreciation I thought of my own life, of my country and our civilization. I had learned here to appreciate the riches of comfort and learning, the wealth of beauty of sight and sound that surround us from our birth. Secure in our heritage we are often blind to it. Surrounded by so much, we are often too lazy to stretch out our hands for even the nearest. I had come here from a life so fabulous that this new language I had learned had no words to speak it in.

I had come from one world to live in another. These two worlds judged by standards so greatly different that translation was often impossible. Partly for this reason, partly because of my job, I had often seemed to agree where I did not. One cannot do field work by saying, "Of course, it is impossible for a man, allegedly a witch, to turn himself into an animal; by what fiction do you account for his retransformation?" The mere suspicion that his beliefs are ridiculed will silence a man permanently. Now I had to show myself to them as a liar and a hypocrite or abide by what they knew I understood and thought I approved and believed. I had been right, last night, to resolve to break through my enforced isolation. But I could not do so by giving in to them.

I stood up, to shake myself free of indecision. Their laughter at suffering was merely one symbol of the gulf between their world and mine. Today, for the first time, I began to realize that our kindness to the crippled and unfortunate is a luxury born of our ability to spare help and resources. But that luxury has become a moral obligation. I must not abandon it. I had known that where existence is precarious, the weak go under. But I found it horrible that those who were safe should laugh at the sight. Even if they knew they too might perish on the morrow, even then, especially then, should they not rather pity than laugh? Where people laughed at human misery, our doctrine of kindness to animals, for the sake of mere kindness without intent to use or worship, seemed the wildest extravagance. They would accept, I thought, the notion that a god would mark the fall of a sparrow—but with a hunter's eye, for I did not think they could imagine any being free of the fear of hunger.

No, I didn't want to be like them. At the moment I didn't particularly care if I liked them, or they liked me. But like me or not, I would not let them lump me. I had work to do here; I would not go home a failure. I needed to restate my impartiality and a certain professional indifference, not only for their benefit but for mine. If they would not let me be equally friendly with everyone, I could be equally cool to everyone. In a mood for cold-blooded intrigue—as far from my normal state as my earlier self-pitying wish to be loved—I sat down again, to plot and plan.

I stepped outside. "Ikpoom?"

He heard, but he paid no attention. He had again remembered that I was being ostracized.

I challenged him. "Ikpoom, which of us two is senior?"

Still Ikpoom said nothing, but he looked hard at me.

"Come, Ikpoom. I am not to be treated thus. You may speak to me as Redwoman, your friend, or you may speak to me as a stranger and a European."

At that, Ikpoom came to me, as I had expected. But I had not expected to see him grin. "Yes, Redwoman?" His amusement was not at my expense, and his sudden yielding left me at a loss. He saw it. "You made Kako agree to let my wife remain, Redwoman. Nevertheless, Kako is my elder brother and he is the chief." As far as anyone could see, Ikpoom had nothing further to say. He barely breathed the rest. "You have shown us all that you are a witch, but it is not I alone who believe your heart is good." He turned away.

I stood stock still. Ikpoom had chosen his words carefully. He had told me that it was Kako whom I must fight and that there would be those who would support me. The more I thought about it, the more likely it seemed. Kako might not have much against me personally, but it was an open secret that he resented the presence of a European in his chiefdom: it inhibited his usual methods. It would be like Kako to seize this opportunity to damage both me and Yabo.

Well, there was only one thing to do. Have it out. But how? I could not admit the possibility of defeat. I walked slowly toward Kako's reception hut. Ikpoom might be right, that others still liked me, but he would not openly help me. I couldn't think who else would. Yabo was discredited. The pro-European element in the community didn't include more than one or two worthless youngsters. But Kako had enemies, and I still had a certain prestige. After all, Kako was still exceedingly polite to me, and Kako always had a reason. It might be no more than not wanting me openly against him. That was a slender weapon. I would have to feel my way.

I greeted Kako. Face to face with him—distant, civil and self-possessed—forcing the issue seemed far from a simple matter. This would be no gentleman's agreement, reached in privacy. I girded myself for an open fight and held Kako in casual conversation until the elders began to drift into his reception hut, as some of them did daily, running the affairs of the community by these almost happenchance meetings.

Old Tar gave me my opening with the greeting, common enough at such occasions: "Have you come to hear things?"

"Indeed," I replied, "but I have also come to ask." I purposely chose the word that meant to interrogate, cross-examine and accuse. It was a formula that must be answered by the most senior man present.

"Ask away." Kako sounded not at all enthusiastic.

Innocently, as though I had meant the word in its most innocuous sense, I began by asking Kako the sort of general question they were all used to hearing from me. This time, however, I inquired about the hidden matters of magic and witchcraft which Yabo had revealed to me.

Kako assured me that I was asking about things that did not exist. "Perhaps, Redwoman, there are superstitious folk among the tribes to our south who believe such nonsense. But not among us. Someone has been stringing you along."

"That is possible, Kako. Indeed, that is why I have come to you, here, before the elders. Did you not tell me when I first came here what you had already told the European

233

administrator: that you would teach me the great things of your country, and truly?"

Kako looked his most paternal. It had not been wise to mention Sackerton. I shifted my approach. "I am perplexed, Kako," I resumed. "Long ago, when Poorgbilin's wife was so ill, everyone praised you because you forbade the owls that had come to his homestead. If owls are really witches, as I have been told, then you did well and showed that your heart was good and also strong. But you say now that owls are just birds."

This was the right tack. The elders were avoiding each others' eyes and Kako's. I persisted. "Surely, I didn't hear you right?"

"Now which wife of Poorgbilin's was that?" Kako wrinkled his forehead.

"His second wife."

Kako had caught me off guard and seized his advantage. "Ah, yes," he said thoughtfully. "The one from Nder's country." He turned to one of the elders. "Do you remember her father's sister's son who stole a goat from this market?" The owner of the goat was present. I would have to wait for another opening. Kako had won that round hands down.

While I waited for them to finish with the goat, I decided to abandon Poorgbilin's owls. I prayed for some advantageous opening in the conversation. By making my attack before the elders, I had staked heavily. It was win all, lose all now. If Kako continued to evade my questions, if none of them spoke now, none of them would ever speak. My work would lie at Kako's mercy. I tried to recall everything Yabo had ever told me, even while I listened attentively to the elders' talk. One of them was saying they ought to seize payment for the goat from the first close relative of the thief who came near.

"No," objected Kako, one eye on the European in their midst. "That is not done these days. It leads to trouble."

"What else are we to do? What else have we ever done?

I'm tired of waiting for compensation." The owner of the goat was snappish.

Kako, having refused the obvious remedy, started a soothing but unhelpful reply. However, he had been thinking as he spoke, for he broke off in the midst of a sentence. "I have it. Tomorrow Aghegh is coming. He will use his influence, if I ask him to . . ."

I lost his next words. Aghegh was an unusual name; I had heard it before in some important connection. Of course. He was a famous magical expert, one of the few who could perform the Doiyor ceremony. What had Yabo said about the Doiyor magic? Remembering, I prepared to break in on Kako's last word, if necessary to shout down the owner of the goat.

"To perform the Doiyor?" I barely got in my phrase, but it was enough.

"Huh? What?" Kako was startled. There was a stir among the elders.

"Aghegh," I said distinctly. "You have, no doubt, asked him here to perform the Doiyor ceremony for Ikpoom's wife? To cure her madness."

"Doiyor ceremony? Never heard of such a thing. Ikpoom's wife? Certainly not! That is . . ." It was the first time I had ever seen Kako rattled.

"It is true," I resumed with an air of judiciously weighing the one factor against the other, "that the Doiyor is very expensive, but then you are a chief, wealthy and generous, a man who can afford to help his younger brother."

I paused. Still Kako made no reply. Sunk back in his chair, head bent like a buffalo about to charge, his mask of benevolence lowered, he peered at me from under his brows.

It was now or never. "There are those who say you do not help Ikpoom's wife because you yourself are bewitching her." I named the precise variety of witchcraft.

"Yabo lies! No one but Yabo can do that." Kako was stung into retort, though just a few moments ago he had denied, before us all, the very existence of that means of witchcraft.

"Does he?" I asked. "I do not know what to believe, Kako. Until this morning I have not asked"—I meant accuse now—"because at Amara's funeral you did not ask me. But now I do ask. Is Ikpoom's wife to remain mad? Why do you deny your knowledge? Is it because you wish me to think you cannot bewitch her?"

"I am no witch. I have a good heart." Kako again had himself in hand.

"Why, then, did you drive her away to wander alone in the bush? Was it not so you could kill her secretly and in secret greed eat her flesh alone?"

So serious an indictment must be answered with violent indignation. Kako sprang to his feet shouting protest. Habit was as strong as I had prayed it would be. The elders also jumped to their feet to shout. As soon as some of them began to defend Kako, their enemies swung over to my side. "You ask well, Redwoman." "Let us hear your voice, Kako."

"Never would I do such a thing. My heart is good, I tell you. You, why do you make this accusation? What proof have you?" I let Kako shout. I had learned much from Yabo. They would be curious. I waited till everyone was quiet and then, like Yabo, accused from my chair, speaking slowly that each question might sink in.

"Indeed, Kako, I hope I am wrong. But if I am wrong, why do you pretend to know nothing of the Doiyor ceremony? It can only be to avoid helping Ikpoom's wife. Nothing else can. Or can it be because you really do not know? But so ignorant a man should not be chief. Or do you wish to insult me? Are you seeking a quarrel with me, Kako?"

It was an attack Kako could not ignore. He could not assent to any one of my accusations without giving ammunition to some of his enemies. If he did answer, he would have to admit he had been lying to me. We waited, I with some anxiety, for Kako was a slippery opponent.

Kako gave a hearty laugh and sat down. Again he was

wearing his paternal, benevolent expression. "Seek a quarrel with you, Redwoman?" His voice made the very idea incredible. "Never. But we saw that you are young and a woman, therefore we spoke carefully before you. But now that we have all seen you have a strong heart, a heart strong enough to bear such knowledge, we will tell you what you wish to know. Of course Aghegh is coming to do the Doiyor for Ikpoom's wife. Shall I spare expense or trouble for my brother's wife? The ceremony must be performed behind closed doors and at night, but you shall sit beside me and watch it. Shall it not be so?" He looked at the elders.

Over their chorus, "It shall be so," I grinned at Kako and got from him a look of amused appreciation. I had finally won his respect. Kako, I suddenly realized, was one of those men who made friends only among potential enemies who might be dangerous. That was just as well, for I intended to press my advantage. I addressed them all. "You know I have come here to learn your ways. You know I visit all those who teach me. Thus it is that I visit Yabo. You are all of one country and brothers. Who am I to decide if you or Yabo are right? When brothers quarrel, does a stranger intervene?"

I paused for the inevitable "Of course not" produced by that proverb. Yes, I must remain a stranger. That was my answer. Meanwhile, I looked first at Kako, then at the elders who liked him least.

Kako, correctly interpreting my glance, assured me that this was my only correct position. Paternally he added, "Go to see Yabo, my child. He has never sought a quarrel with you. None of us seek a quarrel with you. We are all glad to have you here."

With bland and fulsome reassurance, we took leave of each other.

Within a day, everything was as smooth and cordial as it had ever been. Only my heart had cooled and withdrawn.

Chapter Eighteen

THOSE early November nights through which Lucia sang were the last rains. They were followed by hot, still weather. Sometimes there was thunder on the horizon. Sometimes rain seemed to hang above our heads. Not a single drop fell. I had had enough rain. I welcomed the coming harmattan wind with its dry heat and attributed the dull lethargy that fogged my mind to the heavy between-season weather. I needed a change, and not just a change of weather. After all, I had been in bush since late July, almost four months.

And it was still seven weeks until Christmas. I couldn't very well go back to the station before then. At least, I thought I couldn't—not after what I had told Sackerton about being so happy in bush. To keep myself from weakening, I sent Rogo in to confirm the date of the truck's coming. I ruffled the pages of my diary impatiently. I was perfectly all right, I told myself. It was merely a matter of hanging on to my resolution never again to forget who and what I was: an anthropologist and an American, an heir to civilization.

The English were quite right. One had to dress for dinner. One needed a symbol, some external sign, to assist daily remembrance of what one was. It did not occur to me that the need for such artificial aids was alien to me and a sign that I was no longer myself. Instead, to help me over the next seven weeks, I called the cook and gave detailed orders for a Thanksgiving dinner. At the same time

I told Sunday to lay out evening clothes, set the table with my best, and put out all the liquor in a fine array. I was no longer trying to learn how to survive in my new environment; I was concerned with sealing myself off from it. Since my set-to with Kako I had fostered the sentiment that business was business; after hours, one should try to forget it.

But on Thanksgiving evening I found myself thinking shop. I had spent all day with the elders at Poorgbilin's homestead. In the best Thanksgiving tradition I had gone without lunch and was very hungry. Also, I told myself, I had good reason to celebrate. All day Kako had kept me beside him, explaining freely and lucidly. We were on better terms than ever before, for we had each realized that we could not afford to neglect the other. Only on one point had Kako refused to say more than "Wait and see." Reasonable advice, since that point concerned the future. But it also concerned Yabo.

Yabo and Poorgbilin had the same great-grandfather. The day's business could not be settled unless all the male descendants of that ancestor were present. They could continue to ostracize Yabo only by slighting their own and pressing business. People here lived so closely together that almost every movement of one irritated another. Yet they were so dependent on each other that continuing a feud or indulging a spite was a luxury taxed with personal disadvantage.

Yabo was called to the meeting and came. At first, he was treated to the same cold civility that had been my lot. However, the polite manner is incompatible with their debating technique. One cannot shout and brandish a spear with reserve. Inevitably, as soon as people began to find their interests threatened, they began to stamp and scream. Yabo was out in the middle, yelling with the best of them. It was an angry scene, but a very normal one. Yabo, I felt, was back in.

Soon Yabo had the center of the stage. In his opinion Poorgbilin's cousin Shosho had one marriage ward too

239

many and must give one of them up. Kako stayed out of it. He and the elders had come to arbitrate if necessary, but primarily to witness. The argument swayed and surged. Gradually, it became clear that Yabo's opinion would be accepted. The elders were supporting him with loud comment.

Eventually only Shosho, who had a ward to lose, disagreed. He strode up and down before the elders, shaking his fist, shouting abuse at Yabo, bringing up again with new arguments all the points that had already been settled.

People began to shout at him. "Sit down." "Shut up." "The matter is finished." "Who are you to talk?"—with heavy sarcasm—"An elder?" "Keep quiet."

Yabo had been standing in the middle of the yard. Now that it was clear that public judgment had been passed and that it only remained to make Shosho accept it, Yabo started back to his seat. As he passed behind Shosho, Shosho whirled about and struck him hard on the side of the head.

Yabo reeled back.

Shosho, hand raised to strike again, was muttering words clearly audible in the silence, "Leave me alone, you! Leave me alone. I'll kill you. Leave me alone, I say."

Yabo feigned to ignore him. While the elders still sat silent and open-mouthed, he coolly commented, "This is your youngster, Poorgbilin. Do you approve of his deed?"

"No, of course not." Poorgbilin's rich voice was thin with shock. "Shosho! Stop it." Two young men of the homestead approached at Poorgbilin's sign, ready to seize Shosho if necessary. It wasn't.

Poorgbilin went heavily up to his young cousin. "Shosho, do you understand? I don't agree. Once before you struck an elder kinsman. I meant what I said then." Poorgbilin turned to the elders. "Is it not so?"

Shosho made a queer gesture, half of protest, half of appeal.

"It is so." A full chorus and unanimous. They were the elders, whom the young must be taught to respect.

"And it shall be as we said?" Kako now spoke, questioning Poorgbilin. I was perplexed at the scene and by the words. Only Shosho's reaction and the attitude of the elders showed me that what took place was significant.

"It shall be so." Poorgbilin pulled his toga tight about his girth in emphatic agreement.

Shosho looked toward the elders. He was afraid now. I couldn't understand. The elders answered Shosho's look of appeal. "It shall be so."

Kako himself addressed Shosho, who now seemed half stunned. "We do not agree to what you have done. We warned you before. Now we will no longer protect you." He turned to Yabo. "We do not refuse. If Shosho calls us, we will not come."

Yabo smiled—a thin, vicious smile. As he turned to leave the homestead, he looked at Shosho and smiled again. Before that smile, Shosho reeled as though under a blow.

These were the comments Kako had refused to explain to me. Not merely Kako. Everyone else replied, "Wait and see." They did tell me that some years ago Shosho had lost his temper and struck one of his uncles. The elders had come to witness their reconciliation; at that occasion the elders told Shosho he must never again do such a thing, or . . . The threat was implied. Whatever happened to Shosho, they would not intervene. I myself must wait and see. But Shosho was a truculent young man with a nasty temper. I felt he deserved anything that might be coming to him. It was nice to see Yabo once more aligned with the angels. It was certainly nice to see him taking part in things again. He drew sparks from everyone, and those sparks . . .

I abandoned metaphor, and Yabo. It was Thanksgiving evening: I was stretched out in my deck chair and dressed, to Sunday's delight, in my very best clothes. I dipped into the fresh roasted peanuts and prepared to enjoy myself. There would be nothing else to celebrate until Christmas.

Then I would be in the station. Tonight, I dedicated myself to the last bit of my best bottle. Solemnly I stood up, my own M.C., and raised my glass to the wall lizards agilely catching insects behind my lamp, a living audience and no less attentive than the usual banquet guests. I gave them "The Pilgrims and Thanksgiving." I had no intention of saving my toasts till after dinner. When one is both host and guest, one needs no sign to break up the party. It takes all one's efforts to get into the proper mood.

Like my formal dress, Sunday's best uniform and the formally set table established the fact that this was a party and not a solitary binge. He had put his whole heart into the occasion. My usual way of life gave his love for the elaborate only one outlet: whatever I ate, however I dressed, my napkin appeared before me in complicated folds. Sunday spent hours torturing innocent cloth into birds and animals that could be destroyed with one casual flip. Tonight he had outdone himself in complexity.

Sunday produced wine, poured a bit for me to taste, then at my nod, filled the glass. I approved the ritual, even though I did have enough sense left to realize how futile it was on the last bottle. Grandly, Sunday bore in the main dish. His gait implied a train of following footmen; his arms seemed to bear the weight of roast swan; his proud solemnity would have suited one who bore the Christmas pudding flaming with brandy. A few months before I would have had to put my napkin to my lips to hide a smile. Now, I shared his mood. I carved the roast chicken as though it were fat turkey. Punctiliously, I relayed my compliments to the kitchen.

My compliments were deserved. The cook had boned the chicken and stuffed it superbly. Even after I had eaten all I wished of it, my sense of duty obliged me to eat on. Such labor should not go unappreciated. And, judging by the murmurs from the kitchen as Monday bore out the almost empty platter, the cook was gratified. I had left little room for anything else. Eating had become a duty. Guest to my own staff, I approached the remainder of the meal with the reluctant appetite of one who does not wish to insult his hostess. I had eaten till I could eat no more. It was, no doubt, this drowsy after-dinner state which made Thanksgiving with strangers so difficult. One doesn't have to make conversation within the family. I nursed my liqueur. I didn't have to make conversation with anyone but myself. By my own line of reasoning, that should be even better. But it wasn't.

I sat on in lonely splendor. I grew bored with my own company, but I had no other retreat from the noisy, drumming world outside. The night I had danced at Ihugh's wedding came back to torment my mind with contrast. I knew what had gone wrong, I scolded myself. I had grown too dependent on the company and good opinion of my neighbors. I must learn to be consistent and self-sufficient. Two minutes later I swept out of my hut to go show Udama my finery.

The days that followed were days of vacillation. I had been burned—by Amara's death, by the enforced isolation that had followed. I wanted to divorce myself from all emotional ties. But old habit was strong. Sometimes I could forget my scars, and pass the day with old friends in natural life and laughter. More often I held myself aloof. Now that I had once seen these people as savages, in a moment of bitter emotional reaction, little things that had not bothered me before grated on my nerves. Dirt, crude manners, lack of sensibility.

Then the new season came to cheer me. The earth lost its humidity. The threatening clouds became a fine haze of dust. The wind rose and veered fitfully from south to north and south again. One morning, I woke to find the sun dim, the water cold, and a strong wind from the north blowing Sahara dust into one's eyes, over one's food, sheets, clothes, boxes, turning everything a reddish gray with dust. The harmattan had come, and with it the fine exhilaration of wind and dry heat. Desert bred, I revived. I was able to walk long distances with a new vigor. The faint rub of dust on everything I touched made it seem like home.

When Ikpoom told me I mustn't go to Poorgbilin's because there was water on the path, I thought he had gone as crazy as his wife. The heat of the bone-dry ground burned through my shoes. I told him so.

"There's water there. You must not go. Don't you understand?"

"No," I answered bluntly, "how can there be water?"

"It was poured over Poorgbilin's homestead."

"Who poured what over Poorgbilin's homestead?" I could talk in riddles too, if that was what Ikpoom wanted.

Ikpoom lowered his voice. "Water has been poured over Shosho."

I looked at Ikpoom. He obviously thought he was making four out of two and two. I couldn't see it. Half aloud I repeated, "They poured water over Shosho."

"No," Ikpoom corrected.

"You said they did."

"No. I said it was poured." Ikpoom leaned a few inches toward me. "He poured it."

I glared at him. Denying a whole statement because one word was off was one of their favorite tricks. However, Ikpoom had been kind enough to explain which word instead of stopping with a bare "no" as most of them did. They, he, what difference did it make?

My memory began to click. "Yabo!" I ejaculated.

"You know." Ikpoom's voice was deeply satisfied. He went back inside his hut.

I was outside the homestead and on the path before I realized that I still didn't know why I shouldn't go to Poorgbilin's. Yabo had poured water over Shosho. A man's age mates, I knew, when he got above himself, sometimes spoiled his best clothes by pouring beer over him at some dance or market. I couldn't see Shosho taking such treatment from anyone. Anyhow, why wait so long to pour water over him and why not do it before the elders? I didn't see anything so dreadful about that. It was nothing to make Shosho turn gray and reel with fear at the prospect. Why should the elders intervene to save a man a drenching? Water never hurt anyone—not even in flooded rivers. With a shudder I remembered the swollen stream through which Ihugh had dragged me on that premise.

On the path I met Poorgbilin, followed by all his wives carrying household equipment on their heads. "Where are you going?" I demanded.

"To the farms," he replied. "All of us."

"But . . ." In protest I waved at the stuff they were carrying.

"We will sleep out on the farms. We shall stay there permanently until it is finished."

"What is finished?" I hadn't been so hopelessly bewildered by apparently simple, word-of-one-syllable statements since my first arrival.

"Water," replied Poorgbilin, "has entered our homestead." He stopped as though the situation, that one fact given, became self-evident.

"Lots of water?" I asked feebly.

"No," said Poorgbilin, "just Shosho. That is why we are leaving."

While I stood there completely baffled, Poorgbilin and his wives went on. I was still rooted to the spot, when some more people from Poorgbilin's homestead came filing down the path. In the hope of getting a little further with the conversation, I started where the other had ended. "You are going to the farms because of the water?"

"Yes"—this was one of Poorgbilin's talkative brothers. "Who would stay where there is water?"

It might be uncomfortable at that, but they couldn't mean plain, ordinary water. "Is no one staying?" I asked desperately.

"Only his mother. A foolish woman: she heard the elders refuse, and now she tries to make them come."

"I see," I said, not quite truthfully. "Shosho's mother."

They started off down the path. "Hey," I yelped after them, "what about Yabo?"

Over his shoulder Poorgbilin's brother tossed back, "Shosho's mother has gone to plead with him. Perhaps he will come. It is not our affair. We didn't forbid it." They passed out of sight, behind the tall grass.

Well, I told myself stepping out resolutely, there was only one thing to do about this water that had been poured over Shosho in punishment and that was somehow dangerous to others. Go see for myself what had happened to Shosho.

There was a strip of raffia strung across the path turning off into Poorgbilin's. On it were hung various magical emblems, representing the evils that would afflict anyone who might infringe the purpose for which they had been put up. I knew them mainly from the farms, where they hung to prevent theft. If these had been put here to keep people out and I passed under them, I would get dysentery, a bad skin rash and have my nose fall in. Involuntarily hoping they were there for some other reason, I ducked underneath and went rather slowly into the silent homestead. I called. A voice answered feebly from under the eaves of one of the huts. As I went closer, I saw a man was lying on a plank bed. Closer still I recognized Shosho. Still closer. I stopped short.

Smallpox.

"Water," I found myself muttering in a voice I didn't recognize. "Yabo poured water over you."

Smallpox. A disease so dreaded that even my boys would not name it in their own language. A disease caused by witchcraft and considered always fatal unless the witch himself agreed to cure it. "Wait and see," they had all told me. Again coincidence had worked to enhance Yabo's reputation as a witch. It must be coincidence. It had to be.

Shosho spoke with effort. "Yabo, make Yabo come. I will agree to anything. Only make Yabo come. He will laugh at my mother."

Glad of the excuse, I turned to go. For once Yabo had not laughed. He was coming into the homestead with Shosho's mother. Shosho needed taking down a notch. I knew it. But his self-abasement before Yabo made me writhe. Yabo got his apology, and more. Finally Yabo asked the old woman to bring a calabash of water. Before he drank and sprayed out the water in sign of forgiveness, Yabo turned to me. "Do you bear witness, Redwoman, and do you watch me give Shosho medicine. Watch and tell the elders what I have done that they may know I have a good heart. They did not forbid it; nevertheless, I will not kill Shosho."

I hurried back home to hold a series of earnest consultations. My boys, fortunately, had been recently vaccinated. I demanded curiously why no one in Kako's part of the country had been. In their voluble replies, I detected a certain evasiveness which left me uneasy. People were afraid of it, so said my boys, because the vaccination almost always infected badly. This particular end of the country was very "bush"; everyone fled when the administration sent down a vaccination team. Putting on a look of mingled innocence and superiority, my boys said such an attitude was pure foolishness. They themselves could see no reason for it.

I talked with Kako. He heard with interest that Yabo was giving Shosho medicine and, while twisting the affair to Yabo's discredit, had quite a bit else to say. "Yabo wishes to show us that his heart is not bad. One never knows just what Yabo will do." Kako, who never acted on impulse when sober, spoke disapprovingly. "Whenever we do refuse and tell him he must not bewitch, he goes his own way. This time, when we told him that we would not protect Shosho from him, he does not kill." He paused and added in a grumble, "He knows perfectly well Shosho is no good. We would be well rid of him."

"But," I said perplexed, "what about Poorgbilin? What did he do?"

Kako seemed to think I was changing the subject.

"Well," I amplified, "Poorgbilin's whole homestead fled to the farms for fear of the water."

Kako sighed in a way that made me feel especially stupid. "Yabo poured water over Shosho only. Shosho, of course, feels resentment because Poorgbilin withdrew his protection. Therefore, they fear Shosho might in turn bring water to them. Therefore they went away to the farms where they would be out of his reach—for Shosho is young and doesn't know things."

Kako's explanation in words of one syllable had only added another riddle. That Shosho didn't know things meant Shosho was not a witch. Nevertheless, he could cause smallpox, and in the innocent at that. Then they must know the disease was contagious. Perhaps they explained only the first case in terms of witchcraft. Why not? Come to think of it, I didn't know how one could get smallpox without catching it from someone. Of course, Shosho might have been exposed to it at market, or someplace else. But it was their beliefs I was concerned with. There I was confused. I hoped for future enlightenment.

I received none. It was I who had to answer questions, in a conversation that took place so often, with such stereotyped words and glances, that I grew bored with it.

"Tell me, Redwoman, do you not fear to go where there is water?"

"No, for the water cannot touch me." Since my vaccination mark was high on my thigh, I avoided demonstration. "I have had that medicine which protects me."

"Then," with a curious and rather veiled look from the corner of the eyes, "water was once brought to you?"

This seemed a rather good way of putting it. I agreed, adding, "My parents had the water brought to me when I was very young, that I might be strong and never fear water."

This information was usually digested in silence. Several times I was tempted to throw in a lecture on the benefits of vaccination. I never did. Even if I didn't put their backs up, who was there to vaccinate them? Besides it looked as though no one else was coming down with smallpox.

Indeed, Shosho eventually recovered. His hut and everything in it, except the plank bed which was scrubbed and sunned, was burned. Then Poorgbilin and his people moved back. People occasionally referred to the affair, generally when they wished to point out to me how necessary it was to get along with one's kinfolk. "If you keep making trouble, they withdraw their protection. Then you are alone and helpless."

Then Rogo returned. He brought word that the truck would meet me on the road on December twenty-fourth. He also told me that a great smallpox epidemic raged to the north of us: "There is water all over the land, and everywhere people are fleeing before it."

I asked him, as I had asked my other boys, whether he had been vaccinated. Unlike the others, he did not understand the phrase—one invented by the medical missionaries. I looked at his bare arm. The vaccination scar was there, but I still didn't know how long ago it had been done. I resorted to the terms of my standard conversation on the subject. "Rogo, when was water brought to you?"

Rogo shook his head sadly, "My grandfather died before I was old enough to learn such matters."

It was often difficult to keep Rogo to the point. "Look, Rogo," I said firmly, "while you were gone, water was poured over Shosho, and you walked through water on your way back here."

"I walked around it," Rogo corrected. "It is dangerous to walk where people are in fear of water. But I do not fear anything here: it is too far from my own relatives; they cannot bewitch me at this distance. And you, my mother, even if you owed the witches food, you would give them one of your other children before me."

I don't think I did a double-take. I know I grew dizzy. I pointed to the vaccination mark on Rogo's shoulder. "When was that done?"

"That?" It was Rogo's turn to think I was changing the subject. "In the station. Just before you found me at the market of papers. I worked a week for a man; he sent me to the hospital with a paper and this was done."

"It is our medicine," I told him, "to protect you from water."

"That is possible," Rogo said politely. "It is not important." He came to the point. "It is you, my mother, who will protect me from the water. You have told everyone that water was brought to you when you were a child. Even at Nder's they know it. I knew you had a strong heart," his voice held admiration, "but I didn't know you could pour water over others. Now everyone will be afraid of you, and we, your children, will be safe under your protection."

I had been talking about vaccination. People had interpreted what I said in terms of witchcraft. From my words they understood that as a small child my parents had first exposed me to smallpox and then taught me the black art of causing it in others. I had branded myself a witch and a braggart. Humor and perspective lost, I, like Yabo, turned for refuge to an inner and contemptuous superiority over this foolish world. Let them fear me. It had its uses. As long as my work was not impeded, I didn't care. I was past laughter.

Chapter Nineteen

THE HARMATTAN wind blew, persistently, monotonously, flaying us with daily whips of hot dust and dying away every evening only to leave us in a stifling oppression of still red air. No single motes of dust could be seen swimming in the stream of light that poured through my open window. We lived in an aquarium of dust through which we saw the sky gray or primrose, but never blue. In this atmosphere my first exhilaration sank into depression; now and then wind lashed into gusts of irritability as sudden as the dust devils that whirled through the homestead yard.

Soon after dark the wind would rise again, to blow chill through the homestead. Everyone stayed inside by their fires and behind closed doors. My tropical clothes were not proof against this cold, and I was driven early to bed to lie awake shivering under my blanket and listening to the owls. In the mornings I huddled late in bed for warmth, while outside in the chilly gray light, people whispered of the witch owls that had come in the night. There was contagion in their fear. I caught it from my boys, from the people, from Lucia, from the very air. Convinced that the owls were sounding her doom in their nightly chorus, Lucia once more sat and sang her queer, uncanny songs. Worse again, she no longer hoed my bare yard or gathered, as sauce plants, weeds from which she cooked impossible messes for her husband. Lucia's madness showed naked the fears others tried to mask, and her terror worked in turn on our fears.

Whatever caused the tense nervousness that held us all—perhaps it was the wind, perhaps it was the water to the north, perhaps only the tradition that at this time of year the witches returned from their Sabbath—the witch owls would not let it die. I could not help listening to the owls: first in the distance a soft "huu, huu"; a pause, as though waiting for an answer, and then, from the darkness, a reply. Even I thought of them as witch owls when they flew straight toward us to sit outside the homestead in the night, calling—for whom? In the morning people whispered with averted eyes. Someone owed the witches human flesh. They were calling in the night for that debt, and no one knew who the victim would be.

I would not admit that I had been infected by their fears. Because I would not admit that I was nervous, I was angry that my boys were afraid, angry at the sound of the boxes they shifted across their hut door at night. I had a vicious desire to mock their fears into hiding. Only my job forbade it—that, and the knowledge that any open reversion on my part to the European viewpoint that witches did not exist would be taken as the sheerest hypocrisy.

One morning, when I was washing up after sick call, Sunday came in to say that Yabo had brought me a gift of meat. I was pleased. Meat had been difficult to buy lately; chicken and bully beef soon pall. "It was well you told me it was meat, Sunday," I approved. "I will go accept it now, so that it may be cooked at once." It was a very hot day.

Yabo untied a leaf-wrapped bundle. It contained two rather thin slices of liver. Pausing only to yell at Monday to come take the gift to the cook, I added to my thanks a sincere confession that I liked meat. I handed the meat to Monday: "Tell the cook I will eat it now." I resumed my grateful phrases to Yabo. "I never have enough meat. I could eat it every day."

Monday overheard. He looked at me as Luther, without an inkpot handy, might have looked at the Devil: a look of dismay, confirmed belief and despair at having nothing to throw. His appalled face, Yabo's mirthless hoot of appreciative laughter, and the lengthy conferences that my boys held in the kitchen that day made me realize that I had added another unsavory note to my reputation by accepting and eating the meat of so well known and feared a witch.

I knew what I had done. They thought I had accepted human flesh and that I would now owe Yabo a victim. Rogo's blithe confidence that I would kill one of my domestic servants before I killed my scribe drew a grim smile from me. But I made no move to reassure them. Let them think the owls were witches calling me to give them a feast. My boys ought to trust me. Anyhow, owls were just birds. I wrote my jumbled resentment in my diary. Not until I reread it in the station to improve my New Year's resolutions did I see that I had become incapable of thinking or feeling clearly either in their terms or in mine.

I did realize that I was waiting for release like a prisoner. I found myself counting the days too often not to realize it. Perhaps it was unfortunate that I did, for it enabled me to attribute my nervous irritability to the well-known phenomenon of "going bush." It seemed sufficient remedy to vow never again to isolate myself from my own people for more than three months. Meanwhile, I could do nothing but "carry on as usual." I called on my last resources of self-discipline.

Discipline was not enough. I realized that when I found myself talking to the owls.

One chilly night I sat close to my lamp, for warmth as well as light, translating fables. Through the scratch of my pen and the hissing of my lamp, I was very conscious of the hooting of the owls congregated in the distance. Stubbornly, I refused to admit that it made me nervous. After all, I knew owls were just owls. There was nothing I could do about the boys; it was silly to be infected by their fear. It would show a serious lack of discipline to stop my translating and catch up on notes instead, just so that I might have the companionable noise of my typewriter. I concentrated on the page before me. I finished my task. Resolutely, I put out the light and went to bed.

Resolution is sleep's worst enemy. Trying to sleep, I tried to banish all thoughts from my mind. A blank mind was only the more receptive to the sound of calling owls. Suddenly childish, I buried my head under the pillow in an ineffectual attempt to shut out the sound of neighboring doors being barricaded and to seal off the sound that was causing their fear.

The owls disbanded. We could hear them calling to each other as they flew apart. Some came nearer. With a steady, unswerving approach that seemed willed and purposeful, one came toward us, calling, calling, ever closer, past my door to settle in my mango tree. Maddened by Lucia's now hysterical singing, furious that my rest should be disturbed, I jumped out of bed and opened the door. There I checked myself and waited for Kako's voice: it was his homestead; it was for him to tell the witch owls to go away.

I listened in vain. Even Lucia was quiet. The silence was broken only by faint movements in the huts near by and by the hooting of the owl in my mango tree. I was suddenly irritated past endurance—at the owl, at Kako, at myself for standing there. I called petulantly and in English: "Oh, go away." Then, carried away by a whirlwind of temper, I found myself screaming in the language of the country the words I had so often heard. "Go away! I owe you no flesh! I have eaten none of your kin. Go away!"

A taunting, leisurely hoot.

"Beat it, you feathered fool!" The angry American valediction tore from my throat. "Beat it, I said."

The owl soared gracefully from his perch, a dark shadow that was absorbed into the night, and hooted ever more faintly into silence.

I clung to the door, weak and shaken by sheer physical reaction to fear and anger. I tried to pull myself together. "Poe just didn't know how to handle that raven." I bit the sentence short. I must not start talking to myself like this.

To keep from it, I sat down and wrote a letter. I tore it up, the next morning.

The next morning, Rogo and my boys came in delegation. Their long prologue of trivia made me realize they had something of importance to say. I controlled my impatience with difficulty. Only a few more weeks, I reminded myself. It would be a pity to blow up. Still they skirted the subject. I looked at Rogo. He broke in on Sunday's parentheses. "I told them that of course you are a witch but that you will use your witchcraft to protect us."

"It was the owls," Monday blurted out, "the owls and your eating Yabo's meat. Then you chased them last night."

"But we are afraid when they come."

"We want you to go tell Kako and Yabo that the witches must no longer come here as owls."

My thoughts raced. I could not bring myself to give such a message to any man. No one could control the movements of wild birds. Kako would take it seriously, so would everyone else—except the birds. If I delivered such an ultimatum and still the owls returned, my boys would be more terrified than ever. They would distrust either my good intentions or my ability.

"We nearly ran away." Monday was penitent.

I inquired with a look. The cook nodded. "I have been twenty-five years with Europeans, but I have never been with one who was a witch. We are afraid. We will believe you, if you say you mean to protect us. Rogo says you do. But Kako says you mean to increase your prestige among the witches by killing us for a witches' feast."

My eyes blurred with rage. Kako again! So he was still trying to get rid of me. Well, he wouldn't. I waved the boys into silence. I must control my anger if I were to think clearly. It must have been for this reason that Kako did not speak last night when the owl came to my mango tree. And if it hadn't taken flight at my shouting . . . But it had. The first round went to me. There must be no mistake this time. I must do something, and it must leave no loophole for Kako.

I turned to Rogo. "Can Kako, I, or any human being control the birds and animals of the bush?" A plan was slowly forming in my mind.

"Of course not. Only the sprites can do that."

"Never mind the sprites. I ask you this: is it not true that it is only the witch owls that you fear and only the witch owls that can be controlled by man?"

There was a chorus of complete assent. They thought me stupid to stress the obvious, but the distinction was essential to my purpose.

"I cannot control the birds of the bush. I will not try to control the witch owls that come to any other part of this homestead, for it is Kako's homestead. How can I know what lies between him and the other witches?"

Rogo voiced their approval. "That is Kako's affair. He who intervenes in the dispute between a man and his brother is not thanked but severely beaten by them both."

"Then," I insisted, "it is only those witch owls who come to our tree, here, that concern me." I had recalled one of my mother's bird-scaring devices that might just scare owls as well.

"Then leave me, for I must make preparations." I had to do some fast thinking. "Soon I will come outside to perform one of the most potent ceremonies of our country. After it is done, I swear to you"—what is truth? the letter or the spirit?—"that not one witch will come as an owl to sit on your huts or in our mango tree. Any owl that comes thereafter will be naught but a harmless bird of the bush."

Rogo, at least, believed me implicitly. The others had still to be wholly convinced. I looked straight at them. "You yourselves say I am the first European you have met who is a witch."

The cook apologized. "It is more difficult to help than to harm. The witches of our country are old. You are young and a woman."

He was sincere now. So was my reply, "In all the history of our country the worst witches have been young women."

The boys scattered. I sat and thought hard. Despite my

reputation, I might have been able to convince my boys—
if it had not been for Kako. He had started a whispering
campaign against me. I must kill it, thoroughly. I couldn't
afford to let Kako get the upper hand, and I couldn't afford to have my boys run out on me. By hook or by crook
. . . Again I tested my plan. Its success was wholly dependent on the faith I could inspire in myself and the
hocus-pocus I intended.

I walked outside. Kako, the elders who had been with
him in his reception hut, the entire homestead stood about.
Kako shot me a wary glance. "Your children tell us you are
about to forbid the witch owls."

"No owl," I told Kako, "that is not a bush owl will come
here." If I were to carry conviction, I must stick to the
truth, in the letter and in the traditions of the West. I ordered Monday to cut and hack several bright tin cans into
pieces. These were the bird-scarers my mother had used in
her vegetable garden: two bright pieces of metal, strung
together like clappers. "What I do, my ancestors have
taught me," I told Kako.

I sent Sunday off to peel bark for string from certain
plants here believed efficacious against witches. I did not
have to explain this part to them. I assembled the bright
metal clappers and strung them ready to be hung. Again I
turned to Kako. He'd asked for it; it was up to me to make
it good. "This," I said touching the bark, "you know. I
must use it, for the plants of our country do not grow here.
Metal," I said touching the tin, "is feared by witches.
Those witches of our country who transform themselves
into wolves must be killed with a silver bullet. These will
suffice for witch owls."

"We hear, Redwoman, and we learn. Thus far," Kako
was not impressed, "I can do what you have done."

"It might be well if you did so, Kako. Unless you agree
to witch owls, of course." Before he could recover, I drew
a small, obsidian arrowhead—my good-luck charm—from
my pocket. "This is what I prepared within and secretly. I
can tell you only that it is a thing of the people of long

ago, so long ago that the ancestors of my country were not yet born."

Kako was intent now. Everyone watched me closely as I marked a cross on each piece of metal. "To ward off evil." I used the deep, sepulchral tone they adopt for magical purposes. I inscribed a rather crude magical pentacle on the obverse sides of the metal pieces. "What was known by those of old and feared by witches."

An incantation was necessary now. I prayed, and I prayed sincerely—for I was not sure that what I was doing would succeed or that it was right. For better effect, and to keep in the spirit of the thing, I kept to Latin. Twice I repeated the paternoster. I continued, for they hadn't had enough, with snatches remembered from the Vulgate: fragments of Psalms, snippets from the Song of Songs. Still too brief by their standards. I repeated myself. Suddenly, by unconscious and imperceptible transition from Solomon's Song I found myself in the midst of one of Catullus' more impassioned love lyrics. The sudden awareness of the incongruity between means and end, the quiet schoolroom where I had learned and the present scene in which I repeated, brought me to an abrupt stop.

In any case, it was enough. I had the bits of metal hung, some in the mango tree, one by each hut door. I noticed that the boys were careful to place them where no one could accidentally brush against them, and Monday, before he would agree to climb the mango tree holding my charms, insisted on being touched by my arrowhead.

I was pleased with myself, and I had a second drink in self-congratulation. I had convinced my boys that only bush owls would come near us. And I thought I had put up a good performance. I scowled at the thought of Kako's unscrupulous attempt to terrify my boys. He was clever. I was rather uneasy about him. He would have no hesitation in taking advantage of any weakness he could find in me. I was too absorbed in my duel with Kako to consider the morning's events in any other light.

The next few nights were owl-less. I couldn't count on

such continuing good fortune. Kako's "Wait and see" attitude still bothered me. I hoped something would turn up to take our minds off owls. Something soon happened, but the owls got mixed up in it before it was over.

One day Kako came to tell me that a skilled "cutter" had come to circumcise all the boys in the homestead. I nerved myself to witness, and tried to drum up some enthusiasm by telling myself I was lucky to have the chance. In a tribe where there are no bush schools, no regular circumcision ceremonies, only a conviction that men must be circumcised before they had anything to do with women, an opportunity to see the thing done and make sure that what they had told me was so could only happen by chance. Still, I didn't relish it.

However, Accident, who was among those to be operated on, was almost exuberant at the prospect. "Then I shall be a man," he told me proudly. With all the energy of his eight years he ran round and round the homestead with a boasting shout, "After tomorrow let all women beware of me. Oi! But I shall be a man indeed!"

We met early the next morning—blood, like oil, congeals in the chill of the morning; no one would perform such an operation at noon when the blood flows freely. We all watched Kako manipulate ritual symbols as he ceremonially removed all magical danger from the fourteen boys. If all magical precautions were taken and witches were successfully warded off, there could be no danger in the operation.

Men, women and children gathered around to watch and hearten the lads. Myself pale and shaken from mere watching, I paid full tribute to the endurance they showed. Most of the boys bit their lips in silence; any stifled moan that escaped them was drowned in the shouted encouragement of the by-standers: "Have courage!" "Strengthen your heart!" "Now you are a man!" A few, like Accident, managed to gasp out faint bawdiness, "Whittle carefully there. Many women shall judge your work!" No matter how feeble the jest, such sallies were greeted with great applause. "Our little brother has a strong heart." "He who jokes under the knife will not fear lions."

Their courage put me to shame. My stomach, queasy and rebellious, shoved my heart into my throat. Vividly, almost blotting out the sight before me, I saw the old English prints: the patient strapped to the operating table, the solicitous relatives, the grim surgeon, the bottle that was the only shield against the shock of pain. I couldn't have taken it. My knees shook. This could be done at the hospital. Such pain was unnecessary. Accident had proved his courage. My father's voice rose out of the past: "Grin and bear it." Learn to laugh on the gallows. But why stand on the gallows? Accident's mother had watched, apparently unmoved. "It is nothing, my son." But her knees were shaking too.

No, it was not callousness. Not exactly. Not the callousness of a single heart, but the callousness of a whole culture, a protection against the pain that had to be borne. Like their bare, horny feet. I couldn't walk where they did. Taking advantage of a man's blindness to make him jump was part of it. Laugh at the man on the gallows, for you may stand there tomorrow. I was used to shoes and anesthetics, had a thin skin and thin nerves and feared cruel laughter.

The smallest boy, only three, was screaming his heart out. Beside me his mother turned away, held on to me. "He is not old enough. He doesn't know. He can't understand. He does not know it must be. How, then, can he jest? How can he be brave?"

What must be, can be endured. Of all the people there, only I knew it didn't have to be. They had not learned to cry in their anguish, "This must not be! Surely there must be a way!" That rebellious cry had encouraged us to find a way. I had been used to mock at visionaries and reformers. Face to face with the alternative, I was humbled. I myself was not one who cried, "There must be a way." I had never seen the need, for I had been born to a pleasant world. But here—where people said, "It must be as it is. It must be endured": where their only solution was "Grin and bear it," where I could not say, "This is the best of all possible worlds"—here I was forced to consider the possibility that even my world might be improved. I banished the thought. I had grown fearful of the constant temptation to question my own values that these people and this world afforded me.

Kako was talking at me. I hadn't been listening, and had to ask him to repeat. The boys were being taken into his reception hut, where he could protect them against witches, where their elder brothers could tend them, and where the women would find it easier to feed them the special diet that was thought to expedite their healing.

That night the owls came again, a dark horde of owls, calling, mocking us from the trees. Lucia was nearly frantic. Kako himself stood out in the middle of the homestead yard, bellowing at the owls, "Go away! There is nothing here for you. The blood you smell is not for you. Go away. I refuse. Go!" Ikpoom was grappling with Lucia. With all the noise, the owls did go away. That time. But they came back twice during the night.

In the morning people conferred together in anxious little clusters. There was no doubt in anyone's mind that the witches had been seeking to attack the newly circumcised boys, for they were in an unusually vulnerable condition. Only my own household looked happier. Not a single owl had perched around our huts or in our tree. I put little reliance on this: the owls had been hooting from the trees around the homestead; not a single owl had actually come into the yard. For this measure of aloofness, Kako got all the credit. Until a bit later in the morning.

Kako was worried by this attempt against the circumcised boys. He came to ask me if I had any medicine for them. While we were standing talking under my mango tree, my bird-scaring tin cans twirling in the wind and clattering above us, Yabo came into the homestead. Kako watched his advance with deep suspicion. Reserve broken under his load of worries, he muttered in my ear, "That's the man. It's he who led the witches last night. It's he who is my enemy and would like to be in my place. Don't let him fool you, Redwoman; he thinks himself stronger than either of us. You would be wise to stick with me. What can your charms do against him?"

Just then Yabo looked up and over at us. The metal hanging from the mango tree glinted in the sun, bright mirrors for its beams. Yabo, looking straight at them in curiosity—for he had not witnessed my conjuring—put a startled hand up to his eyes. Yabo was surprised into loud speech: "Something has pierced my eye!"

We all turned to watch him. Again he looked to see. Once more, as from a flashing mirror, light beat against his astonished gaze. "What is it, Redwoman?" he growled. "What do you keep there that strikes people in the eyes?"

Kako chuckled. "What's the matter, Yabo? Are you surprised that what is done by night can be seen by day?"

Yabo growled some contemptuous nastiness, but he held his eyes carefully averted as he walked toward us.

"Or do you not know, Yabo," Kako mocked him, "that owls came here last night and that Redwoman does not agree to owls."

"Redwoman." Yabo's pronunciation dismissed me.

"Yes, Yabo, Redwoman." Kako patted me on the shoulder. "You and I have taught her well. She has too strong a heart to worry for herself. Only when her children were frightened"—a nice way of describing the panic he had tried to instigate among them—"did she put up that which protects." He waved at the bright metal above him, before he added with meaning: "It is odd, Yabo, that this which protects against owls has hit no one else."

I tried not to show my relief. I was less than ever sure how far Kako had been taken in by my mumbo jumbo. It didn't really matter. It had become politic for Kako to announce publicly that my charms were real and potent. I no longer had to fear the effect of witch owls on my boys.

Yabo was leaning on his spear. He considered us as we stood there. Then, as he had done at Amara's funeral, he

262

took the credit of false accusation. He did not deny Kako's words. He countered with a single retort. "In that case, Kako, you had best move into Redwoman's reception hut."

Kako didn't. But for ten days my reception hut was full of freshly circumcised boys. And for the first time, Kako called me "friend." It did not occur to me to doubt his insincerity.

Chapter Twenty

I BEGAN to notice the strangers. Everywhere I went there were visiting relatives, many of them with their wives and children. Even Yabo's homestead was full again, full of strangers and distant kin. I could imagine no reason for such a vast gathering, yet I could not think it altogether chance. I asked everywhere, and everywhere I was told, "One likes to see one's kinsmen." One or two answered obliquely, "This is a good country." Superficial answers, all of them, which I could not penetrate. The strangers had not come together. Each of them might have come for the reason he said. Yet never before had there been a similar gathering, never before such movement of people around the countryside. And over them all was a faint air of uneasiness, as fine, thin and unmistakably present as the harmattan dust which covered us all.

Possibly I was attributing my own nervy irritation to them. I didn't think so. Their jesting was edged; their laughter was forced. People who had always rubbed along smoothly now seemed to feel some grittiness between them, some irritant that turned their lightest teasing into anger. Once or twice it occurred to me that like myself they were waiting for something, but for something unpleasant. Then I dismissed the thought and told myself that the taint of suspicion I sensed lay in the strangers who did not know me or what I was doing. There were so many strangers. It was almost like the first weeks I had spent here, when every face was unknown and every heart secret.

Only Kako's behavior convinced me that there was something wrong. Kako, whose hospitality was renowned, was refusing people food. Kako, who liked to impress travelers with his generosity, was driving harmless, perfectly well-behaved strangers out of his homestead and out of his chiefdom. Strangest of all, the very people who most deplored any sign of stinginess in a chief were praising him for his present meanness. Kako's temper, usually so well controlled, had grown short and uncertain. I turned to Udama with my inquiries. She was brusque in reply. "Those people wouldn't do anything to you or Kako. It is to protect the rest of us that he sends them away." Her answer told me only that her nerves also were frayed.

Once more I turned to Yabo. One would have to add much more than a grain of salt to anything he said about Kako, but if it were to Kako's discredit, he would certainly tell me. Nevertheless, Yabo hesitated to commit himself until I repeated Udama's comment. Yabo leered, "To protect others, indeed, only to protect others. Do you see me, who can indeed protect others, turning strangers away from my household? No, for I am strong."

Of a sudden Yabo was sober. "They are fleeing from the water. It is coming very near." The seriousness of his voice and face made me feel that we were on a perilous sandbank of safety, a refuge over which the water might soon, at any time, rise.

From Yabo I heard how the smallpox was spreading, coming ever closer. People who lived next to the infected areas were fleeing to kinsmen who were still more remote from the danger. If they fled in time, they found refuge. But once the epidemic struck, they could not escape. None would receive them. These were the men I had seen Kako chase. Only one place must they be accepted: in the land of their fathers' and their fathers' fathers before them. Thence they could not be driven. "But," said Yabo, "there they may be killed."

"Why should you fear the water, Yabo?" Shosho's lesson was on the tip of my tongue.

265

"Need you ask?" Yabo's gaze was deep and curious. "Who does not know the terror and the death and the hate that it brings? I fear nothing else, but I fear the water." And Yabo looked to the north whence the water was spreading. "Do you not know that fear, you of your country?"

"Once we did. Long ago." I stopped short and left him. His question evoked words in my mind—plague and pest—words that I would gladly have forgotten. They come from a distant past, but horror still clings to them. Not here, and not to me; it could not happen. Protest was vain. I too looked to the north.

The somber countryside suited my thoughts. Since the end of the rains, the grass had been slowly, almost imperceptibly dying. Now the remaining green looked shabby under the dry, tall stalks that scabbed the living vegetation with a dead brown. Lest their homes be consumed by fire, people had burned the strips of grass around the homesteads early, while there was still moisture in the ground. Now, every evening when the wind sank, the bush was fired. We were surrounded by a reddened sky, even while the true sunset was obscured with smoke and dust. The nights were lurid with fires marching rapaciously through the dry grass. By day we saw the fire's path black on the ground, black trees and sullenly smoldering stumps. Flame-withered, fire-reddened leaves rustled to the ground to gossip with those already fallen—a fellowship of whispering ghosts. Only the cane grass still stood, lifeless rods of pale brown against the black earth.

While I walked through the dying landscape, I tried to weigh Yabo's news calmly, objectively. I must separate the real from the shadow threat. Our vaccinations probably assured the physical safety of my boys and myself. It was their state of mind I had to worry about. The owl incident had proved that their fear of witchcraft was easily worked on, and smallpox was its most virulent manifestation. On the other hand, the owl incident had also proved my good will toward them. The unknown and unknowable factor remained: the people themselves. How calm would they remain? So far this was still a place of refuge. If people here began to flee . . .

Well, there was nothing to do but wait for the truck. Two more weeks. I could not know how fast smallpox might spread. Who of us can remember? However, they seemed to be taking sensible isolation precautions. If no one were allowed in from the areas where the disease was already rampant, surely it could not spread. At least not very rapidly.

And so, for a while, it seemed. The water came no nearer —by now I thought of smallpox as water, as a treacherous, hungry sea beating steadily against crumbling dikes. Too long tensed against danger, foreseen but unpredictable and invincible, nerves frayed and broke. Day and night we heard—not singing nor laughter, nor the pleasant, merry patter of rain through the leaves—but the voracious fires crunching the dry grass like celery stalks and sharp voices in thrust and riposte, crackling with quick, explosive anger.

The smallpox spread: only two miles now. Kako's market was deserted. The strangers began to leave, moving still further from danger, only to halt and return again. There was smallpox all about. We were islanded, save for a few slim bridges that led out into an unknown distance. At the first advance of the water, the countryside had seethed and boiled with the movement of people fleeing before it. Now almost all movement had ceased. We were cut off from news. Kako allowed no more strangers in and those now in safety, however threatened, feared to wander in search of greater safety lest they find greater peril.

The magical symbols that I had seen hung before Poorgbilin's homestead when Shosho had smallpox now hung across the paths, demarking Kako's limited domain of safety. No stranger could pass through these barriers without peril to himself. We were as though besieged, without hope of succor. The enemy might pass us by. Otherwise we were lost; we had no weapons with which to fight. I had to think in such analogies. The only horror known to our generation in the West is the horror of war. But the people around me knew, and knew directly, what it was that they feared. I couldn't tell whether they lacked faith in their magical bulwarks against outside evil or whether they feared treachery within. I knew they were afraid. Fear crept shadowlike over their faces; it jerked at their gestures, sharpened their voices and sapped their hearts. Fear eddied in the air like the black smuts from the burning grass; it marked us all and left the sign for others to read.

Fear kept my eyes on my calendar. Fear drove the boys to me, every day, to ask, "How long now?" Only one more week. Seven days. "Wait for the truck," we told each other. "It isn't long now. Nothing can happen in so short a time." And what else could we do? Walk up the road to meet the truck? On the road we would find neither food nor shelter. On either side there was, or might be, smallpox. Nevertheless, I arranged with Kako for carriers, a task I usually left till a day or two before I was to leave. Just having their names in my book seemed to us all to bring the day of escape nearer.

Five more days, four more—then the smallpox came, and came to our very doors. I was standing under my mango tree, dispensing medicines for stomach aches and headaches and sores. It was the late afternoon, when women pound yams for the evening meal, when men sit about resting, and the children play through the homestead, telling riddles, chasing each other, climbing trees. From the tall, temptingly branched locust tree just outside the homestead, we heard the shrill news screamed out. "Water!"

The word touched us into silent statues, grotesquely figuring interrupted movement. Then, eyes widened and nostrils dilated, our heads turned.

"Water! Saar has it. On his face, his body. Here, on the path. I can see."

They ran. Scrambling to their feet, dropping everything they held, they ran far behind the huts on the other side of the homestead. Kako ran into his hut, stumbling over the threshold. My boys ran, to stand clustered close behind me. Only Lucia stood still, laughing hysterically.

"Water! Don't you hear it? It's water, here, on the path."

While the boy's terrified voice still shrilled danger, Kako came running back out to face it. In his right hand he had his most powerful magic; he swung the heavy, soot-blackened pot before him like a censer. In his left he bore a frond of the leafy plant that protects against witchcraft.

Running, Kako went to turn back danger. He was afraid, but he ran forward, shouting hoarsely, "I forbid you to enter. By that which I carry, I forbid you to enter." He was at the path entrance now. "I forbid evil to enter. You, our child, have brought evil to the land of your fathers. Once before you brought hate to this homestead and I sent you forth." It was Saar, Saar who had hated Ticha and been sent from the land. "Again I forbid you to enter. Go to the farms! You shall walk alone and sleep alone. Let all men shun you, for you have brought evil among us."

As though Kako's voice were a shield, some of the braver men crept back into the homestead yard. "Go!" Kako's voice was a stern imperative. "Go alone to the farms. None shall visit you nor speak to you. Go!"

I could not see what was on the path. I had no power to move from where I stood.

"He's going!" Another shrill cry from the tree. A few more people came back into the homestead. Kako was digging a hole in the path; there he placed the sacred plant by which he had adjured Saar, who would have brought evil among us. Silently, gradually—as though speech and movement were forgotten arts that must be learned again and slowly—the men drifted toward my mango tree. I was the first to speak. In the shock of crisis I obeyed the peculiar Western notion that one should go on as though nothing had happened. "Does anyone else want any medicine tonight?"

"Have you medicine for death, Redwoman?" Ihugh was derisive.

Question and counterquestion undammed a torrent of

voices, blaming, accusing, in a confused roar of speech. Saar had left with hate in his heart. Saar had gone where there was smallpox—in their horror they uttered that deadly word. He must have gone there deliberately, deliberately to bring back smallpox. He was evil. His heart craved vengeance. He wanted to kill his people, his own kinsmen. Why else would he have gone where there was smallpox? He had eaten the food of witches. He was a witch. Who else would deliberately take up water?

There was no pity here. Kako had turned back the evil of smallpox, but hate and fear had crept through his defenses. Exhausted, Kako had crept back into his reception hut, speaking no word of reassurance to his people. There were hasty movements in and among the huts. Again, as before at Yabo's and at Poorgbilin's, women were tying together a few poor belongings and preparing to flee. Not courage marked out who would stay, but smallpox. Udama left, without a word to husband or children. Ihugh's new wife rocked back and forth in an agony of terror. "A husband whom I do not know, and there is smallpox at my father's." Ihugh noticed her as soon as I did. He strode to her: "Go! or shut up!" Still she cried. Only those who thought their fathers' homes still free from the disease had any place to go. The rest were caught between two fires, like Ihugh's wife. One blow silenced her. Ihugh slid her unconscious body into the hut.

I stood on underneath the mango tree, mind too numb to translate what my eyes and ears told me. I saw the women leaving. None took their children, for a child has right only in his father's homestead. Without comprehension I watched the men cutting inches from the low thatch above their doors, saw them examine the doorway itself minutely. "What is it?" I mumbled to my boys. They were paralyzed with fear. Only Rogo gave a sudden, sharp grunt. He went to my kitchen, got my matchet, and started to trim the thatch on our huts.

Lucia was struggling madly in the arms of her husband. I heard and saw her frantic terror and knew Ikpoom's soothing words to her as false as those of a captain calming passengers in a shipwreck. Lucia was too lost in terror and madness to understand her husband's confident words, but she could sense his fear. She twisted wildly from him and ran screaming out of the homestead straight over the sere, burned land and into the tinder bush. Like a man who sees something precious fall from his hand into perilous water, Ikpoom stood and stared for an infinite second before he plunged after her.

It was not yet dark, but already those who still remained, went into their huts and barricaded the doors behind them, after a last, long look at the threshold. Ihugh stepped back out again. He came over to me. He glanced at Rogo's work. "You too are my mother, Redwoman, and you remain. I will make sure." He bent over to examine every splinter in my rough door. "It's all right. Don't go out in the night. Don't leave your hut in the morning until you have looked."

"What is it?" Fear held me close now, and everything I could not understand was terrible.

Rogo answered. "They are afraid Saar will come in the night." He went on, with an occasional helping word from Ihugh. I listened in silence, feeling my mind cleared and sharpened by the day's shocks. Yet, like one who has suffered shock, I thought myself more self-possessed than I was and longed for the false relief of hysterical laughter.

Indeed, they knew smallpox was contagious, or rather, they knew how to make it so. They knew of vaccination. They knew it well. Only the purpose was different—homicide.

Smallpox can be given in two ways: by witchcraft, as Yabo had given it to Shosho, and by "vaccination." Take a splinter, dip it into your own pus-filled sores, creep in the night into the silent, sleeping homestead and place these envenomed darts in the thatch and doorways of your friends and kinsmen so that in the morning the poisoned sliver will pierce them. Why should you suffer alone? Give them all smallpox: to your wives, your brothers, your par-

271

ents and your children. You were given smallpox thus, or by witchcraft. And if you cannot avenge yourself on the witch himself, take vengeance on those whom he loves, kill all his dependents so he will have to sit alone, in a silent homestead. If you do not know the witch, you know at least that he must be among your closest kin. No one else has the power. You may kill a few of the innocent; they may be those dearest to you. But they are not really innocent, not really dear—or they would have protected you.

Terror and death and hate. Terror and death and hate. Yabo's words tolled through my mind and heart all that night. I sat in the cold white light of my hut, behind barred doors and windows. I too was afraid. Afraid of fear, afraid of hate and most afraid of that wretched outlaw Saar, driven out in his misery to live or die as best he might, quite alone. He had a shelter of sorts, the thatched roof built on every farm. He would have no fire, no food, no vessel in which to carry water even if he had the strength to go for it. He must be very cold. I was cold, here in my hut. And I was afraid, afraid to take him succor, and cold with fear lest he come to me seeking help. In every sound I heard the footfall of a hideous figure creeping into that moonlit homestead to crouch in the black shadow by the doorway, black hate in his heart. I was afraid. I had no medicine, could give him nothing. Thus denied, that hate might turn against me too. Terror and death and hate; the words whispered over.

I could give him food and water. I should take food and water to him. Protected by vaccination from disease, knowing it a terrible moral wrong to abandon the needy and helpless, I could have no excuse. He must be helped. I could not. If it were known that I had been with him, who would give me food and water, who would stay with me, who would protect me against the hate and fear in which I too would then be included?

I had been ostracized merely for visiting the witch Yabo. Under these circumstances, I could not foresee the penalty but I could guess its terror-driven severity. Fear makes every man cruel, and there was a great fear abroad to-night, the like of which I had never dreamed. Only for one purpose would anyone now visit Saar. That anyone would be a witch—no one else could be safe—and that purpose would be to acquire smallpox venom in order to infect those whom he could not bewitch, because they were not his kinsmen. And I, a stranger and for my actions considered a witch, would indeed fit the description. I was the person. They would assume the purpose. Every accusation that had been shouted against Saar would be shouted against me.

In the cold light of dawn, weary of the torment of mind and heart that had driven me pacing the night about my hut, I knew myself a coward. It would be extremely dangerous to go to Saar's aid, dangerous for myself and even more dangerous for my boys whose only protection I was. I knew too much of the panic that could hold these people in its grip, too well how easily they slipped the control of their elders, not to be afraid. At the best it would mean abandoning my job in this community: no one would ever again accept me after an action so evil in their eyes. At the worst it might mean an arrow in my back. There was no doubt in my mind—and there is none now—that it would have been foolhardy in the extreme to go to Saar's assistance. There was no doubt in my mind—and there is none now—that by leaving him to his fate I denied the greatest of our moral values: one must not withhold help which it is in one's power to give. The dilemma was naked before me, and before it I shrank back in naked inadequacy.

Shriveled with my own futility, I crept out into the light. There was some absurdity in the way doors were slowly opened, the way heads cautiously peered out to make a painstaking scrutiny of every projection, every roughness on the door where the deadly poison might lurk. Men wandered miserably about seeking some more fortunate brother or uncle whose wife was still with him and who would have cooked food to share. My boys' faces were pinched with hunger; they had been fed by Udama, and

273

she had run away. Ihugh brought them food. "It is not well cooked. I could not beat all the fear out of my wife."

Across the homestead yard, I could see Iripa, one of the younger matrons of the homestead, sulkily throwing more tubers into her mortar to be pounded as the hungry crowd of relatives gathered about her husband. Her two children, both terribly disfigured by yaws, sat listlessly at her feet.

"You must leave, Redwoman, now, today." I had never seen Ihugh afraid. He was not afraid now. One can fear only so long as one can still hope. "I will carry for you, and my younger brother. Ikpoom, too, and Cholo."

"But I have the names of ten who would carry for me." Ihugh just looked at me. "I must have six at least." Then I remembered. Cowardice might be the greater part of prudence, but I need not be wholly a coward. I need not take escape at any price. "Listen, Ihugh, it is on the third day that the truck comes to the road. I do not leave until then."

Across the yard Iripa pounded yams and sang a mean little song: her husband's relatives were consuming her food, even as the locusts consume the grain. It suited the day: this creeping, unconquerable plague, all the more terrible for its associations with evil and witchcraft, was contaminating us all.

"I have no cause to fear the water."

"Redwoman, can't you understand!" Ihugh's enormous hand held me by the shoulder and shook me in exasperation. I didn't mind. For all my words, I was afraid, and Ihugh was an ally against my fear. "When the water comes thus . . ."

"I couldn't find her," the voice at our elbows was exhausted. I turned to see Ikpoom, sooty from the burned land, scratched by the dry cane grass, his face drawn with weariness. "I couldn't find my wife, and what will happen to her? She is mad; she cannot take care of herself. And now, now," there was agony in his voice, "when brother turns against brother, when the water destroys the land with death and terror, what will become of her? She is alone and lost and I cannot find her."

"No one will harm her, Ikpoom." Ihugh was gentle. "All those who see her will know that she is among those hated by the witches. Go eat, and rest."

Each additional grief twisted my heart; I hated myself for having little sensibilities about which I could do nothing.

Ikpoom wandered over to join the group around Iripa. Her husband offered him food. Iripa slammed down the pestle, cracking it viciously against the sides of the mortar. "Where has Ikpoom been all night? Where? Am I to feed those who come bringing water to the homestead?"

"I go to summon Cholo." Ihugh went, and I didn't try to stop him.

"Answer us, Ikpoom, where have you been and what evil do you bring?" A confused babble was Iripa's only answer. Ikpoom was too weary to raise his voice, but the rest—even those who said they believed him—were too afraid to be sure, and yet themselves too tired to deny his reasonable statement that one who wishes evil does not come to do it during the daytime.

While they still hesitated, Iripa raised her voice in rapid, hysterical accusation. Now she was waving her six-foot mahogany pestle, still aimlessly, still merely gesturing. One of her children came over to Ikpoom. All the children liked him, for he was kind. Ikpoom put his hand on the child's shoulder.

"Leave my child alone, you!"

Taken aback, Ikpoom just stared at the furious woman, his hand still on her child.

"Leave my child alone!" Using that formidable pestle as a club, Iripa gave Ikpoom a mighty blow on the head. The berserk light was in her eye. Even while Ikpoom was still falling, she started to lay about among the other men, twirling the pestle about her head, screaming obscenities, strong with hate and frantic with fear. The men scattered, ran from her, hid. Only her child sat crying by Ikpoom's unconscious figure.

Now Iripa's husband, armed with a tremendous log of firewood, came up behind her. He called. She turned, caught the blow full across her stomach, and doubled up like a bolster hanging across the line. He paused only to fling the pestle safely out of his wife's reach; then he made straight for Ikpoom, his relative. Now everyone was out in the yard, excited, jabbering, shocked. "She must go." "We will not have such women here." "Ikpoom must go. He brought water." "Chase them both out." "Ikpoom went for water." "He was gone all night." "They are both evil." Fear made them cruel.

Ikpoom staggered to his feet. "I'm going. I have brought no evil here. It is you who have done evil to me. But I'm going. And when I find my wife, I'll return, do you hear?"

Perhaps to that crowd of nervous, frightened people there was some menace in his voice, or perhaps it was just the shadow of fear and hate that lay over us all. They turned on him: "Get out! Get out!" And they chased him out as hounds chase a hare, until Ikpoom, like his wife, disappeared into the dead grass beyond the homestead.

While they still shouted over Iripa's moaning, writhing body, I too decided to go. "Pack," I told the boys, "pack quickly." I believed Ihugh now, and Ikpoom was gone. "Only three loads; what you want you must take yourselves."

They had kicked Iripa to her feet and were chasing her as they had chased Ikpoom. Kako rushed out. He began to shout for silence. "My children . . ." he began but he did not finish.

There was a high-pitched call from the distance. "Kaakooooo. Kaaaa-kooool" Somewhere there was death or danger. Only then does a man stand in the middle of his homestead, raise his voice and pitch it to shout a heralded message understandable for over a mile, though it can be heard even further. "Kaaa-kooo!"

"Where's Ihugh?" rasped Kako. "His voice is the loudest for answer."

"Gone for Cholo," I heard myself say. "I am going."

"It is well."

"Kaaa-kooo!" In this manner word of war, of dangerous game, of any disaster is rapidly relayed across the countryside. "Kaakooo!"

"It's from Poorgbilin's," someone muttered.

Ihugh came back, with Cholo and a stranger.

"Ihugh!" Kako yelled at him. "Come to listen and reply."

"What shall we pack?" Sunday was stupid with panic.

"Kaaa-kooo!"

"Kaakooo hears!" Ihugh's voice, pitched and vibrant, penetrated our ears, shutting out the senseless babble of the homestead and carrying far across farm and homestead.

"Kaa-koo. It is our brother Apu who has called. There is water in his homestead."

Kako stood at Ihugh's elbow while the message was thrice repeated, and muttered the reply in Ihugh's ear.

"Apuu. Apuuuu! You are to sit in your own huts and on your own farms."

"Sunday!" He was gray and afraid and useless. "Sunday! hear me!" I swore. "Rogo!" He was afraid, but he trusted me, and he heard. "Rogo. Tell this fool to come to his senses or I'll have him beaten, I'll give him to the witches!" Fear made us all cruel.

Terror and death and hate. Ihugh's wife stumbled from her hut, and collapsed on the path sobbing, afraid to go, afraid to stay.

"Kaa-kooo!" Another call, from another homestead. "Kaaa-kooo!"

"Kaakoo hears."

"One box with food and the water filter. Make him listen, Rogo."

"Kaa-koo! It is Tar. A woman, our daughter, was given water by her husband and has brought it here. Kaa-koooo! The smallpox has come to our homestead."

"The bed, net and blankets. Clothes for the station."

"Kako hears. Send her to the farms and sit alone."

"There are four to carry. I have told you three loads. The fourth I will pack myself." My notes. I felt myself a refugee, intent on saving what was most precious.

"Children of Kakooo!" Ihugh's voice swept the countryside. "Children of Kaa-kooo! I call you all!"

Cholo grasped my wrist. "Yabo asks: have you learned that which you did not know?"

Terror and death and hate.

"I am learning, Cholo, fast. And Yabo?"

"Sits armed in his reception hut."

"Children of Kaa-kooo! Water has entered our land. You are to sit alone and walk alone. You shall visit none and speak to none. Children of Kako. Do you hear?"

"We hear." The response from the nearest homesteads. Then they called to those further away. "Children of Kaakooo!" The call was taken up from Poorgbilin's from Yabo's. "Water has entered our land." It was shouted and re-echoed ever further into the distance. "You are to sit alone and walk alone." Till it became indistinct. "Visit none, speak to none." And we could hear no more.

Kako had not forgotten me. "It is not safe here," he whispered. "You must go to the station. Through Nder's. It is the only way. They will think I and Yabo—all of us who are elders and witches—have agreed to the water. Go back to the station, Redwoman, but tell us that you will return and that you do not agree to the murder of witches."

"You speak my heart. Have Ihugh tell them." While I packed my notes, while Ihugh's loud voice rang through my hut, I still heard Yabo's voice—"Terror and death and hate. I fear nothing else, but I fear the water"—and Cholo's —"He sits armed in his reception hut." We ourselves have seen fear rule the mob. There was fear, here, and the mob. And the elders were the witches: Kako, Yabo, Tar, Poorgbilin. "Witches are only people." "One must kill before one is killed."

"Redwoman!" It was Rogo. "Hurry. Ihugh and Cholo

are holding Yabo's guest by the wrists. If you do not hurry, he will flee."

"I come." I thrust my last papers hurriedly into the box. My boys were outside, each with a small sleeping mat on his head. Ihugh led the way. Cholo drove his father's "guest" before him. We paid no heed to the heat of the day. There was terror behind us, and we fled. Everywhere we saw the magical symbols that marked danger but had failed to ward it off. Here there were some people out on the farms. Smallpox had entered their homesteads. They had left brothers and children and wives to die, and fled here for refuge.

"*Dies irae,* day of wrath." I kept time to my walking. "Day of wrath and fear."

"Water, water!" A warning call perhaps, or the plea of the sick and thirsty, from the something huddled under the farm shelter. "Water!" We didn't stop to see.

We entered no homestead. "If there is no water among them," Ihugh warned me, "they will think we bring it."

We needed shade and we needed rest. "I will go. The water cannot touch me."

"An arrow can."

I kept on the path. Remembered words in my ear set the pace. "He sits armed, in his hut. *Dies irae.* He sits armed. Day of wrath, day of fear."

There were people on the path now, with their possessions on their heads. Some were wives fleeing from their husbands. Some were whole families fleeing from an outbreak in the homestead itself. Here we met a dreadful hurrying panic.

"*Timor mortis conturbat me.*" My feet marched on; independent, seeking safety. "The fear of death . . ." Not the death of one person. Not the death of Amara. That was grief, and sanity, and the decency of human love. Not this terror. "*Dies irae.* Day of wrath." Terror and death and hate.

The heralding calls from the homesteads where the dread plague had struck sang us on our way. The sun sank low.

We skirted a homestead. There were people within it, but they were filled with a terrible, defeated lassitude. "Water, water."

It must be thus when empires fall, and a whole society goes crashing into ruin. The fear that tears father from child, brother from brother, husband from wife. Where there is no law but nightmare.

In the gray harmattan dusk we parlayed outside a homestead. It was free of disease. But they would not take us in. "Where shall we sleep?"

"There is danger here." Ihugh whispered in my ear as he had whispered when we walked through the market place where there had been fire. "There is a moon. We will rest on the path, till we can walk again. Come, Redwoman."

We walked. First one foot and then the other. It was very important to remember that. I sank down on the path. "We must rest." Sunday had packed six cans of sardines and two of bully beef. The cook had brought some bread. The nine of us shared food in the cold night and moonlight.

We went on again. I was limping, but I walked on. There was no refuge here. "The fear of death . . ." The old medieval songs clanged in my ears. *Timor mortis conturbat me.* We have no vocabulary left for terror. We live safe. "Day of wrath." Our tragedy is the death of one. "Day of fear." We turn for amusement to the old accounts of the plague and the pest. "That day of weeping." Europe conquered the pesthouse and created Belsen. "That terrible day, when the earth shall be shaken." And people run screaming from each other, when fear transforms kinsmen into frightened strangers and enemies.

We fled through the night, till I could go no further. By a stream, where the path had been beaten wide by bathers' feet, we rested for what remained of the night: I lay on my bed, with the eight who were with me on the ground about me. At dawn we started again. All day we walked over the hot dry paths through a desolate burned country, empty of life and laughter. At midday we rested again by a stream and watched the people pass, all going the same way in groups of three and four. They too were fleeing from the smallpox. None paused to speak with us. They passed with a swift side glance of mingled fear and curiosity, took a quick handful of water to drink from the stream, and then went on.

We followed. Still we saw no one working on the farms. There was smallpox here too. But here people could still flee. They were not yet isolated. We became sure of escape, and my thoughts turned again to their analogies to press and urge my feet forward. We were refugees fleeing before an invasion. We were soon to reach freedom. But it was not so: our welcome was not the welcome given to fugitives from war, but the welcome given those who have fled the plague and may bear it with them. No one would take us in; no one would give us food; no one would let us rest in the shade of his tree.

On and on. There is no stronger emotion than terror, but there is one thing greater than terror: fatigue. We walked. There was nothing left in our minds, our hearts or nerves or bodies to show that we lived, but we walked. We reached Nder's. He let us in. The truck had come. This night it would rest on the road, early tomorrow go on to Kako's. Nder was speaking with the nervous rapidity of moderate fear. It had brought him a team of vaccinators from the station at his request. "I worked for Europeans once and I know. Let them call me a witch; I'll see my own homestead is safe."

He too was afraid, but not past sanity. "Let Ihugh and the rest stay here with me as long as they wish." He still feared Europeans more than he feared anything else. A progressive chief. I would tell Sackerton so.

I went on to the road, afraid the truck might yet slip on without me. On and on through the heat of the afternoon, through the countryside seething with refugees as Kako's had before the smallpox struck. Sunburned, weary, blistered and lame, too tired to rest and still driven by terror in my flight to safety, I bullied the driver into going now, though we would arrive at night.

I swayed and bumped on the springless seat, mind blank, as we jounced over the rutted road. I could not yet realize that we were safe, that we had escaped the fear and the violence. We reached the station.

"The administrator's house," I told the driver. I found myself leaning forward tensely, eyes fixed on the bright light of the pressure lamp that stood out on Sackerton's lawn. We stopped there, before this strangely peaceful scene of people, clean and unafraid, sitting in a bright light.

"Yes?" Sackerton peered into darkness. "Oh! How nice you could come early." He helped me down. "Won't you join us?"

They were drinking coffee from demitasses. And they stared at me as I stood there, haggard and filthy, on Sackerton's well-pressed arm, laughing, laughing as though I would never stop.

Chapter Twenty-One

I HADN'T been in the station long before I began to wonder how I could ever go back. No one about me in the station saw any difficulty. They knew there was a smallpox epidemic. They thought it very sensible of me to have come out while I could still get any carriers at all. And they could not understand the fear. I could find no words that had meaning for them. I could tell them of Amara's death and make them weep. They did know what it is to watch a loved person die. It might never have happened to them, but they had been instructed by endless novels and by sentimental nannies' instructions—beginning with the death of a pet cat.

There were two people, two who almost understood. Sackerton, who remembered his Pepys and his Boccaccio, but it was only from the printed page that he knew two people held by the tenderest bond of love and affection could, when plague struck, leave each other to die in lonely terror. Sackerton, and the little French priest who had seen women leave their children in the open, on the fear and refugee-choked roads, when death struck from the skies. The priest knew, but he could not help me. "Be forgiven, forget, and start a new page." I felt myself entitled to forgiveness only from those I might have harmed: from Saar whom I had given no aid, from the people who had cried for help from their farm shelters and whom I had passed with deaf ears. I could not forget. And I had to go back. How could I turn over a new page?

I went back. My possessions were still there. My work had yet to be finished. And I could never live in peace with myself if I knew that I had run away and never gone back. But I went as one who goes to make atonement and do penance. I went back, and was shamed. They too had come back, but without ostentation and without false pride. They had run away. Only those who had no escape had stayed. Those who had stayed welcomed those who came back. Those who came back were able to return without turning over a new leaf to hide the sores and failures of the past. In their own souls they could admit failure in their past, know that they would fail again in the future, and still live. It was very humbly that I sat among them on my return.

Everyone welcomed me. "Now it will be as it was." If, like me, they were conscious of those so newly dead—so many, and so many of them children—they made no sign. Indeed, none mourned publicly. The raw, red mounds of earth that marked the path-side graves were too many and too fresh for us to forget, but there had been so much hate and fear that even the desire of vengeance gave way to the longing for peace and quiet living with one's neighbor.

It was enough that once more the living sat together, brother with brother, wife with husband, parent with child. We all greeted old acquaintances with real delight. We asked after none we did not see. It was too soon to stir the shallow graves. Not until we could be sure we would rouse grief rather than hate or fear would we do so. We went out of our way to be pleasant to each other. The social bonds that hold men together were too recently mended for any to wish to strain them. Even Yabo kept a courteous tongue.

On the second day of my return, Kako came to invite me to an evening of storytelling. It was to be in my honor. He had invited the famous fable tellers of the vicinity to come tell their tales—in a few days, when the moon would be full. I thanked him. I couldn't look forward to several hours of rapidly told animal tales; some of them, as written by Rogo, were quite amusing, but the storyteller's singsong still made understanding difficult for me.

Still Kako lingered. I thought perhaps my thanks had not been vociferous enough. I redoubled them. I wanted to show the gratitude I felt for the welcome they had given me after my desertion. I was to be allowed to do so: Kako wanted me to bring my pressure lamp; moonlight was all very well, but a big lamp like mine lent prestige to an occasion. I grinned, and promised, and marveled again that they could make it so easy to mend broken threads.

A few nights later we sat under the cold moon of the harmattan in a circle in Kako's homestead yard. My pressure lamp was carefully placed, under Kako's personal direction, to illuminate the storytellers as they passed before us and the assembled elders. Gradually the people gathered from the neighboring homesteads. They brought their wives and children, and they brought wood for fire and stools to sit on. The homestead was full of preparatory bustle as people borrowed coals to start their fires and jostled each other for a place close to the front. Then, places staked out with fire and stool, people circulated to greet each other, as people do in a theater lobby. The air was filled with the happy hum of an audience sure of good entertainment.

Behind Kako's reception hut there was a great coming and going, whispering and giggling, very much like the noise of people plotting charades. Cholo, who was to tell the first tale, squatted before me in brief, friendly greeting and gave me news of his sister: Atakpa was well; her cowife had been blinded by smallpox. "It makes more work for Atakpa. They're both after their husband now, to get them a little wife to help."

"Cholo!"

"I'm coming," Cholo shouted toward Kako's reception hut. He glanced at the gathered audience and left. He waved Ihugh to join him. Soon Ihugh was running toward

285

his hut, consulting with his uncles, and then back to join Cholo behind the reception hut. People settled down to wait, with anticipation.

Cholo came out before the lamp, and, with many gestures, began the story of the hare and the elephant.

The hare went hunting one day. He armed himself with a club made of cane grass and, knowing his weapon weak, wore a ferocious mask to petrify his prey with fear.

Here Cholo began to sing, stopping to instruct us all in the chorus of his song: nonsense syllables with a rousing rhythm and a lilting tune. I got interested. This would be far more fun than mere storytelling.

First the hare met a mouse. The mouse screamed with fear when he saw the terrible mask, but instead of standing trembling and ready to the hare's club, the mouse turned to flee.

Again Cholo waved us into the chorus.

As the hare pursued the mouse, his mask slipped down over his eyes. But the hare has long ears, and he was able to follow his prey by the rustling in the dry grass. In his flight, the mouse ran straight into an elephant and the elephant also began to run. The hare, unable to see, now followed the elephant and beat him with his cane club. The elephant, thinking this the tickle of the mouse's whiskers, ran ever faster.

Again the chorus. Then Cholo disappeared. I had enjoyed the song, and prepared for the next story. But this one was not yet finished. Cholo returned. This time he was the hare. To his head he had tied two waving fronds as ears, over his face a cloth daubed with mud, and in his hands he held a weak blade of cane grass. He mimed his story, dancing before us, searching for game, finding the mouse and pursuing it blindly.

Then out came the elephant, roaring: a long bed tied to a man's back—those huge, splay feet could be no one's but Ihugh's—covered with two dark togas that swayed with the elephant's dancing. The youngest children screamed most satisfactorily and had to be comforted by their parents, while the older children told them with great superiority that the elephant was really a man. Cholo now struck the elephant boldly with his grass blade, now used it as a baton to wave us all into his song and chorus. One or two of the young men beat sticks against their chairs, the better to mark the rhythm while the hare and the elephant danced. In a final surge of enthusiastic singing and dancing, the hare and the elephant disappeared.

Immediately one of Ihugh's cousins sprang into the center of the circle and began his tale of the goat who was a blacksmith and how he was tricked by the hare. He too had a song for his story, for the fables themselves are common property, and a storyteller makes his fame with his songs and dancing. Again I found myself laughing wholeheartedly and joining in the singing. I was enjoying myself immensely.

As the evening wore on, other men also rose to tell their stories, pressing brothers and cousins into service in the charades and commandeering props from the women of the homestead. A pot tied snoutlike over the face made a hippopotamus. Sheepskins, leaves and cloth-covered stools created strange monsters and sprites. There was not a single dull story. The audience wouldn't allow it. They were as loud in their criticism as in their praise, and people shouted down any fable teller who failed to hold their attention: "That's too long." "Your song's no good." "You've got the story wrong." "Learn to dance." Sometimes it needed only the momentary inattention of part of the audience to embolden one of the other storytellers to jump into the center even while another fable was being told. Then for a few moments we heard two tales, two songs at once. Soon people would take up only the one chorus and the other fable teller would sit down.

Mainly it was a contest between Gbodi and Ikpoom, who were the two great storytellers of the country. Gbodi, a short stocky little man with a huge voice, excelled as a dancer and tumbler. In the tale of the cricket and the praying mantis, he danced holding a heavy mahogany mortar in his hands. First, as the praying mantis, he held it over his head, then, placing the mortar on the ground, he continued to dance on it upside down, his hands grasping the edge of the mortar, his feet in the air—and singing all the while.

Ikpoom excelled in mime. His ugly face was extraordinarily expressive, and he was at his best when he could himself act out all parts of the story at once. Now he was telling the tale of the chief's daughter who refused to marry any man, for she knew she was far too good for any suitor who came to court her. Ikpoom's voice was shrilly angry when, as the girl, he warned lovers off the farm and threatened to shoot them with bow and arrow. His voice was eerie and his song uncanny as he portrayed the chief of the underworld sprites, Agundu, who is a head with wild, red eyes and with gouts of blood on the raw cut neck that terminates the creature. He showed us how Agundu borrowed the radiance of the sun and moon and with them dazzled the girl, how she followed this bright illusion away from her own people whom she had scorned, and how at the very gates of the underworld Agundu gave back to the sun his glory and to the moon her beauty. Only then, when it was too late, did the girl see what monster she had chosen, and then, too late and in vain, she longed for a human mate.

I had no need to hear the shouted proverb that marks the end of each story. I knew the moral of this tale. Especially now, in this situation in which our common humanity and pleasure in amusement was so evident, the dangers of parting from one's own to follow beckoning strangeness loomed perilous and sad.

Ikpoom sang the lament of the girl whom blind pride had shut in a strange, dark world away from the sun and familiar light. I wondered where Lucia had wandered. In the confusion and terror, Ikpoom had not been able to find her. She had once more fled from her own people and from the real world, perhaps in pursuit of some strange illusion . . . Memory returned in a sickening wave. In terror. In blind flight from a reality that was not to be endured. But we had come back. She still fled. The sadness of Ikpoom's song might all be art, but I remembered his face when he had seen Lucia run from him into night and the waters of death.

Thoughts of Lucia and the lost nights I had spent listening to her song drew my attention from the fable telling. I had been driven back here by the same kind of blind compulsion that had made me leave. I could not spend the months that still remained in the moral and emotional vacillation that had whipped me from rest and composure in the past. I tried not to think. That had been my remedy in the past.

Ikpoom sang for Agundu, for the grinning skeleton of the world that underlies all illusion. One can ignore Agundu. But those who follow him may never return, for they have seen and can never forget.

No, I could not forget. I had followed Agundu. My soul's protest was so deep that I nearly cried aloud: I can look on Agundu, on reality, unafraid, but I cannot see my own naked being. I had followed science out here, as one follows a will-o'-the-wisp, seeing only what beckoned from the distance, paying no heed to the earth I spurned beneath my feet, seeing naught about me. I had served anthropology well. Notebook upon notebook, good stuff, and accurate, and I had the knowledge to work it soundly so that I might stand, with a craftsman's pride, before the finished work and say, "This is mine."

I had followed Agundu. There was no jury, no god, before whom I could stand unashamed to say, "This is me." *Me*, as I sat there, the product of my pettiness and my cowardice. But not *I*. I was still unfinished, could still change, could still return. I had learned. I had discovered that there were moral values which I could not willfully abandon, no matter what the dictates and interests of science and no matter how impossible it had been for me to live up to those standards. I had run away from the choice when I had finally seen it—like Lucia. I would always have to live with that knowledge of personal inadequacy. Very well, I could benefit from the smarting salt of humility.

But they knew. All these people laughing around me. They knew how to come back. I had still to learn.

Gbodi was telling a tale now, of the hare's attempt to pass himself off as one of the bush sprites in their own country. Great a trickster as the hare is, infinite as is his ingenuity, he was unable to act and feel as did the bush sprites. At first this enabled him to deceive them the better and to steal the toga that bears one along like the wind, but ultimately this lack of understanding and this difference was his undoing. "This time," sang Gbodi, "the sprites killed the hare and ate him. The fable has killed the hare."

The hare would soon be resurrected in another fable. The trickster is immortal as a type no matter how often any one trickster tricks himself into disaster. But even the greatest trickster cannot transform himself. His personal habits always betray him, as they betray all of us for what we are; we ourselves are the only ones to see ourselves as what we think we ought to be or what we would like to be thought.

Many of my moral dilemmas had sprung from the very nature of my work, which had made me a trickster: one who seems to be what he is not and who professes faith in what he does not believe. But this realization is of little help. It is not enough to be true to oneself. The self may be bad and need to be changed, or it may change unawares into something strange and new. I had changed. Whatever the merits of anthropology to the world or of my work to anthropology, this experience had wrought many changes in me as a human being—and I had thought that what wasn't grist for my notebooks would be adventure.

I had held that knowledge is worth the acquisition. I had willingly accepted the supposition that one cannot learn save by suppressing one's prejudices, or, at the very least, holding them morally in abeyance. The trouble lay in my careless assumption that it would be only my "prejudices" that were to be involved, and never my "principles" —it had not occurred to me that the distinction between "prejudice" and "principle" is itself a matter of prejudice.

It is an error to assume that to know is to understand and that to understand is to like. The greater the extent to which one has lived and participated in a genuinely foreign culture and understood it, the greater the extent to which one realizes that one could not, without violence to one's personal integrity, be of it. This importance of fidelity to one's own culture and one's own standards is mutual. That is what tolerance means: allowing each man his own integrity. Not an eclectic picking of convenient moral maxims for oneself.

Like the practice of free speech, free thought and free reading, the act of immersion in a wholly foreign culture demands the will and ability to think out the consequences. More than ever I realized that one may not accept what is as what should be, on the mere grounds that "it is so." More than ever I had to admit that Poorgbilin's senior wife had been right: I had the heart of a child and had yet to learn wisdom.

I had lost track of the fable being told. It was a long one, and I couldn't keep the characters straight. Neither, it seemed, could Accident—energetic as ever and quite unchanged save for a few pockmarks on his nose. Perhaps, though, it was just his sense of mischief that made him bounce up from his seat beside his brother and take the stage with the storyteller. "I don't understand. Would you repeat more slowly?"

There was a startled gasp. Then a roar of laughter, even from the interrupted storyteller. "What was his great-great-grandfather's name? And where did he learn to perform that ceremony?" continued Accident, so broadly that I too began to laugh, for it was my own accent and my own questions that Accident was imitating. Aware that he had lost his audience, the fable teller began to play informant to Accident's anthropologist. Accident in turn looked eager or baffled, scribbled in the air as though in a notebook, wiped imaginary glasses, adjusted imaginary skirts and took off my accent, gestures, errors of grammar and habits of phrase with such unmerciful accuracy that even as I laughed myself sore I resolved on improvement. Accident finally sat down under a shower of pennies and approving applause.

He set a brief style, for both Cholo and Ikpoom now took turns at imitating Europeans. Using Ihugh as a stooge, Cholo presented a missionary hopeful of a convert. He lectured Ihugh on the benefits of Christian morality; as proof, he told Ihugh that all men were brothers. Ihugh successfully looked both pleased and puzzled. He asked to hear more on the thesis that all men were brothers and through just what genealogical ramifications. To show that he was prepared to listen at length, he started to sit down. But the missionary forbade Ihugh to sit in his presence, for he was a European. He began his lecture. But Ihugh, muttering that brothers didn't behave like that, took himself off.

The topic was one that interested people very little, and Ikpoom had no difficulty in interrupting the missionary's fervor with his portrait of an administrator on tour. As a shaky old man seeking justice, he embarked on a long story involving the complicated marriages, adulteries, loans and general finagling of four generations. As the administrator, Ikpoom was first patient, and then, with each successive complication of the old man's tale, more and more annoyed and abrupt. As the interpreter between them, Ikpoom floundered, piled confusion on confusion, substituted women for goats and nephews for uncles. Soon Ikpoom had created a tangle of wild misunderstandings and exasperated exhortation from which an entirely irrelevant decision emerged on wholly erroneous grounds.

We were all laughing so that we could scarcely hear Ikpoom, who, waiting for each gale of mirth to subside, looked perplexed in the different ways appropriate to the old man, the interpreter or the administrator—picking his teeth with a spear, fiddling with his badge, or tugging at a nonexistent mustache so vividly that I saw Sackerton himself.

"That is the way it is," gasped Kako, choking in an effort to regain his composure. "It is thus indeed!" And again he burst out laughing as Ikpoom tottered off behind the reception hut weeping the futile tears of an old man robbed of wives and money in the name of justice. "It is so. They judge us, but they do not understand us, and what can we do?"

Gbodi, not to be outdone in comedy, came out holding one end of a cane, with Accident at the other end, leading him. Gbodi's uncertain step confirmed Accident's comments. "Don't stumble over the root, father." We sat back to watch a blind man being led into adventure. "There's the tree, father."

And Gbodi, wrenching the staff from the child's grasp, poked wildly about with it till he had whacked the mango tree just to our left.

"Higher, father, and to the right."

Gbodi slid the stick cautiously up the bark, entangled himself in the roots and fell down. "Where is the stick, my son?"

"Over there, father."

"Where, my son?"

"There! But your cloth is disarranged, father. No, over there."

And the people laughed while Gbodi groped helplessly about for his stick and fussed with his cloth, while Accident improvised brilliantly misleading remarks. Eventually Accident picked up the stick. Each time he proffered it to Gbodi, calling "Here, father, over here!" Gbodi stumbled to a complete miss or lurched against the stick with a sharp, hurting thwack.

I was the only one not laughing. On principle I was not amused, nor was Gbodi funny enough to betray me into laughter. But before the audience could tire of the blind man's wild grabs in the dark, Gbodi took the stick and started leaping and prodding among the branches of the mango tree as he sang and shouted. Meanwhile Accident retreated further and further away and cried, "Careful, father. Higher, father. Be careful."

Gbodi's frantic jumps and his tripping over the roots on which he landed blindly and inaccurately, his teetering in wild attempts to regain lost balance, formed such a magnificent display of acrobatic skill that I forgot everything else in breathless watching. Suddenly Gbodi thwacked a high branch. Then, in descent and still midair, he gave the contorted twist of a man unexpectedly stung in a tender spot.

"Bees!" an anguished cry.

"Run, father," cried Accident, setting the example. But Gbodi obstinately prodded and leaped and writhed and and slapped while I, like everyone else, shouted and hooted at his contortions.

Out of breath, Gbodi stood still a moment to teach us his song. While we sang, he resumed his dancing, leaping and stumbling, and I, singing the words as well as I could for laughing, didn't consider that perhaps it was no kinder to watch a blind man trying to gather honey defended by bees than to watch a blind man jump. I couldn't stop laughing. Gbodi was funny. Anyhow, he wasn't really blind. The whole thing was funny.

One of Kako's brothers who had been partially blinded by the smallpox was laughing with the best of us. "That is the way it is," he gasped. "Indeed, it is so. What can one do?" It was Kako's comment about the administrator. I had understood it in that context.

Gbodi, overwhelmed by stinging bees, staggered, abandoned all hope of honey and lurched off the scene, shouting wildly for his son and his stick.

Ikpoom, who hadn't waited to see the end of Gbodi's act, hobbled from behind the reception hut. His preparations had been elaborate. With mud and the blood-red sap of a gummy tree, he had made of himself a loathsome imitation of a man crippled by elephantiasis, tertiary yaws and running tropical sores. He wore the rags and dirt of a man crushed by illness and poverty. In a cracked tremolo he quavered an ardent love song. We began to laugh. This crippled beggar hoped to marry the chief's daughter.

The chief, who knew the suitor well, demanded a fantastic sum for his daughter. The cripple, who had no kin, no farms, no resources of any sort, was for just a few seconds dejected enough to complain of his estate in an unhappy little chant. He tried to persuade the chief that a man as powerful as he would not need a powerful son-in-law. He was refused in no uncertain terms and went off to court the chief's daughter in secret, for he thought that his personal charms might persuade her to elopement.

Ihugh, large and awkward as the chief's daughter, had to be prompted by Ikpoom in a loud stage whisper to each unkind retort, for the storyteller's disguise prevented his playing both parts himself. Nevertheless, Ihugh's bashful giggles, the incongruity of such a man playing such a role, and the cruel wit to which he was tutored all heightened our appreciation of the cripple's ardor and his incurable and crazy optimism.

Even when we did not laugh, our mouths like our hearts were twisted with a wry mirth. The cripple must be a fool not to realize . . . A fool? Or mad. In such a situation one must either laugh or go mad, laugh at the reality or be mad in the illusion.

Only in a very sheltered life of the sort made possible by civilization can one maintain a fine and serious sense of the tragedy of misfortune. In an environment in which tragedy is genuine and frequent, laughter is essential to sanity. Such laughter is neither callous nor humorous. It is both to one of us, for behind the protecting curtains of ease and resource which civilization has woven we grow sensitive. For us, to be indifferent to suffering is to kill in ourselves that sympathy without which we become dead to our fellows and ultimately to ourselves.

The endurance these people had developed is not the same thing as the scar tissue that arises from an unwillingness to be hurt again, and that, having originally given protection, then slowly smothers and kills what it was first designed to shelter. But these people were not individually callous; they were weather-beaten by their constant exposure to disease and famine. Unable to escape the knife, they admired those who, like little Accident, were able to jest under it.

The chief's daughter would reject the cripple. Rejected, he would have to admit himself the poor, loathsome creature he was, or we would know him mad. There were those whom such knowledge might drive mad. Those who see the reality but cannot face it have no refuge but insanity, a flight from their life, their culture and their society. The ivory tower is a similar refuge. To withdraw from the world or to allow illusion to govern one in one's dealings with oneself or the world are both a flight into madness.

The cripple looked into the mirror of scorn held up for him by the chief's daughter and saw himself through her eyes. Ikpoom's song cursed the witches who had made him so and mocked himself for exposing himself to mockery. Then with his own eyes he looked at himself and found something better than her picture and worse than his hopes. "Thus it is," his song ended, "and what can one do?"

These people had developed none of the sciences or arts of civilization. They had not learned to change that which is, to wish for a better life so greatly that they would stake the familiar good that might be lost with the familiar evil. They were not, as we are, greedy for the future. We concern ourselves with the reality of what is, because we wish to direct change wisely, hoping thus to preserve the good on which we are agreed while yet attaining what we believe should be. They did not seek to learn thus purposely. If they knew a grim reality, it was because their fate rubbed it into their very souls.

The storytelling was ended. People wrapped their cloths close against the chill as they made ready to leave the fires and go home. Slowly, with the happy murmur of pleasant recollection and reminiscent laughter that marks the home-going audience in Africa as in St. James' theater, they filed out of the firelit homestead yard into the quiet night.

I stood for a while, looking after them. They knew how to live at close quarters with tragedy, how to live with their own failure and yet laugh. They knew the terror of a broken society, where brother's hand is raised against brother in hate and fear; they knew how to come back, brother to brother, and create life anew. We give succor to the unfortunate and the crippled, who here are laughing-stocks. But we abandon those who have proved themselves weak and faithless. And these people, who have no succor to give, who have all been weak and unfortunate, who all know they may themselves be faithless and crippled, and who all know that they build on shifting sand, have yet the courage to build what they know will fall.

These people know the reality and laugh at it. Such laughter has little concern with what is funny. It is often bitter and sometimes a little mad, for it is the laugh under the mask of tragedy, and also the laughter that masks tears. They are the same. It is the laughter of people who value love and friendship and plenty, who have lived with terror and death and hate.

> To be worst,
> The lowest and most dejected thing of fortune,
> Stands still in esperance, lives not in fear;
> The lamentable change is from the best,
> The worst returns to laughter.